WHY?

WHY?

Alex Lizzi Jr.

Dedication

I would like to dedicate this book to my loving father, Alex Lizzi Sr. Thank you, Dad, for instilling in me a strong work ethic and the belief that you can do anything if you want it bad enough. Thank you for teaching me how to be a good father through your example as a loving father. Love you, Dad.

Alex

I would like to give special thanks to the following individuals: to Sarah Thomas, for designing and creating the book cover; to Colleen Lippert, for her awesome job, as always, of editing; to Captain John Davis, a pilot who flew the very route depicted in the book; to Richard C Gove and to all my wonderful clients for their input (you know who you are); and last, but not least, a very special thanks to my wife, Janice, for her patience while I wrote *Why?*

Table of Contents

Chapter One

Her heart pounded in her chest as she struggled to breathe. A bead of perspiration, starting at her forehead, slowly made its way down her nose, balancing for what seemed an eternity before making its descent into the canyon of her cleavage. Her knuckles turned white as she gripped the armrests of her seat.

"Miss, are you all right?" asked the man seated beside her.

Rachel Hickenine, a plump, 42-year-old accountant, her hair disheveled and perspiration now starting to bead on her forehead, sat fidgeting in her seat, mentally preparing herself for takeoff. She let out a little sigh as the man next to her rolled his eyes.

Flying petrified Rachel. She had hoped to take the train to the home office in Houston, but it would have taken three days each way and that would mean using up most of her vacation days. She detested being required to attend the annual Christmas party, especially since it seemed to be nothing more than a bunch of overweight balding men, who reeked of stale cigar smoke and Old Spice aftershave, standing around and patting each other on the back, thinking that the festive holiday spirit gave them the right to a free feel or a sloppy kiss. She didn't know which was worse, the Christmas party or flying.

With her stomach churning like a cheap blender from the Dollar Tree, Rachel could feel the vibrations of the plane as they accelerated down the runway. It reminded her of the coin-operated bed in the cheap motel that she had slept in after last year's Christmas party, minus the smell of smoke and cheap perfume that lingered in the room. Her company was first class, right down to the buffet that they provided at the Howard Johnson hotel.

As Rachel gripped the armrests of her seat, she felt the plane leave the ground. The vibrations suddenly stopped as abruptly as the bed at the motel when her quarter's worth of time had ended. She let out a sigh of relief as perspiration trickled down her spine and one of her barrel curls dangled in her face. She could feel the tension in her body starting to ebb. Suddenly, she heard a loud crash against her window and a sickening whining noise from the plane's engine. A shuddering vibration passed through the plane, causing her to let out a blood-curdling scream. She turned to look at the window and saw that it was covered in blood.

A flight attendant came running down the aisle, not knowing what to expect.

"Miss, it's all right. It was only a flock of geese. It happens quite often."

Rachel looked up at the flight attendant in total disbelief. The man sitting to her right shrank back into his seat, wishing he could be anywhere else but sitting next to this mad woman. Though she didn't fly very often, she had never experienced flying into a flock of geese. She noticed that the other passengers were staring at her, and feeling her face turning as red as a chili pepper with embarrassment, she closed her eyes, wishing that it was all a bad dream.

"Ladies and gentlemen, this is the captain speaking," said a voice over the cabin's loudspeakers. "Some of you may have noticed that we've had a minor encounter with a flock of geese."

Minor, thought Rachel. There was blood and other debris all over her window. The flight attendant, a little disheveled from her run down the aisle, politely instructed Rachel to pull down the blind on her window.

"Pull down the blind? No," said Rachel. "I would like another seat, please."

"I'm sorry, ma'am, but the plane is full. I don't have another seat to offer you."

Forget her, thought the man sitting to Rachel's right. *What about the rest of us?*

"Would you like a complementary drink?"

"I don't drink!" Rachel blurted out, before she could even think about what the flight attendant had asked.

"I'm sorry. Is there anything else that I can do for you?"

"On second thought, why not?"

Rachel asked for a glass of wine, and then slugged it down like a miner who had just finished a twelve-hour shift.

"May I have another?" Rachel asked, letting out a little burp. "Excuse me," she giggled.

Four glasses of wine later, the Fasten Your Seatbelt light had come on and they were preparing to land.

Once the bird-battered plane was emptied of its human cargo and luggage, it was brought into a hanger where it could be inspected for any damage that the geese might have caused. Brad, the lead mechanic on the night shift, picked up the work order and began to read it. He pushed his glasses back up his nose as he walked over to the plane. The pilot's report stated that a passenger in row 28 complained of geese hitting her window and that the crew felt a small surge in the left engine that corresponded with the complaint.

Great, thought Brad, *what a way to start a shift.*

Brad started his inspection by checking the engines first. There were goose parts all over one of the engines.

"What a mess," he muttered under his breath. "And the smell. You would think that after flying over eight hundred miles that it wouldn't smell so bad."

The engine would have to be cleaned and then repaired. Brad hoped that the damage wasn't too extensive. Next, he checked the window. He knew it would have to be power-washed before he could determine whether it needed to be replaced.

And my wife wonders why I became a vegetarian, he thought.

After Brad made his evaluation, he brought a copy to his boss, Herman.

"What, are you kidding?" said Herman. He was a short, portly balding man in his late fifties, and as he took a drag on his cigarette, he let out a hacking cough. "This plane is scheduled for Rio tomorrow. It's Christmas Eve. It's booked solid."

"I know," said Brad as he rolled his eyes and pushed his glasses back up his nose. "But I really think we should tear down that engine. It looks like it's missing a few fins. I really can't tell unless I tear it down. And I think we should replace the window as well." Brad already knew what his boss's reply would be.

"And just what world do you live in?" asked Herman as he took another pull on his cigarette.

Brad thought, *Here we go again.*

"We can't afford to have this plane out of commission that long. Besides, we don't have a plane to replace it."

Brad had heard this speech a thousand times before. "When do we ever have a plane to swap out for another one? Half of our planes are held together with bailing wire and duct tape."

"I'll tell you what. You can replace the window if it's cracked, but just hose out the engine!" barked Herman as he took another drag on his cigarette.

"But if I replace the window, it won't have enough time to set up."

"Tape it," said Herman, fighting off a coughing jag. "The tape will hold it till the glue sets up."

"I really don't like doing things that way."

Herman's face was turning blue from a lack of oxygen due to coughing and trying to talk at the same time.

"I didn't ask you what you like doing. And, Brad, get me another cup of that tar they call coffee before you start working on that plane."

Chapter Two

The plane was approaching the airport. As the seatbelt sign flashed, Billy could feel the plane rolling from side to side and shuddering. It felt like he was in an old pickup driving down a washboard road. He felt the plane's landing gear being lowered as it rapidly descended from the clouds. Looking out his window, he couldn't tell if it was snowing or if it was just the thick moisture of the clouds that they were passing through. Then he felt a cold shiver run down his spine, something he had not experienced for over a year in the sweltering heat and humidity of Vietnam.

When the plane broke through the clouds, he could see that it was snowing; it was a heavy, wet snow. The runway was covered in deep slush, and the plane's wings were still heaving from side to side. Billy gazed out the window and saw rusty orange smoke billowing from the smoke stacks of the steel mill, leaving the snow-covered ground a rusty orange.

He thought of Vietnam, with its war-torn countryside, where bombs riddled towns and villages, and people lived in constant fear for their lives, not knowing where their next meal would come from or if there would even be a next meal. Then he thought of his fellow soldiers on patrol in the jungle, and the constant rain, the snakes, the booby traps, and the shelling that kept him up all night. He thought of the friends who had died just days before their time in Vietnam was up.

With a sudden jolt, Billy felt the plane touch down on the runway. He had butterflies in his stomach. *Why am I so nervous? I'm home, safe and sound. I didn't come home in a box like so many of my friends have,* he thought. It made him sick to think of it. Actually, it made him feel guilty. Why had he come home without a scratch while so many others had come home dead or, worse, in pieces?

Billy, wearing his Army dress uniform, approached the gate. The first thing he heard was war protesters chanting their anti-war slogans. Then he was met by people with signs, news cameras, and policemen as he exited into the waiting area. Billy scanned the crowd and finally spotted his mother standing away from the protesters. Some other family members and friends were holding up signs saying, "Welcome home! We love you!" His mother was clearly upset with the protesters. She looked gaunt and her hair had turned mostly grey. He didn't remember it being so grey before he left. He noticed that his dad was losing his hair. What little he had left was now in a comb over. He had also aged in the year that Billy had been away.

A man wearing a sweatshirt with a peace symbol on the front of it, and sporting long greasy hair, held a sign saying, "Baby killers!" He suddenly jumped out and stood between Billy and his family. Billy felt a surge of rage coursing through his veins. A policeman grabbed the protester and moved him out of Billy's path. His mother started to weep and it made his eyes begin to water. He swore that he wouldn't cry, but he couldn't hold back the tears once he locked eyes with his mother and saw the tears of joy flowing down her face.

Billy sat in the back seat of the family car, a red Ford Country Squire. His mother loved red. He gazed out the window at all the war protesters while his dad and brother riddled him with questions.

"Give the boy a chance to catch his breath. He just got home! He's not going anywhere. He's home now," said his mother as she let out a sigh of relief.

Billy felt another attack of guilt, even before his mother had finished her sentence, because he'd be leaving again in just a few short days. He had even entertained the thought of going to Brazil straight from Germany but he knew that would have killed his mother, especially since Christmas was just a few days away.

As they made their way down Elm Street, Billy could see what looked like a small crowd gathered in front of his family's home. He felt a knot forming in his stomach. *Not more protesters,* he thought. *Not in front of my own home.* It was cold and windy, and he couldn't read the signs through the blowing snow. As they drew closer, he could see that they weren't protesters, they were well wishers. Billy immediately felt overwhelmed. It seemed as if the whole town of Rochester had come to welcome him home.

Mr. Edwards, a tall, thin hunch-backed man with weary eyes, said, "Welcome home, son." He hugged Billy so tightly that he could hardly breathe. Mr. Edwards's only son, Tom, hadn't been so lucky. He was killed by a land mine just three weeks after arriving in Vietnam. The travesty had left the Edwards with little to live for.

6

"Thank you, sir. It's great to be home. I'm sorry about your son. Tommy was a brave soldier."

Now the guilt was greater than ever. Why had he lived and Tommy died?

Melinda, wearing a dress two sizes too small, pulled on his arm, turning him around.

"Let me see your war medal! Wow! You're a real war hero!"

Not Melinda, he thought. *I'm really not in the mood to deal with her.*

Melinda lived three doors down the street from him and had had a crush on him since the third grade.

"Congratulations," said Mr. Edwards. "I read in the paper about you being awarded the Bronze Star."

"I heard that you got it for your selfless heroism, indomitable fighting spirit, and extraordinary gallantry, and that you were directly responsible for saving the lives of several of your comrades while inflicting serious damage on the enemy," said Melinda proudly as she hung on Billy's shoulder.

"Tell Mr. Edwards how you single-handedly took out two enemy bunkers, and how you carried two wounded soldiers to safety and then returned to the fight, and how you destroyed a machine gun nest and carried out another wounded soldier," Melinda gushed, as if she were one of the wounded soldiers that he had carried out of harm's way.

Billy looked embarrassed. He hated thinking about that day, it made him sick to his stomach. He hadn't done anything special, at least not anything that any other guy in his squad would have done in the same situation.

Melinda noticed that Billy looked annoyed.

"I was only telling Mr. Edwards what a war hero you are." Quickly changing the subject, she put her arm around Billy as if they were long-lost lovers and said, "You men look absolutely starved. We've got a mountain of food for you all. I don't know that I've ever seen so much food in one place, and it all looks so delicious. You're so thin now, Billy. Why don't you let me fix you a plate?"

"I'm fine, really."

"I won't hear of it. A war hero like you needs some special attention."

"No, that's all right, really."

7

"I won't hear of it," she repeated. "I'm going to fix you and Mr. Edwards a plate."

As Melinda walked over to a table laden with food, Mr. Edwards said in a tired, drawn voice, "No thank you, Melinda. I really need to get home and check on Elma."

"Can I fix a plate for Mrs. Edwards?" asked Melinda.

"That's sweet of you, dear, but it would only go to waste. She hasn't had much of an appetite since Tommy died. Nothing's the same now that he's gone. I think I'll just be running along now."

"I'm sorry to hear that, Mr. Edwards," Billy interjected, feeling another wave of guilt. He had to get away. There were too many reminders of what he had just been through. There must have been at least three other families there who had lost a son.

Mr. Edwards gave Billy another hug goodbye, and then Melinda grabbed Billy by the arm and said, "How about a little fresh air?"

Seeing how uncomfortable Billy looked with Melinda, Mark Adams, Billy's friend from high school, went over to them and said, "Hey, Billy, how are you?"

"We were just going to grab a little fresh air," said Melinda, trying to guide Billy away from Mark.

"That sounds good right about now. I could use some fresh air myself. I'll join you. Melinda, why don't you grab us a few beers and meet us outside."

Billy woke to the familiar smell of his mother's coffee brewing and the sound of bacon frying. He could hear the excitement in her voice as she told his father her plans for the day. He felt sick with guilt. He didn't want to disappoint his mother, especially since she had worked so hard to make his welcome home party special, and now she was making all these plans for him and the family. When would he tell her?

Billy looked around his room. His mother had kept it clean for him and had pressed all of his clothes, even his favorite sweatshirt, which was hanging in his closet.

"Honey, are you awake?" asked his mother as she peeked into his room.

"I'm up," he replied.

"I've got breakfast for you, dear."

"Be right down."

Billy threw on a pair of jeans and his favorite old sweatshirt and went downstairs to the kitchen. He couldn't believe how clean the house was after the party the night before. His mother must have stayed up all night cleaning.

When he walked into the kitchen, he saw his father sitting in his same old chair, reading the paper like he'd seen him do a thousand times before. His mother, in her floral apron, was standing by the stove, just as she did every morning. The coffee smelled great and the food looked even better.

"Sit," said his mother as she poured him a cup of coffee. "I made your eggs sunny side up, just the way you like them. You still like them that way, don't you?"

"You bet, Mom. But you must be exhausted."

"Are you kidding?" said his dad, looking over the top of his paper from the other end of the table. "Your mother has been dying to wait on you. She's been going crazy, waiting for you to come home. She has big plans for Midnight Mass."

"Bill, stop that." Turning to Billy, his mother said, "It's just wonderful to have you home. I still can't believe it's really you sitting there."

Then she started to weep with happiness.

"Mom," said Billy as he rose from his chair and hugged his mother.

Bill didn't notice that Mildred had started to cry because he was so used to her tears, and he just rambled on with his conversation.

"Billy, I've been talking to Bob Richardson down at the mill. You remember Bob, don't you?"

Mildred, drying her tears, went back to busying herself at the stove.

"He said to send you down first thing right after New Year's. You know the mill always closes down for two weeks at the end of the year for the holidays. Half the workers call in sick anyway, so they just close down for two weeks."

"I know, Dad. They've been closed over the holidays ever since I've been alive."

Billy thought about how some things never changed and how lucky he was to have such great parents.

"Bill, stop all that talk about the mill and let the boy eat."

"Well, son, you sure do look thin."

"Bill, if you would let him eat…."

9

"Ah, Mildred, I'm just glad to see him, that's all."

"Where's Frankie?" asked Billy, trying to change the subject.

"Your little brother got up early and went over to Jimmy Park's. Jimmy's dad needed help at the dairy," said Mildred.

"I can't picture little Frankie milking cows," said Billy.

"How about that Melinda?" Said Bill. "She sure is a beauty. I saw you two together yesterday, with her arm around you and that big plate of food she made up for you. You know, I don't think a day went by that Melinda didn't stop in and ask about you."

"Bill, let the boy eat already."

"Eat up, son. Your mother and I have a little surprise for you."

"Bill."

"Yeah? What is it?" Billy asked, seeing the joy on his father's face and hoping it had nothing to do with Melinda.

"What the hell. I might as well tell you now. I landed us some tickets to the Steelers game this afternoon. Franco Harris is red hot, him and his Italian army!"

"Mom, you're going to a football game?"

"Are you kidding me? Your mother would sit on a frozen lake and ice fish if it meant spending time with you."

On the way home from the football game Mildred couldn't stop talking about her first pro football game.

"Can you believe that game, Pittsburgh beating Cleveland 24 to 21 in overtime. What a great game!" Said Bill. "I think I'll turn in for the night."

After Bill went upstairs, Mildred asked, "Billy, are you all right? You hardly touched your food at the restaurant."

"I'm fine. Tired is all."

"Are you sure, Billy?"

"Yeah, I'm sure, Mom. It's just been a long day and I think I'm still a little jet lagged."

Billy couldn't hold it in any longer, it was eating a hole in his stomach. He didn't know what to do. His dad was in the bathroom getting ready for bed and his mother had turned back to the television to watch the news. The newscaster had just announced the daily death toll in Vietnam. Mildred hated how they brought the war into everyone's living room.

"Mom, I need to talk."

Mildred turned around with a look of terror on her face, thinking that the newscast had upset Billy. She got up and turned the TV off.

"Mom, I love you so much. You and Dad have been so great, I'm so lucky."

"No, son, we're the lucky ones."

"No, Mom, I'm the lucky one. I've got something to tell you. Please hear me out before I lose my nerve."

Mildred could feel her heart start to race.

"There wasn't a day over there in Vietnam that I didn't thank God for you two. I don't know how I would have made it without your letters. I would read them and then I would reread them."

"Billy," said his mother, her heart feeling as if it were going to explode.

"I felt so lucky. There were a lot of guys who didn't get any mail. I hope you don't mind, but I shared my letters with some of those guys."

Feeling her tears starting to swell, Mildred said, "God knows that I would have written those boys if I would've known."

"Mom, you were great, and Dad...I love you two so much. I don't know how to tell you this."

Billy paused as he tried to find the right words.

"What, son? What is it?"

"Mom, I won't be here for Christmas," said Billy, wanting to die as soon as the words left his mouth.

"What are you saying, Billy? Sure you'll be here for Christmas, where else would you be? You just got home and Christmas is only a few days from now," said Mildred, her voice starting to crack.

"Mom, I have to see Ana."

11

"I thought that was over." Mildred's tone suddenly changed. "I haven't heard you speak of her, I mean, you never said anything about Ana in your letters." She started to cry. "Billy, you can't leave, you just got here. Bill? Bill, come down here!"

"What's the matter?" he yelled down a little too loudly. He had already taken out his hearing aid for the night.

"Billy's leaving."

"What, are you crazy, Mildred?" said Bill as he came down the steps, hair on end and slippers clunking. "He just got here! Where's he running off to now? Billy, what's going on?"

"Dad, I'm going to Brazil just as soon as I can get a ticket. I'm going to ask Ana to marry me."

"What, are you crazy?"

"No, Dad, I'm in love."

"Love? How can you be in love? You haven't even seen Ana in almost two years."

"We've been writing."

"Billy, why don't you wait until after Christmas? Then, hell, I'll send Ana a ticket and she could visit us."

"No, Dad. I can't wait that long. I'm going as soon as I can get a ticket."

"Billy, look, you're breaking your mother's heart."

"Bill, let him go," said Mildred soberly.

"Mom, I'll be back in a couple of weeks. I'm bringing Ana home so all of you can meet her."

"Let's go to bed, Bill," said Mildred as she turned and headed up the stairs. "Bill, come to bed."

The next morning, Billy called the Rochester Travel Agency.

"This is Mary Logan. How may I help you?"

"Hello, Mary, this is Billy Sunday."

"Billy! I heard you were home. Thank God. Now what can I help you with?"

"I need to buy a ticket to Brazil."

12

"Brazil," said Mary, clearly surprised by the request. "Where in Brazil? It's a big place, you know."

"I'm sorry. I meant to say Rio."

"Rio…when would you like to go?"

"As soon as possible."

"You mean after Christmas?"

"No, I mean right away."

"Billy, I know it's none of my business, but didn't you just get home a few days ago?"

"Yeah."

"Billy, your mother would kill me if I were to sell you a ticket before Christmas."

Mary and Mildred were old friends. They both belonged to the Christian mother's group at St. Cecilia's Catholic Church. Mary knew that if the tables were turned, she would be livid with Mildred Sunday.

"Don't worry, Mary. We've discussed it."

"All right, then," said Mary, still a little hesitant. "Let me take a look. There's a flight leaving on the twenty-fourth that connects in Houston for the overnight flight to Rio, arriving on Christmas Day."

"Nothing sooner?" asked Billy, overwhelmed with guilt but still wanting to leave that afternoon.

"No, I'm sorry."

"Well, if that's the best you can do, I'll take it."

"Billy, again, I know this is none of my business, but can I ask you what's so important that you need to be in Rio before Christmas?"

Billy hesitated, and then said, "It's Ana. I'm going to ask her to marry me."

"Marry you!" Mary was surprised that Mildred hadn't even mentioned that Billy had a girlfriend. "Well, I hope she says yes."

"Thanks, Mary. That makes two of us."

Chapter Three

At the airport in Houston, Billy sat in the waiting area at his gate people watching while waiting for his connecting flight to Brazil. He wondered where all those people could be going on Christmas Eve. Then he thought about his pals still fighting in Vietnam. How could the world be so different? Just a week ago, he was living in hell witnessing death everyday, and now he was in a busy airport full of happy people. Everywhere he looked there were bright lights and people singing Christmas- carols. What were his friends he left behind in Vietnam doing?

Stop, he thought.

Billy turned his head and saw a little girl who was holding her baby doll she was sitting with her parents, waiting to board their plane. Behind the little girl were two lovers holding hands. He turned his head left and saw grandparents playing with their grandchildren. He looked behind him; people were laughing in the bar as Christmas music played throughout the airport.

"T'is the season to be jolly! Fa la la la la, la la la la…."

Jolly, he thought. *Was Charlie jolly when he taped a grenade to a child before sending him into an American camp to beg for food? How could there be so much happiness and so much sadness at the same time?*

Billy needed a drink.

The bar behind him was full of people, and he was tired of sitting alone, so he walked in and ordered a beer and a shot, and then he tried to find a seat. He spotted one by the window, walked over to it, and sat down. He found himself between a middle-aged couple who were deeply engaged in a conversation filled with laughter and hadn't even noticed him when he sat down and a lonely looking middle-aged man with a long salt-and-pepper beard. The man was thin and he stared out the window with a faraway look.

14

Billy wondered if he was a Vietnam vet; he'd seen that empty look before. He noticed that the man's glass was empty.

"Hey, man, let me buy you a beer," Billy offered.

The lonely looking man turned slowly and looked straight into Billy's eyes without speaking.

"Merry Christmas! I'd like to buy you a beer. My name's Billy Sunday."

Billy extended his hand. There was a long pause and Billy was beginning to wish that he had minded his own business. Then the man took his hand.

"Hector Garcia. Thanks, and happy holidays to you as well."

"I didn't mean to disturb you."

"No problem, I was just lost in thought. It's fine. Actually, it's nice to talk to somebody."

"I know the feeling. Where are you headed?"

Hector paused for a moment before replying, "Rio."

"Me too!"

"No kidding? That's bizarre."

"Yeah, what are the odds?"

Hector turned away abruptly as a loud, fat man walked by. He turned back to Billy after the man sat down at a nearby table occupied by an attractive woman. Billy was getting the feeling that he should have left Hector alone.

"Hey, man, what takes you to Brazil? No, wait, let me guess. It's a woman, a very pretty woman," Hector said with a large toothy smile.

It was amazing. It was as if Billy had been talking to two different people.

"You got that right. She's a looker."

"Be careful, my friend. Those Brazilian women can be very dangerous."

Billy was perplexed. He didn't know how to read Hector. One minute he was sad and lonely and the next he was as jolly as could be. Now he was serious and foreboding.

"I'm kidding," said Hector, after noticing the look on Billy's face. "My wife, she was from Brazil. What a woman…I think it's that hot Latin blood, nothing in the world like it. What am I saying? I'm telling you?"

"No, you're right. There's no one like Ana."

15

"Ana. That's a good name. That was my wife's name," said Hector, his mood shifting once again to sadness.

With some reluctance, Billy asked, "What takes you to Rio, Hector?"

Hector ignored the question.

"I'm starving," said Billy, trying to change the subject. "I wonder if the food in this place is any good."

There was a long pause. Hector looked over at the fat man's table, and then he said, "Don't know, man, but you can bet it ain't cheap."

Billy flagged down a waitress and ordered a cheeseburger and fries. "How about you, Hector, you want anything?"

"No, man, I'm good. Thanks anyway."

Billy noticed Hector staring at the fat man and the attractive woman a few tables away. They were getting up to leave.

"Hey, man, it's been good talking with you, and thanks for the beer. Maybe I'll see you around."

Hector stood up and walked away before Billy could even answer him. The waitress brought Billy his food.

"Will there be anything else for you?"

"No thanks, ma'am," replied Billy as he paid for his food and tipped her five dollars.

"Thanks!" said the waitress. "And Merry Christmas!"

"You too," he said, feeling better after seeing the smile on her face.

Billy tried to call Ana after he left the bar but she was out. The housekeeper said that Ana had been waiting for his call but she had to go to dinner with her grandparents. She told Billy to try calling again before he boarded his plane.

As the plane was starting to board, Billy noticed that all the phone booths were occupied. He decided that he couldn't wait for a booth to open up and risk missing his flight, so he reluctantly boarded the plane. He soon discovered that his seat was all the way in the back, right next to the restroom. *Great, I guess this is what you get when you buy your ticket at the last minute...the smelliest seat and at top dollar to boot,* he thought.

As Billy made his way to his seat, he noticed that Hector was only a few rows in front of him. Hector didn't acknowledge him as he went by, even though he seemed to be looking right at him. Billy buckled in and tried to relax, preparing for the long flight ahead of him. Waiting for takeoff, his eyes wandered to the back of Hector's head. Billy wondered what had happened to him to make him so edgy. At the same time, Hector was replaying in his mind what had led him to where he was now, on a flight to Rio. He tried to stop thinking about it, but the images kept flashing by in an endless loop. He was close now, but he just wanted it to be over.

Hector followed the Lincoln into a crowded mall parking lot full of scurrying holiday shoppers. An old woman loaded down with packages struggled to open the door of her car, as the driver of the Lincoln tried to squeeze his land yacht into the parking space next to her. He tapped impatiently on his horn, startling the woman and causing her to drop her holiday packages in front of the car, further frustrating the man, who now leaned on his horn.

Hector reached for the gun on the seat of his pickup, tempted to rid the world of such a self-serving vermin. A security guard walked up from Hector's blind side and knocked on the Lincoln's window. Hector, who was sitting in his truck behind the Lincoln, waiting for it to park, slowly pulled around the car and circled around the parking lot. He found another parking space two rows over where he could still see the Lincoln.

The security guard helped the elderly woman pick up her packages and secure them in her car while standing in front of the Lincoln. After the woman safely backed out of her parking space and drove away, the security guard allowed the Lincoln to pull into the vacant parking space. Then he returned to his truck to continue his surveillance.

The driver of the Lincoln sat in his car, waiting.

Hector was puzzled. The man seemed to be in such a hurry but now he just sat there in his car. It looked as if he were reading the paper. Hector surveyed the parking lot. The security guard had gone around to the other side of the mall. It seemed to be quiet. Hector reached for the pistol, slid it into the pocket of his jacket, and got out of his truck. He walked slowly toward the Lincoln, staying out of the driver's view. Hector could feel his heart pounding, drowning in the emotions that were driving him to send this man to Hell where he surely belonged.

A taxi pulled up behind Hector and blew his horn just as Hector was pulling the pistol from his jacket pocket.

"Hey, bud, you the guy who called for a taxi?" asked the taxi driver.

Hector stood paralyzed.

A fat man opened the door of the Lincoln without noticing Hector's presence and shouted, "Here! What the hell took you so long? I've got a plane to catch and now I'm going to be late."

Hector kept walking, making his way back to his truck.

Billy became acquainted with many of the passengers after a few hours in the air, as people started up a conversation with him when they stood in line to use the restroom.

Billy was tired he wanted to try to get a couple of hours sleep before they reached Rio.

Billy woke with a startle when a fat man waddling down the aisle bumped him as he made his way to the restroom. It was the same man that Hector had stared at when they were in the bar. It was a good thing that the restroom was unoccupied at that moment. If the man had to wait to get in, he'd practically be sitting on Billy's lap. Having a seat next to the restroom was an experience that Billy didn't want to repeat. As soon as he landed, he would buy return tickets with seats closer to the front of the plane. He couldn't imagine Ana having to sit in the back next to the restroom.

Without warning, the plane started to shake and then suddenly surged before dropping in altitude. Billy felt like he was on an amusement park ride. The Fasten Your Seatbelt light came on and Captain John Davis spoke over the loudspeaker.

"Ladies and gentlemen, this is your captain speaking. At this time, I'd like to ask all passengers and flight attendants to return to your seats and fasten your seatbelts. We'll be experiencing some turbulence as we make our way around a bit of rough weather, so it'll be a bumpy ride for awhile. As soon as we get through it, I'll shut off the Fasten Your Seatbelt light and you'll be free to move about the cabin. Thank you for your cooperation."

18

In the cockpit, Drew Collins, the co-pilot, said, "Some turbulence. It feels like we're being shaken apart. These Andes Mountains can really play havoc with the weather this time of the year."

"I'm going to drop her down, try to get below this storm," said John.

"Do you think that would be a good idea in this weather, especially with these mountains all around us?" Drew asked. "We're entering Brazilian airspace now. Let me check with the tower in Rio and see if they can find us a smoother route."

Billy hadn't seen the fat man come out of the restroom yet. *Maybe he's too scared to come out, or maybe he's stuck,* he thought, wincing at the possibility.

Suddenly, the plane dropped steeply. It felt like a mile but Billy was sure it must have been only a dozen yards. No matter how far it actually was, it was enough to cause screams of panic. Some of the overhead compartments flew open, spilling out their contents. Carry-on baggage and packages slammed into unaware passengers, causing even more panic.

Billy heard a loud scream. He looked toward the front of the plane to see what was going on. The first class restroom door had flown open when the plane hit the air pocket. A woman tumbled out of the restroom and landed on a man's lap. The woman let out another scream as she attempted to free herself from the man. She was having a hard time moving because her pantyhose were bunched around her ankles. With the man's help, she finally got to her feet and stood in the aisle. Bending over, she frantically tried to pull up her pantyhose, but the plane suddenly hit another air pocket and she fell headfirst to the floor, rolling down the aisle. By this time, her pantyhose had torn, freeing one leg and allowing her to get to her feet. Kicking off her shoes, she reached down again and tore at her pantyhose, trying in vain to regain any sense of composure.

"Ladies and gentlemen, this is your captain speaking once again. We are experiencing quite a bit more turbulence than we had anticipated, but please remain calm. The flight attendants will be around to help anyone who is injured. Once we get through this weather, things will smooth out. We are now in Brazilian airspace and we are approaching the final leg of our trip, so it shouldn't be much longer until we get you to your final destination. Once again, thank you for your patience and cooperation."

"Captain," said Drew, "the left engine light is on. I think we may be losing it."

John looked down at the light on the control panel. Then he grabbed the checklist and flipped to the section detailing emergency procedures.

In row 28, Louise Thompson was sitting in the window seat. She had banged her head against the window when the plane dropped and she could feel a lump starting to swell. She turned to her husband and said, "Lyle, I hit my head. Am I bleeding?"

Lyle rolled his eyes as he pressed the call button for a flight attendant.

"Lyle, you didn't even look."

He rolled his eyes again as he turned to look at his wife's head.

"I saw stars when I hit my head," said Louise, and then she paused.

"What is it now?"

They'd been married for forty years and if there was anything he knew for sure, it was that his wife was a drama queen.

A flight attendant came to their row to see what they needed. The flight was starting to smooth out at the lower altitude.

"It's my wife. She's hit her head."

"Are you bleeding, ma'am?"

"I don't know. My husband never answered me."

Lyle rolled his eyes. He was used to this routine.

"Are you having any blurred vision? Do you feel nauseous?"

"Yes, I do feel a bit nauseous."

"I'll bring you some Ginger Ale and crackers then."

"But, miss, you haven't checked to see if I'm bleeding."

Lyle remained silent to avoid encouraging his wife's dramatics.

"Lyle, do you hear that?"

"Hear what?"

"That hissing sound."

He wanted to say, "It's probably the flight attendant having to deal with a drama queen," but he knew better. Instead, he said, "No, dear, I don't hear a thing."

Now annoyed, Louise asked, "Do you have your hearing aid on?"

The flight attendant returned with a cup of Ginger Ale and a few packets of crackers. "I'm sorry it took me so long, but we have some injured passengers that I needed to attend to."

"Well, dear, what am I?" said Louise, glaring coldly at the flight attendant. Then her eyes opened wide and she said, "Miss, do you hear that?"

"Hear what, ma'am?" The flight attendant was growing a little impatient with Louise. There were some people who actually needed help.

"That hissing sound."

Yeah, that hissing sound is me boiling over, thought the flight attendant. "No, ma'am, I'm sorry, I don't hear it. It's really noisy in here as it is and things are a little tense—"

"There it is again! And now there's a whining noise!"

"Well, yes, I hear—"

The flight attendant was cut off by a loud explosion, which ripped a three-foot hole in the plane next to Louise's head. The breach caused such a tremendous vacuum that it tore Louise from her seat sucking her along with the flight attendant through the gapping hole in the plane. Lyle and the male passenger sitting to his right had become wedged in the hole. The oxygen masks deployed, and paper, clothing, snacks, cups, cameras, tote bags, and anything that wasn't tied down was making its way to the breach in row 28.

The debris, along with Lyle and the other man, had temporally plugged the hole in the plane, which suddenly went into a nosedive. Passengers and carry-on baggage flew everywhere. Billy grabbed his oxygen mask, put it on, and then tried to help the woman to his right who sat screaming insanely. He saw a baby fly helplessly through the air and a flight attendant hit the ceiling of the plane.

The plane went into another dive and a flight attendant flew through the cabin as if she had been shot from a cannon. She slammed into the wall at the back of the plane, sending a serving cart airborne. Cans of beer and soda and pitchers of coffee spilled from its interior as it came to rest on the passengers seated in row 14.

Billy could feel the plane struggling to right itself as passengers and debris again went tumbling inside the cabin. Then the engine screamed and the plane shuttered. It seemed to be leveling out and slowing down, and everything seemed to be happening in slow motion. Passengers were bleeding and screaming as they struggled to free themselves and locate their loved ones.

As the captain struggled to keep the plane airborne with just one engine, he made an announcement.

"Ladies and gentlemen, I realize this is a difficult request to make under the circumstances, but I must ask you to please remain calm. We now have the plane under control and we should be landing shortly. Again, please remain calm, and if you are able, please look after your fellow passengers until we are able to land and get everyone out safely."

Inside the cockpit, the navigator issued a Mayday call.

"Mayday, this is Flight 153. Mayday, mayday, we are going down. Our flight coordinates are 120 degrees southeast...."

Under control! thought Billy as he looked at the carnage around him. There were bodies and debris everywhere. People were crying, screaming, pushing, and shoving, trying to get out of their seats. *Where do they think they're going? We're still in the air, at night and over the middle of a jungle no less.*

Two of the flight attendants were still able to function, though they were bleeding and one had an eye that was swollen shut. Their uniforms were torn and bloodstained. With total disregard for their own well-being, they did whatever they could to stop the hysteria within the cabin.

Billy could tell that they were running on only one engine because the plane felt as if it wanted to roll. Then it started to shake again and he saw a bright flash of light. *Enemy fire!* He thought. *No, wait, we're in Brazil, not Vietnam.*

It was lightning. They were flying into a thunderstorm. The captain's voice echoed throughout the ravaged cabin one last time.

"Ladies and gentlemen, we are losing altitude quickly and will have to make an emergency landing. To prepare for landing, please remain in your seats with your seatbelt buckled, and head down and on your lap. We will do our best to land this aircraft safely. Good luck and God bless."

Then there was silence.

Suddenly, the plane dropped as the pilot lowered the landing gear, shearing off the tops of the trees. The noise was deafening. Billy could feel trees being sheared off by the wings, and then the plane felt as if it were cartwheeling end over end in slow motion. Through the flashes of lightning, Billy could see bodies fly in every direction. Then he felt a rush of air and rain on his face. The plane seemed to be going in two different directions at once before it finally came to a stop.

Chapter Four

After Ana had returned from dinner with her grandparents, Rosesa, the housekeeper, said, "Mr. Billy called not more than twenty minutes after you left."

"Didn't you tell him to call back?" asked Ana in a panic.

"Si," said Rosesa in a calm, soothing voice. "I'm sure Mr. Billy tried to call again. Maybe he couldn't get to a phone. He told me that he had to wait forty-five minutes to make his first call."

"I know, you're right," said Ana, disappointed. "It's just that I'm so excited to see him. It's been two very long years since we've been together."

"He will be here soon," said Rosesa as she hugged Ana. She thought about when she was a young girl in love. "I'll draw you a hot bath so you can relax and get some sleep.

"Sleep said Ana, Ill lye a wake all night thinking of Billy."

"You better try to sleep Ana, you don't want to have bags under your eyes when you go to meet Mr. Billy"

I'll be back in the morning, I will help you get dressed and Heraldo can drive you to the airport. Mr. Billy should be here in no time."

The night was long, it seem to take a lifetime waiting for morning to arrive. "Which dress should I wear?" Giggled Ana

She held up the dress that she had lain out earlier.

"I don't think it's revealing enough," she murmured as she walked back to her closet and stared at the rows of dresses. She picked through them, looking for the one that would stick in Billy's memory like the first time he'd ever been kissed. She was pleased at how she had blossomed. She was no longer the skinny girl that he'd left two years ago. She had sent Billy sexy photos of herself while he was in Vietnam, and she was sure that at least half of his unit dreamed about her at night.

"My goodness, you are going to give that young man a heart attack," said Heraldo as he opened Ana's door for her. "And maybe this old man, too."

"Heraldo, you're a dirty old man," said Anna.

"I'm not dead yet," he replied, wishing he were young again. "Mothers of the saints, look at all of this traffic."

"It's Christmas. Where do you think all these people are going?" asked Ana. "You would think they would all be at home with their families."

"I have no idea, but I wish they would get wherever they're going. This traffic is making me crazy!"

A man in the car behind them pressed on his horn impatiently.

"Give it a rest!" Heraldo shouted as he gave the rude driver a universal hand gesture.

"Heraldo, I saw that."

"Sorry," he said, shrugging his shoulders in embarrassment. "But where does he think I can go? I can't drive over the car in front of me."

"I see the airport!" squealed Ana, which caused Heraldo to slam on the brakes and the driver behind them to press on his horn again.

"Heraldo, I can hardly breathe! I'm so excited!"

He just shrugged and thought, *that lucky devil.*

"Do you want me to come in with you?"

"Yes, please, Heraldo."

"Then I will drop you at the door and park the car."

The car was actually a limousine. As it was too long to fit into a regular parking space, Heraldo parked in the shuttle lot and waited for the shuttle bus to take him back to the terminal. He hated to ride the shuttle bus because the foreign drivers made him nervous.

The airport was exceptionally crowded. There was a live nativity scene in the lobby, with sheep, goats, and a crying baby adding to the festive spirit of Christmas. Ana thought she saw Billy making his way through the crowd.

"Billy! Billy!"

A fat man with his wife and kids stepped in front of Ana, blocking her view.

"Excuse me," Ana said as she tried to squeeze past the man. He was pushing a stroller with two screaming children aboard and one of them spilled his drink onto Ana's dress. Startled by the wet, sticky fluid running down her leg, Ana let out a scream.

"I'm so sorry," said the man as he reached to wipe Ana's leg.

"Stop!" she cried, trying to push the man's hand away from her.

Ana skirted her way around the stroller and swung her head around, frantically searching for Billy's face in the crowd.

Meanwhile, the shuttle bus carrying Heraldo to the main airport lumbered through the entire parking lot row by row, picking up passengers.

"Hey, pal. Do you think we could speed it up a bit?"

The driver gave Heraldo a look of annoyance.

"I'm sorry, sir. I am required to have a full load before leaving the parking lot."

"How much longer will this take? This bus is only half full."

"Well, after I make my way down all the rows...," he paused as he looked at the car parking two rows over, "I can proceed to the airport. You know you should allow yourself two hours before your flight." The driver looked at Heraldo in his rearview mirror.

"I'm not flying, I'm picking someone up."

"Didn't you just park a limo? You know, you could have just picked them up outside where it says Arrivals. They have a waiting area for limos," said the bus driver, while looking at Heraldo in the rearview mirror.

Where did they find this guy? Heraldo thought. He hoped he wouldn't be on the same shuttle bus when he had to go back to pick up the limo.

When Heraldo finally entered the lobby of the airport, he heard his name being called over the loudspeakers.

"Heraldo Gonzales, please report to the information desk. Heraldo Gonzales, please report to the information desk."

"All right already," he muttered. "Give it a rest."

"Heraldo, where have you been?" asked Ana, as if she were his mother and Heraldo was late for supper.

"I had to park the car, remember?" sighed Heraldo, rolling his eyes.

"I thought I saw Billy but now I can't find him."

"What happened to your dress?"

"Heraldo, didn't you hear what I just said?"

"Yes, you said you thought you saw Mr. Billy." Heraldo thought, *Great! I just got here and I haven't even had time to get a coffee. Now I've got to get back on that damn shuttle bus and get the car.* "Well, then, I'll go get the car."

"Heraldo, you aren't listening!"

"What?"

"I said I *thought* I saw Billy. I couldn't find him so I had him paged."

Now Heraldo wasn't feeling so bad; she was paging Mr. Billy as well.

"The woman at the information desk asked me what flight he was on and when I told her, she said that his flight had been delayed."

Great! Thought Heraldo, *I can go get a coffee after all!*

"Why has the flight been delayed? When do you think Billy's plane will arrive?"

"I don't know." Heraldo shrugged, his outstretched hands palms up. "I hope not too long." Secretly, he hoped that the delay would be long enough to give him a good excuse not to go to Christmas Mass with his wife. He hated going to church. Up and down, sit, kneel and stand. He couldn't understand why they couldn't just sit still in church.

"Heraldo, go over to the desk and ask them just how late Billy's flight is going to be."

"I can do that," he said, sticking out his lower lip and bobbing his head. "What's the flight number?"

"It's Flight 153 out of Houston."

"I'll be right back."

As Ana waited for Heraldo to return, she wondered if she would have time to buy a new dress at one of the shops in the airport. If so, she hoped she would be able to find a dress as sexy as the one she was wearing, now stained with red juice.

Heraldo overheard the gate agent at the counter talking to a man. The agent's badge declared that he was Pedro Santos.

"Flight 153 has been delayed, sir."

"When do you expect it to arrive?"

"We're not sure at this time."

"What is that supposed to mean?"

"I'm sorry, sir, I'm only giving you the information that I was given."

"Who gave you the information?"

"My manager, sir."

"Then I'd like to speak with the manager."

"I'm sorry, sir, but he's very busy."

Pedro knew that his manager, Mr. Lopez, was trying to contact the airport in Houston.

"My wife and daughter are on that plane."

A woman near the man said, "My husband is on that plane, too. This delay will ruin my plans for Christmas."

Pedro didn't want to be reminded that it was Christmas. His wife had already been down that road with him, wanting to know why he had to work even though he had seniority. In truth, he didn't have to work. He had signed up for the shift because he hated going to his in-laws' house every Christmas. The house was very small and his mother-in-law was a poor housekeeper. The dining room table was piled high with newspapers and old magazines. In the twenty years that he'd been married, he had never actually seen the top of the table. When it was time to eat, they ate buffet-style. After filling your plate, you were left standing, trying to eat your dinner while juggling your plate and drink, with kids and dogs running all over the place.

A short, barrel-shaped man wearing yellow Bermuda shorts and a large sun hat spoke up.

"The plane is over two hours late. What's going on here?"

"Sir, I'm sorry," said Pedro, wiping the sweat off his forehead with his handkerchief. "I will be more than happy to relay the information to you just as soon as I have any to give. I assure you, I also wish that the plane would get here soon. It is Christmas after all, and I would like to be with my family just as I am sure you would rather be with yours."

The barrel-shaped man was at a loss for words after such a deluge.

Then, a Catholic priest spoke in a very calm but authoritative voice.

"I would like to speak to the manager, please."

Pedro looked at the priest, focusing on his collar and the crucifix that dangled around his neck. "I'll get him right away," he replied as he reached for his handkerchief.

Pedro knocked on Mr. Lopez's office door. When there was no answer, Pedro slowly opened the door. Mr. Lopez was on the phone. Pedro winced when he saw the stress on Mr. Lopez's face as he listened to a voice on the other end of the line.

"What do you mean you don't know where it is? I've got a mob of people down here wanting to know where that plane is!"

Pedro hoping that Mr. Lopez hadn't seen him attempted to duck out of the office, thinking that Christmas dinner at his mother-in-law's house didn't seem so bad after all. Unfortunately, Mr. Lopez had seen him trying to retreat and motioned for him to come in.

"What is it?" Mr. Lopez asked, holding his hand over the phone's mouthpiece.

"Sir, I can see that you're busy."

"Spit it out!"

"Well, sir, there is a priest and a group of people who would like to speak with you."

"About what? Can't you see that I'm busy?"

"Yes, sir. It's about Flight 153. They want to know where it is."

"Damn it, that's what I'm trying to find out! Go and tell them that I'm on the phone with Houston right now."

Chapter Five

The glare from the fire was blinding, and the sickening smell of burning flesh mixed with jet fuel hung thickly in the humid air. Terrible screams of pain and cries for help rang in Billy's ears. Still strapped in his seat, Billy felt the woman seated beside him leaning heavily against his shoulder. He unfastened his seatbelt and turned to help her, but her glazed-over eyes told him that she hadn't made it.

Billy then noticed the large gaping hole in the plane not more than four rows from where his seat was. It looked like the plane had been cut in half, as if a giant guillotine had severed the tail section from the rest of the fuselage. He saw that the main part of the fuselage, half submerged in the swamp with a wing still attached, was burning. In the

29

light of the fire, debris could be seen hanging from the trees, and what looked like human carnage floated in the swamp.

There were cries of pain in the distance, and Billy could swear he heard screams coming from the trees. Red dots started to appear in the swamp, along with reflections of the burning fuselage. Suddenly, Billy heard horrifying screams and thrashing sounds in the water, then silence. A woman cried for help and he strained to see where the cry was coming from. Making his way to the muffled cries, he saw two bodies, one on top of the other. Then he saw a bloody hand squirming out from between the bodies, fingers wiggling as if they were playing the piano. It appeared that the two bodies were atop a third person.

Billy struggled to lift the battered corpse of a fat man off a nun. The man was missing an arm and part of his face. Billy felt his stomach roll. The nun was missing a leg and both of her arms had been brutally broken; they dangled as he lifted her off the trapped woman. The woman's bloody hand reached up and grabbed the front of his shirt.

The hand held Billy's shirt with a death grip. Billy could hear what sounded like a young woman pleading for help. Billy grabbed the young woman's hand from his shirt pulling her through the carnage. The young woman gasped for breath. The young woman was a nun. Billy asked the young nun if she was all right? Still gasping for breath the nun praised God for still being alive. Thank you sir for your help I couldn't breathe. "Your name sir?"

"Billy, Billy Sunday, taken with the young nuns beauty.

"My name is sister Mary Alice."

Billy broke from his trance, wondering why such a beautiful young woman would be a nun.

In the firelight of the wreckage, with blood glistening on his arm and a long lock of blond hair dangling over one eye, a man frantically pulled at the twisted metal that trapped his young wife in a row of mangled seats. The young man was hysterical, crying out, "Lara! Lara!" And then, "God, why? Why?"

Alfred still remembered the glow on Lara's face as she was telling her parents about their upcoming great adventure. Lara was proud that Alfred and her were travailing

30

to south east Brazil from a little town of Milnor North Dakota to work as missionaries among the Kerenal Indian tribe.

Now, sitting among the wreckage while holding Lara's lifeless hand, he suddenly broke down crying. He looked to the sky and whispered hoarsely, "Why? Why?"

Without Lara by his side, Alfred had lost the will to live. He decided that the only way to be with her again was through death. He carefully lifted her limp body and cradled her in his arms. Then he lowered himself, with Lara still in his arms, into the water and slowly began to make his way through the swamp, away from the plane and away from the life he once knew.

Lou woke with Betty's head face down in his lap. Betty body was twisted at an odd angel. Lou took a deep breath and looked up praying to God that Betty was just unconscious. But he knew better, when Lou reached down to lift Betty's head from his lap he could tell that her neck was broken.

Lucy miller woke screaming. What was left of a stocking covered leg wearing a black laced up shoe was laying a crossed her shoulder. Billy ran to the historical screaming woman and pulled away the leg, freeing the screaming woman. But Lucy still kept screaming. Billy smacked the woman's face several times trying to stop her screaming. Billy was getting ready to shake the screaming woman, when sister Mary Alice stopped him gently moving Billy aside and wrapped her arms around the screaming woman and pulled her in close to her bosom. Billy thought that maybe he should start scream still in Ahh of sister Mary Alice's beauty.

Billy looked around the cabin of the plane. The light was poor at best, what light there was, was coming from the burning fuselage of the plane. Hector was now seated one row back from where the tail of the plane broke free of the fuselage. Billy noticed that Hector wasn't moving. Billy made his way to Hector; Billy shook Hector he didn't respond. Billy put his hand on Hectors chest, he was still breathing but very shallow. Billy, tried to release Hectors seatbelt, it was stuck. Billy pulled on it franticly. While trying to release hectors seatbelt Billy heard a loud hiss. He looked up not ten feet from where Billy stood were two red glowing eyes, and they were coming closer. Billy reached into his pocket pulling out his Buck 110 pocketknife and cut the seatbelt away from

Hector. As Billy went to reach for Hector he woke up and freaked out on Billy grabbing for Billy's knife.

"Hold on there, partner I'm only trying to help you."

Hector stopped fighting Billy for the knife and looked up at Billy.

"What, happened asked Hector?"

"The plane crashed said Billy.

"Crashed? No said Hector it couldn't have."

"It did said Billy" as he reached for Hector trying to get him away from the edge of the plane before Hector noticed the fast approaching alligator. Billy slowly put his knife away before guiding Hector away from the broken edge of the plane.

As Billy helped Hector to safety he noticed a woman move her hand.

Billy, looked at the woman, she was coved with blood. But there it was again her hand moved slowly reaching up and touching her head.

Lou had freed himself from Betty and his seatbelt he gently laid Betty back in what was left of her seat as he tried to stand.

After Billy sat Hector down in a seat at the rear of the plane he went back to help the blood covered woman.

Billy spoke softly to the woman telling her that she was going to be all right, hopping that she wouldn't start screaming like the woman that sister Mary Alice was holding. Julie didn't scream, she grabbed onto Billy like she was in a very deep lake and she was drowning. Billy pushed her back from him and shouted, its okay you're going to be fine.

"Fine! The woman shouted back. Do I look fine to you? I'm covered with blood."

"At least it not your blood that you are covered in."

Billy could see the woman sitting beside Julie had a deep laceration in her neck cutting her jugular vein. Her heart kept pumping her blood out onto Julie till it ran out.

The twisted remains of the plane's nose were half submerged in the swamp among the shredded trees and vines. It looked as if it had been torn from the fuselage by a giant's hand and then tossed aside like a piece of litter.

32

"Listen. Someone's calling for help," said Hector.

"I hear it," said the nun, straining her eyes to see where the cry was coming from.

An alligator came out from under the wreckage of the tail section that they were standing on and began to hiss.

"Damn, they're everywhere!" said Hector, his heart pounding hard against his chest.

"Free lunch," said Billy. "There'll be a feeding frenzy with all that blood in the water. Every alligator within ten miles is on its way."

A cold shiver ran up Sister Mary Alice's spine. Then she heard the cry for help again.

"I think it's coming from the nose of the plane, the part that's buried in that heap of trees, though I can't quite make it out yet."

"No, listen," said a short, portly man wearing a flowered shirt and blue shorts. "I think it's coming from the restroom."

He tried to open the door but it was jammed. He put his ear against the door. He was sure there was someone inside. He looked around and spotted a piece of metal from the wreckage. He wedged it into the doorframe and pushed with all he had, but the metal just bent.

"We have to find something else," he said and started digging through the debris. He found a piece of heavier gauge metal and worked it into the doorframe. He gave it a good push and the door finally sprang open. There, still seated on the toilet with his pants around his ankles, was the fat man Billy had seen enter the restroom before they crashed. His nose was bloody and he was covered with blue liquid. He was trapped by one wall that had been pushed in on impact.

Hector did nothing but stare at the man, who cried out, "You got to get me out of here! I'm claustrophobic and I'm losing my mind!"

"Do you have any injuries?" asked Billy.

"I think my nose is broken."

The man in the flowered shirt tried to push against the wall that had trapped the man. It wouldn't budge.

"I've got an idea," he said. He took out his Swiss army knife and cut off a couple of seatbelts from the seats nearby. "If we tie these seatbelts together and slide them around him and then pulled, we should be able to dislodge him from the toilet."

"Now wait a minute. Do I look like a stump in a field or a car stuck in the mud? I have a name."

"Excuse me, what would your name be?"

"Dick Frost."

"Lou Smiley."

Lou slid the seatbelts around Dick.

"Okay, on three. One...two...three!"

Dick let out a loud bellow as his body lifted from the toilet and squeezed past the collapsed wall.

The dim morning light peeked its way into what was left of the tail section. Smelly and dripping, Dick started complaining about the airline's incompetence even before he had taken the time to thank the men for rescuing him from the toilet. He vowed to sue the company for all it was worth.

"I'm a lawyer," said Dick. "I can help anyone who's interested. I'll even cut my rate to twenty-five percent. After all, we're sharing the same miseries."

"You're ready to sue, but what about saying thanks for pulling your fat ass out of the toilet?" said Lou.

Dick started to reply but Billy said, "That's enough. We need to stop bickering. We have to think about how we're going to get out of here before worrying about whose fault it is."

"We know whose fault it is," said Dick.

"Enough already!" Lou shouted. "Billy's right. We need to focus on getting out of here. But first we have to get the dead out of the cabin."

"What do you mean?" asked Julie York, a 67-year-old widow still covered in blood who was flying to Rio to visit her daughter Bridgett for the holidays. "Can't we leave them here for the rescue people?"

34

"Yes, let's just wait for the rescue people," said Lucy Miller, a 52-year-old redhead from Minnesota who was traveling with her girlfriend Sally, hoping to enjoy the sun and beaches of Rio.

"No, we can't wait," said Billy. "We need to get them out of here before they start attracting predators." He was thinking about the alligators he had already seen.

"But the rescue people should be here soon," said Julie, looking out through the torn opening of the wreckage.

The man held his hand to his head. He felt a large bump starting to form. He was groggy and felt like he was awakening from a deep sleep. Then he heard buzzing and felt stinging sensations. The plane felt like it was leaning forward. He tried to turn his head but there was something pushing against the back of his seat. He could see shadows flickering on the bulkhead wall in front of him and he could smell something burning.

Jesus, he thought as he regained his senses. *We've crashed! The flippin' plane has crashed!*

Feeling panic spread throughout his body, he struggled to unfasten his seatbelt. Then he pushed off the limp body seated beside him. He got to his feet and thought; *I've got to get out of here.* As he turned to make his way out of the cabin, he felt something dripping on the back of his neck. He looked up and saw a man skewered upon a limb jutting out of the bulkhead above him. He became sick to his stomach and vomited.

The woman felt someone shaking her shoulder and she heard a voice far off in the distance. Then she felt a pain in her right leg. *Why is it dark? Where am I?* She thought.

Then the voice became louder.

"Are you all right?"

She looked up to see a large man in glasses with blood on his shirt.

"What the hell is this!" she shouted, hoping that this was a bad dream from the anchovy pizza that she ate during the flight.

"Are you all right, miss?"

She looked at the man and screamed, hoping that she would wake herself up.

"Please," said the man, "don't scream. I can help you get out."

"Out! Out, of what? Where am I?" she shouted as she reached for her handbag, which held a small canister of mace.

"It's all right. We've crashed, but everything is going to be fine."

"Fine?" she screeched. "Of course it will because this is just a dream, right?" Her hand fumbled in her handbag for the canister of mace.

"No, you aren't dreaming," said the man as he tried to calm her down. "We've crashed in the jungle and the plane has broken apart."

"Tell me you're kidding," she said, panic spreading through her body like wildfire. "How could this be happening? I was supposed to go to the beach, get a tan, and maybe, if I was lucky, get laid. But, a plane crash? That was definitely not on my wish list."

The man gripped her arm gently.

"My name is Fred Dowding. And yours?"

"It's Jan Lombardi."

"Jan, please, let me help you get out of here. I'm afraid the plane might catch fire."

In the cabin just behind the cockpit, the man woke and found himself pinned under a row of seats. The pain in his right arm and leg was unbearable. Then he realized what had happened. He began to shout for help.

He was in the coffee business and had been traveling to Brazil for years. He was a bachelor with no family to speak of, except a couple of cousins that he hadn't talked to in years. The people at his office probably didn't even notice that he was gone. As for his neighbors, he barely knew them, even though he had been living at the same address for fifteen years. Now he was trapped in the wreckage of an airplane, where he was sure that he would die, not that anyone would really miss him.

As Fred and Jan made their way to the open end of the cabin, they couldn't believe what they saw. It was like something from a Hollywood movie. The wreckage of the plane was scattered over fifty yards in all directions, and the main fuselage lay burning with one wing still attached. The tail of the plane was twisted among a pile of sheared off trees. Debris hung from the trees as monkeys howled and birds screamed. Little red dots could be seen everywhere and they were moving.

"What the hell are those red dots?" asked Jan, still holding on to the remote possibility that this was all a bad dream.

"I think they're alligators," said Fred, wishing he had thought before he spoke.

"Alligators! Don't be messing with me, man. I am definitely not in the mood."

They heard a man call for help. Fred turned back toward the cabin. "Did you hear that?"

"Yeah, but I can't tell where it came from."

A monkey let out a loud howl. It sounded as if it was sitting right on top of the wreckage.

"There it is again," said Fred as he made his way back into the cabin. "It's coming from over there." He strained his eyes, looking into the dark cabin for signs of movement.

Jan followed Fred, afraid to let him out of her sight.

Fred stumbled over something in the aisle. He looked back to see what it was and realized that it was a severed leg, still clothed in trousers. He started to vomit again.

"Oh my God, Irene," Jan mumbled as she began to vomit, too.

The man cried out again, half in pain and half in fright.

Fred, trying to regain his composure, forced himself to find the origin of the cries. Jan turned away, trying to find some fresh air, but the smell of both the vomit and the jet fuel were too much for her. She fainted and hit the floor with a loud thud. Fred, too busy frantically pulling at the wreckage to reach the injured passenger, didn't hear her fall.

"Hold on, buddy. Just a little longer."

Fred looked behind him and saw Jan on the floor, trying to sit up.

"Jan, what happened? Are you all right?"

Jan nodded weakly as Fred went back to trying to free the man from the row of seats. As Fred pulled off what was left of the seat that had pinned the man down, the man let out a scream of pain. A piece of metal from the seat had punctured his mangled leg.

"Crap," said Fred, realizing what he just did. "Hold on there, buddy," he said as he tied his belt around the man's leg.

Then Fred heard another cry for help. He got the man to a sitting position and said, "Jan, you stay here with—sorry, buddy, what's your name?"

"Coleman," gasped the man.

"I think there's someone in the cockpit. You two stay here while I go check it out."

Fred wrestled with the cockpit door and finally got through. The cockpit was in shambles. A tree had pierced the nose of the plane, killing the co-pilot, the flight engineer, and the navigator. The second flight engineer sat motionless in his seat. His broken neck was unable to sustain the weight of his head, which was twisted away from his body and resting on his left shoulder. The pilot, who was pinned under the control panel, drifting in and out of consciousness, managed to survive the crash.

"Captain, can you hear me?" Fred shouted.

He nodded and then winced in pain. "Can you help?"

"Hang in there. I'll get you out."

By the time Fred got Captain Davis into the cabin with Jan and Coleman, it had started to rain. Fred wondered if there were any other survivors besides just the four of them in the nose of the plane. He went to the edge of the cabin and looked toward the tail section. Through the pouring rain, he thought he saw movement and began shouting.

"I see them!" said Jan, hoping it was a rescue helicopter.

Fred yelled louder.

Billy heard Fred's shouts, and waved and shouted back, "Do you have a raft?"

"Captain, do we have a raft on board?"

"Yes, we do! I can't believe I forgot about the life raft and survival gear. Must have been that landing," he quipped.

"Yeah, we have a raft!" yelled Fred. "Give us a few minutes to find it." Then, to Captain Davis, he asked, "Where is it?"

"It's up there, in the ceiling," he said and pointed to where it was stored. "Right up there. There's not much of the ceiling left but the raft should still be there."

Fred realized that he would have to free the man impaled by the tree in order to reach the raft.

"What are we going to do with a raft?" asked Jan.

"It's the only way to get to the tail section, especially with all those alligators," said Fred.

"So you expect us to paddle through an alligator-infested swamp in a flimsy raft? I don't think so. Why can't we just wait here for the helicopter?"

"We would probably die before anyone found us."

"Die? What do you mean?"

"Just that. What are we going to eat? What are we going to drink?"

"Well how long do you figure it will take before we're rescued?"

"Fred's right," said Captain Davis weakly. "They haven't even missed us yet."

"What are you talking about? You're the captain. Surely you told someone what was going on," said Jan.

"I'm sorry. We did send out a Mayday call but now that we've crashed in the middle of a jungle, there's no way for anyone to know where we are."

"What are you talking about?" said Jan, her voice now quivering. "What about the radar screen? Wouldn't they have seen us drop off the screen?"

"No," said Captain Davis as he bit his lip in pain, "because there is no radar screen."

"Sure there is," said Jan. "I saw it in the movies."

"I'm afraid that it's only in the movies."

Fred turned white. He knew that it would take some time before anyone reached them due to the terrain, but if they hadn't seen them disappear from the radar screen—because there was no screen—then their chances of ever being found were slim to none.

"Captain, I thought there was a screen," said Fred.

"Nope," said Captain Davis with a quiver in his voice. The pain was becoming overwhelming.

"Then how do they know where to look for us?" asked Fred.

"They don't," he replied, beginning to shiver uncontrollably.

"That's bullshit!" shouted Jan. "I would have never got on this frickin' plane if I'd known that they don't keep track of where the planes are going. That's just great! We crashed in some frickin' jungle and nobody even knows that we're missing or where to look for us." *Just like my ex-boyfriend. I could be gone a couple of days before he even noticed,* she thought.

"That's about right," said Captain Davis. "If it's any consolation to you, I don't like it, either."

"Now what do we do?" asked Jan.

Captain Davis bit his lip again. The pain was making him queasy and lightheaded. "We'll have to find our own way out."

"Are you kidding me?" said Jan. "I can't find my way around the block without getting lost and you want me to find my way out of a frickin' jungle?"

"Jan, let's worry about that later. Right now I'm going to need you to help me free this man from the tree."

"Freddy, are you nuts? This guy tells me I have to find my way out of a frickin' jungle and now you want me to pull a corpse out of a tree?"

"Listen, we need the raft to get out of this jungle and I can't move him myself. Captain Davis and Coleman both have broken legs, so that leaves you."

"Thanks, Freddy. Don't get pissed off at me if Irene spills her cookies all over you."

"Who's Irene?"

"That's my stomach. And let me tell you, she ain't too happy."

Jan reluctantly followed Fred. She felt Irene starting to rumble as she peered up at the man. He looked like a frog on the end of a spear. Fred reached up and started pulling on the man. His arms and legs started to quiver. Jan screamed and then hit the floor. Fred let go of the man and started to slap Jan's face lightly, trying to bring her back to consciousness.

Jan came to and felt Fred slapping her face. She kicked him between the legs and Fred's eyes crossed. He fell to the floor and went into a fetal position, trying to catch his breath. Jan realized that Fred was just trying to revive her.

"I'm sorry, Fred! I freaked out when I woke up to you slapping me in the face."

Fred just stared up in disbelief. When he finally caught his breath and could stand, he motioned for Jan to help him. Jan closed her eyes as they slid the man from the tree. They dragged his remains to the cut-off end of the cabin and dropped him into the water,

40

where it splashed loudly. Almost immediately, two alligators latched on to the body and pulled at it fiercely.

Jan turned away and started to cry.

"We need to get the rest of the dead out of the cabin before the alligators try climbing up in here," said Fred. Then he reached up and retrieved the raft, pulling it to the edge of the cabin. He pulled a cord and the raft began to inflate.

"Fred, you aren't really thinking of putting that raft in the water, are you?"

Fred looked at Jan for a moment before replying, "Yeah, that's usually what you do with a raft. You put it in the water."

"But you just said we shouldn't be attracting the alligators."

"They won't bother you in the raft," said Captain Davis.

"They aren't going to bother me 'cause my little white ass ain't going anywhere near that raft."

"Just help me lower it down," said Fred.

"Didn't you just see what those alligators did to that poor man's body a few minutes ago?"

"Please, Jan, just give me a hand lowering the raft. Then, if you could just hold the line tight while I get in, I would appreciate it."

As Jan helped Fred lower the raft into the water, the red glowing eyes started to move closer to the raft. A cold shiver ran down Jan's spine.

"Freddy, there's a big knife in this bag. You'd better take it with you," said Jan.

"That's a machete," said Captain Davis. "There should be two of them, along with a flare gun and a first aid kit."

" A machete? I can't believe there's a machete on a commercial airline."

" There on all the plane that fly over countries with jungles" Said Capitan Davis

His bowels turning to liquid, Fred reluctantly took one of the machetes. *With my luck, I'd miss the alligator and sink the raft,* he thought.

"Look! There's a man in a raft!" shouted Lou.

Fred paddled slowly across the swamp as the red beady eyes followed his every movement. He could feel the sweat beading on his forehead as he tried to focus on the tail of the plane and forget about the alligators. Suddenly, a large monkey started howling in

41

the tree right above him. Fred looked up and froze. A large anaconda snake was slowly extending itself toward him.

"Paddle, man!" yelled Hector.

Fred looked at Hector and began to paddle harder. The tail was only about fifty yards away from the nose but it seemed more like fifty miles.

Billy and Hector climbed down and stood on a piece of metal hanging from the tail. Hector reached out to Fred as the large snake entered the water, its head raised like a periscope.

"Hey, man," said Hector, "don't look behind you. Just grab my hand."

Fred panicked and froze, picturing himself being wrapped up by the huge snake and then being pulled into the water, where the alligators would fight over him.

Billy jumped down into the raft and grabbed Fred's arm.

"Hector, give me a hand!"

Hector hesitated, his gaze fixed on the snake.

"Come on, Hector! We don't want to tear a hole in the raft. It's our only way out."

The snake spotted a corpse floating in the water and abruptly turned away from the raft. When the snake turned away, Hector grabbed Billy's hand, pulling him and Fred to the safety of the plane.

"Hey, man, I'm Billy." Pointing to each person in turn, he said, "This here is Hector, Lou, Dick, Julie, Lucy, and Sister Mary Alice."

"I'm Fred."

"How many of you survived?" asked Billy?

"Including me, four. Two men, Captain Davis and Coleman—they both have broken legs—and a woman, Jan, who's relatively unharmed."

Just then, Lucy cried out, "When are we going to be rescued?"

"Well, to be honest, I don't think that we will be rescued," said Fred.

"What are you talking about? Of course we'll be rescued," said Lou.

Fred paused for a moment before he spoke.

"Captain Davis said that they don't even know that we've crashed."

"That's nonsense," said Lou. "We crashed hours ago. They would have seen us drop off the radar screen."

"That's what I thought, but Captain Davis said that there is no radar screen."

"Bull," said Lou as everyone chimed in in agreement. "I've seen it on TV."

"That's it. Unfortunately, it's only on TV and in the movies. In real life, they don't have a clue where we are."

Lucy began to weep.

"Why, that's bullshit!" shouted Dick. "When will they start looking for us?"

"Captain Davis said that they would start looking in a couple of days, at the earliest."

"A couple of days? Are you mad?" said Dick.

"I think I'm heading in that direction," said Fred.

"Have you forgotten that today is Christmas?"

"Christmas? What does that have to do with them rescuing us? This is Brazil and we are lost in the jungle. The jungle is a very large place. It could take weeks to find us. You would have better luck finding a needle in a haystack or even a field of haystacks. I'm just telling you what the captain said and I think he would know. And if anyone's in a hurry to be rescued, I think he would be at the top of the list. His leg's broken pretty badly and he's in a lot of pain."

"Then what do we do now?" asked Lou.

"We have to find our own way out."

"That doesn't answer my question about Christmas," said Dick.

"Being that it is Christmas, in Brazil, most airports will be running with a skeleton crew. The first thing they'll do is check to see whether we landed at another airport."

"Hold on there, pal. There aren't too many airports that we could've landed at, so how hard could it be for them to realize that we didn't land?"

"You would think it wouldn't be a big deal, but I'm just telling you what the captain told me."

"Then what do we do?" asked Dick, panic flickering in his voice.

"Like I said, we have to find our own way out."

"But we don't even know where we are. How are we supposed to know what direction to go in?"

"I think we should head east."

"East? Why east?"

"Well, we were heading southeast to get to Rio and the Andes are to the west."

"Hold on. How do you know that we aren't on the other side of the Andes?"

"I don't. I'm just making an educated guess."

"Educated?"

"Yeah, educated," said Fred, becoming a little annoyed. "Dick, it makes sense that we are on the east side of the Andes. So if we continue east, we're bound to run into a river that will take us out of this jungle."

"What about food?"

"What about it? What do you think you'll be eating if you choose to stay here and wait to be rescued?"

"Well, don't they have emergency rations on the plane?"

"No, there are no emergency rations. We might be able to search through the wreckage for the food carts, but even if we did find food, it would most likely be spoiled by now with this heat and the rain."

"Then what will we eat while we're trying to find our way out of here?"

"Whatever we can find along the way. I'm sure we could kill something or catch some fish. Hell, maybe we could even kill one of those alligators."

"What about the injured? They'll just slow us down. And what if they die along the way?"

"We can't just leave them behind. They'll never make it. We'll have to take them with us."

"Dick, he's right," said Hector. "We have no choice. We have to take our chances and take them with us."

"Okay, so you all agree we should try to find our way out of here?" asked Fred.

Everyone except Dick nodded. When they all turned to him, staring, he finally said, "Yeah, all right, I'm in."

"Then the first thing we need to do is to get the other survivors over here where they'll be safe and somewhat out of the weather. After we get the injured settled, we need to start salvaging everything that we can carry."

44

Daybreak finally arrived. The light of the new day, Christmas, 1971, illuminated a horrific sight of battered and torn bodies and debris from what was once Flight 153. The smell of smoke and death hung heavily in the hot, humid air. Pieces of clothing hung dripping from the trees. Monkeys howled and birds screamed in the jungle. A large snake slithered through the water, while an alligator dragged away the remains of a passenger. The body was so mangled it was hard to tell if it was a man or a woman. Staring in total disbelief, the survivors of Flight 153 had never witnessed so much human carnage.

Except for one.

Weighted down with casualties, the soldiers were hunkered in the tall elephant grass, taking heavy enemy fire from the North Vietnamese as they awaited rescue. A helicopter appeared on the horizon, stopped, and then hovered. Billy stared up at the Huey as if it was an angel sent straight from God. He fired a green smoke bomb into the sky, giving the helicopter their location and providing some cover as the Huey lowered itself to the ground. As it touched down, the Vietcong's attack intensified.

Keeping low to the ground, the marines began transporting the wounded to the helicopter. Its rotors chopped at the air, creating a cyclone of dust and flattening the elephant grass to the ground. One soldier who was running with a wounded man on his back fell to the ground. Part of his leg had been shot off from a round fired from a fifty-caliber machine gun. Both men screamed in agony as they hit the ground.

Billy grabbed what was left of the soldier's badly mangled leg and quickly applied a tourniquet, while another soldier picked up the wounded man and loaded him into the helicopter. As it powered up its engines to lift up into the sky, Billy loaded the soldier with the tourniquet into the helicopter. The bullet-riddled Huey, straining under the weight of the wounded, finally lifted off the ground and took flight.

As the helicopter made its way to the horizon, a single RGP streaked skyward toward it. Suddenly, the Huey exploded into a fireball. Hot metal and human remains rained down to the ground below, as Billy and his patrol lay flat, seeking cover in the tall elephant grass from heavy enemy fire. It was a sight that would replay in Billy's mind forever.

Billy and Hector helped Fred into the raft first before getting in themselves. They paddled back across the swamp to the nose of the plane, where the others were patiently waiting. When they reached the nose and got out of the raft, Fred introduced Billy and Hector to Jan, Coleman, and Captain Davis.

"How many alive?" asked Captain Davis.

"Including Billy and Hector, seven," said Fred.

"I can see that you and Coleman are bad off," said Billy. "We need to keep your broken legs from moving so they don't get worse or get infected. Maybe we could make splints using some inflated flotation devices and seatbelts. But we need something solid to keep your legs straight."

"How about the curtain rods in the galley, would they work?" asked Jan.

"Yeah, I think they'll do just fine," said Billy.

They quickly went to work making the splints. Then, as gingerly as they could, they strapped the splints to the men's legs. Coleman and Captain Davis tried not to cry out but the pain was excruciating. After resting for a few minutes, they were loaded into the raft, followed by Jan and the others. Seeing Jan trembling with fear, Fred reassured her that the alligators wouldn't bother them as long as they stayed in the raft.

They were only ten yards from the tail when the sky opened up on them. It rained so hard that they could no longer see the tail of the plane. Hector kept paddling and then Billy made him stop.

"Why are we stopping?" cried Jan. She thought the rain would soon swamp the raft, leaving them defenseless against the alligators.

"We can't risk puncturing the raft on the jagged edges of the plane," said Billy.

"How long can we sit here before we sink?"

"We won't sink as long as we bail out the water."

"With what?"

"With our hands if we have to."

Fifteen minutes later, the rain stopped and the sun came out. When they reached the tail of the plane, Fred, Hector, and Billy lifted Coleman and Captain Davis onto the

46

tail section and then got back into the raft to look for supplies from the wreckage of the plane. Sunlight poured through the gaping hole of the jungle's canopy. They looked up and watched a monkey drag a bright red dress up into the trees.

"With any luck, he'll leave it at the top of the tree so the spotters can find us," said Fred.

"Look over there," said Hector, pointing as he swatted another mosquito. "What's that blue thing?"

There were clouds of mosquitoes all around them; it was as if they were traveling through fog. As the raft approached the blue container, an alligator raised its head and let out a loud hiss, startling the men. Two bodies floated among the debris surrounding the blue container.

"Now what?" said Hector, with a shudder of fear?

"Remember this place. We'll come back to it after that gator's belly is full," said Fred.

They paddled through the debris, picking up suitcases and boxes until the raft could hold no more.

"Stop!" Hector shouted as Billy reached for another suitcase. "You want to sink us? I don't know about you, but I'm in no hurry to feed these alligators."

Back at the tail section, Lucy cried, "I know we're all going to die and be eaten by those awful alligators!" She was lying huddled in a corner, holding her side and groaning she was suffering from what appeared to be internal injuries. The pain grew more intense each time she tried to talk, so eventually she spoke less, to the relief of the other survivors.

All that Lucy had wanted was to lie on the beach and experience a little nightlife, but she didn't want to do it alone. It took awhile, but she finally persuaded her friend Sally to accompany her, even though Sally had wanted to spend Christmas with her daughter and her family in Cleveland. Lucy hadn't been with a man for years and thought she could find one in Rio, even if she had to pay him. She thought her chances would improve if she had a sidekick. Lucy now realized that her selfishness had cost Sally her life and it would more than likely cost her her own life.

47

The men arrived with a pile of soggy suitcases and boxes and unloaded them into the cabin. The others stood in silence as they stared at the belongings of those who didn't survive. With more curiosity than a three-year-old on Christmas morning, Dick was the first one to dig into the pile, grabbing an expensive-looking piece of luggage and frantically pulling at its latches. They were locked.

"Damn it! How are we going to open these damn locks?"

The others looked at him with disgust.

"If you would be more patient, I'll show you," said Fred, deciding that he really didn't like the man.

"Did you find any of the blue containers?" asked Captain Davis.

"We found one," said Hector, "but we couldn't reach it. An alligator had already laid claims on it."

"I hope there's food in one of those boxes. We're all getting a little hungry," said Lou, his stomach growling.

"What happened to the packets of peanuts and crackers and those little bottles of booze that we found earlier?"

The group turned and stared at Dick.

"What? I needed something for my pain. I've got a broken nose, not that any of you care," he said sheepishly while putting a hand up to his nose.

"What about the crackers and the peanuts?" asked Lou.

"I couldn't drink on an empty stomach. I've got an ulcer."

"Stop bickering," said Captain Davis. "Since I'm in no condition to lead, I'm putting Fred in charge. From now on, he'll make the decisions, especially when it comes to rationing food and supplies."

Fred's mouth dropped open. "Me? But I've never been in this sort of situation before," he protested, not wanting the responsibility.

"You'll do fine," said Jan, digging through the soggy pile for something to eat. "What's in this box?" she asked as she desperately tried to open it. It was marked "Perishable" and "Sisters of Christ."

"That must be one of the boxes we were bringing to the missions," said Sister Mary Alice.

"What's in it?" asked Jan, not having any luck opening it.

"I have no idea. It could be food."

Lou got out his Swiss army knife and cut into the box.

"Beans and corned beef hash!" he cried. He really didn't care for beans. His ex-wife cooked them five nights a week, and after they had divorced, Lou had vowed that he would never eat beans again.

"Open them!" said Dick, his mouth salivating like a creek in the spring after a hard thunderstorm.

"Corned beef hash. I don't know that I've ever eaten it from a can before," said Jan. But it beat the hell out of beans. Beans and Irene didn't get along.

The rain had started again. The jungle seemed to come alive, with birds squawking and monkeys howling, and alligators hissing as they fought over the remains of those who had perished.

"I can't take it!" cried Lucy. "Those awful sounds...I'm losing my mind!"

Sister Mary Alice went over to comfort her. Lucy buried her face in the nun's habit and sobbed uncontrollably.

Jan went to check on Coleman. He was burning up with a fever but shivering uncontrollably.

"Fred, Coleman isn't doing very well. Can you go and try to retrieve that medical container you found earlier?"

"I'll have Billy and Hector go back out," said Fred.

Dick, overhearing Fred and Jan's conversation, said, "That sounds like a good idea. My nose is killing me and my head is pounding."

"Maybe you'd like to give them a hand then," said Fred.

"I would, but I'm in way too much pain."

"That headache is more than likely from all the booze that you drank."

Dick gave Fred the finger and told him to screw himself.

Fred, seeing red, silently counted to ten instead of reaching out and driving Dick's fat nose through the other side of his head. After he was done counting, he said, "You know, we have enough to worry about without wasting our time on you."

Dick just waved his finger in front of Fred's face.

Jan stood between them and got right in Dick's face. "Grow up!" she shouted.

Dick turned and walked away. He was going crazy. He'd been hooked on painkillers and booze for years and now he was starting to get the shakes. He needed at least a little booze to make him forget that he was trapped in the tail of a wrecked plane in the middle of a jungle. To make matters worse, he was trapped with a nun, two whiny old ladies, a broad who wore her handbag strapped across her chest as if she were guarding her life savings, a guy in a stupid flowered shirt, a know-it-all who was now supposedly in charge, a Mexican, a young soldier, a guy who looked like he wasn't going to make it, and a crackpot pilot who had gotten him into this mess to begin with. *How could this be happening to me?* He thought.

Hector and Billy slipped back into the raft just as the sun was breaking out of the clouds. It blazed through the ragged tear in the canopy. Everything glistened in the sun and clouds of insects filled the air. A parrot glided leisurely over the raft. It was as if every living thing were feasting on the sun's life-giving rays.

Suddenly, they heard an odd sound like thunder, but it was coming from the water. The men stopped paddling and focused on the sound. The raft slowly drifted to a stop. The thunder roared again, followed by a whistle and a bark. Hector turned abruptly. Several triangles sticking out of the water raced toward them. Then the thunder clapped behind them, exploding from the water. One of the triangles suddenly emerged from the water in the jaws of the largest alligator that either man had ever seen. It was black and as long as a station wagon. The men were petrified with fear, too scared to take a breath, as the prehistoric reptile vanished beneath the murky water.

Moments passed before either of them spoke. Then Hector whispered, "Wh-what the hell was that?"

"I think it was an alligator," replied Billy, also whispering.

"Man, I don't know. I've never seen no alligator like that. It was longer than my pickup truck. And what the hell was that thing in its mouth? It looked like a goddamn giant rat."

Still frozen with fear, Billy's eyes surveyed the water around them. A solitary monkey howled, like a sentinel sounding the alarm.

"We've got to get the hell out of here," said Hector, beginning to panic.

An eerie calm came over Billy as he remembered the panic in the jungles of Vietnam, where enemy fire seemed to come from nowhere as they lay on the jungle floor awaiting death.

Back in the cabin, Lou worked to remove several rows of twisted seats with the tools he found in one of the shipping crates.

"They've been gone a long time."

"That medical container was a ways off," said Fred.

Coleman continued to burn up with fever while shivering uncontrollably. Captain Davis and Lucy had fallen asleep. Jan had found them some sleeping pills and codeine in luggage labeled "Mrs. Thelma Wilson." She knew that Mrs. Wilson wouldn't need them anymore.

Lou had managed to get the restroom back in order by pulling out the collapsed panel and clearing out the debris. The door didn't close all the way but at least it allowed them to relieve themselves without incurring the dangers of the swamp.

As if someone had flicked a switch, rain began to pour down so hard that it was like standing under a waterfall.

"Those poor men are going to drown," said Jan. Never in her life had she been in a place where it rained with such ferocity.

"I'm freaking out, man," said Hector. "I can't see my hand in front of my face, the raft is filling up with water, and there's a freaking prehistoric monster bigger than my pickup somewhere out there."

"Just bail," said Billy.

They had retrieved the medical container and had the plane in sight when it started to pour again.

"Oh my God!" screamed Hector as he frantically grabbed at his throat. "Get it off! Get it off me! Get it off!"

A flying snake had collided with Hector. Although those kinds of snakes didn't have wings, they were able to flatten their bodies and propel themselves from tree to tree by creating a whipping motion, traveling fifty feet or more in search of prey or to flee from a predator. Paradise tree snakes and golden tree snakes were not uncommon in that part of the jungle.

It was raining so hard that Billy could hardly see Hector. Blindly reaching for him, he felt something wrap around his arm and knew it was a snake. With Hector still screaming, Billy grabbed the snake with his other hand and cracked it like a whip, flinging it into the water.

"Calm down, Hector, it's gone. Now settle down before you flip us over."

Hector, frozen with fear, was numb. All he could think about was being eaten by that black monster. They sat motionless for what seemed to be an eternity, though in reality it was only twenty minutes.

While the rest of the group was waiting for Billy and Hector to return, a cloud of mosquitoes filled the tail section. Jan slapped them and scratched at her skin.

"You know, there are more than twenty-five hundred different species of mosquitoes in the jungles of Brazil," said Fred. "But only female mosquitoes will bite you, sucking blood up to three times their body weight and taking up to ninety seconds to get their fill before lumbering off to digest their meal."

"I could have gone all day without that little tidbit of knowledge," said Jan.

"The female mosquito needs protein from the blood to produce her larvae. Only certain species of mosquitoes, such as *Aedes aegypti*, transmit deadly diseases like malaria, yellow fever, the HIV virus, and dengue fever. They transfer the diseases through their saliva after penetrating their victim's skin."

"Fred, stop it! You're freaking me out. This is hell! Forget the fire and selling my soul for a drink of water. How about selling my soul to get rid of these damn mosquitoes?"

"Don't be so quick with the water. The only fresh water around here will be what we trap."

"I wish you'd trap some of these mosquitoes. I'm just about one big welt," said Jan, slapping at another mosquito.

Darkness began to envelop the swamp as a new chorus of sounds awoke in the jungle. Sounds of thunder rumbled as Hector and Billy arrived in the raft, Hector all but walking on water to get to the safety of the cabin.

"You men are positively heroic," said Sister Mary Alice. "I've nearly worn out my rosary beads with worry."

Lou reached down to give the men a hand, while Captain Davis, pulling himself to an upright position, asked, "Did you find the medical container?"

Dick watched with anticipation, hoping the container would be full of pain medication. His nose was killing him and Fred was being stingy with the codeine that they had found in Mrs. Wilson's luggage, allowing Dick just one tablet.

I'll bet he's never experienced how painful a broken nose is, Dick thought. *But I could help him with that.*

After Billy opened the container, he and Hector peered inside. Billy reached in and picked up a jumble of items.

Dick, staring in disbelief, asked, "What is that stuff?"

"I would have to say that it looks like blood pressure equipment."

"That's it?" said Dick in disbelief, envisioning a container full of morphine.

"We risked being eaten by that black monster for medical equipment?" said Hector as another clap of thunder rang out.

"I don't see any lightning," said Lou, gazing at the sky from the edge of the cabin.

Hector began to shake uncontrollably.

"You're soaked," said Sister Mary Alice. "Let me wrap you in a blanket. It's a little damp but it should help you with your chill."

Fred lit the makeshift lantern that he constructed, fueling it with some hydraulic fluid that he was able to salvage from the tail of the plane.

Suddenly, a roar of thunder filled their tiny space.

"My God!" Jan gasped. "That gave me gooseflesh. I've never heard thunder that close to me before."

"Where's the lightning?" asked Lou. "I've heard of dry lightning but I've never heard of dry thunder."

53

Another roar of thunder was followed by a very loud hiss. The hair on the back of Fred's neck stood at attention. "That's not thunder," he said.

"It has to be," said Lou. "Must be that the trees are blocking the lightning."

"I wish you were right," said Fred, "but I've heard that sound before."

"Who hasn't?" Dick said sarcastically, grinning and thinking, *Just my luck, being stuck with a group of idiots.*

After another round of thunder and hissing, everyone squeezed together in the back of the plane. Jan sat on top of a seatback, making the sign of the cross.

"Sister, you'd better be cracking out those rosary beads. What the hell is that?" Jan screamed.

"It's a black caiman!" shouted Fred.

"A what? What the hell is a black caiman? It sounds like some kind of tribal witch doctor!"

"It's a black alligator that can grow to about twenty feet or so and can weigh around three thousand pounds."

Jan's mouth dropped open as she gasped. A mosquito as large as a fly landed on her nose. She was in a trance until the mosquito started drawing blood, and then she howled, "I can't take one more creepy thing!" as she slapped the mosquito away.

The thunder woke Lucy and she started to scream, "Coleman! Oh my God, Coleman's dead!"

He'd been lying next to Lucy on the floor at the back of the plane where Lou had removed the seats. The putrid odor of death rose in the thick, humid air.

The alligator hissed loudly, and suddenly there was a pair of eyes staring at them.

"Oh my God, what's that?" cried Lucy.

"It looks like the alligator's trying to climb in," said Fred.

Lucy fainted and fell to the floor.

Fred grabbed the medical container and threw it at the approaching alligator. The black caiman attacked it with such ferocity that bits of the plastic container flew back into the cabin. Jan screamed, pulling at her hair.

"We need a barrier! Billy, help me!" Fred shouted.

The men frantically grabbed the seats that Lou had unbolted and stacked them in front of the opening.

"We're going to die," Jan moaned. "Why didn't I just die in the crash?" She began crying.

Dick stood with his back against the wall, as far back in the end of the cabin as he could get, pushing Jan out in front of him. She screamed as he shoved her toward the alligator.

"I hope it doesn't mess with our raft," said Billy. "That's our only chance of getting out of here."

"Maybe not," said Captain Davis. "We haven't tried the plane's radio yet."

"Are you kidding?" said Dick. "That's negligence! You mean I've been here suffering while you knew we could use the radio?"

"I didn't say that. I said we haven't *tried* to see if it still works."

The alligator came roaring back.

"He wants Coleman," said Fred. "He can smell him."

"Well, give him to it!" said Dick. "All he's doing is stinking up the place and endangering the rest of us!"

"We can't just feed Coleman to the alligator!" screamed Jan.

"Why not? Better him than me. I've got a lot to live for!"

The group stared at Dick in disgust.

"All right, then, Dick. You drag Coleman over here and feed him to the alligator yourself."

Sister Mary Alice's face turned white as she worked the beads of her rosary.

Dick, in defiance, stood as still as a statue.

"Dick, let's go!" shouted Fred.

Dick still didn't move, staring Fred down.

"Billy, give me a hand."

Jan turned her head. She couldn't watch. Irene was starting to rumble.

Fred and Billy dropped Coleman over the seats and heard another roar of thunder as his body hit the water, which thrashed as the monster fought over the remains of the forgotten salesman.

55

It seemed to take an eternity for the night to pass, and no one slept. When morning finally came, the alligators, including the black caiman, had moved on and a toucan called out, waking the jungle to a new day. Fred and Billy got in the raft and headed for the cockpit at first light.

Chapter Six

Blotting the perspiration from his forehead, Mr. Lopez, with Pedro on his heels, arrived at the ticket counter.

"Ladies and gentlemen, may I have your attention please. My name is Mr. Lopez. I am the manager of the airline. I apologize for your inconvenience due to the delay of Flight 153. I know that it's Christmas and you all have very busy holiday plans. I've checked with Houston regarding the plane's delay and they are checking on the plane's whereabouts as we speak."

"What do you mean 'the plane's whereabouts'?" asked a short, plump woman wearing a brightly colored muumuu.

"Just that," said Mr. Lopez. "Houston is checking to see what's causing the delay."

"Excuse me, Mr. Lopez. Why can't *you* check on the plane?" asked a skinny man smoking a large cigar.

"We have," said Mr. Lopez. "However, the plane's crew has not responded."

"The plane is more than two hours late. Shouldn't you have heard *something* by now?" asked a large woman wearing a very short dress and a Santa Claus hat.

"It could be that the weather is interfering with their reception," said Mr. Lopez.

"But the weather has been clear," said the woman with the Santa Claus hat.

"Please understand, the Andes Mountain Range can create its own weather, and it's the rainy season in the Amazon jungle. I assure you that I will let you all know what is going on just as soon as I hear from Houston," said Mr. Lopez. A long strand of his comb over dangled over his left ear. "Please enjoy some refreshments complements of the airline. My ticket agent, Mr. Santos, has brought out coffee and cookies for you to enjoy while you wait."

Heraldo went over to where he had left Ana.

"What did they say? Why is the plane late? When will it land?"

"One question at a time, Ana. They think maybe it's the weather that's holding up the plane."

"They *think* it's the weather? They don't know for sure?"

"No, they're not sure. They're waiting to hear from Houston."

A crowd started to form at the ticket counter again. The plane was now nearly three hours late and there was no word from Mr. Lopez. Pedro kept reassuring people that he would let them know any news as soon as he had received it.

Mr. Lopez went back to his office and tried calling Houston again. Houston hadn't had any luck in tracking down Flight 153. They'd contacted Belize, Nicaragua, Costa Rica, Haiti, and the Dominican Republic, and none of those countries had had any contact with Flight 153. Houston was still waiting to hear back from Panama, Venezuela, and Trinidad and Tobago, and they were still working on contacting French Guiana,

Columbia, Ecuador, and Peru. They had contacted Cuba, but the country had denied knowing anything about Flight 153. They wanted Mr. Lopez to check with Belem, which was the contact station for Northern Brazil, and then to contact Santiago, Manaus, Brasília, Santarem, Belo Horizonte, and Cuiaba.

After Mr. Lopez thanked Houston and hung up, he diligently began making phone calls, starting with Belem. He dialed the check station but the phone rang and rang. Finally, the operator came on the line.

"I'm sorry, there is no one answering. Would you like to try back later?"

"No! This is an emergency! There's a plane missing and it's essential that I talk to the check station!" shouted Mr. Lopez, his voice quavering. The operator reconnected him; the phone rang for a full fifteen minutes with no answer.

Mr. Lopez hung up and tried calling the Santiago check station. There was no answer.

This is ridiculous, he thought as he dialed the station in Manaus. Once again, there was no answer.

Then he dialed Brasília Airport. At long last, he had made a connection and relayed his information to the control tower. The manager at the tower told Mr. Lopez that they had had no contact with Flight 153, but they would call him if they received any new information.

The plane was now well over three hours late, and Pedro needed to know what to tell the people waiting for Flight 153. The airport was nearly empty. There were no more flights coming or going to the airport that night, which was left with a skeleton crew to run operations until morning.

Pedro knocked gently on Mr. Lopez's door.

"Yes? What is it?"

"Sir, the people…well, they are beginning to become more than a little upset."

"I haven't been able to get a hold of many stations, and the ones that have answered have no information on Flight 153."

"Sir, what should we do with all the people waiting?"

"Send them to the Parrot Lounge. I've called over and had them keep some of their staff on duty with instructions that drinks, food, whatever they want is complementary. I'll be there in half an hour to answer any questions."

Pedro scurried from Mr. Lopez's office and did as he was told, moving the crowd of people over to the Parrot Lounge.

"Miss Ana, we're being asked to wait in the Parrot Lounge," said Heraldo.

"I've got to call Daddy. He must be worried sick."

Ana walked over to a bank of telephones and started dialing. "Daddy? It's me. Billy's plane is more than three hours late and they have no idea why. They assured us that the plane had definitely landed, and now we've been asked to wait in the Parrot Lounge until the airline confirms which airport the plane has landed at."

"Billy will be fine. This happens quite often at this time of year," said Franco Silva, Ana's father. "This is the rainy season and it's Christmas, so many people have taken the day off. That's why they haven't heard where the plane has landed. He should be here first thing in the morning, so have Heraldo bring you home. Leave the phone number to the house at the information desk so they can call you in the morning."

Chapter Seven

A terrible odor came from the cockpit as Billy approached its entrance. Flies buzzed all around the cabin.

"What's that smell?"

Billy gagged as he pulled his shirt up to cover his nose.

"I forgot to tell you," said Fred. "That's the rest of the flight crew."

When the men entered the cockpit, Fred started to vomit. There were ants everywhere, engulfing the co-pilot. His uniform moved as if he were struggling to get out of it. The ants had already eaten away most of his exposed flesh.

Fred turned to Billy and said, "I can't go in there."

"We have to, Fred. We've got to see if the radio works."

Fred gasped for fresh air and asked himself why he had volunteered for this. He should have been on his way to the Consulate, not searching for a radio in the wreckage of a plane. An anthropologist by trade, he had been hired by the Brazilian government for his knowledge of the Xingu tribal culture. The government wanted to build a hydroelectric dam to harness the Xingu River, a river nine hundred miles long that flowed northeast and emptied into the Amazon River.

Fifteen different Xingu tribes lived along the river. Most of the tribes had been moved to the Xingu Indigenous Park Reserve, but there were still a few small tribes that had refused to move and they stayed hidden in the jungle. These tribes had been suspected of killing and wounding several of the government's surveyors.

Fred was a virgin to the real jungle. Most of what he knew about the Xingu people and their culture he had learned in the classroom. He'd also watched documentary films and studied with a professor who had lived in Cuiaba. The job was based in Rio, but he was expected to do much of his fieldwork in the jungle. He had planned to meet with government officials before heading out into the jungle. He never imagined that he would be in a plane crash, survive, and become stuck in the middle of the jungle.

Billy suppressed the urge to vomit, wrapping his shirt over his nose and mouth, and holding his breath and then taking only small gasps of air when he needed to. The smell was all too familiar to him.

The cockpit was a disaster. The radio was covered with blood and who knew what else. Billy looked for the switch to turn it on but there were switches everywhere. Then he stopped to think. The radio would have been on when they crashed. As he looked around the cockpit, he saw that most of the switches were in the on position. He suddenly felt lightheaded. He needed some fresh air, so he turned and headed out of the cockpit.

Fred sat waiting in the raft. "Does it work?"

"It looks like it's still intact but there's no power. You'd think there would be a backup power system."

"I'm sure there is, but I wouldn't have a clue where to look. I'm an anthropologist. I don't know much about airplanes. I guess we should have thought to ask Captain Davis about that before we paddled over."

It started to rain. Fred jumped at the sudden crack of thunder.

"Damn! I hope that's not those damn alligators back for seconds."

"It's just thunder," said Billy as lightning flashed.

"I'm usually an optimist, but things aren't looking very good. What are we going to do now?"

"We'll just have to find our way out somehow."

"What about Captain Davis, with his broken leg, and Lucy Miller?"

"We'll do the best we can with them. This swamp has got to drain into a river somewhere."

"You're right about draining into a river somewhere, but do you have any idea how big this wetland can be?"

"I don't know. Ten, twenty miles across?"

"Try the size of Colorado. And even if it were only ten miles across, the vegetation is so thick we may have trouble getting the raft through the swamp to the river. And if we do get to a river, who knows how long it will take us to get down it, if it's even navigable."

Fred paused for a moment.

"I'm sorry, I'm just venting. I know we have no other choice."

"That's fine, Fred, you can vent to me. But when we get back to the others, I want you to stay as positive and upbeat as you can. It's going to be hard enough as it is to get this group motivated enough to get through what lies ahead."

Billy joined Fred in the raft and began paddling back to the tail section.

"Well, did it work? Tell me it worked. Tell me they're on their way to rescue us," said Jan, standing at the water's edge as Billy and Fred climbed up from the raft. Fred looked up at her and shook his head.

"Damn! Then tell me the radio works but you got cut off."

Fred continued to shake his head. Jan started to cry.

"Captain Davis, is there a backup power system?" asked Billy.

"There is."

Billy felt a stab of hope.

"Where is it?"

"Under the cockpit."

The sudden feeling of hope disappeared as quickly as it had come.

"I was afraid of that. The underbelly of the cockpit is buried in the swamp and it's full of water. That explains why I couldn't get any power when I hit the auxiliary switch. Is there any other power source that you can think of?"

Captain Davis furrowed his brow. The painkillers were making him groggy.

"I think we're out of luck then. The only other power source would be located in the main fuselage and that was destroyed in the crash."

"We're doomed!" Dick bellowed.

"We're not doomed," said Fred. "We have some supplies and we have the raft. We'll find our way out of here and to the river."

"The river, and then what?"

"We follow it."

"To where?"

"To wherever it leads us."

"To our deaths is more likely. We might as well stay here and wait to be rescued."

"You are more than free to do so."

Fred secretly hoped that Dick would stay behind. Finding their way out was going to be hard enough without listening to him whine the entire time.

Jan and Lou had found some more painkillers and sleeping pills along with Xanax. They had kept the find to themselves so that Dick wouldn't pester them for some pills or try to steal them. They were determined to dispense them as needed, hoping to make them last as long as they could.

"I think we should leave in the morning," said Fred. "There's still a little daylight left, so we should make good use of the time. We need to go through this luggage and see what we can use."

"Like what?" asked Lou?

"Clothing, for one. Sister, see if you can find some pants and a shirt. That habit you're wearing will make travelling in the jungle difficult for you. Not to mention, it would become an anchor if you were to fall out of the raft. Jan, you might want to find some pants for you, Lucy, and Julie as well. We'll all need to cover as much of our exposed skin as possible or the mosquitoes will eat us alive."

"Tell me something I don't know," said Jan.

"We'll have limited room in the raft. With ten people and food and supplies, it'll be a little tight," said Fred.

"We should leave the captain and the old lady behind," said Dick. "They'll just slow us down."

"Why don't we leave you here?" said Lou. "You're more trouble and complain more than both of them together."

"We're not leaving anyone behind," said Fred. "Let's stop bickering and start getting things together so we can be ready to leave at first light."

The night was long. The alligators returned after dark, making thunderous sounds half the night, but they didn't attempt to enter the plane. Lucy let out little crying sounds all night, while Dick complained about his nose and terrible headaches, keeping everyone up most of the night. Worst of all, the mosquitoes were murderous.

Billy lay awake, thinking about Ana. *She must be sick with worry,* he thought. Then he thought about his mother and father. He wondered if they even knew that the plane was missing. It had only been two days, so he doubted that it made the news back in the States yet.

Fred lay awake, thinking about how they would find their way out. How far were they from a river? How far would they be able to travel with Captain Davis and Lucy? Then his mind started to race. The jungle had so many challenges. Would any of them make it out alive?

Morning came but no one needed awakening; the jungle was alive and well. The mosquitoes must have gained ten pounds overnight. Everyone was scratching at the bites on their skin.

"I don't think I have a spot left that a mosquito hasn't already taken a bite out of," said Jan.

Fred had made a makeshift canopy for the raft to help keep the rain out, as well as the sun whenever they got out from under the jungle's leafy darkness. He had also rigged up a drip system to catch rainwater. He had removed the freshwater holding tank from the rear lavatory of the plane and placed it in the center of the raft. Billy packed the rest of their supplies around the water tank to help stabilize it. Without fresh water, they had no chance of getting out of the jungle alive.

"When are we going to eat? I'm starving," whined Dick.

"After we get this raft loaded," said Lou, looking at Dick with disgust.

Jan gave Captain Davis and Lucy each another pain pill and some cold beans.

"What about me? Where's my pain pill?" whined Dick.

"We don't have that many left, and Captain Davis and Lucy are in a lot more pain than you are," said Jan.

"How do you know? Who made you the pain authority?"

"I did," said Fred. "Now give us a hand loading this raft."

Dick stood defiantly at the edge of the plane.

"I'd like to see you make me, fat boy."

Fred's blood started to boil. Inwardly, he counted to ten and then said, "Lou, Hector, can you give Billy and me a hand getting Captain Davis into the raft?"

The men carefully loaded the captain into the raft, leaning him up against the pile of supplies in the center of the raft. Next, they loaded Lucy and Julie into the raft on either side of the captain. Then the rest of the group climbed into the raft.

Fred took one more look around the plane's tail section. He felt like he was forgetting something. Then it came to him. He should leave a note to any would-be rescuers, telling them who had survived, when they left, and what direction they were headed. He picked up the marker that they had found in a tote bag and wrote his note on the cabin wall.

To whom it may concern: On this day, December 27, 1971, the survivors of Flight 153 are Fred Dowding, Billy Sunday, Lou Smiley, Julie York, Lucy Miller, Jan

Lombardi, Captain John Davis, Hector Garcia, Sister Mary Alice Grant, and Dick Frost. We have set out at daybreak in the plane's rescue raft, heading due east.

Fred then climbed aboard the raft as Billy and Hector slowly started paddling.

"What took you so long?" asked Dick impatiently.

"I left a note."

"A note? Are you kidding me? Who's going to read it, a monkey?"

"Good thinking, Fred," said Captain Davis. "I should have thought of that but with these pain pills and the pain in my leg, I'm just not thinking very clearly."

"Yeah, like when you were flying the plane," said Dick. "You weren't thinking too clearly then, either."

"That's enough out of you," said Fred through gritted teeth. "I've had all that I'm going to take. Now unless you want to make a go of getting out of this jungle on your own, I'd advise you to mind your manners."

Everyone in the group turned and looked at Dick, as if to say they were in full agreement with what Fred had just said.

Dick turned and looked away from them.

The sun climbed high into the sky. Occasionally, they saw rays of sunlight peaking through the jungle's canopy. It looked just like the pictures on the calendar that they handed out at church. The raft drifted in and out of clouds of mosquitoes, and they watched monkeys swinging from tree to tree, howling as if to warn the jungle of their intrusion.

"These bugs are biting my bites," said Jan, looking as if she had a bad case of chicken pox.

"They're not biting me," said Dick.

"Then it must be true what they say about lawyers," said Jan, drawing a chuckle from the otherwise solemn group.

Lou and Fred relieved Billy and Hector at the paddles.

"I can help paddle," offered Sister Mary Alice.

"Thanks, Sister, but we've got it."

It started to rain, causing Hector to tense up. He feared the rain, thinking of the giant black alligator and the snake that flew out of the tree, wrapping itself around his neck.

As night began to fall, the jungle seemed to grow louder.

"Is it my imagination, or does it seem like the jungle has turned up the volume a couple of notches?" asked Jan. She felt gooseflesh rising over her mosquito bites.

"We'd better start looking for a safe place to spend the night. We can't risk puncturing the raft in the dark," said Fred.

After securing the raft to a large tree, Hector strained his eyes to see where all the noise was coming from. The jungle had become completely black. Jan couldn't remember ever being in such complete darkness. She couldn't even see her hand in front of her face.

"Aren't you going to light the lantern?" asked Dick.

"No," said Fred. "We can't risk using up what little fuel we have. Besides, it would only attract more insects and the bugs are thick enough as it is. I'll take the first watch," he said as he checked his watch. The glowing hands of his watch said it was only 7:30. "Hector, you take the second watch. I'll wake you in three hours, so try to get some sleep. Morning will be here before we know it."

Fat chance of that, thought Jan. *This is going to be the longest night of my life.*

At 10:30, Fred said, "Hector? It's your watch."

"I'm awake. I should have just volunteered to take watch all night. I can't sleep."

"I don't think I'll be able to sleep, either, but I'm going to try."

Hector sat listening to the nightlife of the jungle and to Dick snoring. He thought of his wife and daughter and he felt so alone without them. The pain caused by the tragic death of his wife and slowly watching his daughter die was still fresh in his mind.
The hate inside Hector was growing stronger by the day. How could anyone steal the money to care for an injured child knowing that without it she would die? Let alone a lawyer that was representing her. If it weren't for his unfinished business, he would've already joined them. He grew sad at the thought of how long his daughter had suffered before she died, of how she had withered away before his eyes. He couldn't stop his mind

66

from racing. He decided that he would let Fred and Billy sleep until morning, knowing that there was little chance of him falling asleep himself.

Suddenly, a loud scream pierced the darkness, followed by another loud scream. Jan screamed herself as she reached out for Fred.

"What the hell was that?"

"I don't know for sure."

"It sounds like a howler monkey," said Billy.

It started to rain again. Billy was thankful for the jury-rigged canopy that Fred had made. He could only imagine how uncomfortable they would be sitting in the dark in the pouring rain.

Morning came slowly and the rain had slowed to a drizzle. A large snake was stretched along a tree limb twenty yards away from the raft. It had what looked like a monkey, half swallowed, sticking out of its mouth.

"Well, there's your answer to what was screaming last night," said Fred.

"So much for breakfast," said Jan as she felt Irene about to lose her cookies.

"Good," said Dick. "I'll eat your share."

He stood next to Sister Mary Alice and peed over the side of the raft, making sure she got a good look.

"Dick, have a little respect," said Lou, wishing he had left the vulgar man stuck in the john.

"A man's got to relieve himself," said Dick as he continued peeing.

"Yeah, well, why don't you try relieving yourself behind the blanket that we hung for that very purpose?"

Hector untied the raft and started paddling, hoping that Dick would fall into the water. He knew the water wasn't deep enough for him to drown in, but maybe they would get lucky and an alligator or some other creature would take Dick off their hands.

Dick fell back into the raft, showering himself with his own urine.

"Damn it, asshole! Couldn't you wait until I was finished?"

A thought struck Fred as he watched Dick peeing into the water.

"I just remembered something very important."

"What?" asked Jan, thinking it was an odd time to remember something.

67

"The Willy fish. It's the most feared creature of the Amazon."

"I thought the piranha was the most feared," said Lou.

"No, it's got to be that damn black alligator. The one that's as big as my pickup truck," said Hector.

"No, it's the Willy fish. It's also called the toothpick fish or the vampire fish."

"Stop!" Jan shouted. "I don't need anything else creeping me out. Now you want me to worry about vampires? I'm not in the mood for any more creatures, thank you."

"I'm not fooling around. The fish's real name is Candiru. They live mostly along riverbanks in shaded areas. They're transparent and—"

"Fred, you're freaking me out! This isn't funny."

"It's not a joke. They're anywhere from one inch to six inches long, and they're attracted by the scent of ammonia discharged by other fish through their gills. They got the name vampire fish from the way they eat. After finding their victim, they swim into the fish's gills and extend their fins, which act as barbs so the fish can't expel them. Then, using their little sharp teeth, similar to piranha teeth, they gnaw at the fish's insides, causing it to bleed. Then they gorge on their victim's blood before releasing their barbs, allowing the fish to expel it, and then they sink to the bottom of the river to digest the food."

"Wait a minute," said Dick. "What's all this got to do with us taking a leak?"

"There's ammonia in urine," said Fred.

"What, it's going to swim up my dick?" laughed Dick.

"Exactly. That's why it's the most feared creature of the Amazon. It smells the scent of ammonia and swims right up the urethra tube. The bad news is that it can't get out on its own; it has to be surgically removed. If you don't get to a doctor soon enough, your bladder will burst because you can't discharge your urine. After the Candiru eats its way into your bladder, it keeps going. By then you hope you're dead, although some people have been known to live up to four days before they finally die."

"You're full of shit," said Dick. "I don't believe a word of it."

"I'm afraid he's telling the truth," said Sister Mary Alice. "I've read about it in our literature for our missions. They gave very strong warnings against swimming in the rivers and urinating, especially in shaded shallow water."

"Yeah, well, I'm not buying it," said Dick.

"You've been warned," said Fred.

Hector turned white. What else was he going to have to worry about? Now he was afraid to pee.

Sister Mary Alice turned and checked on Captain Davis. She felt his head, still burning up with fever, and tried to get him to open his eyes, but he wouldn't respond.

"I think Captain Davis has taken a turn for the worse," she informed the others. "We must do something for him quickly."

Fred leaned over and felt Captain Davis's head.

"Wet some rags and lay them on his forehead."

A snake dropped out of a tree next to Lucy and she started screaming, pulling at her hair. The frightened snake crawled over to Julie. She stood up to try to get away from the snake but lost her balance and fell into the water, screaming.

"Grab her!" yelled Fred.

Hector tried to reach over the side of the raft to grab Julie. Then he froze with fear, thinking about the vampire fish.

Jan grabbed Lucy, wrapping her arms around her to try to calm her down.

"Billy, help me hold Lucy down!"

Lucy struggled, kicking and screaming.

Billy punched Lucy on the point of her jaw, knocking her unconscious.

"She's in shock," said Sister Mary Alice. "I think she's going mad. Perhaps we should restrain her before she wakes up."

Lou, a bit unnerved by the incident, said, "There's some duct tape in the red bag."

Fred tried to reach over Hector to get at Julie but the raft had drifted too far from her. He tried to hold out one of the paddles to her but it was beyond her reach. She began to sink into the murky waters, gurgling and flailing as she tried desperately to keep her head above water. They watched helplessly as she finally gave in to the swamp.

"I didn't think that the water was deep enough to drown in," said Lou as they all looked on in disbelief.

Fred kept quiet, not wanting to cause any more alarm. He knew the reason Julie had drifted away from the raft so quickly was that something was slowly pulling her. He turned his attention to Lucy.

"I think you should give her a Xanax when she comes around."

"Xanax? Who has Xanax?" asked Dick. "Why didn't somebody offer me one?"

After a while, it stopped raining. The sun peaked through the canopy of the jungle, and the sky became more and more visible as they continued traveling east. The swamp that they had been traveling in for a day and a half began to narrow, and a current began to pull them along. Then the channel widened again before spilling them into a river, the dim jungle light giving way to sudden brightness.

"Look at the sky!" Jan exclaimed as she scratched her insect bites.

The river was enormous. At nearly a hundred feet wide, it was a giant flow of brown. As they joined the current near the riverbank, Fred grabbed a thin tree and brought the raft to a halt, tying it to the tree.

"What are you doing?" Dick asked, looking at Fred in disbelief.

"There's only about an hour of daylight left and we have no idea what lies downriver," Fred replied.

"Are you mad? There could be a town or a village right up the river. We could be saved!"

"Or there could be rapids leading to a waterfall. I think we should stay here for the night. I would hate to be caught up in fast-moving water in the dark and not be able to see where we're going. Remember, we have injured people on this raft. Captain Davis still has a high fever, and he's been slipping in and out of consciousness."

"I want to vote on it," Dick demanded.

Chapter Eight

Heraldo brought Ana back home. There seemed to be more people at the house than at the airport. Her mother loved to entertain, and since her father was the CEO of an oil company, there were always many people to entertain. Ana made her rounds dutifully, although she was in no mood to celebrate at the Christmas party her parents were throwing. She had really looked forward to showing Billy off to her friends. Now that she had come home without him, she really didn't feel like talking, but she also didn't want to sit alone in her room.

"Ana, I was so looking forward to meeting Billy," said Carla, her friend from college. Carla was gorgeous, with long legs that drove all the boys at school crazy. Ana knew that the real reason Carla had come to the party was to see if she could get Billy to turn his head. Ana knew Billy wouldn't because Carla was definitely not his type.

The party seemed to last forever. Ana just wanted it to be morning so she could have Heraldo take her back to the airport to pick up Billy. Ana's father had come up to her room after he had ushered out the last few guests.

"Ana, Billy's plane should be in by noon," said her father.

"Noon? I thought you said Billy would be here in the morning."

"He very well could be, but it's more likely that it'll be closer to noon. People will be moving a little slower after celebrating the holiday. I'll tell you what. I don't have to be at the office for a few more days, so why don't I go to the airport with you?"

"Oh, would you, Daddy? That would be great! I love you, Daddy."

"I'll have Rosesa bring up a sleeping pill for you. That way you won't be lying awake all night worrying. You'll want to look your best when we pick up Billy."

The next morning, Ana woke at ten o'clock. Tying the belt of her robe, she made her way to the dining room. Her father was sitting at the table reading the paper, and Rosesa had her breakfast waiting.

"Good morning, sunshine! It's a beautiful day," said Franco.

"Did the airport call yet?" asked Ana. She was upset with herself for sleeping in.

"Not yet, but I'm sure they'll be calling any minute to tell us what time Billy's flight will land."

"I'm going to run your bath," said Rosesa. "Try to eat something, Miss Ana."

"I can't eat. I'm too excited."

"You heard Rosesa," said Franco. "Please, try to eat something."

Ana, picked at her food before going up to her bath.

71

"What would you like to wear today, Miss Ana? It's going to be hot, but not as hot as you're going to look for that boy."

"Oh, Rosesa," said Ana, blushing.

"Why, look at you, you're beautiful!" said Rosesa. "That's one lucky boy. I could dress you in a flour sack and you would still make that boy cross-eyed."

"I want to wear the pink dress," said Ana as she lowered herself into her bath. The hot water felt good and it smelled of roses. She tingled all over knowing that Billy would be there in just a few short hours.

The phone rang. Ana held her breath, trying to hear who was calling. "Rosesa, was that the airport calling?"

"No, dear, it was just Heraldo wanting to know if he should come pick you up. It sounded like he had a bit of a hangover and his wife was not happy about it. He said he would be right over."

Ana stepped out of the bath, dried herself, and put on the pink dress. Then she sat down at her dressing table to finish getting ready. After making sure that she looked perfect, she slipped into her matching heels, grabbed her handbag, and headed to the kitchen to wait with the others. Heraldo sat at the island sipping black coffee, while Rosesa stood at the sink washing the breakfast dishes. Noon came and went.

"Daddy, I thought you said Billy's plane would be in by noon."

"I'll call the airport and see what's going on," Franco replied.

When he called the airport, he asked to speak with Mr. Lopez, the airline manager.

"This is Mr. Lopez. How can I help you?" he answered exhaustedly.

"Good afternoon, Mr. Lopez. This is Franco Silva speaking. I'm calling to inquire about Flight 153. It should have landed yesterday but we understand that it was diverted and would be arriving sometime today. Do you have any word on its scheduled arrival?"

"I'm sorry, Mr. Silva, but we still have no word on the whereabouts of Flight 153."

"What do you mean you haven't heard a word? Have you called Houston?"

"Yes, Mr. Silva. They haven't heard a word, either."

"Why, it's been almost a full day now. Somebody should know where that plane is."

"Yes, sir, I am aware of that. We're working as hard as we can to find out where Flight 153 is and when we can expect them to land. As of now, I am waiting on word from Houston."

"Well that's not good enough. I want you to call General Russo. Tell him that Franco Silva wants him to start searching for that plane, and I mean right now!"

"But, Mr. Silva, I can't do that until I hear from the home office in Houston."

"Give me the number. I'll call them myself."

"I could get into trouble if I give you that number, sir."

"Trouble? You don't know the meaning of trouble. I'll have your airline shut down!"

"Please, Mr. Silva. There's no need for threats."

"I assure you, Mr. Lopez, that these are not idle threats."

Mr. Lopez finally gave in and gave Franco the number to the airline in Houston. As soon as he hung up, the phone started to ring. It was Billy's parents.

"Hello, Mr. Silva? This is Bill Sunday, Billy's father. Merry Christmas to you and your family."

"Happy holidays to you and your family as well, Mr. Sunday."

"Mr. Silva—"

"Please, call me Franco."

"All right then. Franco, listen, I know Billy was probably so excited about finally seeing Ana again that he forgot to call us when he landed. Could I please have a word with him?"

They don't know, thought Franco.

"Hello, Franco? Are you still there?"

"Yes, Bill, I'm still here."

"Franco, would it be possible to talk to my son?"

"I'm sorry, Bill. I thought you would have heard by now. Billy's plane hasn't landed yet."

"What do you mean?" asked Bill, his voice rising with panic.

73

"I'm sure he's fine. I was just getting ready to call Houston to find out where the plane landed. They more than likely had to land at another airport due to weather or trouble with the plane. And with the Christmas holiday, they could have a hard time getting the plane fixed. You know things down here aren't like they are in the States," Franco replied, feeling as if he were rambling.

Bill didn't know what to say. After worrying for thirteen months while Billy was in Vietnam, to think of losing him in a plane crash just days after he got back from the war was unthinkable. What was he going to tell Mildred?

Chapter Nine

"All right," said Fred. "All those in favor of forging ahead, raise your hands."

Everyone looked at one another and then back at Fred.

"Raise your hand if you want to forge ahead," Fred repeated.

Dick was the only one with a hand raised in the air.

"Well, then, that settles it. Hector, give me a hand tying us up for the night."

"I can't believe that you people want to spend another night sitting in this raft tied to a tree when help could be right around the next bend!" Dick shouted.

"Listen, Dick! I've had enough of your wind for a lifetime!" said Lou. "I don't know why God stuck me in a raft in the middle of the jungle with the likes of you, but He must have had a good reason. It could be like reading a bad book. It sure makes you appreciate a good one."

"Screw you," said Dick.

Jan couldn't help thinking about what Dick had said, that help could be as close as the next bend in the river. But Irene was telling her that Fred was right about going down a huge river in the dark. It would be like playing Russian roulette.

That night felt like their longest yet. All anyone could think of was what was around the next bend. When morning finally arrived, their third day in the jungle since the crash, everyone was ready to go.

The raft drifted lazily down the muddy river, and there was no need to waste any energy paddling. As the sun rose higher, the raft had traveled much further beyond the first bend in the river without any sign of a village or a town.

Jan was waiting for Dick to shoot off his big mouth, telling Fred how much further they could have been down the river and that much closer to being rescued if they would have listened to him and taken a chance yesterday. But Dick did nothing more than act like a big baboon warming himself in the morning sun as the raft floated along. Jan found that the river had a seductive effect on her. It was like looking into the eyes of a great snake whose powerful, hypnotic gaze drew in its victim and gently wound it within its coils. That's what the river was like, a big snake. It lulled them and drew them in, and before they knew it, they would be in the great snake's belly.

The day grew hot and the raft drifted slowly in the lazy current of the muddy river, while a pungent odor of rotting plants hung in the hot, humid air. Everyone was hot, sweaty, and tired. The crash, people dying, the insects, the noise, and their

75

uncertainty of being in the jungle for the last couple of nights had taken its toll. Before long, they drifted off to sleep, one by one, but Fred struggled to stay awake, his head bobbing like an ornamental dog in the back window of a '57 Chevy. As the rest of the group lay sleeping against one another, they unconsciously swatted at the insects that continuously landing on their sweaty, sticky bodies. The slow-moving river finally overwhelmed Fred, and he fell into a fitful sleep among the others.

Chapter Ten

The pain in his side was unbearable. He was bent over in an alley, hiding behind an overflowing dumpster, heaving and trying to catch his breath.

"Who were those guys?" Dick gasped, still holding his side. It felt like someone was pulling his intestines through his left ribs. "Don't they know I'm good for it? I just need a few more days. Damn, I only owe them twenty grand. I can make that back in one good night if the cards would only come my way for a change. Think, think. Calm down."

As the pain eased, he straightened up and peaked around the dumpster. It smelled bad; he couldn't imagine what it smelled like in the summer. He could feel his heart pounding hard. He looked down, half-expecting to see his heart protruding from his chest. Then he took two steps out from behind the dumpster and heard a loud, metallic crash behind him.

Dick's bladder suddenly emptied. He could feel the hot urine trickling down his leg. A large alley cat leapt from atop the dumpster and ran by him down the alley.

"An effin' cat! Jesus effin' Christ, an effin' cat! Get a grip, Dick," he muttered. Then he realized that he had just pissed his pants.

Dick looked cautiously out into the street. There were two cabs sitting at the end of the block. He flagged one, pulled the door open, and jumped in before the cab had come to a complete stop.

"In a hurry, buddy?" asked the cab driver. "Damn, what's that smell? Ah, Christ. Tell me you didn't piss yourself back there in my cab."

"I didn't," said Dick.

"You sure as hell stink," said the cabbie. "Where to, buddy? I hope it ain't far."

Dick didn't know where to go. He needed some clean pants that was for sure.

The cab stopped at a red light and the cabbie turned around, facing Dick.

"Shit! You did piss yourself! Get the hell out of my cab! That's twenty bucks, you asshole!"

Dick opened the door and got out, giving the cabbie the finger as he ran from the cab and spotted a bus. He reached the bus just as it was pulling away and grabbed the handrail at the bottom of the steps. He pushed a few coins into the fare box as the bus driver looked at him with disgust.

Dick found a seat near the back of the bus and thought about which case he could settle. There was that fat black chick, what was her name? She got hit by an old lady backing out of a parking space at McDonald's while she was digging into her fries. Cornelius. Cornelius Bell, that was it.

The old lady's insurance company would settle for fifty grand, and Cornelius was already spending the money. He had to figure out a way to get a bigger cut, especially since he told Cornelius that the case was worth at least a hundred thousand.

It suddenly came to him. He would tell her that the insurance company had photos of her dancing at a club, and there was a guy willing to testify that she took him home and screwed his brains out. Dick laughed at how stupid his clients were.

"Thirty percent of fifty grand is fifteen grand. That should give me a little breathing room. I just got to get to work without them seeing me," Dick said to himself.

The next day, Dick's secretary, Betty, buzzed him.

"Mr. Frost, there's a Mr. Gambezze on line one."

"Tell him I'm busy, that I'll call him back."

"Mr. Frost, he said that he really needs to talk to you. It's urgent he said."

Dick didn't want to talk to Gambezze. He hadn't heard back from the insurance company yet, but he knew he couldn't put off Gambezze much longer.

"Fine, put him through then. Jimmy, how's it going?"

"Not too good. You gave my guys the slip last night."

"Jimmy, give me a chance to explain. They weren't being reasonable. I told them that I would have the money by the end of the week, and then one of them tore my suit jacket. That suit cost me a thousand bucks."

"Dickey, you shouldn't buy such expensive suits when you owe me so much money. Besides, that's what you told me last week and I didn't see a thin dime."

"Jimmy, I'm waiting on this broad's insurance company to pay up. They're being a little cheap but they finally settled this morning. I can get you fifteen of that twenty I owe you in a couple of days."

"Twenty-five. It's going to cost you a little in interest."

"Damn, Jimmy! Where am I going to get another ten grand?"

"You'll think of something. I'll give you a week."

"Jimmy, next week is Christmas."

The line went dead and Dick began to sweat. Then the phone buzzed again.

"Mr. Frost, it's your ex-wife on line two."

"Which one?" cried Dick, now thoroughly agitated?

"I think its wife number two."

"Fine, put her through."

"Hello, Dickey. Merry Christmas!" said Jennifer, who was indeed wife number two. "You do know that it's Christmas next week, don't you? You haven't paid me my child support this month, not to mention you haven't paid my alimony for the past three months. And the school called. There're not going to let the kids go back after Christmas if you don't pay the back tuition that you owe them."

"The kids can go to public school then."

"Dickey, you know what the divorce decree says. You have to pay to keep them in the school that they were in when you ran off with little miss hot pants."

"Anything else?"

"What about Christmas, Dickey?"

"What about it? And stop calling me Dickey, it's Dick."

"I already know that you're a dick, Dickey. You did remember that it's your year to have the kids during the holidays, didn't you?"

"No, in fact, I did not remember."

"Well I've got plans, Dickey. You'll have to take them."

"What kind of plans?" asked Dick, wondering what in the hell he was going to do with two whiny brats.

"It's none of your business. Now, Dickey, when are you going to give me my money? Or would you rather spend Christmas in jail?"

Dick's secretary buzzed him again.

"Listen, Jennifer, I'll have to call you back. I have to take this call."

"Don't you pull that shit on me Dickey? I was married to you, remember? I know all your bullshit excuses!"

Dick hung up with wife number two and buzzed Betty. "Yeah, what is it now?"

"It's Cornelius Bell, line one."

"What does she want?"

"I really don't know, but she sounds upset."

"Great, this is just what I need. Put her through. Hello, Ms. Bell, what can I do for you?"

"You can start by telling me who this guy is that I supposedly screwed."

"You got my message then."

"Uh-huh, yeah. And just what do you mean you're only going to settle for half of what you promised me?"

"I'm sorry, Ms. Bell, but you shouldn't be out dancing all night and then picking up Johns when you're supposed to be disabled."

"I haven't been out dancin' or screwin' nobody!" shouted Cornelius.

"What about the pictures?"

"I don't know about no pictures."

"The insurance company has pictures of you dancing and screwing."

"Did you see the pictures?"

"Yes, I'm afraid I have."

"And you're sure it was me?"

"Well, I've got to admit, it was a little hard to tell one hundred percent for sure that it was you in the position you were in."

"See then? If you can't tell it's me and you're my lawyer, then ain't nobody gonna tell it's me?"

"Are you willing to risk getting nothing? If a judge sees those pictures of you doing it doggie style, well…I think you know what I'm trying to say."

"What about that money your friend Jimmy gave me?"

Ah, shit, thought Dick. He forgot that Jimmy had advanced her money on her settlement.

"How much did he lend you?"

"Lend me? I thought you said not to worry about it, that you would get the insurance company to pay it?"

"Well, they will pay it, but it comes out of your settlement."

"You all didn't say that before!"

"Sure I did, Ms. Bell. Who do you think I am, Santa Claus?"

"You lawyers are all scum! Just how much money am I gonna get? And when am I gonna get it?"

"Calm down. You'll get it in a couple of days."

"You still didn't say how much."

"I'm not sure right now, but it's a lot more than you would have got without me. I've got another call coming in, Ms. Bell. I'll get back to you in a few days."

"But—"

Dick hung up the phone and it immediately buzzed again.

"Yeah, what is it now?"

"Mr. Frost, I'm just calling to remind you that you have a meeting in the boardroom in ten minutes."

"Thanks. And, Betty, if that Bell broad calls again, take a message."

Dick gathered up his things for the meeting and headed down the hall to the boardroom. Jerry Goldstein, the firm's senior partner, approached him before he could reach the door.

"Dick, can I talk to you for a minute after the meeting?"

"Sure, Jerry."

After the meeting, the other lawyers filed out while Dick stayed behind. He was starting to sweat. He could tell by the tone of Jerry's voice when they met in the hall before the meeting that he wasn't there to get good news.

"Dick, is everything all right?"

"Yeah, sure, Jerry, why do you ask?"

"Well, Dick, it seems that you're overdrawn on your company credit card. And when I had my secretary go over the billing statements, there were about three thousand dollars of personal charges on the card."

Jerry gave Dick one of those long stares that he gave defendants sitting on the witness stand.

Dick felt his face growing red as he thought of how he was going to explain himself. Jerry didn't give him time to think of a good answer.

"Now, Dick, I've seen some of those charges myself, really Dick happy endings? What is that? I hope it isn't what I think it is. You know that we are a reputable law firm."

"No, Jerry, it's nothing like that. I threw out my back, and it was late, and I thought maybe if I got a massage it wouldn't—"

"Dick, your back must have really been bothering you, considering there were six or seven charges to that business last month alone. I haven't had a chance to go through all your statements but I have turned them over to accounting. They'll be giving me a full briefing on your charges."

Dick felt sick to his stomach. He'd had it with Jerry's bullshit. He knew that Jerry used his company credit card for his own personal use all the time. And some of those young girls he saw Jerry go out to dinner with sure weren't his clients. More like a little pro *bone*-o work. One thing was for sure; they earned every penny screwing Jerry's fat ass.

"Dick, we have another little problem that we need to fix."

What now? Christ, like I need more bullshit, thought Dick.

"The firm was served with garnishment papers today."

"Wait a minute. I just talked to Jennifer this morning."

"Jennifer? Don't tell me you owe her money as well? I was talking about Nicky, your first wife. It seems you owe her thirty thousand at twelve percent interest. Dick, if you don't mind me asking, how could you owe someone so much money?"

Jerry seemed to be enjoying the grilling he was giving Dick.

"We pay you a good salary, somewhere around one fifty before bonuses, and how much would you say you made in bonuses last year? Another fifty thousand or so?"

"Something like that."

"Then, Dick, tell me what's going on."

Dick wanted to kick Jerry's fat pompous ass. He was going to make Jerry pay. Who did he think he was?

"I make this firm a lot of money. They can afford to pay my credit card bill. Shit, show me one partner who hasn't used his company credit card for his own personal use. I don't know what to tell you, Jerry."

"Dick, you're going to have to do better than that."

Dick was getting pissed.

"Who are you, my dad now, Jerry? What crawled up your ass?"

Jerry's jaw dropped.

"Let's cut the crap, Jerry. I know that you screw around on Barb all the time, and you know as well as I do that I'm not the only one using my company credit card for personal use. So tell me what's really going on."

Jerry stood up, bewildered and at a sudden loss for words. Then he stammered, "Dick, we've been having some complaints."

"What kind of complaints?"

"Some of your creditors have been calling me."

"Like who?" *It better not be effin' Jimmy Gambezze*, thought Dick.

"I'd rather not say."

"That's chicken shit, Jerry, and you know it."

"I've got the reputation of the firm to think about."

"Shit, Jerry, we are one of the sleaziest law firms in the city. Who are you kidding?"

"Dick, I don't want to lose you. You've made our firm a lot of money over the years. But you're becoming a liability, so I'm telling you to clean up your act or you're through."

"I'm through now!" said Dick, standing up and balling his fists.

"This meeting is over, Dick. I think you get the message."

Jerry held the door open and motioned for Dick to exit.

"And, Dick, I really don't think it would be a good idea for you to come to the company Christmas party. People are talking and it might be a little uncomfortable. You understand, right?"

Dick stormed out of the boardroom and headed to his office. He couldn't believe the day he was having. It seemed like the whole world was out to get him. He needed to calm down and think. He went into his office and closed the door behind him. Betty had put a pile of mail on his desk while he was out. He was glad that she was out to lunch.

That meant that he could ignore his phone calls, which would give him time to clear his head.

Dick looked through his mail. There were a few Christmas cards from business associates and a card with a letter and a picture of a young girl inside.

Dear Mr. Frost,

I'd like to wish you and your family a Merry Christmas. Mr. Frost, you killed my child, so Christmas at my house won't be very merry. I'd be careful if I were you, Mr. Frost, because I'm going to kill you. So have a Merry Christmas. Your day of reckoning is coming soon.

Sincerely,
An unsatisfied customer

Dick looked at the envelope for a return address but it didn't have one. Then he checked the postmark. It was from Pittsburgh. Go figure. Ninety-nine percent of his clients were from Pittsburgh. *Can anything else go wrong today?* He thought.

He decided not to hang around to find out.

Dick left his office and headed downtown for lunch and a drink. He settled on Callahan's because the food was decent and cheap, and he was sure he wouldn't have to worry about running into anyone from the office. His head was pounding. He tried to remember what Jerry was talking about at the meeting.

A waitress came to his table, handed him a menu, and asked, "Can I get you something to drink?"

"Sure. Bring me a Rolling Rock and a shot of Crown. And could you bring me a couple of aspirins? My head is killing me."

"Sure thing," said the waitress, and she walked over to the bar with his order.

Dick suddenly remembered what it was. Jerry had said that the insurance company agreed to pay five million dollars on that railroad worker's accident, but the union boss wanted to wait until after the first of the year to pay it out. *That must mean that it'll be deposited into the firm's escrow account,* he thought. His headache was starting to fade away, even without the aspirin. He actually felt a little festive and thought about doing some Christmas shopping for himself. *Maybe Christmas won't be so bad after all,* he thought.

Dick arrived at the office late on December 23. His head was killing him from too much booze the night before and his back hurt. *So much for trying to take care of that at Happy Endings*, he thought.

"Good morning, Mr. Frost. Can I get you some coffee?" asked Betty. Her hair was done up in a beehive style and she had twinkling lights woven through her barrel curls. Dick did a double take when he noticed the little Christmas lights blinking in his secretary's hair.

"How about a couple of aspirins to go with that coffee, Betty?"

"Coming right up. And Mr. Frost, Ms. Bell called and left three more messages." Betty returned with Dick's coffee and aspirins. "Sorry, I forgot to ask. Would you like a pastry or some Christmas cookies?"

"No, I think I'm good."

Dick was still trying to figure out why his secretary had Christmas lights blinking in her hair.

"Mr. Frost, I see that you've noticed my hairdo. What do you think?"

You really don't want to know what I think, thought Dick. "It looks very nice. What's the occasion?"

"Don't you remember? The company Christmas party is tonight. I can hardly wait! I was hoping to leave a little early to get ready, if that would be okay with you, Mr. Frost."

"That would be fine," said Dick, still not understanding why a grown woman would walk around with Christmas lights in her hair.

"Thank you, Mr. Frost. I'll leave around three o'clock then."

"Why don't you just take off when you go on your lunch break? It's the holidays and there's not much going on anyway."

"Thank you, Mr. Frost! Are you sure you'll be all right?"

"Yeah, I'm sure. I think I might leave a little early myself."

Betty left Dick's office, pulling the door closed behind her. Dick popped the aspirins into his mouth and took a sip of coffee. Time was running out. He needed to pay Jimmy the next day. *And all the business I sent his way*, he thought. *He should be paying me.*

Dick unlocked the bottom drawer of his desk and pulled out a file with the numbers to his offshore account. He used the account to hide money from his ex-wives and their thieving attorneys. He called the bank and gave the teller his account number and password, and then asked for his balance.

"Only two hundred dollars? Never mind, I'll be making a large wire transfer to my account tomorrow."

"Actually, sir, you'll need to complete the transaction by 4 PM tomorrow or it'll have to wait until the following business day after Christmas. Where are you calling from?"

"Pittsburgh, Pennsylvania, in the United States."

"Then you'll need to complete the transaction before 10 AM, your time."

"That early? Okay, I'll see what I can do. Thanks."

Dick hung up the phone, deep in thought. How could he get the transaction done before ten o'clock? His phone buzzed, startling him.

What now? He thought. He picked up the receiver and sighed.

"Mr. Frost, it's your ex-wife Jennifer on line one. I told her you were busy but she insisted on talking to you. She said it was about you picking up the children for Christmas."

"Thank you, Betty," said Dick as he punched the button to line one.

"Dickey, I still don't have my check and I need to do some Christmas shopping."

"I sent your check yesterday."

"Dickey, that's bullshit and you know it. I'm tired of your lies! I'm coming over to your office right now to get my money, and I'm bringing the kids and the sheriff with me. If you don't pay up, I will cause a scene that your office will never forget, not to mention I'll have you arrested for contempt of court for not paying child support, especially at Christmas! You know how much the sheriff's department loves lawyers who keep putting criminals back on the streets."

86

"But I'm not a criminal lawyer."

"No, you're just a criminal."

"Fine. How much do you need?"

"All of it."

"How much is all of it?"

"As of today, you owe me forty-five hundred dollars."

"Forty-five hundred? Do you think I carry that kind of cash in my pocket?"

"You did when I met you."

"That was two marriages and four kids ago."

"Sounds like a personal problem to me."

"Can't this wait until tomorrow when I come over to pick up the kids?"

"No, it cannot! I told you I need to buy the kids their Christmas presents!"

"How about I come over this morning and bring you the money?"

"Fine. You have one hour. After that, I'm calling the sheriff and we'll be at your office pronto with the children in tow. And, Dickey, I want cash this time, not one of your rubber checks."

"Don't worry. I'll go to the bank and get the cash before I come by. I'll be there as soon as I can."

"One hour," said Jennifer before she hung up the phone.

"Bitch," said Dick into the dead phone line.

"If you would like to make a call, please hang up and try again," said a recorded voice.

"Screw you, too!" Dick shouted into the receiver before slamming it back down on its cradle.

I don't need this right now, he thought as he tried to clear his head. His Christmas bonus should be in the bank by now, but he hated like hell to give forty-five hundred of it to Jennifer.

Dick got up and grabbed his coat.

"Betty, I've got to run a few errands. If I'm not back by lunch, you have a Merry Christmas."

"I'll see you at the Christmas party tonight, Mr. Frost. I want to introduce you to my new boyfriend."

"I'd love to meet him," said Dick as he turned and headed out the door for the bank.

Dick handed the teller a withdrawal slip for forty-five hundred dollars. She looked at the slip and asked Dick for his ID. Then she walked over to the assistant manager's desk. She looked back at Dick, as did the assistant manager. Then the teller picked up Dick's driver's license and walked back to the counter where he was waiting, impatiently tapping his foot and looking at his watch. He was running out of time.

"I'm sorry, Mr. Frost, but we can't process your withdrawal request at this time."

"What do you mean? Are you closing for lunch or something?"

"No, sir. I'm afraid it's because you don't have enough funds in your account."

"There must be a mistake. My Christmas bonus should have been deposited yesterday. It was for twenty-five thousand dollars."

"Mr. Frost, I'm not showing a deposit for that amount," said the teller politely.

"Then what amount are you showing?" asked Dick, feeling his face growing red.

"I'm not showing a deposit for any amount."

"There has to be a mistake," Dick muttered as he looked at his watch. He only had thirty minutes to get across town before Jennifer headed to his office with the sheriff and kids at her heels.

"Mr. Frost, you are more than welcome to talk to the manager. Mr. Wilson will be more than happy to assist you. Please, let me show you to his office."

"I can see his office from here," said Dick rudely as he walked over to Mr. Wilson's office.

Mr. Wilson stood up when Dick entered his office unannounced. "How may I be of service?" he asked.

"You can start by getting my withdrawal."

"Let me have a look at your account. Hmm. I'm sorry, Mr. Frost, we're not showing a deposit at all. Not yesterday or today."

"Can I use your phone?" asked Dick, reaching for it without waiting for a reply. He dialed his office. "Betty, this is Dick. Put me through to Jerry's office."

"Yes, sir. Just a moment."

Dick waited impatiently while he was on hold, tapping his foot rapidly on the floor.

"Sorry for the delay, Mr. Frost. Mr. Goldstein has gone home for the day. Is there someone else I can get for you?"

"Yeah. Put me through to payroll."

"Just one moment," said Betty as she put Dick back on hold.

Dick looked at his watch. He only had fifteen minutes left. He would have to call Jennifer and tell her that he was going to be late.

"Good morning, Mr. Frost. How can I help you today?"

"Sally, I think there might be some sort of mistake with my Christmas bonus. I'm at my bank and they're not showing that it's been deposited."

"Let me check for you, Mr. Frost. Just one moment."

Dick looked at his watch again.

"Mr. Frost, I'm sorry, but there was a judgment for thirty-five thousand dollars."

"They took it all? That's impossible!"

"I'm sorry, Mr. Frost, but I'm afraid it is possible."

"What about my paycheck?"

"Payroll isn't until next Friday."

"All right. Thanks, Sally." Dick hung up the phone. "Well, I guess that's that. Mr. Wilson, I need a loan."

"I'm afraid that I won't be able to help you with that, Mr. Frost."

"Why not?"

"Well, sir, because you're two months behind on your car payment."

"Then what about a second on my house?"

"I'm sorry, but you already have a second mortgage on your house. Actually, I'm showing that you're five days late on that payment as well."

"Fine. How about an advance on my credit card then?"

"I'll need to check on that. If you'll excuse me," said Mr. Wilson as he got up and left his office.

Dick checked his watch. He only had five minutes left. He reached for Mr. Wilson's phone and dialed Jennifer's number.

"Hello?"

"Jennifer, this is Dick."

"Where are you? You're supposed to be here in five minutes according to the timer on my stove."

"Since when do you know how to use a stove?"

"Screw you, Dickey. When the buzzer goes off, I'm hanging up and calling the sheriff."

"Calm down. I'm at the bank now getting your money."

"Sure you are, Dickey. Uh oh, what's that? That's right, it's the buzzer ringing. I've got to go now. See you at your office."

"Jennifer, wait! I—"

It was too late. Jennifer had already hung up.

"Christ," said Dick under his breath.

"Mr. Frost?" said Mr. Wilson as he came back into his office. "I'm sorry, Mr. Frost, but the credit card company has asked that you surrender your card."

Jennifer, the kids, and the deputy sheriff walked into the lobby of Dick's law firm. Jennifer ignored the receptionist at the front desk and went directly to Dick's office.

"May I help you?" asked Betty.

The deputy and the kids stared at Betty's hairdo, now at full blink.

"I'm here to see Dickey," said Jennifer, eyeing Betty's hair with envy.

"I'm sorry. Mr. Frost isn't here right now. Who should I say was asking for him?"

Jennifer walked past Betty and looked into Dick's office.

"I told you that Mr. Frost wasn't in," said Betty, her voice quivering because the deputy was still staring at her.

"I knew this was going to happen! I never should have agreed to let him come over and pay me."

Betty suddenly felt embarrassed for her boss.

"When will he be back?"

90

"He didn't say. He wished me Merry Christmas early in case he didn't get back from his errands by the time I left for the day. I told him that I'd see him at the Christmas party tonight."

Betty quickly put her hand over her mouth, realizing that she'd just let Jennifer know where to find her boss. Then she thought about how embarrassing it would be for him to be arrested at the Christmas party in front of everyone. There was no way she was missing the Christmas party, especially after all the money she had spent getting her hair done. If her boss asked her how his ex-wife knew he'd be there, she'd just play innocent.

Dick parked two blocks from his office and walked to his building. From the street, he could see that his office lights were off.

Thank God my personal account's not at the company's bank, Dick thought. *If I went in tomorrow morning and tried to transfer five million to an offshore account, they'd be calling the police.*

He went through the back entrance and up the stairs, avoiding the elevator for fear of running into anyone. Then he slowly opened the door to the hallway and peeked around the door. He heard voices in the hallway. *Damn! Everyone should be at the Christmas party downstairs. Who's still here?* He thought. Then he heard laughing.

"Stop that!" giggled a woman.

I know that voice, thought Dick.

"Stop! You're going to leave a mark! Let's go, we can't be late for the party. Your wife will be there."

"Don't worry so much," said a man.

Dick heard the bell of the elevator as the doors opened. He waited for at least a minute, until he no longer heard the couple. He made his way down the hall to his office. When he turned on the lights, he noticed a note on his desk.

Mr. Frost, while you were out, your ex-wife, two of your children, and a sheriff's deputy came here looking for you. When I told them you were gone for the day, she flipped out and said she was coming back here tonight to look for you at the company Christmas party. I hope you get this message before you get to the party.

I think your ex-wife is hell-bent on making a scene. Maybe you should skip the Christmas party. Merry Christmas. Betty.

"The joke's on her," laughed Dick. "I hope they're there waiting all night."

Still laughing, Dick went down the hall to Jerry's office. He heard a bell ring. Then he heard laughter, followed by another bell ring. He tried to open the door but it was locked. *This can't be happening,* he thought as he quickly crossed the hall and ducked into his office.

Dick thought he recognized the voices of the couple who had stopped in the hall outside his office. He could see the man's shoulder resting against the frosted glass of his office window. There seemed to be an odd blinking light, then more giggling and talking.

"I don't know," giggled the woman. "What about your wife?"

"Don't worry about her," said the man.

"But we could get fired if we get caught."

"Don't worry! I'll be a partner soon."

"Really?"

"Yeah, Jerry told me this morning. He's going to make it official after the first of the year. Can you keep a secret?"

"Sure!" said the woman, giggling again.

"Jerry told me that he's getting rid of Dick Frost."

Dick couldn't believe what he was hearing. He was right, it was Tom Mahoney, but who was the woman? It was taking all Dick had not to confront the two of them when he heard the knob to his office door turn. *Thank God I remembered to lock it,* he thought.

"Let's go to my office."

"It's all right, I've got a key."

What? Thought Dick. *Betty's the only other person who has a key to my office. Damn, I should have guessed it was her when I saw the blinking lights.* He heard the jangle of keys and quickly made it back into his private office, locking the door behind him.

"Let's use Dick's couch."

"I couldn't do that," said Betty as she locked the office door behind her.

92

Dick was trapped. At least Betty had the decency not to want to use his couch. *Let's hope Tom out there is speedy,* he thought.

Tom wasted no time. He got right down to business.

Betty said, "We really should have gotten a room."

"Nah, this is safer."

"Aren't you even going to take your clothes off?"

Tom was standing with his trousers and underwear pooled around his feet. "Just pull up your dress and take off your panties," he said.

"I don't know," said Betty, looking at Tom's small erection. His penis looked a little crooked, too.

"Come on. You can be my private secretary."

"I-I think I've had too much to drink. I'm feeling a little sick."

Tom was getting impatient standing there with his pants down around his ankles.

"You're going to need a new job when they fire Dick, aren't you?"

Why, that little shit! Thought Dick. *That's Betty's new boyfriend?*

"I think we should go now," said Betty.

"Not yet. We have a little unfinished business to take care of first."

"I think you should let your wife take care of it. It's too small of a job for me."

Tom's small, crooked erection quickly disappeared as he struggled to pull up his pants.

"You'll regret this. When Dick's gone, this will be my office and you'll be out of a job."

"Well right now this is still Mr. Frost's office, and if you're trying to threaten me, that sword cuts both ways."

Dick waited a full twenty minutes after Tom and Betty left before coming out of his office. Then he snuck downstairs to the lobby. From the main receptionist's desk, Dick retrieved the key to Jerry's office, crept back upstairs, and unlocked the door. He found the company checkbook in the bottom drawer of Jerry's desk. He removed a check from the checkbook and laid it on Jerry's desk, and then he found a letter with Jerry's signature on it and placed it over the check. He slowly traced Jerry's signature onto the check. Then he took a fountain pen from the desk drawer and inked over the traced signature. He waited for the ink to dry, and then he put the check into the typewriter. He made it out for five million dollars.

Dick spent most of the night in his car, which was parked a block away from the bank. He checked his watch for about the fiftieth time and found that it was just before nine. *Just five more minutes,* he thought. He'd planned on being their first customer of the day, thinking that the day before Christmas shouldn't be that busy. He got out of his car and started walking to the bank.

When Dick rounded the corner, he was astonished. There were about fifteen people waiting at the door. Dick could see the old bank guard standing on the other side of the bank's door, holding a bunch of keys and looking at his pocket watch. At precisely nine o'clock, the guard unlocked the door. Dick pushed his way to the front of the line.

"Hey, buddy, what's your rush? You all but knocked that lady onto the floor."

Dick ignored the guard and went to one of the tellers' windows. The teller had noticed Dick's rude behavior as well.

"How may I help you, sir," she said crisply.

"I'd like to cash this check and have it wired to this account," said Dick as he handed over the check and the account number.

The teller looked at the check, then back at Dick.

"Sir, I'm going to have to see your ID."

Dick removed his wallet from his pocket, took out his driver's license, and handed it to the teller. She looked at the driver's license, then back at Dick.

"Sir, I'm going to have to have my manager approve this. I'll just be a moment."

The teller took Dick's driver's license and the check and walked over to the assistant manager's desk. Dick could see her talking to him but he couldn't hear what she was saying. The assistant manager looked over at Dick, then back down at his desk, then back at Dick. Then the teller walked over to Dick and, avoiding eye contact, said, "Mr. Frost, please follow me."

They walked over to the assistant manager's desk and he stood up as Dick approached.

"Good morning, Mr. Frost. I'm Mr. Sneed."

94

The skinny assistant manager held out his hand to Dick, and Dick reached out to shake it. It was mushy, limp, and cold and Dick quickly withdrew his hand.

"Please, have a seat. Now, Mr. Frost, I'm not sure that I can deposit your check and wire it to your account," said Mr. Sneed.

"Why not? The check's good."

"Well, it is an unusual request."

"What's so unusual about depositing a check and wiring it to a different account?"

"It's the amount of the check, sir."

"The check's good," Dick repeated. "My firm has been banking here since we've opened."

"I have checked your account, Mr. Frost, and five million would leave you with only a little over four hundred thousand."

"So? Is that a crime?"

"I'm sorry, Mr. Frost. I cannot release this amount of money without talking to Mr. Goldstein first. Now if you'll excuse me."

Mr. Sneed rose abruptly from his desk and went into his manager's office. Dick saw him go behind his boss's desk and sit in his boss's big leather chair. He watched Mr. Sneed pick up the phone and dial a number. When he stopped dialing, he stared at Dick. Dick tried not to look nervous, though in reality he was about to come out of his skin.

Dick turned at the sound of a commotion at the front door. The guard was trying to keep a disheveled man out of the bank.

"Sir, if you don't have an account at this bank, there is no reason for you to be here."

Dick noticed that the guard had his hand resting on the handle of his ancient revolver. The man turned from the guard and reached into his tattered duffel bag resting on the floor behind him. The guard took a step back and drew his gun. A woman screamed and another woman fell to the floor, covering her head. The assistant manager came to the window of his boss's office, still holding the receiver to his ear. The man pulled a bank passbook from his bag and handed it to the guard. The guard cautiously took the passbook from the man's hand, still clutching his gun. He studied the passbook, keeping one eye on the man, and then he slowly handed back the passbook to the man as he holstered his revolver. The man made his way through the lobby and helped himself to Christmas cookies and a cup of hot coffee.

Dick looked back at Mr. Sneed as he was hanging up the phone. Then Mr. Sneed came back over to his desk and sat down in front of Dick.

"I'm sorry," said Mr. Sneed, "but I'm unable to reach Mr. Goldstein. He'll be out of the office until the second."

Dick put on his trial face, looked Mr. Sneed in the eye, and said, "If I can't make this transaction happen, we'll have to close the firm's account, with the remaining funds in cash, immediately."

"I can't do that."

"Why not?" said Dick, now standing and leaning over the desk, staring Mr. Sneed in the eye. He could see that Mr. Sneed was starting to crack.

"I'm not sure that you have the authority to close the firm's account," said Mr. Sneed in a quivering voice.

"Then I'll see to it that you're fired for refusing to make this transaction. As full partner in the firm, I'm not only authorized to close the firm's account, I'm also authorized to sue your bank for defamation of character."

"Defamation of character? Whatever do you mean?"

"I mean look around you, Mr. Sneed. Everyone in this bank is staring at us. Look, your guard has his hand on his revolver. He's a little gun happy, don't you think, Mr. Sneed? While I'm at it, I think I'll file a lawsuit on behalf of that poor man your guard stopped at the door; you know, the one he held at gunpoint while he checked his passbook."

"Please, Mr. Frost, let's be reasonable," said Mr. Sneed, perspiring heavily. "Can't this wait until after Christmas? The bank manager will be back from his holiday then, and I'm sure he will help you with whatever your firm needs."

Dick looked at his watch. It was 9:50. He had just ten minutes left to make the transaction or he'd be screwed. Hell, if this didn't work, he could never come back to this bank again. But if he ended up walking out without the money, at least he had his plane tickets. Dick continued to stare Mr. Sneed down, even as the assistant manager struggled to break eye contact.

"Call your bank president and explain what's going on here or I'm going to sue him personally for leaving such an incompetent man in charge."

Dick could see the man weighing his options. Mr. Sneed looked over at the teller and waved her over to them. Then he took a very deep breath and looked at Dick one last time. Dick looked at his watch. It was 9:55.

To the teller, Mr. Sneed said, "Please take care of Mr. Frost's transaction." Then he turned back to Dick and said, "Merry Christmas, Mr. Frost," before walking to the men's room, where Dick was sure the man was going to throw up.

The teller handed Dick his receipt. He looked at it and saw that it was stamped "9:59 AM." He turned and headed for the door.

Chapter Eleven

A burning sting from an insect bite woke Dick from his nightmare. He was dreaming of the mess he'd left back in Pittsburgh, wondering if the plane crash was karma. *Forget Pittsburgh,* he thought. *Rio's home now, with all those hot, young Latin women, topless beaches, no ex-wives and child support, and no more death threats from unhappy clients. But now this, what are the odds of me being in a plane crash in the middle of the jungle?*

He looked over at Sister Mary Alice.

I'll bet that nun is still a virgin bride of Christ. I'll show her what being a bride is all about.

Dick stared at Sister Mary Alice. She was stretched out on the raft and her blouse was pushed up. Her sweaty body revealed shapely breasts with dark pink nipples. They stood up like an eraser on a pencil and it wasn't even cold. He made up his mind. He was going to have a piece of that before this was over. He saw the way she looked at his manhood when he was taking a piss. She wanted him.

The raft suddenly got caught on a log, sending Lou into the water. Two alligators wasted no time jetting into the water from shore. Jan screamed as she watched the alligator's race toward Lou. Fred and Billy reached over the side of the raft, desperately trying to grab hold of Lou as he thrust his hand into the air. Billy grabbed Lou's hand and with one fluid motion jerked him right out of the water.

As he pulled Lou into the raft, Billy lost his balance and knocked Fred to the floor of the raft. As he fell, Fred grabbed Billy's shirttail, spinning him around and causing him to land on top of Captain Davis. Hector pulled Billy off Captain Davis, but not before Billy's elbow caught the captain's left eye, causing it to swell. The captain had been unconscious for over twelve hours and probably hadn't felt a thing. Even so, Sister Mary Alice applied cool rags to his eye to keep the swelling down.

After the Xanax had kicked in, Fred removed Lucy's restraints. Lucy, growing very pale, had developed a fever. She wouldn't eat or drink and she lay curled up in a fetal position in one corner of the raft. Sister Mary Alice thought that she might be suffering from malaria.

The raft drifted slowly down the river, passing through thick clouds of black mosquitoes that attacked everyone except Dick. Jan looked as if she had measles on top of chicken pox. Her skin was so raw from scratching at her mosquito bites that she worried that flies might deposit their larvae into her open wounds.

The light slowly began to fade. Billy spotted a cove in the river just ahead that looked like a safe place to spend the night. Just as they positioned the raft into the cove, a large alligator came from atop the bank and lowered itself into the water.

"We could make camp there for the night," said Fred.

"I'm not leaving this raft until you go check it out," said Jan. "There could be a few of his friends still up there."

"Billy, Hector, and Lou, why don't you go check it out. I'll stay here with the others," said Fred.

The riverbank was muddy. Billy slipped and fell just as he reached the top of the bank. He got back up and held out his hand to Lou, pulling him to the top, and then they both reached out to help Hector up. When they entered the clearing, they saw a large pile of sticks and branches, as if someone were preparing to build a bonfire.

"Well I guess we won't have to gather firewood," said Lou.

"This looks pretty safe," said Billy. "Let's get everyone else up here."

Hector went back down to the raft to help Fred with Captain Davis and Lucy as Jan and Dick made their way up the riverbank. When everyone was settled, Hector and Lou started to pull sticks from the large brush pile. Jan scratched her mosquito bites and watched the men tend the fire. She couldn't wait to eat, she was starving. Fred had said that they could heat the beans over the fire, and even though beans and Irene didn't always get along, she could hardly wait to eat something hot.

Hector lifted a large stick and Jan let out a loud scream.

"Hector, look out! There's a snake!"

Before Hector could react, the large bushmaster snake, one of the most deadly snakes in the jungle, lunged at him, striking his boot.

Jan had reached total overload and fainted.

Lou whirled around with a large stick, swinging it at the bushmaster and knocking it off Hector's boot. The snake's fangs hadn't quite penetrated Hectors boot. Instead, the snake's venom ran harmlessly down the boot's leather exterior.

The snake was still angry and kept striking at Lou's stick. As Lou tried to kill the snake with his stick, Billy drew his machete, and with one smooth motion, he cut the snake's head off, leaving its headless body wrapped around Lou's stick. Everyone let out an audible sigh of relief.

After the fire burned down enough for them to cook, they heated tins of beans and corned beef hash.

"I'm getting sick of eating beans and hash," Dick complained.

"Don't let us hold you back from finding something else to eat if you don't want what we've got. Maybe you'd like that dead snake over there," said Lou.

The evening gave way to a darkness that seemed to double the volume of the jungle. Lou volunteered to take the first watch, since he had slept most of the day as they drifted down the river.

The insects were murderous. Jan didn't think she had any more blood to give. She laid down next to Fred, fearful that Dick would try to steal the painkillers that she had been keeping in her shoulder bag.

Hector wondered where the moon and the stars had gone. He was growing tired of the black, noisy nights. They had taken a tarp from the raft and made a little lean-to. Unfortunately, the lean-to wasn't big enough for them all to fit under.

It started to rain at about ten o'clock, just as Billy was taking over for Lou, which forced them to squeeze under the tarp together. The rain came down so hard that it put out their campfire. Then the wind picked up and lightning flashed. Loud roars of thunder filled the air, sending chills up their spines. Their memories of the ferocity of the black caiman after they had slipped Coleman's lifeless body into the water back at the plane were still fresh. Through the strobes of lightning, Hector noticed that Sister Mary Alice was praying with her rosary. He started to pray as well.

Morning was a long time coming. As the dim light of dawn grew brighter, Billy and Hector bailed out the raft. Lou tried to light a fire but the wood was too wet. Sister Mary Alice checked on Captain Davis. He was still burning up. She tried to get him to drink some water but most of it dribbled down his neck. She was afraid that if they didn't get him to a hospital soon, he would die. Billy and Hector carried Captain Davis to the raft. As they were climbing up the riverbank, they heard a loud scream.

Lucy Miller was dead.

Chapter Twelve

Franco dialed the number to the airline in Houston and was patched through to a Mr. Charles Fishel. Mr. Fishel was very polite and courteous. In a strong southern accent, he told Franco that they had contacted every airport that Flight 153 could have landed at, and they were now trying to check to see who last had contact with the plane.

"Wouldn't the other airports know that?" asked Franco.

"Not necessarily," said Mr. Fishel. "The plane has to check in every hour, but that doesn't mean that they make contact. If the weather is bad or the person running the check station isn't by the radio, they could fly for hours in who knows what direction."

"Wait a minute. What do you mean by 'fly for hours in who knows what direction'?"

"Just that. If they were to run into a bad thunderstorm—and we do know that there were some pretty big systems moving through the area on Christmas Eve—the plane most likely would have tried to fly around the storm, causing it to travel off course. That would leave us with a pretty big grid to search. And, as I'm sure you know, the Amazon jungle is a pretty big place to look for an airplane. The jungle canopy is so thick that we could fly right over them without seeing them."

"Well that's why we must start searching for them right away," said Franco impatiently.

"I assure you, Mr. Silva, we will contact Rio and start the search just as soon as we know where to look."

"I'm going to call General Russo just as soon as we hang up and have him begin searching for the plane immediately."

"Mr. Silva, I understand your need to start the search, but what good would we be doing if we don't know where to look. All we would accomplish is wasting the time and energy of the search party that may be looking hundreds of miles from where the plane has landed."

"You mean crashed, don't you?" said Franco, becoming annoyed with Mr. Fishel's reticence at sending out a search and rescue team.

"Please be patient. I assure you that we want to locate Flight 153 as badly as you do. If you would please give me a number where I can reach you, I will call you just as soon as I know something."

Franco gave Mr. Fishel his phone number and then called General Russo.

"We have two search planes ready to go at a moment's notice, just as soon as we have a general idea where to search. You know, Franco, the jungle is a very big place, and these planes can only fly for eight hours before they have to refuel. Depending on where the plane has landed—"

"You mean crashed."

"I like to look on the bright side, Franco. You know how poor our communication system is. They may have landed at some out-of-the-way airfield. It's been done before. Now, Franco, try to be patient. I'm your friend. You know I'll do everything in my power to find this plane and your daughter's boyfriend."

"Thank you, general. It's just hard to be patient when I look into my daughter's sad brown eyes."

"I will let you know what we find just as soon as I know. Good day, Franco."

"Daddy, what did General Russo say?"

"He said he would let us know where the plane is as soon as he knows."

"Does that mean they think Billy's plane has crashed?" Ana asked as she trembled and started to cry.

Franco put his arms around her.

"No, dear. General Russo thinks that they may have landed at a small airstrip. You know how poor our communication system is. He's sure that everyone is fine, and he will let us know where they are just as soon as he finds out."

"We need to call Billy's parents and let them know what's happening."

"You're right, Ana."

Franco made the call to the Sundays. They were sick with worry. They had called the airline and were told the same thing that Franco was told. The Sundays thanked Franco for calling and assured him that they would let him and Ana know of any news just as soon as they heard anything. Franco assured them that he would do the same.

"Daddy, what do we do now?"

"We wait. And we pray."

At 6:00 PM, General Russo called the Silvas. He had just gotten word that an air traffic controller at Manaus Airport thought that he might have heard a Mayday call early

103

on Christmas morning, but he wasn't sure because it was garbled and he only heard it once. Nonetheless, he had noted it in his report.

"I'll have two planes begin searching from Manaus Airport," said General Russo. "We will send one plane north to cover one search grid and another south to cover another search grid. I will let you know what the search planes find as soon as I hear from them."

Chapter Thirteen

It was the fourth day after the crash. Lucy lay curled in a fetal position, her body cold to the touch. Sister Mary Alice had tried to wake her, grasping her arm to roll her over. As she did so, a giant centipede crawled out from Lucy's mouth and Sister Mary Alice screamed. She jumped back and screamed again, and then ran toward the men, grabbing Lou by his shirtsleeve and trying to put him between her and Lucy. Lou wrapped his arms around Sister Mary Alice, holding her tightly as she shook uncontrollably. She had had enough.

Jan ran over to see what was happening, but Lou shouted for her to stop. "Just turn around and head back to the raft!"

Jan did as she was told. She too was reaching the far ends of her own sanity.

Hector and Billy ran up the hill at the sound of the screams. They found Fred whacking at a giant centipede with a stick. The centipede quickly scurried away into the undergrowth.

Upon hearing word of a giant centipede in their camp, Dick ran down to the raft, knocking Jan out of his way.

Fred yelled, "Hey! Get back up here and give us a hand with Lucy."

Dick climbed into the raft and sat there, not saying a word. He now knew he had gone from the pan and into the fire.

Billy and Hector helped Fred dig a shallow grave with the two machetes and a hatchet. Lou helped Sister Mary Alice get down to the raft, and Jan gave her two Xanax pills to calm her down before taking one herself. *This is going to be one long day,* she thought.

"This isn't much of a grave," said Hector. He was growing very tired of death.

"It's the best we can do in these conditions," said Fred.

"What is it with this place? It's like we've crashed into some lost land like you see in a sci-fi movie. Everything down here is gigantic, like that black alligator and those giant rats and that centipede. Jeez, the snake that ate the monkey must of weighed four hundred pounds. What'll we find next?"

The men made their way back to the raft, and Fred sarcastically thanked Dick for helping them. Dick just stared at Fred, wishing he were anywhere but there on the raft stuck in the middle of the jungle.

The rain stopped abruptly, as if a switch had been turned off. Within five minutes, the sun was blazing. The beauty of the jungle was majestic. All the colorful birds, the plants, the flowers, and the leaves sparkled like diamonds as the sun soaked up the drops left behind by the rain.

The raft drifted slowly down the muddy river. Everyone was thinking about Lucy. Who would be next? Would any of them get out of the wretched jungle alive? Then they all became lost in their own thoughts.

Lou thought of Betty and of how long they had been planning this vacation. Betty was a widow and Lou had asked her several times to marry him, but the answer was always no. She told Lou that she loved him but thought it was a bad idea for them to get married because she would lose her late husband's pension. She could see no reason why living together wasn't good enough for him. Lou just liked the security of marriage. He told her that he made enough money, so they didn't need the pension.

Oh well, water under the bridge, he thought. Betty was dead and by the looks of things, the rest of them wouldn't be far behind her. They were running out of food, and no one had a clue where they were. Fred had thought that they might be on the Xingu River or one of its tributaries, but that was only a guess. They were dying off one by one, and that thing that crawled out of Lucy's mouth was enough to give anyone nightmares.

The travel agent never told Lou about any of the things that lived in the Amazon, especially the vampire fish that Fred talked about. He wondered if they were real or if Fred had made it up to give Dick a scare. Well it sure scared him. He planned to be as far away from the water as he could before taking a pee.

Lou kept thinking about having to leave Betty's body back in the swamp, knowing that the alligators…well, he just didn't want to think about it anymore. He would pray for her instead. Then he thought *if I do make it out of this damn jungle, how am I going to tell Betty's children what happened to their mother?* Betty's daughter hadn't wanted them to go to Rio. She wondered why they couldn't be happy with going to Florida like all the other old people from her church. Boy, how Lou wished he had listened to her.

He wondered if his own children knew of their fate, that his plane had crashed. Was it on the news? He knew he had promised to call them on Christmas. What day was it anyway? Was it day four or five after the crash? Had they started to search for them yet? Would they search for them? The jungle was so big, how would they even know where to start looking? Captain Davis had said that they had sent out a Mayday call, but had anyone heard it? *You really do have to live every day as if it were your last,* Lou thought.

He remembered sitting and laughing with Betty in the airport lounge in Houston before they got on the plane. Who would have thought that they were only hours away from crashing? He remembered teasing Betty about going topless at the beach. She said she would if he would wear a Speedo. He laughed, picturing his bird legs, flat butt, and potbelly in a Speedo. *What a sight that would be,* he thought.

Jan was also lost in her thoughts. What would be worse, dying or being the only one left alive and having to find your way out of the jungle on your own? She tried not to think about it.

"Good thoughts. Only good thoughts," she kept repeating to herself.

It was no use. Jan could not get Coleman, Julie, or Lucy out of her head. She hated closing her eyes because she kept seeing that monstrous black alligator tearing into Coleman's dead body. Or she would see Lucy, screaming and pulling her hair out as Julie, struggling to stay afloat, slipped under the black, muddy surface of the swamp.

She was glad that Lou had warned her about Lucy. She didn't know what she would have done if she had seen a giant centipede crawl out of Lucy's mouth. Just knowing that it had happened sent chills up her spine. She would have nightmares for the rest of her life, however long that would be, perhaps just a few more days by the looks of things.

A colorful bird on the riverbank caught Jan's eye. She had never seen so many different brightly colored feathers on a bird before. She wondered what kind of bird it was.

"Fred, look at that bird over there."

As Fred turned and looked, Jan could swear that she had seen a face in the jungle, but then it was gone.

"Where?"

"It must have gone behind one of those trees," said Jan, wondering how it could have disappeared so quickly.

Fred watched for a while until his eyelids grew heavy and he dozed off. He had hardly slept a wink the night before in the rain, and he was exhausted. He didn't know how he was going to keep on going. He wondered how much longer Captain Davis would hold on. He'd been in and out of consciousness going on four days, or was it five days? He couldn't remember.

"Look, there it is again! Wait, there are two of them," said Jan.

Fred, roused from his slumber, turned and looked. Fear ran up his spine. They weren't birds they were Kayapo people, native to Brazil. They were the reason the Brazilian government had hired him. They were the tribe being blamed for the deaths of the surveyors of the dam. Fred didn't say a thing. He knew he couldn't let the others know about them.

"Do you see them?"

"Yeah, I see them."

Chapter Fourteen

General Russo had the search planes out the next morning. Each plane had two men, a pilot and a spotter. The search planes were instructed to fly in a grid pattern, flying ten miles in one direction and then flying ten miles back in the other direction. When they came to a river, they were instructed to fly directly over it, knowing that would be their best chance of spotting any survivors.

The northern search plane flew over the Negro River. Its headwaters started in Colombia and flowed southeast, emptying into the Amazon River. The southern search plane flew down the Amazon River, and then south along the Madeira River. Both planes flew until dark, spotting only normal traffic on the rivers and nothing to indicate that a crash had occurred in the jungle. After the planes had landed for the night, General Russo called Franco.

"The planes flew all day, Franco, but they didn't find any sign of the plane. They'll start searching again first thing in the morning."

"Can't you send out more than two search planes?"

"I'm sorry, but we only have enough money in the budget for two planes."

"That's absurd! If we don't find those people soon, they'll have little chance of surviving."

"Let's look on the positive side. We still can't rule out that they landed on some out-of-the-way airstrip."

"General, I beg your pardon, but I am not some stupid tourist. I know as well as you do that the plane has crashed somewhere in the jungle, and that every moment that ticks by decreases their chance of survival. If we don't find that plane in the next few days, our chances of finding anyone alive are slim at best."

"I understand your concern, Franco, but I assure you that I am doing all that I can."

"What about the American Coast Guard?"

"We've put in a call to them and are waiting to hear back."

"Have you called the airline in Houston?"

"Yes, Franco, I have. They are also working on getting help from the Coast Guard. I know it's hard to be patient but please try, my friend. We are doing all we can. Now let me call you tomorrow with good news, I hope."

109

"I apologize for my impatience, general. Thank you for all you are doing. I'll wait to hear from you tomorrow then. Good night."

"Daddy, what did General Russo say?"

"He said that they looked all day but had no luck. They will continue searching in the morning."

"Can't you do something?"

Franco was frustrated. He knew that there wasn't much more that anyone could do. The jungle was so big and they really didn't know where to look. But he couldn't stand seeing the sadness in his daughter's eyes.

"Can't you send your helicopter to help?"

"It's not my helicopter, Ana. It belongs to my company."

"But you run the company."

"That's true, but I couldn't spend the shareholders' money searching for an airplane that has nothing to do with the company."

"But think of all those people who are lost, and their families. Please, Daddy. Surely your shareholders would understand that this is a special circumstance."

Franco thought about what Ana was proposing. It would be good public relations for his company, especially if they were to find the plane and rescue the survivors—if there were any survivors.

"All right, I'll send the helicopter out tomorrow."

The next morning, Franco called General Russo to tell him that he was authorizing his company helicopter to join the search. General Russo suggested that he start his search out of Itaituba and fly along the Tapajós River. He would make sure that his search pilots were in contact with the helicopter. Franco agreed and thanked the general before hanging up.

"Daddy, can we go on the helicopter and help with the search?" asked Ana.

Franco was uneasy with her request. What if they were to find the plane and it had crashed? It could be a gruesome sight.

"No, Ana, I don't think that would be a good idea."

"But, Daddy—"

"No, it's too dangerous. I'll tell you what. You can go to the office with me tomorrow and you can listen in on the search pilots as they conduct their search."

Ana was dejected but she didn't want to push her father any further. Listening to the search over the radio was better than nothing.

Chapter Fifteen

The Kayapo people, a warrior tribe, went into seclusion after Christian missionaries entered their land in the early 1940s and 1950s. A medical scientist who had accompanied the missionaries had a new vaccine against measles that he wanted to try, and he persuaded the tribe to be vaccinated before exposing them to the measles virus. The vaccine didn't work and the measles virus ended up killing over forty percent of the Kayapo population. The surviving Kayapo went into hiding, showing aggression to anyone who breached their self-imposed boundaries.

The Kayapo people had very distinctive features. The men wore lip and ear disks that extended their lips and earlobes many times their normal sizes. They also shaved half of their heads and painted geometric designs on their bodies with colorful paints. They wore very colorful headdresses made from the tail feathers of the many exotic birds that inhabited the rainforest.

Hidden in the shadows of the jungle, members of the tribe watched a yellow raft full of people drift down their river. They had seen the great fire in the jungle several nights ago and had visited the site of the crash, not knowing what had fallen from the sky and then burned. What they did know was that the white people didn't belong there.

Fred searched the banks of the river, hoping not to see any more of the Kayapo. Jan thought that the heat must have been getting to her. The face that she thought she saw was distorted, with humongous lips and ears hanging down to its shoulders. She convinced herself that she must be hallucinating. They surly were just birds, odd-looking birds. But what hadn't been odd or unusual since they crashed? Giant alligators, giant rats, giant snakes, giant centipedes, bloodsucking insects of every variety, these were things she never imagined she would see in her lifetime.

"Fred, I know this is going to sound a little crazy, but did you see faces on those birds?"

"You're nuts," said Dick.

"Dick, that's enough," said Fred. "No, Jan, I didn't see any faces, but they were very unusual-looking birds."

"I must be going mad," said Jan. "I don't know how much more of this I can take, and now I'm hallucinating."

"Maybe it's from having too many mosquito bites. You'll be fine, dear," said Sister Mary Alice. "The Lord will watch over us."

"Yeah, well He hasn't done a very good job so far," said Dick.

Everyone looked at Dick with disgust.

The sky became very dark and the wind picked up. Suddenly, the rain came down in sheets. Hector had never been in a place where the weather changed so quickly. He was tired of the rain, tired of the bugs, and tired of eating beans and hash. Even though he was tired of the food, he was grateful for it. He couldn't imagine what it would be like if they had to catch their food or what it would taste like.

The more time Hector spent in the company of Dick Frost, the more he hated him. He daydreamed of ways to kill Dick and of how happy everyone would be without him. How was it that everyone but Dick had been eaten alive by the mosquitoes? Maybe Jan was right. Even the mosquitoes had better taste than to bite Dick.

The raft was picking up speed and it sounded like the river was beginning to churn.

"Fred, why are we going so fast?" asked Jan.

Fred had noticed that the raft was picking up speed but he really couldn't tell what was going on because it was raining so hard. Fred told everyone to put on their life jackets because they could be dealing with some rapids.

"Life jacket, are you kidding me?" said Dick. "How do you put on a seat cushion?"

"Weren't you watching the safety demonstration while we were taxiing? Here, you put your arms through the loops of the cushion like this," said Fred.

"I want to see this. Go ahead, fat boy. Put it on."

Fred felt his blood pressure climb. *Why is this guy such an asshole, challenging everything I say? Why should I care whether he puts on his life jacket,* he thought. "On second thought, Dick, do us all a favor and don't put on your life jacket."

The river was moving faster, and the raft was starting to rise and fall among the crashing waves. Water began to splash into the raft and Jan became frightened.

"I'm not a very good swimmer," she said.

113

"Don't worry," said Fred, "I think we'll be fine. It's just a small stretch of rapids. It's normal, every river has some."

"How do you know what kind of rapids these are?" shouted Dick, the noise of the water becoming louder by the minute.

This guy is the biggest asshole that I ever met, thought Fred.

Hector was petrified. All he could think about was the giant black alligator and the Willy fish that Fred had talked about. He hoped that the water was moving too fast for either one of those predators to be around.

"What should we do about Captain Davis?" asked Sister Mary Alice.

"Tie the life jacket to him," said Fred as the raft came crashing down again. "Billy, try to tie down the supplies."

Lou helped Billy tie down the supplies as Dick struggled to put on his life jacket. The rapids in the river were reaching level five. The canopy tore off from the raft and dragged behind it before becoming completely detached. Water poured over the sides of the raft so fiercely that it was all they could do to stay inside the raft. The roar of the water had become deafening. Then the raft jetted straight into the air like a rocket, spilling everyone into the water.

Hector sank beneath the water and crashed into a rock, which knocked the air from his lungs. Jan bobbed in and out of the water like a buoy in a stormy sea. Sister Mary Alice tried desperately to hold on to Captain Davis but the current was too strong. Dick struggled to keep his head above water, trying to locate the banks of the river. Lou was the lucky one. After being thrown from the raft, he somehow found his way to shore.

Fred was able to grab onto a low-hanging tree limb. He heard Jan screaming as she flailed in the churning water. He lunged for her, still holding on to the limb.

"Jan!" Fred screamed. "Hold on to my arm! I don't know if I have the strength to hold on to you and this tree limb at the same time."

Jan looked terrified. Fred wasn't sure that she heard him. Then Jan reached up to Fred's arm, clamping on so tightly that Fred thought she might pull his arm from its socket. She choked and spit out the muddy river water, clinging to Fred's arm with a death grip.

Billy had tied himself to the raft so he wouldn't lose it, knowing that it was their only chance of getting out of the jungle alive. He fought to keep his head above water. Gasping for air, his lungs burned as if they were on fire. He was becoming dizzy and he couldn't tell where the surface of the water was anymore. He thought of Ana and he thought of his parents, how his mother had begged him not to go.

Sister Mary Alice found herself stuck up against a rock. Her head above the water, she thanked God for His mercy and prayed for a way out of the water. She knew that He would help her, that He hadn't brought her this far only to let her drown.

Fred pulled Jan and himself along the limb to the safety of the shore, where Jan let out a blood-curdling scream. Fred thought his eardrums had been blown. He felt Jan's fingernails dig deeply into his arm. As Fred turned his head, he could see why Jan was screaming. There, at the base of the tree limb that they were clinging too was a bushmaster snake, coiled and ready to strike. Fred could feel his strength fading fast as he clung to the tree's limb, holding not only his own weight against the strong pull of the current but Jan's weight as well.

Hector found his way to the surface of the water, gasping for air. He spit out the rancid-tasting river water, not wanting to die until he completed his task. As he fought to keep his head above water, he saw Sister Mary Alice just upstream, clinging to a rock sticking up out of the river. Hector swam with all his might to reach her and the safety of the rock.

Lou appeared out of nowhere, armed with a large stick, and he whacked the bushmaster snake over the head while it was focusing on Fred and Jan. The snake's body curled around the stick that pinned its head to the ground as Lou struggled to kill it.

Fred felt Jan's body go limp and she started to slip away. He used every ounce of strength left in his body to hold onto her.

"Lou, help me! I can't hold on much longer!"

Lou flung the stick with the snake wrapped around it as far away as he could and struggled to grab Jan, pulling her to safety, and then he reached for Fred. Once on the riverbank, Fred knelt on all fours, coughing out the river water that had made its way into his lungs as he struggled to keep Jan's head above the water.

Billy could feel himself falling. He thought that he had died and he was falling into wherever you go when you die. Then he felt a sharp pain in his side. He didn't think he should be feeling any pain if he was dead. Then he felt as if he were climbing upward. His head emerged from the water and he felt himself bumping to a stop. He gasped for air, and then he opened his eyes. He could feel something pulling him gently. He realized that he had gone over a waterfall and was now resting in a pool away from the falls. The raft was still attached, and he was alive, but what about the others? What had happened to them? Were they still alive? Or was he now all alone?

Dick panicked when he reached the bank of the river. He was frightened. Was he the only one left alive? How would he get out of the jungle? He knew nothing about survival. His nose was killing him. He must have bumped it on a rock when he was thrown from the raft.

Shit, it's bleeding, he thought. He was lucky that piranhas hadn't attacked him. Then he had a happy thought. Maybe they attacked Fred instead. He would have loved to have seen Fred become fish food.

The rain had stopped and the sun came out. It soon became unbearably hot. Dick could feel his clothes baking in the sun. The river was still deafening. He started to shout, hoping that someone would hear him.

Hector held on to Sister Mary Alice as they both clung to the rock. "We have to get out of here!" Hector shouted.

"But how?" she cried.

"I'm not sure," he replied as he searched for the safest way to the shore. "How good of a swimmer are you?"

"Fair, at best."

"Do you see where the river starts to curve over there? Do you think you can swim to the bank? You would have to swim with the current and then swim hard to the right as the river starts to make its curve."

"I think I can do it."

"Stay to my right. That way I can help you if you feel you're being pulled by the river. On three," said Hector as he gave Sister Mary Alice a little hug before they pushed off from the rock.

The current was stronger than Hector had thought it would be, but Sister Mary Alice held her own as they made their way down the river.

Fred was performing CPR on Jan. As she started to spit up water, he gave her mouth-to-mouth breaths as Lou looked on, fearful that Jan had drank too much of the river water. She stared to cough. Fred turned her on her side and she began to vomit. Jan gasped for air in between heaves.

"I think she's going to make it," said Lou with a sigh of relief.

Billy pulled himself up onto the bank of the river, and then he pulled the raft ashore. He lay back, looking up. There wasn't a cloud in the sky, even though not five minutes earlier, it was raining so hard that he couldn't see ten yards in front of him. It was the same weather that they had in Vietnam, only this time nobody was shooting at him.

Hector and Sister Mary Alice pulled themselves up onto the bank of the river, where they lay gasping for air.

"I sure am glad that Fred had me change out of that habit. I know that there would have been no way I could have swam while wearing it. It would have been just as Fred had said, I would have sunk like a rock," Sister Mary Alice said as she rolled over and looked up at the sky, thanking God for His mercy.

"Do you think anyone else survived?"

"I sure hope so."

"It sounds as if there's a waterfall just up ahead. I can't imagine anyone surviving that."

"Well maybe they got out like we did, before the falls. Wait! What about Captain Davis? I tried to hold on to him but—"

"I think he's gone. There's no way he could've survived. He was so weak that he couldn't even raise himself up in the raft. Besides, it was all we could do to save ourselves."

Sister Mary Alice was silent as she prayed for the soul of Captain Davis. She had become very attached to him over the last few days.

"There's only a few hours of daylight left, at most. We need to find the others. Then we need to find a safe place to spend the night."

Dick started to panic. He shouted at the top of his lungs as he ran up and down the bank of the river searching for the others. He heard a loud hiss and realized that he had run right over the top of an alligator lying in the mud. He kept running as the alligator emerged from the mud, snapping. Then it slid into the water. Dick leaned over with his hands on his knees and wished that he had a clean pair of shorts, because he needed them after that encounter.

Fred and Lou sat Jan up against a tree so she could regain her senses.

"What are we going to do now?" asked Lou.

"I don't know," Fred replied. "We need to find the others, if there are any others to find."

"But there's only an hour or two of daylight left. We need to find a safe place to spend the night, and we'll need to gather some firewood and build a fire to keep the critters away."

"How are we going to build a fire?"

"I still have my Zippo."

"Thank you, God. Lou, you are amazing. Do you want to sit with Jan as she comes to, or do you want to start looking for the others?"

"I really don't think we should go too far from one another."

"All right. Let's give Jan a little more time to rest and then we'll all go together. Does that sound good to you, Jan?"

Jan nodded weakly.

"Sounds good to me, too," said Lou.

Hector and Sister Mary Alice got to their feet and started shouting, but the roar of the river was too great for anyone to hear them.

"I think we should look for a place to spend the night," said Hector. "I don't think that we should go too far from shore. We need to gather some firewood and start a fire. Maybe the others will see the smoke and come to us. I think we'll have a better chance of surviving that way."

"I think you're right," said Sister Mary Alice as they made their way into the jungle.

Lou gathered some wood. Fred had decided that Jan was too weak for them to go anywhere until the morning, so they would stay put until then.

"I sure am hungry," said Lou. "I know how much I complained about those beans and hash but I sure would like to have some right about now."

"I know what you mean," said Fred. "I'm just glad to be alive."

The jungle started to get dark. The only good thing about being so close to the roar of the river was that it drowned out the night cries of the jungle. Lou had the fire going in no time.

"Hold on, Fred, I'll be right back," said Lou and he disappeared into the jungle. He returned about five minutes later with something attached to a long stick and held it over the fire.

"What's that?" asked Fred.

"Dinner," said Lou, with a huge smile on his face.

"You must have been a Boy Scout."

"Sure was. I actually made it to Eagle Scout."

"It doesn't surprise me," said Fred, chuckling.

Jan was finally regaining her strength. "I had a terrible dream," she said. "I was drowning and there was this big snake."

"It was only a dream," said Fred, not wanting to upset her. He was starting to take a shine to her.

"Thank God. I don't think I can take one more thing. I'm surprised that I'm still sane as it is. I would have never in my wildest dreams imagined that I could have survived what we've been through already."

Fred put his arm around Jan and pulled her close. To his surprise, Jan snuggled into his embrace.

Lou took a deep breath, glad to be sitting near a fire with Fred and Jan. At least he wasn't alone.

"Well, who's hungry?" Lou asked.

"I'm starving," said Jan as Lou pulled a piece of the roasted meat from the stick and handed it to her.

"That smells wonderful. My God, this is wonderful! I was really getting tired of those beans and hash. What is this?"

"Just a little something I managed to trap," said Lou, not wanting to tell her it was the snake that made her pass out.

While the others were making camp for the night, Billy settled in alone. He had spent many nights alone in the dark, wet jungle while learning how to survive. The first thing he remembered was to keep cool and not to panic. He had seen too many people get killed in Vietnam because they lost their cool and panicked, running in the jungle only to stumble upon an enemy booby-trap. The best thing to do was to stay put and wait for daylight.

Dick was also alone; however, he had never been through survival training, so he had never learned the importance of remaining calm and not panicking. He couldn't believe that he had just stepped onto the back of an alligator and lived to tell about it. But would he live through the night? and if he did then what? How was he going to get out of the jungle? He started to worry that his ex-wife was right, that karma would eventually catch up with him.

Dick tried to distract himself by thinking about what was probably going on back home in Pittsburgh. He knew that his partners were going to be pissed when they found out that he had stolen all the money in the company's bank account. He hadn't left them a dime. He would have liked to have seen Jerry's face when the bank called him to tell him that he was overdrawn.

Jerry most likely spent most of his Christmas holiday dreaming up ways to cheat the clients of the five million dollar class-action suit. He knew that Jerry had bought his wife and his girlfriend new Porsches for Christmas and that Jerry planned to take his girlfriend to Paris right after New Years on the pretense of business. Dick knew that Jerry's wife really didn't care where he went or with whom because she had her own life.

Jerry would probably go crazy if he knew that while he was off with his girlfriend, Dick had been banging his pretty little wife. And he would probably really freak out if he found out that his wife and his sweet little secretary were having a fling. Dick was sure that Jerry didn't know that his wife liked it both ways. If he ever got out of the damn jungle, he'd set it up so that Jerry would find out about his secretary and his wife. His only regret would be that he wouldn't be there to see his face, providing that he still had a face.

Jerry was in deep with the wrong people, but Dick was involved with them just as deep, if not deeper. The firm needed money a few years back when they lost a big lawsuit, so they had to borrow money to keep afloat. They went to the same people that they sent their clients to when they needed to borrow money to tide them over until they got their settlement money.

Jimmy didn't have a problem lending them money because they were his cash cow, but he wanted a little more than just interest in return. He wanted a piece of the rock; he wanted thirty percent of the company. Jerry and Dick didn't want to give him any percentage of the company but they had no choice. If they didn't have the cash they needed to stay in business, they were done, not to mention that Jimmy was going to drop the dime on them for stealing from their clients, so they had no choice but to borrow money from Jimmy on his terms.

What Jimmy didn't know was that they were cooking the books. Jerry and Dick had been hiding cash for years. Jimmy was no dummy. He knew they were cheating him but he looked the other way, waiting on the big settlements. It was one of the main reason Dick stole the money and high-tailed it out of town.

Dick suddenly felt the hair on the back of his neck stand on end as a howler monkey let out a loud scream. Howler monkeys, the loudest land animal in South America, could be heard from as far away as three miles. Dick was starting to panic as it grew darker. *Where are those assholes?* He thought. *Somebody else had to have survived.*

The jungle was completely black. Dick had never been in a place where the rain started and stopped as if someone were turning a valve on and off, the creatures were all on steroids, and when it got dark, it was beyond black. He was beginning to sweat. He hadn't taken the time to see where he was or what was around him before it got dark. All he knew was that he was still by the river. *Great, that's where the alligators like to hang out, and don't they like to feed mostly at night?* He thought.

The howler monkey let out another scream. Dick could feel his heart start to race as if he were about to have a heart attack. He could feel his nose begin to throb. He hoped that his bloody nose hadn't put out a blood scent. Who knew what would come out of the jungle to try to eat him. Dick vowed that if he ever got out of the jungle, he was leaving Brazil forever. Instead, he would find a safe beach that wasn't full of things wanting to eat him.

Chapter Sixteen

It was now five days after Flight 153 went down in the jungle. General Russo called Franco to let him know that the U.S. Coast Guard had joined the search and that they were sending out two HU-16e Albatrosses. They would be focusing their search along the Xingu River and its tributaries, while his men continued their search along the Madeira and Machado Rivers.

He asked Franco to keep searching along the Tapajós River for another day, and then have his men move down to Cachimbo and search along the tributaries of the Tapajós River, the Juruena River, and the Teles Piras River. General Russo told him that everyone was instructed to use channel three so that they all would know what was going on. Before he hung up, he wished Franco good luck and promised to stay in touch.

Ana was excited that the Coast Guard had finally joined the search. She couldn't understand what had taken them so long, since the plane had gone missing five days ago. She was starting to lose hope but she didn't want to give up. She knew that Billy was all right and that he was making his way back to her. He was a survivor.

The two U.S. Coast Guard planes started flying at daybreak. One flew north along the Xingu River and the other flew south. Their plan was to follow the river first, and then work their way back and forth ten miles out on each side of the river.

The Xingu River was a very large river, over 900 miles long and lined with dense vegetation. There were hundreds of square miles of jungle between the rivers that would have to be searched. Trying to find where a plane might have landed in that jungle would be more difficult than finding a needle in a haystack, a cliché that the pilots never grew tired of using.

As the planes set out, the skies were clear and all the pilots checked in with search and rescue headquarters. By order of Major Reno, who General Russo had put in charge of the operation, all planes were to check in at the top of the hour, unless they had found something.

Lieutenants Robert Smith and Mike Johnson piloted the U.S. Coast Guard planes. Their spotters were Ensigns Jimmy Porter and Frank Street.

Lieutenant Smith and Ensign Porter started their search at the mouth of the Xingu River, while Lieutenant Johnson and Ensign Street started their search at the mouth of the Iriri River, a tributary of the Xingu River.

Lieutenant Smith flew down the Xingu River. There was very little river traffic, no more than a few small fishing boats, canoes, and cattle boats near the mouth of the river that flowed into a lake. The further that Lieutenant Smith flew, the less traffic they saw, until several hundred miles up the river there was no sign of human existence.

Lieutenant Johnson and Ensign Street flew for several hours before spotting what looked like someone standing on the bank of the river. Lieutenant Johnson turned the plane back toward the riverbank, but when the two men returned to the spot, no one was there.

"I think my eyes must be playing tricks on me," said Ensign Street.

The men returned to their search, following a grid ten miles wide on each side of the river.

Franco Silva's men had no better luck. The helicopter spotter's eyes grew weary as the day gave way to twilight. Their fuel was running low, so they headed back to Itaituba to refuel and call it a day. General Russo's men were also running low on fuel, so they headed back to the airport for the night.

As Lieutenant Johnson turned the Albatross to return to headquarters, Ensign Street called out, "Sir, I see a large hole in the jungle's canopy at three o'clock. Could you bring her in a little closer so I can get a better look?"

Lieutenant Johnson swung the Albatross around.

"Sir, can you bring her in a little lower?"

Lieutenant Johnson brought the Albatross in as low as he could. The light was beginning to fade, which interfered with Ensign Street's line of sight.

"Wait! There's a plane, sir! I can see what's left of its tail!"

"Are you certain, Street?"

"Yes, sir, it's a tail. I'm certain."

"Do you see any survivors?"

"No, sir, that's a negative."

"I'm marking the coordinates and then I'll radio them in."

When Lieutenant Johnson called in to report that they had spotted a tail of an airplane, Major Reno wanted them to fly by once more to check for survivors.

"I'd be happy to, sir, but the light is fading fast. I doubt we'll be able to see anything," replied Lieutenant Johnson.

"Maybe you could see a light," Major Reno suggested.

"10-4," said Lieutenant Johnson, but when they flew by the wreckage, all they could see was darkness.

Major Reno told them to head back to headquarters and that they'd get a chopper there first thing in the morning.

General Russo called Franco to give him an update.

"Franco, my friend, did you hear the news?"

"Yes, general, I heard it on the radio today. My daughter wanted me to have the helicopter pick her up and bring her to the site."

"I don't think that would have been a very good idea."

"That's what I told her, that it's a military operation and that the only thing we could do would be to listen to their progress on the radio."

"Good, my friend. Let's keep our fingers crossed. I will keep you informed."

"Thank you again, general. You are very kind to offer so much help."

"Daddy, what did he say?" asked Ana.

"He said it was too dark to see anything and that he was sending out a helicopter in the morning."

"When do we leave?"

"Ana, as I've told you, this is a military operation. He said he would keep us informed via the radio."

"Daddy, can you have your helicopter be on standby in case they find Billy?"

"Let's take it one step at a time."

"We should call Billy's parents and let them know that they might have found the plane."

"I think we should wait until we hear back from General Russo."

"But, Daddy, they're probably out of their minds with worry."

"I know, dear, but it would be worse if it doesn't turn out how we hoped it would."

"What do you mean?"

"I just think we should wait and be sure. Now try to get some sleep. Tomorrow is going to be another long day."

"I won't be able to sleep. All I can think about is Billy being trapped out there in the jungle."

"I don't mean to sound callous, but Billy is used to being in the jungle. The good news is that no one is shooting at him."

"But what about the Indians?"

"Let's hope they leave them alone. Morning will be here before you know it."

Major Reno had the rescue team fly out at first light to the coordinates that the Coast Guard pilot had given them. The helicopters were having a hard time finding a place to land because the rainy season had turned the jungle into a large swamp. The helicopters circled around the crash site but saw no signs of life. All they could see was debris and the tail section of the plane. The pilot called back to Major Reno, explaining the situation.

Major Reno instructed them to hover close to the water so they could launch a raft with a search team. The pilot did what he was told, glad that he wasn't one of the men climbing into the raft. It had now been six days since the plane went down and he couldn't imagine what the men would find. They lowered a raft into the water and then lowered four men into the raft. As the helicopter hovered at a safe distance, the men went to explore the wreckage.

Ana and her father heard the helicopter pilot and Major Reno's conversation.

"Daddy, I can't stand it!"

"Be patient, they're doing the best that they can."

It seemed like hours before Ana heard the men reporting back to Major Reno.

"Sir? Sergeant Rico says that this is not the plane that we are looking for."

"What! What! What are you saying? It's the only plane missing."

"Sir, I know that there have been no other reports of a missing plane, but Sergeant Rico said that this one's a cargo plane, and by the looks of it they were smuggling drugs."

"Drugs? Are there any survivors?"

"No, sir. It looks like the flight crew and those travelling with them have been dead for a few weeks. There isn't much left of them according to Sergeant Rico. He said that there's a lot of money still in the plane and quite a lot of cocaine as well."

"Retrieve the money," said Major Reno, "and then set fire to the plane to destroy the cocaine."

"Yes, sir," said the pilot.

"Daddy, how could that be?"

"I don't know."

"What do we do now?"

"I don't know. I would imagine that they would resume their search."

Chapter Seventeen

Day six dawned slowly. Fred woke and found Jan curled up next to him, her head resting on his chest. Lou was stoking the fire.

"Are you cooking breakfast?" asked Fred.

"Don't I wish I had something to cook," said Lou, pausing. "Do you hear that?"

"What?" said Fred as he strained his ears? "I can't hear anything above the roar of that water. There must be a waterfall nearby. Oh my God! I wonder if that's what happened to the rest of the group."

"Well it wouldn't break my heart if Dick went over it. Wait! Do you hear it? It's back again!"

"No, I don't hear anything. My hearing's not what it used to be."

"It sounds like a helicopter."

Fred tried desperately to hear what Lou was hearing.

Jan sat up and asked, "What do you hear, Lou?"

"It sounded like a helicopter," he replied, but he couldn't hear it anymore.

Hector woke with Sister Mary Alice spooning him. Hector hadn't felt a woman curled next to him since his wife had died. It felt good.

Sister Mary Alice was embarrassed when she woke to find herself spooned up against Hector, but to her surprise, she liked it. Suddenly, she jumped to her feet but it wasn't because of her embarrassment. She thought she had heard a helicopter, and she looked up just in time to see it fly away.

"No!" she cried. "Come back!"

"What? Who?" Asked Hector.

"A helicopter! There was a helicopter up there!"

Hector ran to the water's edge and looked up into the sky. He didn't see anything. "Where? Are you sure you weren't still dreaming?" All Hector could hear was the roaring river.

"No, I wasn't dreaming. I saw it. It was right over there. But now it's gone."

Sister Mary Alice sat down and started to cry.

Hector came over and put his arms around her, pulling her face to his chest. "It's going to be all right," he said. "They'll be back. We just need to stay near the water where they can see us."

Billy was lying on his back looking at the sky. In the clouds, he thought he could see Ana's face. She had such a beautiful face, with her large brown eyes. Then he thought he saw a helicopter. It was bright red with some kind of insignia on its side. He jumped to his feet and started waving, but the helicopter was heading in the wrong direction and then it disappeared. Billy started to curse. He wished he'd left the raft out where they could have seen it, but he was afraid that the current would take it away, and he knew that it was his only chance of getting out of the jungle.

Billy was hungry, wet, and tired. He wondered where the others were. Surely someone had survived, they all couldn't have died. He hadn't seen any bodies floating in the river but they could have been downriver from him. He decided that he should find something to eat.

As he walked along the shore, he spotted a deep pool of water not far from where he'd spent the night. There were several large catfish swimming in it. Billy walked to the raft and retrieved the machete from a wet bag. Then he cut a long branch to make a spear and he speared a large catfish on his first try.

Billy gathered some branches to make a fire. The wood was wet and smoked a bit but he didn't care. After he got the fire going, he threaded the fish onto a green stick and roasted it until its skin was crispy.

Dick was exhausted. He thought the night would never end. He couldn't believe that he was still alive, half-expecting some creature to jump out and attack him. Maybe Jan was right. It wasn't so bad being a lawyer.

Dick had smelled smoke the night before and thought that maybe he could still smell smoke. It wasn't quite light enough to start wandering around but it seemed like the smoke wasn't too far away. The minutes seemed like hours as Dick waited for it to become light enough for him to walk safely along the riverbank.

129

He thought he could see a wisp of smoke around the bend in the river so he started to walk in that direction, poking the ground with a stick that he had found lying on the ground before taking a step. Dick had no intention of stepping on another alligator.

Jan asked, "Lou, do you have any more of whatever that was that you cooked last night?"

"Sorry," said Lou. "I've been keeping my eyes open but I haven't found anything else to cook."

"What about all those Brazil nuts that you hear people talk about? You'd think we would be tripping on them."

"I don't know how we would eat one if we found one," said Fred.

"What do you mean?"

"Well, Brazil nuts come in a very hard shell. Even if we had a hammer, we would still have trouble cracking one open."

"Are you kidding me?"

"No, it's true. The average Brazil nut weighs between six or seven pounds and is as hard as a cannon ball. The Brazil nut grows about a hundred and thirty feet off the ground in the crown of the Brazil nut tree. I don't see any trees that tall growing around here."

"Then what are we going to eat?"

"Whatever we—" Lou stopped in mid-sentence, looking upriver.

"What is it?" asked Jan.

"I don't know. I thought I heard something, like a branch breaking."

"I don't think now's a good time to be playing with me, Lou."

"I'm not playing. I heard something."

"I wish I had your hearing," said Fred. "All I can hear is the roar of the river."

Jan screamed as Dick burst out of the undergrowth. He looked awful. The five-hundred-dollar suit that he wore on the plane now looked like a hand-me-down suit from a hobo. Dick's face was covered with scratches. His eyes had black circles under them, and his nose was crooked and swollen. Worst of all, Dick smelled awful.

"Am I ever glad to see you!" said Dick.

"I wish I could say the same," said Lou. "We thought that maybe we got lucky and you drowned."

"Sorry to disappoint you. What do we have to eat?"

"Sorry, pal. We're fresh out of snake."

"Snake!" Jan screeched. "That was a snake that we ate last night?"

"Yeah, one of Dick's cousins."

Jan could feel Irene start to roll over. She thought that she might throw up but she did her best to keep what she had in her stomach down. There was no telling when they would get to eat again.

"Dick, what happen to you?" asked Fred. "Your face is all scratched and you look as if you've been rolling around in the mud. And what's that smell?"

"I fell out of the raft like everyone else."

"I mean, where did you end up? And where did you spend the night? How did you find us?"

"I was lucky. I made my way to shore right away. I had no idea where I was, so I started to run and stepped right onto the back of an alligator."

"It didn't bite you?" asked Lou.

"Sorry to disappoint you again, but obviously I managed to escape. Before I could get up the courage to move again, it was dark. By then I was too afraid to move."

"Imagine that."

"I could smell the smoke from your campfire and it made the night pass even slower, knowing that someone was probably eating and had a way to keep the critters at bay."

"Too bad you couldn't have joined us."

Sister Mary Alice grabbed Hector by the arm. "Look!" she said. "There's smoke over there!"

"I see it!"

Hector and Sister Mary Alice walked along the riverbank in the direction of the lazily rising wisps of smoke. They soon came upon a waterfall that seemed to be about a hundred feet from top to bottom. Somewhere near the bottom was the source of the smoke.

"Do you think the rest of the group went over the falls?" asked Sister Mary Alice.

"I don't know, but someone is down there. Let's take it slow. There's no telling who's down there."

"What do you mean? Whoever's down there has to be someone from our group."

"Not necessarily. I don't think anyone could survive such a great fall."

"Then who else could it be?"

"Indians, drug dealers…hell, it could be headhunters for all we know."

"Hector, that's not the least bit funny."

"I wasn't trying to be funny. It could be someone from our group but I really doubt it. More than likely it's Indians or drug dealers."

"Don't say that. I'm scared enough as it is."

"Do you want to wait here while I check it out?"

"Are you kidding me? I'm on you like white on rice."

The two slowly worked their way down the bank, trying to see where the smoke was coming from. Sister Mary Alice's foot got caught on a vine and she fell into Hector, causing them both to go rolling down the hill.

Billy heard the crashing in the undergrowth and thought it might be peccaries attracted by the smell of his fish cooking. He looked around for any signs of movement.

Hector held on to Sister Mary Alice as they came to a stop at the bottom of the hill.

"Are you all right?" he whispered.

"I think so," she answered, thanking God that they hadn't broken any bones.

Hector motioned for Sister Mary Alice to crouch down and not say a word so they could navigate through the undergrowth as quietly as possible.

Billy, spear ready, stood behind a tree.

Hector peered out into the clearing. He saw a campfire burning but he didn't see anyone near it. He motioned to Sister Mary Alice to stand still. They stood silently for at least five minutes before Hector saw Billy, crouched, come out slowly from behind a tree.

"Billy, it's me, Hector! And Sister Mary Alice!"

Hector looked at the raft pulled up onto the riverbank.

"Billy, did you go over the falls in the raft?"

"Kind of. I tied myself to it, but after I went over and came to the surface, the raft was caught in that pool over there. So I swam for it and pulled it up onto shore before it could be swept downriver."

"Thank God for that," said Hector. "I don't think we have much of a chance of getting out of here without it."

"Enough talk. You two must be starving. I was able to spear a catfish that'll be plenty for the three of us. Let's eat and then we'll talk."

"Great idea!" said Hector as he handed a piece of fish to Sister Mary Alice. She said a prayer of thanks before she ate the fish.

"You're amazing, Sister," said Hector, devouring a large piece of fish. "You pray about everything."

"Leave her alone," said Billy.

"I can't believe you survived these falls," said Sister Mary Alice.

"I think I bruised a few ribs but other than that, I'm fine. Where are the others?"

"We don't know," said Hector, reaching for another piece of fish.

"We were hoping that we weren't the only ones to survive," said Sister Mary Alice. "Well, we found you, Billy. Perhaps we can find the others."

"I think we should stay here for a day and keep a large, smoky fire going. If anyone's still alive, maybe they'll see the smoke and work their way to it," said Billy.

"I'll gather some wood and green branches," said Hector.

"Did you guys see the helicopter early this morning?"

"What? You saw a helicopter, too?"

"Just for a moment. It was gone before I could get to my feet."

"You would've thought that they would've seen the smoke from your campfire."

"I didn't have a fire going yet. And the flare gun was in a sack in the raft."

"Maybe they'll come back through here," Sister Mary Alice offered, silently praying to God.

"I don't know," said Billy. "There's a lot of jungle out here and it didn't look like a search and rescue helicopter."

"What do you mean?" asked Hector.

"It had some kind of logo on its side, like it belonged to a company."

"That could be good news," said Sister Mary Alice. "They may be doing business nearby."

"What kind of business could be out here?" asked Hector.

"It could be mission work. There may be a mission nearby, or perhaps a mining operation or oil exploration."

"I'll buy the mission," said Billy, "but I doubt that they'd be out here mining or looking for oil. How would they get the equipment in here to drill?"

Hector piled the wood and green branches over the campfire. He was going to make sure the smoke was thick and plentiful, knowing that it might help their chances of being rescued. The smoke climbed high into the sky, where it could be seen for miles.

Before long, the others had noticed it.

"Look!" said Lou.

"What do you see?" asked Dick, hoping it was something to eat.

"It's smoke! It looks like it's about a mile or two away."

"I see it," said Fred. "It looks like it's on the other side of the river."

"Great, that would be just our luck," Dick grumbled.

Jan stood up to see what they were talking about but she looked in the wrong direction.

"I don't see any smoke."

"That's because you're looking upriver, you dumb broad," said Dick.

"Hey, wait a minute!" said Fred as he stood between Jan and Dick. "There's no need for name-calling."

Jan turned in the opposite direction and started screaming.

"Damn!" said Dick. "What's wrong with you now? It's just a little smoke. For crying out loud, the jungle's not burning down!"

Jan hid behind Fred.

"What is it, Jan?"

"Didn't you see them?"

"See who?"

Fred strained his eyes in the direction that Jan was looking.

Lou looked too but didn't see anything but jungle.

"She's drugged out," said Dick. "Why don't you share some of those painkillers with me? I sure could use some. I mean, have you seen my nose? You shouldn't be so stingy with them. The captain and those two dead broads don't need them anymore, that's for sure."

Fred turned Jan around and looked into her eyes.

"What exactly did you see?"

Jan just stared at him. Then she broke eye contact, opened her purse, and began digging for the bottle of Xanax.

"I told you she was stoned."

Fred grabbed the bottle from Jan and she tried to take it back from him. Fred held her tightly.

"I think she's gone around the bend," said Lou.

Dick suddenly grabbed Jan's purse, pulling Jan away from Fred in the process. Since the shoulder strap was looped over her head and hung diagonally across her body, Jan was pulled to the ground. Lou grabbed Dick and Fred stepped in.

"Dick, this is going too far!"

Dick stood up.

"Who made you boss, Fred?"

"Captain Davis did," said Lou.

"Yeah, well he's dead."

Fred had had enough. He was about to explode when Dick sucker punched him. Letting go of all his frustration toward Dick, Fred let out a war cry and tackled Dick, pinning him to the ground while throwing punches. Dick's nose exploded and Fred was quickly covered with blood. Jan screamed again. Lou grabbed Fred, and with Jan's help, pulled Fred off Dick. Fred stumbled back, breathing heavily. He looked down at Dick, and then at Dick's blood on his fist.

"Dick, you are free to go your own way. Sue whomever you want when this is over. But if you are going to be part of our group, you will listen to me. To tell you the truth, I wish you would go your own way. It's going to be tough enough getting out of here alive without putting up with your bullshit."

Dick lay on the ground, nose bleeding, wishing he had never met Fred. Unfortunately, he was stuck with him. He couldn't find his way out of a city park without a sign, let alone find his way out of a jungle.

"What's it going to be, Dick?"

Billy speared another fish because they were still hungry. They couldn't remember eating anything that tasted so good.

"Maybe we should go back and look for the others," said Sister Mary Alice.

"I really think we should wait," said Billy. "If they're out there, then they'll see the smoke and come down to us."

"What if they're hurt?" asked Sister Mary Alice.

"Then they're probably going to die."

"Billy, I can't believe you said that!"

"Sister, think about it. It would be hard enough to climb back up that waterfall and try to find them, if they are even up there. For all we know, they may be downriver."

"That's impossible."

"Why's that?"

"They wouldn't have survived the waterfall."

"I did. Why wouldn't they?"

"You're different."

"How?"

"You're young and in shape. Take Dick, for example. I'm sorry to say this, but he's fat and way out of shape. I'm surprised that he made it as far as he has."

"My point exactly. We can't risk it. If they are up there, they'll eventually see the smoke and follow it. Let's give them a day."

"What if they don't show up?"

136

"Then we're going to get back into that raft and try to find our way out of here. Now try to get some rest. And keep looking up in case that helicopter decides to fly over again."

Chapter Eighteen

A week had passed since the crash, and General Russo addressed the search team.

"Men, I know you have searched long and hard without any luck. However, today is the last day of our search. If we don't find something today, I'm afraid we'll have to call it off. It's not likely that any of the survivors would still be alive after a week in the jungle. Now with that in mind, please give it your all. May God bless you all, good luck, men."

The pilots were instructed to conclude their search by covering as much of the Xingu River as they could, keeping to a ten-mile grid along both sides of the river. Lieutenant Smith and Ensign Porter were sent about five hundred miles up the river. Major Reno's two search planes would search a tributary of the Iriri River. Lieutenant Johnson and Ensign Street would search the lower two hundred miles of the river. Finally, Franco's company helicopter would search the last one hundred miles, to the mouth of the Xingu River.

"Daddy, I don't think they should call off the search just yet."

"Ana, we have to be reasonable. This is costing the government a lot of money."

"How can you put a price on those people's heads?"

"The chances of anyone surviving after a full week in the jungle are very slim. They haven't even located the wreckage, let alone found any survivors."

"You have to make them keep searching. I just know that Billy is still alive. I can feel it in my soul."

"I know it's hard to give up but we still have today. Let's go to church and pray. We'll only drive ourselves crazy sitting here, listening to the pilots talk or, even worse, listening to their silence."

"But, Daddy, what if we miss something?"

"I'll have my secretary come find us if there is any news. Now let's go pray."

With the search under way, Major Reno's spotter said, "Sir, I think I see a hole in the canopy."

"Where?"

"At four o'clock, sir. Can you bring her around and a little lower?"

Major Reno swung the plane back around and dropped down to a few hundred feet above the canopy.

"There! There's a burned-out fuselage and a wing. Sir, can you bring her back around again and go just a little slower?"

"I'll try, but I don't want to join them. I'm going as slow as I can while still keeping us airborne."

"I see the tail, sir. If you bring her by one more time, I think I'll be able to see the nose of the plane. There it is! It's about fifty yards north of the tail."

"Do you see any survivors?"

"I'm looking, sir. There sure is a lot of debris hanging from the trees."

"They must have lost power, those poor sons of bitches. It looks like the trees ripped the belly right out of that plane."

"Sir, how could anyone have survived that?"

"We won't know until we get our people down there. Call General Russo and let him know that we found the plane."

"Sir, do you think it's the plane we're looking for?"

"From the looks of the debris in the trees and floating in the swamp, I would say yes, that is our passenger plane. Let's call in the coordinates so we can get a helicopter rescue squad down there."

Chapter Nineteen

Dick was silent. Fred felt sorry for hitting him, especially since he already had a broken nose, but he'd asked for it. Fred told Jan to give Dick a few pain pills. Dick grabbed them and swallowed them dry.

Lou was looking for something that they could eat when he saw the smoke again.

"Fred, look! There's the smoke again and it's thicker than ever. What do you think it is?"

"I would hope that it's the others."

"Who else could it be?"

Fred's first thought was that the Kayapo were building a fire to roast them. He didn't think any one of them could manage to build such a large fire.

"Let's go see where the smoke is coming from," said Lou.

"Maybe I should go alone first, to check it out and tell you what I find," said Fred.

"Are you kidding me?" said Jan. "You're not getting two feet away from me."

"I don't think that would be a good idea, Fred. What if you were to get lost? What would happen to us? I don't think we would be able to find our way out of this jungle without you."

I don't know what they think I know. I've never been in the jungle before, but I better just keep that to myself. We don't need any more drama around here, thought Fred.

"Then what do you suggest, Lou?"

"I think we should all go right away, before that fire dies down and we can't find it."

"Well, if anyone wants my opinion," said Dick, "I think we should build a bigger fire and let them come to us."

"That won't work. That fire is downriver. Chances are that they wouldn't see our fire. And besides, we have to go downriver anyway."

"Then let's get a move on," said Lou.

"Jan, are you going to be all right? Do you feel strong enough to do this?" asked Fred.

"She doesn't have a choice," said Dick. "She either goes with us or she stays here and takes her chances."

"That's enough out of you, Dick. I can see that the leopard doesn't change his spots, or in your case, the hyena."

"What, are you sweet on her, fat boy?"

"That's enough!" Jan shouted. "We can't keep fighting or we'll never make it out of here alive. So let's just go."

"How are we going to keep our eye on the smoke if we're walking through the jungle?"

"We won't be. We're going to walk along the riverbank," said Fred.

"That's going to be hard to do with all the snakes and alligators," said Lou.

"We'll just have to take our time and be careful."

"I've got an idea," said Lou. "Dick can be our point man."

"Screw you. I'm not going to be bait. Put the broad in the lead. She's so chewed up already I doubt that anything else would want her."

"I'll take the lead," said Fred, tired of listening to Dick's insults.

They made their way very slowly along the riverbank, trying desperately not to lose sight of the smoke. They had walked a little over half a mile when they came to a deep creek feeding into the river.

"Now what?"

"I don't know, Dick. What would you suggest?" asked Fred.

"I say that you go up the creek and find us a place to cross, and then come and get us."

"Why, that's a great idea," said Fred, sarcastically. "Except I think you should be the one to find the crossing."

"In your dreams, pal. If I go, we all go."

"Then let's get moving. Who knows how long they'll keep that fire going."

They walked another mile before they came to a tree that had fallen across the creek.

"I wish we had that machete," said Fred. "This undergrowth is really getting thick, and the bugs are as big as rodents."

141

Suddenly, Jan let out a loud scream.

"Now what?" said Dick as he turned to see why she was screaming, as Dick turned his head, he came face to face with a large boa constrictor.

Jan jumped back, running into Lou, who grabbed her, causing her to let out another loud scream.

Fred said, "Just stand still, don't move. I don't think he'll hurt you."

Dick nearly shit his pants for the second time since the raft accident. He didn't know if he should believe Fred or not, since Fred had made it clear that he'd rather be rid of him. Dick decided that he'd rather not take any chances, so he stepped back quickly. The snake lunged at him, wrapping itself around his neck. He fell to the ground, screaming, as the snake tightened its grip. Dick's screams gave way to gasping as he struggled to breathe.

"Somebody do something!" Jan screamed. She hated Dick but she hated the sight of a snake killing him worse.

Lou reached out and grabbed the snake's head. The snake tried desperately to bite Lou, but Lou twisted its head with everything he had. The snake began to release its grip on Dick and started to wrap itself around Lou.

Dick lay on the ground, whimpering and gasping for air. This time he not only shit his pants but he pissed them as well.

The snake twisted violently, trying to break Lou's hold around its neck. Lou couldn't hold on any longer and lost his grip, giving the snake just enough room to set its teeth into his arm.

To everyone's surprise, Jan ran up to the snake, crying like a wild banshee, and sprayed the snake in the face with hair spray. It startled the snake enough to release its teeth from Lou's arm.

Lou fell to the ground, holding his arm and cursing. Fred was able to fling the snake into the creek, where it quickly disappeared.

"Lou, are you all right?"

"He bit me pretty deep, Fred. It hurts like a son of a bitch."

"What about me?" Dick whined. "Does anyone want to know how I'm doing?"

"Not really," said Fred. "I'm surprised, actually. Snake's don't usually bother their own kind."

"Very funny," said Dick as he got to his feet.

"What happened to your pants? You look pitiful, Dick."

"Yeah? Well you'd shit your pants, too, if a snake attacked you."

"Stay downwind, Dick. Better yet, why don't you rinse out your drawers," said Fred. "Jan, tear off a piece of Lou's shirt and wrap it around his arm. And then let's cross this log and make our way back to the river."

Dick was last to cross the log. He swung his head wildly from side to side and up and down, waiting for more snakes to attack him, until he noticed that he was way behind the others. They had crossed the log and had already started back toward the river. Dick hurried, running in a panic to catch up to them.

Fred heard the river ahead. He couldn't believe that they had spent the whole morning walking but seemed no closer to the source of the smoke. When he reached the riverbank, he strained his eyes to find the smoke but he couldn't find it. This made him even more nervous. Maybe the Kayapo had built the fire and not the others. No matter, they were still going to have to make their way downriver if they were going to find their way out of the jungle.

The sound of the river became almost deafening.

There must be a waterfall close by, thought Fred. He could smell smoke but he couldn't see it. Suddenly, he could see smoke in the treetops on the other side of the river. It wasn't as much smoke as they had seen earlier but it was smoke nonetheless.

"Fred, there it is!" cried Jan, relieved that the others must be just across the river. "How are we going to get across?"

"Good question. I have no idea. The water is running too fast for us to swim across, even though Dick could use a bath."

"Screw you."

"Thanks, but I'll pass, Dick. Anyways, here's what I'm thinking. We'll have to climb down these falls first before crossing the river. So let's do that before worrying about what we'll do when we get to the bottom. We'll just take it one step at a time. Are you ready?"

143

Chapter Twenty

General Russo radioed the helicopter crew for an update. The pilot reported that it would take them a couple of hours to reach the crash site. He pointed out that Major Reno hadn't seen a place for the helicopter to land, so that meant they would have to lower a raft of rescuers and then hover above them. That would take a lot of fuel and the pilot wasn't sure his helicopter was capable of pulling that off without crashing itself.

General Russo was not happy with the scenario the pilot had just laid out. He decided that he would have to call the U.S. Coast Guard and see if they could send him a Chinook CH-47. The Coast Guard said they could spare one but couldn't send it out until morning. General Russo thanked them for their support and bid them good night.

Ana and her father were in church praying when Franco's secretary entered. She walked down the aisle silently and genuflected at the pew where Franco and his daughter were kneeling. Then she gently tapped Franco on the shoulder.

"Mr. Silva, I have news from General Russo," she whispered.

Franco turned to Ana. "There's news. Let's go outside."

Once outside the church, Franco asked his secretary to tell him what she knew. Ana was petrified. She didn't know if she wanted to hear it. What if the news was bad? What if Billy was dead?

"Mr. Silva, General Russo called about fifteen minutes ago. I got here as fast as I could."

"What is it? Out with it!"

"Yes, sir. I'm sorry."

Sorry? Thought Ana. Then she was right. Billy must be dead.

"Sir, General Russo said that they found the plane."

"Are they sure it's the right plane this time?"

"I'm not sure, sir. All General Russo told me was that they found the plane at about 2:30 this afternoon."

"Did he say anything about survivors?"

"No, sir, he didn't say."

"Well, didn't you ask him?" Franco demanded loudly.

His secretary took a step back.

"I'm sorry. I've startled you. It's been a long week. Thank you for delivering the news. I'll call General Russo right away. Thank you, again. Please take the rest of the day off, with pay of course."

Franco and Ana made their way back to Franco's office. He dialed General Russo and got a busy signal.

"What's taking so long?" asked Ana.

"It's busy. I'll hang up and try again in a few minutes."

"I can't stand not knowing, Daddy!"

"Try to be patient, dear. We will know something in a few minutes."

Franco picked up the phone and dialed again. This time it was ringing and he gave Ana a thumbs-up signal.

"General Russo's office. How can I help you?" asked the secretary on the other end of the line.

"Yes, this is Franco Silva. I received a message to return General Russo's call. I understand that he has some news for me."

"I'm sorry, Mr. Silva, but General Russo has left for the day. Is there anything else that I can help you with?"

"Perhaps. I need to know the status of the search for the missing plane."

"I'm sorry, Mr. Silva, but I really don't know much about that. I've been out of the office for a few days and General Russo has been out of the office all day."

"But he called me not more than a half hour ago."

"I'm sorry, Mr. Silva. I can try to page him and let him know that you called."

"Thank you, I would appreciate that. Good day."

"What did she say? Is Billy alive? Did they pick him up?"

"Ana, no more questions right now. The general wasn't in and his secretary doesn't know anything new about the plane. I'm sorry, we're just going to have to wait until he returns my call."

Chapter Twenty-One

The waterfall was beautiful, a sheer drop of at least one hundred feet. However, the vegetation was thick and Fred didn't see an easy way down. He could see the smoke more clearly now but not who was fanning the fire. *Boy, I'd love to have a set of binoculars right about now*, he thought as he picked his way through the jungle away from the falls.

"Where are you taking us?" asked Dick. He wasn't keen on going back into the jungle.

"Dick, if you know a better way to get to the bottom, I'm all ears," said Fred.

Dick remained silent.

"I thought so. Come on, let's get a move on."

Lou's arm had become quite swollen. Even though the boa constrictor had no venom, its teeth were loaded with bacteria capable of causing a life-threatening infection.

Two-thirds of the way down the waterfall, Fred slipped and fell. He tried frantically to stop himself from falling off the ledge and going over the falls. He managed to grasp a small vine but he kept sliding uncontrollably down the hill. The vine uncoiled under Fred's weight, bringing him to an abrupt stop at the edge of the falls, where he dangled in the air.

Jan screamed. Dick grabbed on to the nearest tree, not wanting to follow Fred. Lou tried desperately to reach Fred before he went off the edge of the falls. There was a snap and a loud scream, followed by a splash. Lou looked over the edge, clinging to another vine, searching for Fred.

"What was that?" cried Sister Mary Alice.

"What?" asked Hector, looking into the sky in hopes of seeing the red helicopter?

"It sounded like a scream."

"It was probably just a monkey," said Billy as he looked over at Sister Mary Alice.

Lou couldn't see the bottom of the waterfall because of the mist.

"Lou, do you see him?" cried Jan as Dick clung to his tree, thinking that they were really screwed now. He not only wasn't going to get to screw the nun before getting out of the jungle, but he was going to be stuck with Jan and Lou, who didn't know a whole lot more about getting out of the stinking jungle than he did.

Dick started screaming at the top of his lungs.

"Help! Help! Please, somebody help me!"

Sister Mary Alice turned her head toward the waterfall and strained her ears. She could swear that she heard someone crying for help.

"Hector, listen. Do you hear someone shouting?"

Hector turned his head and saw a man floating down the river.

"Billy, there's someone in the water!"

Billy ran to the raft, untied it, and pushed off into the river, paddling as fast as he could with the one remaining paddle. He caught up to the body and reached over the side of the raft, grabbing it by the back of the shirt and lifting its head out of the water. It was Fred. He struggled to get him up out of the water but he couldn't pull him over the side of the raft.

Sister Mary Alice pulled out her rosary beads and began to pray. Hector ran down to the riverbank. He could see that Billy was struggling to get the person over the side of the raft. Then Billy lost his grip and the man sank under the water. Hector dove in, not bothering to think of his own safety.

Billy grabbed Fred's shirt again, letting out a guttural cry. Fred's shirt ripped and he fell back into the water. Billy thought that he had lost him when he saw Hector roll Fred over and start to swim to shore with him. He was relieved until he looked toward the shore. Two alligators were making their way into the water, locked on Hector swimming right at them. Billy began screaming at the top of his lungs as he paddled ferociously at the alligators. The alligators saw Billy's raft bearing down on them and they veered to the side. Billy put the raft between Hector and the alligators, giving Hector the precious seconds he needed to pull Fred to shore. Hector rolled Fred onto his back and started to give him CPR. Fred choked, puked, and coughed, and puked again.

Billy beached the raft as the two alligators followed closely behind. He had never seen such bold alligators before. He knew that the plastic paddle would do him no good and the machete was back at camp. Then it hit him. Billy grabbed the flare gun from the bag and fired it right into the open mouth of the lead alligator. The sulfuric flare exploded

147

in its mouth, completely burning off its lower jaw. The second alligator quickly retreated to the river and swam to the other side.

Sister Mary Alice grasped her rosary beads with a new fervor. She had heard the shot, not knowing that the men had the flare gun. *It must be the drug runners that Hector had spoken about*, she thought. *Please, Lord, spare these men.*

Jan was paralyzed with fear and grief, holding on to a tree and crying uncontrollably. Lou made his way to her.

"He's fine, I'm sure of it. We just need to get ourselves down to the water. I'm sure Fred's waiting there for us."

Lou tried gently to pry Jan's hands from the tree while trying to reassure her that they would be all right. She finally let go of the tree and let herself be led away by him. They walked deeper into the jungle, away from the edge of the waterfall, slowly working their way down the hill.

Dick was still screaming for help when he heard the shot. He turned to look for Lou and Jan but they were gone. Dick started running through the jungle in a panic.

Chapter Twenty-Two

Eight days had elapsed since Flight 153 went down in the jungle. The Chinook CH-47 arrived right at daybreak as promised. General Russo and his team stood ready. The captain of the CH-47 told General Russo that they had their own rescue team and that they only had room for two of his men. General Russo decided to send Major Reno and Sergeant Rico. Then he called Franco to let him know that the Coast Guard's rescue team had departed and that it would take the team about three hours to reach the crash site.

Ana thought that time had never moved as slowly as it did the past week. It seemed like the longest week of her young life. She thought her father should call Billy's parents and let them know that they had located the plane, but her father said it wouldn't be fair to call them until they were one hundred percent sure that they had the right plane and could tell them if there were any survivors.

The Chinook was approaching the hole in the canopy when it ran into a large thunderstorm.

"Not now!" said Major Reno. "Not when we are this close!"

The pilot of the Chinook said that they would have to try to fly around it or turn back. He hadn't seen anywhere that he could set the bird down and sit out the storm. The pilot watched the storm on the radar. They were lucky it was a fast-moving storm and it was moving east of the crash site. He estimated a twenty-minute delay.

After the storm had moved on, the pilot swung the Chinook around and headed for the crash site. Major Reno radioed General Russo, explaining that they were only minutes away from the site, and if he wished to stay on the line, he would keep him informed as events unfolded.

The pilot steadied the helicopter above the remains of the fuselage and hovered as his men got ready to lower the raft. Sergeant Rico joined the Coast Guard's rescue team and was slowly lowered into the swamp below.

He couldn't believe what he saw. The plane had broken into three pieces. The fuselage, with one wing still attached, lay alone in the middle of the swamp. The tail and the nose of the plane were about fifty yards each from the fuselage. The nose of the plane

149

was buried deep in the trees, while the tail looked as if it had been broken off from the plane and was dropped where it sat.

The men rowed slowly to the fuselage, stopping at the wing. Two of the men crawled up onto the wing and checked inside for survivors. As the men looked into the burnt-out hull, they shook their heads. There was nothing left inside apart from the frames of the seats. The men climbed down from the wing and got back into the raft. They slowly paddled over to the nose of the plane.

At the edge of the exposed part of the nose, they found what was left of a head with long, blond hair. The head was planted on a spear decorated with colorful feathers that fluttered in the breeze. It looked like birds had been pecking at it incessantly, feeding on whatever flesh remained. It was a very gruesome sight.

"What the hell is that?" asked one of the Coast Guard men.

"It looks like the work of the Kayapo," said Sergeant Rico.

"What the hell are Kayapo?"

"They're savage Indians. We've been having a little trouble with them lately."

General Russo heard their conversation.

"Rico, what the hell is going on down there?"

"General, sir, it looks like the Kayapo have been here."

"What have they done?"

"We aren't sure yet. So far, we've found what we think is a women's head stuck on a spear in front of the opening at the back of the plane's nose."

"Do you think they killed her?"

"I'm not sure, sir."

"Well, sergeant, find out!"

The men climbed up into the nose. They were soon overwhelmed by a putrefying smell and they were forced to put on their masks. The cabin was a wreck. A tree was sticking out of the cockpit and the door had been pried open. As they entered, the lead man gasped as he looked upon what was left of the co-pilot. He was sitting in his seat with his hand, or what was left of his hand, still on the yoke. He had been completely stripped of his flesh. He was now no more than a skeleton wearing a uniform. The skeletal remains of the navigator hung from the tree that had pierced the cabin, and the remains of three others had slumped to the floor but none of the bodies was missing a head. The remnants of what was once the aircrew were not going to be any fun bagging up and identifying.

The men climbed back into the raft and made their way to the tail section. As they paddled, General Russo asked Sergeant Rico if they had found the rest of the woman.

"No, sir. So far, we've only found five bodies, or skeletons to be more precise, and all of their heads were attached. General, we're on our way to the tail of the plane. I'll keep you informed, sir."

The raft slowly drifted to a stop at the mouth of the tail. None of the men was in a hurry to climb into the tail, not knowing what other gruesome sights they would find. Sergeant Rico accompanied the two Coast Guard men into the tail, expecting to find more skeletons.

The tail section was a mess. All of the seats were torn out and stacked at the opening. It appeared that someone had stacked them there on purpose. There was luggage stacked on one side of the cabin, while other pieces of luggage had been laid open, as if they had been gone through. The men were puzzled. Had there been some survivors holed up in there? If so, what had happened to them? Did the Kayapo tribe capture them?

"Look here," said Sergeant Rico.

On the wall, crudely written in what looked like purple magic marker, was a note:

To whom it may concern: On this day, December 27th, 1971, the survivors of Flight 153 are Fred Dowding, Billy Sunday, Lou Smiley, Julie York, Lucy Miller, Jan Lombardi, Captain John Davis, Hector Garcia, Sister Mary Alice Grant, and Dick Frost. We have set out at daybreak in the plane's rescue raft, heading due east.

Chapter Twenty-Three

Hector stared up at Billy in disbelief. He looked over at the alligator only feet away from him. The alligator's lower jaw was missing and there was smoke still curling from what was left of its mouth.

"Th-th-that was t-t-too close f-for comfort," stuttered Hector right before he passed out.

"Great, how am I going to get them both in the raft on my own," said Billy under his breath.

Fred laid rolled on his side, still choking and gasping, not knowing how close he had come to death right after Hector had saved his life.

Two close calls in about five minute's time is a little much for anybody to deal with, thought Billy, remembering how many times he too should be dead and not knowing why the men around him were killed instead. *Who decides?* Thought Billy. *I mean, really. How could I and three other men be stuck in the same foxhole over a period of twenty minutes and they get shot and I don't? Who decided that I should live while they died? Why?*

"Fred, can you hear me?"

Fred looked as if he might be in shock. Billy smacked him in the face lightly, calling his name.

"Fred, where are the others? Are they still alive? Fred, who's still alive? Are they still at the top of the falls? Fred, do you understand what I'm asking you?"

Billy went over to Hector and tried to revive him but he was out cold.

Sister Mary Alice was losing her mind. She prayed as hard as she could. Who had fired the shot? Were Hector and Billy all right? She didn't know whether to go and see what happened or to stay put.

"Lord, give me strength. Lord, tell me what to do. Do you want me to go or to stay?"

She knelt in the sand, waiting for the Lord to tell her what to do, and suddenly she heard cries for help. It sounded like a woman and a man, and their cries were getting louder. Sister Mary Alice rose from her knees and looked across the water. To her surprise, Lou and Jan stood on the other side, waving and shouting. Then she heard another man cry for help.

That has to be Dick, she thought. *What other man in this group would cry out like that?*

Now Sister Mary Alice had a new problem. What if the drug dealers who had shot at Billy and Hector could hear all the shouting? Maybe they would follow the shouts and shoot at them, too. She really didn't care if they shot at Dick because he was creepy and she didn't like the way he looked at her. It was as if he were undressing her with his eyes.

"Sorry, Lord, I know that wasn't very Christian of me. Please forgive me," she said under her breath.

While Sister Mary Alice was asking for forgiveness, she heard footsteps. When she opened her eyes, she saw Billy.

"Sister, I need your help."

"Billy, where's Hector?"

"He's all right."

"But I heard a shot. He didn't get shot, did he?"

"No, but I think he's in shock."

"But I heard a loud shot," Sister Mary Alice repeated. "Did you run into drug dealers? What happened?"

"I shot an alligator. There were two of them and they were going to attack Hector and Fred, so—"

"Hector *and* Fred? Where did you find Fred?"

"He was the one we saw floating in the river. I tried to get him into the raft but he was too heavy. So Hector dove in after him and swam to shore with him. That's where the alligators come in. I shot one of them with the flare gun and the other one high-tailed it back into the water."

"Well, where are Hector and Fred now?"

"They're a couple hundred yards downriver. Come on, I need you to help me get them into the raft so we can bring them back to camp."

Jan watched Sister Mary Alice and Billy walk away.

"Where are they going?"

"I don't know," said Lou. "Maybe they didn't see us."

Jan grabbed Lou's sore arm and he let out a yelp.

"I'm sorry, Lou. I'm just scared that they didn't see us and they're going to leave without us."

"But Hector wasn't with them. They wouldn't leave without Hector, unless—"

"Oh my God! What about Fred?" Screamed Jan.

Lou was starting to lose his patience and his arm was killing him. He had no idea what had happened to Fred, Jan was about to have a meltdown, Dick was crying like a baby somewhere up the hill from them, and now it looked like Billy and Sister Mary Alice were leaving without them.

Hector and Fred were still lying on the beach where Billy had left them, but the raft was only halfway on the beach. Billy couldn't believe that he hadn't remembered to pull it all the way onto shore before he went back for help. It could have easily been pulled into the current and without the raft, they were doomed.

Sister Mary Alice panicked when Billy started running toward Fred and Hector.

"What's wrong?"

Then she saw Billy grab the raft and drag it up onto shore. She realized just how lucky they were that the raft hadn't floated down the river. She couldn't imagine having to walk out of the jungle. Then again, she was still having trouble believing that they would be able to get out of the jungle at all.

Dick made his way down to where Jan and Lou stood staring downriver. "Where's Fred?" he asked, gasping for breath from his quest down the hill, his new scratches still bleeding.

"I don't know," said Lou.

"He's just gone? It wasn't that far of a drop."

"Not that far of a drop? If it wasn't that far of a drop, then why didn't you just jump off yourself and save yourself the trouble of hiking through all that brush?"

"I thought about it."

"Sure you did," said Lou sarcastically.

"What about the smoke? Who's making the smoke? And I heard a shot."

"Billy and Sister Mary Alice were across the river a minute ago but then they walked away," said Lou.

"What about Hector? Did you see him? And where did Billy and that nun wander off to? Was something chasing them?"

Dick was suddenly worried about being alone in the jungle. He remembered watching Tarzan movies as a kid and the jungle was full of savages.

"I don't know."

"You don't know what?"

"I don't know where they are or if anything was chasing them."

"Then how do you know that's their campfire?"

"I saw them near it."

"You saw them, but you don't know where they are now or if they even saw you?"

"That's right."

"No, that's not all right! I want out of this freakin' jungle! Tell me this then. Do they still have the raft?"

"I don't know."

"Just what do you know?" asked Dick, getting into Lou's face.

"I know I'm about to kick your fat ass if you don't get out of my face. Now back off and find the answers to your questions yourself!"

Billy paddled the raft back to camp. Sister Mary Alice held Hector close to her side and Fred lay in the bottom of the raft, staring into the sky.

"When we get back to camp, we need to get these guys up to the campfire so they can dry off."

Lou saw the raft coming upstream. He started waving and yelling.

155

"Billy! Over here, Billy!"

Billy looked up and waved back. He helped Sister Mary Alice get Fred and Hector settled by the fire.

"You stay here and watch over them. I'm going across the river to pick up Lou and Jan."

"I wonder where Dick is."

"I don't know. I only see Lou and Jan. Maybe we got lucky and Dick didn't make it."

"Billy, that's not very Christian of—"

But before Sister Mary Alice could finish her sentence, she realized that she had had the very same thought.

When Billy got to the other side, he was a little disappointed to see Dick now standing in front of Lou and Jan. He all but knocked them out of the way trying to get in the raft.

"Hold on! Let me get to shore before you try to get in. Do you want to flip it over?"

"We don't know what happened to Fred," said Jan, trying to hold back her tears. "He slipped and went over the falls, and—"

"He's back at the camp with Sister Mary Alice and Hector."

"What? You're kidding! Is he okay?"

Dick didn't know if he was happy or sad about them finding Fred.

"I think he's going to be all right."

"What do you mean you *think* he's going to be all right?"

"He drank half the river before Hector could pull him out. And I think he's suffering from shock. Let's get you over there."

"Do you have anything to eat?" asked Dick.

"Yeah, we've got some catfish."

Dick was starving, and the thought of catfish made him salivate. When Billy pulled the raft to shore, Dick nearly knocked him down on his way to the campfire.

"Where's the fish?"

"Over there," said Billy, pointing.

Dick looked in the direction where Billy was pointing but didn't see any catfish.

"Right there in that little pool."

Dick ran over to the water and, sure enough, there were catfish swimming in it. Dick looked around, and then back at Billy.

"How am I supposed to get them out?"

"That's your problem."

Dick ran into the water, desperately trying to grab one of the fish.

"Dick!" yelled Billy. "Watch out for the vampire fish!"

Dick ran out of the water, squealing like a pig. Then he stood on the shore, angry and wet, looking into the muddy water. He had a feeling that Billy was just having a little fun at his expense. Dick peered into the water, hoping that he hadn't chased the catfish away.

Billy came over to where Dick was standing, his spear ready. He raised the spear and aimed it at the water. Dick let out a loud squeal as the spear went past him. Billy walked over and retrieved it, along with a large catfish stuck on its end.

"I suppose you think that's funny."

"Do you want the fish or not?" asked Billy, holding the fish in front of Dick's face.

"What do you want me to do with it?"

"I thought you were hungry."

"Am I supposed to eat it raw?"

"You can if you want to, but I prefer mine cooked."

"How am I supposed to cook it?"

"I cooked mine over the fire."

Dick grabbed at Billy's spear.

"Hold on there, partner."

"What am I supposed to hold it over the fire with?"

"Get a stick."

Billy shook the fish off the end of his spear and went back over to the water to spear a fish for the others.

Dick fumbled around sheepishly in the brush looking for a stick. He found one, picked up the fish, and pushed the stick down the fish's throat. He held it over the fire and in about five minutes, Dick's stick burnt through and the fish fell into the fire. Dick frantically tried to pick it up out of the fire with the burnt remains of his stick.

"My fish is burning! Isn't someone going to get it out for me?"

Lou said, "Get it out yourself. And next time use a green stick."

"What's the difference?" Dick stared at Lou, hands out in front of him, his palms turned up.

"A live stick," said Jan. She couldn't believe how dumb Dick was. "Green sticks won't burn through."

Jan fed Fred some catfish and he chewed it slowly, his stomach still a little queasy.

"Lou, your arm. It looks awful!" said Sister Mary Alice. "What happened?"

"Snake bite. But don't worry, it wasn't poisonous."

"Let me take a look at that. It looks infected. I'll squeeze out what I can, put some mud on it, and then bandage it. We'd better keep an eye on it."

Chapter Twenty-Four

After nine days with no word on Flight 153, General Russo couldn't believe what he was hearing.

"Sergeant Rico, did you say survivors?"

"Yes, sir. We believe there are ten."

"Sergeant, which tribe do you think discovered the site?"

"I believe it was the Kayapo tribe, sir."

"And why is that?"

"The spear, sir. It has very distinct markings and feathers."

"But don't all tribes use feathers?"

"Yes, sir, they do. But the Kayapo use toucan feathers on their war spears and the feathers on this war spear are definitely toucan feathers. Would you like us to bring back the spear, sir?"

"Yes, sergeant, please bring the spear back with you. You don't think the head on that spear was one of the survivors, do you?"

"I don't think so, sir. There were no signs of a struggle in any section of the plane's remains, and there's no mention of any tribal attacks in the message, sir."

"That's very odd. You don't think that the Kayapo attacked the survivors after they left the crash site, do you?"

"I can't be sure, sir."

"Sergeant, I want you and the other men to make a very thorough search of the site and its adjacent perimeter to look for any signs of a struggle. We need to make sure that the Kayapo haven't butchered those ten survivors before we go looking all over God's green Earth for them."

"Sir, with all due respect, the search area is quite large, and we only have six men and one raft at our disposal. And we have very little time left before we'll have to head back."

"There's still plenty of daylight."

"Yes, sir, there is, but there's nowhere to put the helicopter down. It's been hovering, eating up lots of fuel, and it'll take three hours to get back. Oh, and there's one more thing, sir. What if the Kayapo have taken the survivors prisoner?"

"Damn it, sergeant, I never thought of that scenario. Okay, bring what you can back here. You'll have to return tomorrow and keep investigating."

General Russo had never thought that he would be dealing with the Kayapo tribe in addition to a plane crash. He decided to call the State Department to see if the anthropologist from the States had arrived yet. Maybe he could help them figure out what was going on with the tribe.

"This is General Russo. I need to speak with someone regarding a situation that has developed."

"General, my name is Mr. Lugo. How may I help you?"

"I have a passenger plane that crashed on Christmas Eve."

"Yes, I heard about that. Have you found the plane, sir?"

"Yes, that's why I'm calling you."

"I'm sorry, general, but I'm a little confused. What can we do regarding the plane crash?"

"Mr. Lugo, what I'm going to tell you must be kept in the strictest confidence. I need your word on it."

"Yes, of course, you have my word. I still don't know how I can help you with your plane crash, unless you suspect there was a terrorist attack or the plane was hijacked."

"I surly hope that's not what we're dealing with," said General Russo, though the thought had entered his mind. "Mr. Lugo, what I need your help with is the native people."

"The natives? I'm not sure I understand, general. Did the plane crash into a reservation?"

"No, Mr. Lugo, it did not. The plane crashed deep in the jungle."

"Then, again, general, how can I help you?"

"Mr. Lugo, what I need is to talk to that new anthropologist from the U.S. who's working with you, the expert the hydroelectric department hired to help deal with the Kayapo tribe."

"I'm sorry to disappoint you, general, but he never showed up. He was supposed to be here more than a week ago."

"What do you mean he never showed up? Where is he? Hasn't anyone from the State Department followed up on his whereabouts?"

"Not to my knowledge, general."

"I cannot believe the level of incompetence in this government! Listen, this is very important. Please find out where your missing anthropologist is. Now, while I wait on hold."

"I can try, general. This shouldn't take but a moment."

Mr. Lugo put General Russo on hold and looked up at the clock.

"Great, it's my lunchtime. The general will just have to wait until I return," Mr. Lugo said to himself.

General Russo had been on hold for ten minutes, listening to nothing, not even music. He waited another ten minutes before hanging up and dialing again. On the fourth ring, General Russo got a recording.

"If you receive this message during business hours, I am either on the other line or away from my desk. Please leave a brief message and a phone number, and I will get back to you just as soon as I can. Thank you and have a wonderful day."

I'll give him a wonderful day, thought General Russo. He left a message asking Mr. Lugo to call him as soon as possible, along with the number where he could be reached.

Sergeant Rico and the rescue team returned to the airport with the remains of the five bodies they had found on board and the head on the spear.

"We need to keep this quiet," said General Russo. "And we need to see if we can identify these bodies pronto, especially the head on that spear."

"Sir, with all due respect, that could take quite some time."

"Didn't the airline send us a list of passengers and crew members?"

"Yes, sir, they did."

161

"How many passengers were on the plane?"

"One hundred and eleven, sir. The airline said the plane was full, not an empty seat left."

"Sergeant, how many seats total were on the plane?" asked General Russo, thinking that even the army was incompetent.

"One hundred and forty seats, sir."

"So that leaves us with twenty-nine people not accounted for. How are we going to know who they are?"

"Sir, may I make a suggestion?"

"You may."

"Sir, I think the airline should release a statement asking family members and friends of the passengers to call and confirm that they have been in contact with their loved ones. That way, we may be able to narrow down who's missing."

"Are you out of your mind? Every crackpot missing their dog will call in a name."

"What if they were to send a picture along with the name, sir?"

"Sergeant, we have six faces, not even six faces. More like what's left of six faces. We're missing one hundred and forty bodies now. Even if they sent a picture, what would we compare it to?"

"Sir, if I may interrupt," said Captain Newman of the Chinook helicopter, "we have a list of ten survivors. Is that right, Sergeant Rico?"

"Yes, sir."

"Those ten are the only people who matter right now. We need to confirm that they're on the list the airline has provided."

"You're right," said General Russo. "Sergeant, get that list and see if the names of the survivors are on it."

Sergeant Rico retrieved the list and crosschecked the names on the plane's wall with the names on the list.

"Billy Sunday, a corporal, in the United States Army from Pennsylvania...check. Lou Smiley, a car salesman from Ohio...check. Julie York, from Minnesota, visiting her daughter here in Rio...check. Lucy Miller, from Ohio and also on vacation...check. Jan Lombardi, a headhunter, from Pittsburgh...check. Captain John Davis, the pilot, of the plane...check. Hector Garcia...hmm, he's not on the list. Sister Mary Alice Grant, traveling with three other nuns to Rio...check. Dick Frost...hmm, he's not on the list, either. And Fred Dowding, an anthropologist from Harvard...check."

"Wait, did you say that last one was an anthropologist?"

"Yes, sir. That's what was listed under 'Occupation'."

"It couldn't be, could it?" General Russo murmured to himself.

"Sir?"

"Never mind. So, we have eight out of ten passengers on the list, and the two passengers not on the list are men. The head on the spear appears to be that of a female. I want pictures of the surviving women as soon as possible. We need to identify the head on that spear first before we start looking for the survivors."

"Right away, sir, and, sir. The press is outside. They want a statement. What should I tell them?"

"Tell them that I'll be out in a few minutes."

General Russo went out to meet the press, which was largely made up of reporters from Brazil and the U.S.

"Sir, is it true that after nine days you finally found the plane?"

"Yes, we have located the plane."

"Sir, are there any survivors?"

"Yes, as far as we know."

"How many, sir? Have they been rescued?"

"I am not at liberty to answer that question at this time."

"Sir, why can't you tell us how many survived?"

"Again, I am not at liberty to answer that question at this time."

"When will you be bringing them out? And why didn't you bring them out today if you really did find them?"

"I can't answer that question."

"Sir, it seems a little strange when you say that you've found survivors but you can't tell us how many and whether you'll be bringing them out. Don't you think that's a little strange, sir?"

"I am not at liberty to answer that question at this time."

163

"Sir, why not?"

"I'm sorry, but we must keep the family and friends of the passengers in mind. I will let you know about any survivors as soon as possible. I thank you and bid you all a good night."

General Russo turned away from the reporters and exited the room amid shouts of, "Sir! Wait, sir! We have more questions!" When he entered his office, Sergeant Rico was waiting for him.

"Sir, Franco Silva has been trying to reach you all day. He would like you to call him at your earliest convenience."

General Russo let out a long sigh. "Get him on the line, sergeant. I'll talk to him now." He was dreading the call to Franco. He had a lot of things on his mind and he could feel a migraine coming on.

Franco waited patiently on the line, while Ana stood at his side, exhausted with worry. Her nerves were frayed and she felt as if she were on the brink of collapsing. Who would have thought that a person who had survived the fighting in Vietnam would be in a plane crash once he returned? She had worried for thirteen long months that Billy would be killed or badly wounded in Vietnam. She was so relieved when he called her from Germany to tell her that he was safe and on his way home, Ana snapped back to reality upon hearing her father's voice.

"Thank you for taking the time to call me back, general."

Ana held her breath. She didn't know if she could listen to another word that her father was saying, knowing that at any minute she might hear the words that she dreaded.

"Yes, sir, I know that I must keep this very confidential. I realize that if the press were to get a hold of this information, things could get pretty ugly."

Ana held her hands over her ears and shut her eyes. She started to pray.

"Thank you, general. I will wait for your call tomorrow," said Franco as he turned to his daughter.

Chapter Twenty-Five

Morning came and along with it, a torrent of rain. It was raining so hard that the reunited group had to move their camp off the beach and back into the jungle. Twenty minutes passed, and then another twenty. After an hour of torrential rain, the river started to rise.

"Get into the raft!" Billy ordered. "I'll tie us up to a tree."

Dick knocked Jan into the mud as he climbed into the raft. Fred grabbed him by the back of his shirt and pulled him off balance. Dick fell onto his back into the mud. He looked like a giant turtle trying to right itself. He managed to roll to his side and then onto his feet. He suddenly charged Fred, who stepped aside just as Dick was about to grab him, sending him sliding face first into the mud. Dick tried desperately to get to his feet, yelling, "I'm going to kill you, fat boy!"

"Fat boy? Isn't that like calling the kettle black?"

Dick made it to his feet and charged at Fred again. This time, Fred didn't move. Instead, he caught Dick under the chin with his right fist. Dick hit the muddy ground again, only this time he didn't move. Fred climbed into the raft with the others.

"Fred, you can't leave him lying in the mud like that," said Sister Mary Alice.

"Why not?"

"He might drown."

"I doubt it. The rain will wake him up."

Five minutes had passed and the rain was still pouring down. Sister Mary Alice looked down at Dick. He still wasn't moving.

"Fred, you really should check on Dick."

"Why do you care about what happens to him? No one else does."

"Because he's one of God's children."

"Then let God check on him."

Sister Mary Alice stood up and began to get out of the raft.

"What are you doing?" Hector asked.

"I'm going to make sure that he's still breathing."

"Don't worry, he's too rotten to die. Besides, we couldn't be that lucky."

Sister Mary Alice proceeded to climb out of the raft and managed, with some difficulty, to roll Dick over. He was still breathing, but he had a bloody mouth. It looked like Fred had knocked out Dick's front tooth. She slapped his face repeatedly to bring him around. Dick suddenly opened his eyes and grabbed her wrist, raising his other hand to her as if to strike.

Hector jumped out of the raft and landed on Dick's chest like a cat, knocking the air out of him. Then Billy got out of the raft. He really didn't like Dick but they needed to focus on getting out of the jungle, not beating each other up.

"Stop it! That's enough! I won't have any more outbursts like this. Dick, you need to start pulling your weight around here and start being considerate of others, or you can find your own way out of here."

"I have as much right to that raft as any of you," Dick sputtered, still gasping for air.

"Maybe so, but if we have any chance at all of getting out of here alive, we need to start working together. Now get up and get into the raft."

Dick got up and tried to wipe the mud off his face. As he did, he noticed that there was blood on his hand. He reached up and touched his mouth and teeth until he realized one was missing.

"You asshole, Fred! You knocked out my front tooth!"

"You're lucky that's all I knocked out!"

"Stop it! Dick, get in the raft and shut your mouth before I knock out all your teeth," said Billy.

Dick reluctantly climbed into the raft and sat as far away as he could from the others, thinking of how he was going to make them all pay for his mistreatment. It didn't take long to come up with a plan. As soon as he figured out where they were, he would wait until they were all asleep and then take off in the raft, leaving them stranded. He'd teach them to screw with him.

The rain persisted the rest of the day, forcing them to bail out water all day long.

"Is this wretched rain ever going to stop?" said Lou, soaked to the bone, tired, and hungry. His arm was throbbing, and he felt a little dizzy and he had the chills, but he thought that was to be expected with all the rain.

166

By dusk, the rain had finally slowed to a drizzle. The river had flooded over its banks and into the jungle, creating a swamp.

"I'm hungry," said Dick.

"Who isn't?" said Lou.

"What are we going to eat?" asked Dick, as if there were room service.

"Nothing," said Billy. "The water's too muddy from the rain to spear any fish."

The rain stopped abruptly and the jungle became eerily quiet. Then they heard something moving in the tree above the raft. Jan looked up and screamed. A large snake was letting itself down into the raft. Jan hid her face against Fred's chest. Before anyone could move, Billy decapitated the snake with the machete in one swift movement. The snake's head dropped into the raft, landing on Dick, who screamed even louder than Jan did, and then he fainted. Billy grabbed the snake's writhing, headless body and pulled it into the raft. Everyone leaned as far back away from it as they could.

"Billy!" cried Hector. "What are you doing? Are you mad?"

"Dinner. Just as soon as we can make a fire, we're going to eat this snake."

Jan leaned over the side of the raft and puked.

The snake's headless body wrapped itself around Dick's leg. Hector laughed. "Wait until he wakes up and finds that snake wrapped around his leg!"

Sister Mary Alice found little humor in Hector's remark. She turned to Billy and said, "We're not going to sit in this raft all night with a dead snake at our feet, are we?"

"Sister, I don't know what else we can do."

"Couldn't we hang it over the side of the raft?"

"No, we can't risk attracting alligators, or any other predator or scavenger. That's our dinner or maybe our breakfast. With all this water, it may be lunch tomorrow before we're able to build a fire."

When Dick came to, he didn't find the snake wrapped around his leg very funny. In fact, he fainted again. Billy unwound the snake from Dick's leg and placed it on the floor of the raft. He was worried that the snake wasn't going to keep until morning because of the heat. He decided the best option would be to move on.

"We're going to have to go downriver a bit to see if we can find a dry spot to build a fire so we can cook this snake."

167

"Are you kidding me?" said Jan.

"Are you hungry?"

"Yeah, but I'm not sure that I could eat that snake."

"You ate snake two nights ago with Lou and me," said Fred.

"That was different."

"How?"

"I didn't know that I was eating snake then. Now I do."

"Snake's not all that bad. You'd pay a lot of money to eat snake in a fancy restaurant."

"I doubt that they serve that particular breed of snake. Besides, I wouldn't pay anything to eat snake."

"The moon should be up in another hour. That should give us enough light to paddle downriver a ways," said Billy.

"I don't think that's a very good idea," said Lou. "What if we were to come upon another waterfall? We could all be killed."

"I was a little ways down the river this afternoon when we came across Fred. The river seemed to be pretty slow and wide at that point. There was a nice riverbank there, where Hector pulled Fred out of the river. We should be able to build a small fire there."

"Isn't that where you shot the alligator?" asked Dick.

"It is."

"Are you nuts or just crazy?"

"What do you mean?"

"There's a dead alligator lying there on the riverbank."

"I doubt it's still there. Some other alligator should've dragged it off and eaten it by now."

"My point exactly. The place is probably crawling with alligators. I think we should take a vote."

"A vote on what?"

"A vote on whether to go and eat a dead snake, and maybe be eaten ourselves by alligators, or to stay here and wait until morning, and spear a nice catfish instead."

"Dick, you were the one who wanted to vote on whether we should go down the river at night when we first came to the river."

Sister Mary Alice prayed to God for patience. She was about to lose her mind. She knew that God had wanted her to learn something from the trial that he had laid in her path, but she didn't want to go down the river at night, she didn't want to eat a snake, and she didn't want to take sides with Dick. *Please, God. Help me make the right decision,* she prayed.

"Okay, Dick, let's take a vote. Whoever wants to stay here for the night, raise your hand"?

"That's crazy. It's so dark now that you can't see anyone's hand."

"All right then, we'll do it this way. Fred, stay or go?"

Fred really didn't want to go. He had had enough excitement for one day and he was afraid of the alligators. What if the black caiman ate the alligator Billy had shot and it was still on the riverbank? They'd be the main course, he was certain.

"Fred, what's it going to be?"

Fred was hesitant. He owed Billy his life but he didn't feel like risking it again so soon.

"Fred?"

"I'm really not that hungry. That catfish we ate did it for me."

"I'll take that as a stay."

"I'm sorry, Billy."

"Jan, what about you? Stay or go?"

Damn, I didn't want to be next, thought Jan.

"Jan?"

"Stay. Irene isn't feeling so good right now."

"Hector, what about you?"

"I hate snakes. I vote to stay."

"Sister?"

"Stay."

"Lou?"

"I'm with the others. Stay."

169

"Well, that's that. I hope we can find something to eat in the morning," said Billy as he flung the snake as far away from the raft as he could.

Almost immediately, they heard thrashing in the water. Jan curled up against Fred's shoulder. Sister Mary Alice began to pray. Hector began to shake. Dick had to pee, but he was afraid of falling into the water and feeding whatever was thrashing about. He tried to hold it but the sound of the waterfall intensified his need to go, so he had no choice but to release his bladder. Before he felt the urine run past his knee, Jan said, "Dick, did you piss your pants again? You're disgusting!"

Dick didn't reply. He pretended to be asleep.

They passed the night in the raft fitfully and woke to a repeat of heavy rain. It looked like they'd be stuck right where they were.

Chapter Twenty-Six

It was now day ten since the crash and General Russo couldn't believe their luck. A monsoon had set in. They were calling for heavy rain all day, which meant they wouldn't be able to send the search planes out. It might have been a blessing in disguise since they still hadn't been able to identify the head on the spear. The face was too disfigured to tell who it was, so they would have to try to identify the head using dental records, but that would take some time.

Mr. Lugo from the State Department had called that morning, informing General Russo that their new anthropologist, Fred Dowding, was on the plane that had crashed. That confirmed General Russo's suspicions. The one person with knowledge of the Kayapo tribe was actually out there in the jungle. Or at least he hoped he was.

"General Russo, sir?" said Sergeant Rico.

General Russo was deep in thought and didn't hear him.

"Sir?"

Suddenly roused from his thoughts, he looked up and saw Sergeant Rico at his desk.

"What is it, sergeant?"

"Sir, we're being flooded with phone calls."

"Who's calling?"

"It's more like who isn't, sir. The press wants to talk to you. It seems that somehow they found out about the Kayapo and the head that we found at the crash site. They want to know if it was one of the passengers."

"Well who in the hell leaked that out?"

"I don't know, sir."

"Who else is calling?"

"The airline, the American Embassy, the passengers' families, the Red Cross, print reporters…and then there's Bishop Cheuiche, sir."

"The bishop? What does he want?"

"As you know, there were four nuns on board the plane, sir, and he wants to know whether we have any information on their condition. As you also know, sir, one of the survivors is a nun, Sister Mary Alice Grant."

"Hopefully she doesn't have blond hair."

"Actually, sir, she does."

"Wonderful. What else could go wrong?"

"Mr. Franco Silva has called twice today, sir. He wants to know if you have any more information on a passenger by the name of Billy Sunday. He also wants to know if he should send his helicopter out today."

"Has he looked out the window, sergeant?"

"I'm sure he has, sir."

"Then he should know that there is no way that his helicopter could find anything in that rain. Hell, if he went out there, we'd be searching for his crash site as well."

Franco was waiting impatiently by the phone.

"Daddy, has General Russo called you back yet?"

"No, darling, he hasn't. He must not have any new information to tell us. With this rain, I'm not surprised."

"I know you told me we shouldn't call Billy's parents until we know more, but we do know that Billy survived the crash. Shouldn't we call them and at least let them know?"

"Ana, I just don't know. I wouldn't want to give them false hope."

"If that were me on that plane and his parents knew something, wouldn't you want to know?"

"I suppose you're right. We should call them. What time is it?"

"It's one o'clock so that would be five in the morning there."

"I think we should wait a few more hours."

By four o'clock, Franco hadn't heard back from General Russo. Ana was becoming very impatient. They could no longer put off calling the Sundays.

Franco picked up the phone and slowly started dialing. He had knots in his stomach. He was trying to work out what he would say when they answered. He glanced over at Ana. She was wringing her hands nervously.

"Hello?" answered a tired voice. It was a woman. "Hello? Is anybody there?"

Franco cleared his throat.

"Yes, good morning." He cleared his throat again, not knowing how to begin. This wasn't like him. He was used to running a large corporation. He couldn't remember the last time he was at a loss for words.

"Mr. Silva? Is that you?"

"Yes, and this must be the lovely Mrs. Sunday."

"You are too kind, Mr. Silva. Have you heard any news?" Mildred asked in a quivering voice. She sat down quickly before her legs gave out. She thought she might faint from anticipation of what Mr. Silva had to say. She knew it must be bad news. She had seen the coverage of the plane crash on the news and they were being oddly silent on the chances of there being any survivors.

"Mrs. Sunday, I do have some news for you."

"Yes, Mr. Silva?" Mildred's heart was racing. She wished Bill was home.

"I have been in contact with General Russo. He's the man in charge of the search and rescue efforts. The reason I haven't called you sooner is that I've been waiting for him to call me back."

Ana couldn't stand it.

"Tell her! You're torturing her!"

"I'm sorry, Mrs. Sunday."

When Mildred heard "I'm sorry," it was all she could take. She fainted and hit the floor, leaving the receiver dangling against the wall.

Franco heard a gasp and then a crash.

"Mrs. Sunday, are you all right?"

"Daddy, what's the matter?"

Keeping the receiver to his ear, he turned to Ana and said, "I think she fainted. Or at least I hope that's all that has happened." He felt a rush of guilt wash over him. He knew that if the circumstances were reversed, his heart would just stop beating.

"Daddy, do something!" screamed Ana.

Rosesa ran into the room and wrapped her large arms around Ana. "Shush, baby, shush." She rocked Ana, who had started to cry.

"Mrs. Sunday!" Franco kept shouting, hoping that she'd regain consciousness and answer him.

There was a knock on General Russo's door.

"Sir, Bishop Cheuiche is here to see you," said Sergeant Rico.

"The bishop? Here? What does he want? He knows I'm busy."

"Sir, he said he was tired of you not answering his calls, so he decided to come and talk with you in person."

"Fine. I'll see him."

Sergeant Rico showed Bishop Cheuiche into General Russo's office, and then asked, "Bishop, is there anything I can get for you, some refreshment of some kind? Maybe a glass of wine?"

"Coffee will be fine," he replied.

Sergeant Rico left the room. Bishop Cheuiche had always made him nervous.

"General Russo, it is so good of you to take the time to see me," said Bishop Cheuiche sarcastically.

"No trouble at all. What can I do for you?"

"You can start by telling me what has become of my four lovely nuns."

"Bishop, I've already told you all I know."

"I don't think that you have, actually."

General Russo felt heat racing through his body. *Is this man calling me a liar?* He thought. "Bishop, I can assure you that I have told you all that I know."

There was a knock at the door. Sergeant Rico came in with coffee and cookies and set the tray on General Russo's desk.

"Bishop, would you like cream and sugar with your coffee?" Before the bishop could answer, Sergeant Rico said, "What am I thinking? Of course you do. Your kind always does."

174

Bishop Cheuiche looked up, surprised and annoyed at the audacity of the sergeant.

"I beg your pardon, sergeant? What do you mean by your statement?"

General Russo tried hard not to laugh by looking stern and annoyed with Sergeant Rico.

Sergeant Rico hadn't really thought about what he was saying before it slipped out. Remembering his time as an altar boy, he said, "The nuns always told us that the bishop liked everything sweet and not to hold back on the cream and sugar."

"Which bishop?"

"Why, that was you, sir."

Bishop Cheuiche turned abruptly away from Sergeant Rico and addressed General Russo. "Now where were we before we were so rudely interrupted?"

General Russo wanted to say, "You were just calling me a liar," but thought better of it. Instead, he said, "Bishop, I believe you were telling me that you thought I was withholding information from you."

"Yes, that's right. I would like to know just what happened to my nuns."

"I have already told you that three of the nuns are missing and Sister Mary Alice Grant's name was found on the wall of the plane, along with a list of nine other survivors. I don't know what it is that you think I'm not telling you, Bishop Cheuiche."

"General, there has been word that you found the head of a survivor on the end of one of those wretched Kayapo spears, and that the description of the head found on that spear appears to match the description of our dear Sister Mary Alice."

"Bishop, I do not know where you got your information, but no one from this office has released any information even remotely close to what you have just told me."

"Then you won't have a problem showing me the head from that disgusting spear."

"I really don't think it's necessary, but if you insist. Sergeant, please escort Bishop Cheuiche to the morgue."

"Right this way, bishop."

When they arrived at the morgue, Sergeant Rico escorted Bishop Cheuiche inside.

"Bishop, are you sure you want to do this?"

175

"I assure you, sergeant, that I have witnessed some very gruesome sights in my time."

"Very well."

Sergeant Rico motioned to the mortician to pull open the drawer. When Bishop Cheuiche saw the decaying head, he vomited. He turned away and started for the door, with Sergeant Rico following closely behind him.

"Bishop, is that Sister Mary Alice?"

Chapter Twenty-Seven

Morning came and Lou lay shivering on the floor of the raft in the wet, muddy water. His fever had become worse and his forearm had swollen to twice its normal size. Sister Mary Alice woke first to the sound of the howler monkeys screaming, which still unnerved her. Then she heard Lou moaning.

"Lou!" she cried as she bent down to lift him up.

Hector heard her and woke with a start. Then he went to her side and helped her lift Lou into an upright position.

"Lou," said Sister Mary Alice, "are you all right?"

"Now that's about as dumb of a question as I ever heard," said Dick as he watched them care for Lou.

"He got that snake bite saving you," said Hector. "Is that right? Is that how it happened?"

"Something like that," mumbled Dick.

"I'm sure that if the circumstances were reversed, you would have done the same thing for him, right Dick?" Hector said sarcastically.

Dick looked away and then turned back. "Hey, Billy. Is the water clear enough to spear any fish?"

"Look for yourself," he replied in disgust. "Lou's probably dying and all you can think of is your stomach. No surprise, I guess."

"Billy," said Sister Mary Alice, "we need to find a dry place where we can build a fire. We have to get Lou dry and keep him warm."

Billy untied the raft and began paddling. The river had dropped overnight but it was still muddy. The sky looked as if it would open up at any moment. Billy was deep in thought as the raft drifted down the middle of the river. They needed to make up as much time as they could, and Lou's situation looked like it would only slow them down. They'd already lost two days because of the rafting accident and the rain. He knew that every day they spent in the jungle decreased their odds of getting out of there alive. Billy struggled with what to do about Lou. He knew that Lou would gladly sacrifice himself for the others; he'd already proved that many times. If they stopped and waited until Lou recovered, it could be too late for the rest of them.

"Billy, over there," said Hector. "There's a good spot for a camp, and there's wood already piled up."

Billy brought the raft up to the riverbank.

"Hector, before you go messing with that pile of wood, remember what happened the last time you did that."

How could Hector forget? He was still afraid to go near any brush after his run-in with the snake at the bottom of that last pile of wood they found. Then a terrible thought hit him. That's where Lucy had died.

Billy pulled the raft onto shore and tied it to a large piece of driftwood.

Hector slowly approached the large pile of wood with Billy's spear. When he got within four or five feet of the pile, he heard movement. He could feel his heart in his throat. As he tried calming himself down, out charged four giant rats. In a purely reflexive movement, Hector threw the spear, hitting the last giant rat. It ran about thirty feet before dropping near the river's edge. The other three giant rats had made it into the water.

Jan screamed, clawing at Fred's shoulders. Clinging to Fred's neck, she screamed again, and Fred flipped her to the ground and put his hand over her mouth.

Hector was breathing heavily, looking around to see if there were any other giant creatures ready to charge him.

"Good job, Hector," said Billy as he walked over to the giant rat and finished it off with the machete.

"That's the biggest damn rat I ever saw," said Hector.

"That's not a rat," said Fred.

"It's not? Then what is it?"

"It's a capybara."

"What the hell is a capybara?"

"Well, you're partly right. The capybara is part of the rodent family. In fact, it's the largest member of the rodent family. They can grow to be about one hundred and fifty pounds. You speared one of the smaller ones. I'd guess that it's about ninety-five pounds

178

or so. They mostly eat plants and spend a lot of their time in the water. The native people hunt them for meat, which I've heard is rather tasty."

Jan looked up from the ground and thought, *At least it has legs. Maybe I can make myself believe that it's just pork.*

"I still think it's a damn prehistoric rat," said Hector as he slowly approached the brush pile.

Within an hour, the capybara was roasting over the fire. Billy was worried that the smell of the roasting meat would attract predators, so he kept close watch of their perimeter.

While Dick sat staring into the fire, Hector helped Sister Mary Alice with Lou, and Fred and Jan went down to the water's edge to try to get cleaned up.

Billy wondered if his mother knew that the plane had crashed. How could she not? They'd been out there in the jungle for nine days now, or was it ten? He couldn't remember. His heart grew heavy at the thought of the pain he must be causing his parents, and Ana and her family. Why was this happening? He was beginning to think he was jinxed. That people around him died while he lived still bothered him. He thought about how he was the only one in his foxhole to come out alive, and how the helicopter that didn't have room for him got hit by the RGP and exploded, and now the plane crash. Out of nearly a hundred and fifty people, he was one of only ten who had walked away from the crash so to speak. And now there were only seven.

Billy hated being surrounded by death. He wondered how he was going to get everyone out of the jungle alive. He didn't even know where they were. Then he thought that he should get to know everyone better, that he really hadn't taken the time to find out who they were, and they may be the last people on Earth that he would speak to.

The capybara looked like it was ready to eat. Billy took the machete, cut off a piece, and tried it.

"Not bad."

"Then don't be greedy!" said Dick. "Cut me off a hunk."

"You'll get yours," said Billy, annoyed with Dick. He'd make sure Dick got his share last.

Billy cut off some meat for Sister Mary Alice first and she fed it to Lou. Next, he cut some for Hector, then Jan and Fred. Jan was a little hesitant to try it, but it didn't smell that bad and she was starving. Fred tore into his like a bear waking up after hibernating all winter. Billy cut off a piece for Dick last. He grabbed it like a starving beggar. Maybe beggar was not the right word; beggars at least had a little respect.

Just as they were starting to eat, the sky opened up. The rain came down in a wall of water and they had no shelter. Billy quickly looked around for something that they could form a shelter with. He saw two large pieces of driftwood on the riverbank that he could use to prop up the raft. It would at least create a little relief from the rain. Soon they were all huddled under the raft, trying to stay dry.

Sister Mary Alice sat with Lou's head in her lap. His fever had grown worse and he had slipped into unconsciousness. Sister Mary Alice kept a damp rag across his forehead and prayed through the night but it wasn't enough. By morning, Lou was dead.

Sister Mary Alice cried as Billy and Hector dug another grave.

Billy thought, *now we are six; who will be next?* The rain hadn't let up at all, and Billy knew that if they were still looking for them, they couldn't continue in this weather. Every day that went by without being found meant a day closer to the search being called off, leaving them on their own.

Billy and Hector crawled under the raft to get out of the downpour.

"We're going to have to keep going, rain or no rain," said Billy.

"What if we can't see and the water picks up like last time, and we flip over or go over a waterfall?" Dick demanded.

"Listen, at this point, we only have two options. One, we can stay here and wait until it stops raining and hope we get rescued—personally, I think we'd have a better chance of growing wings and flying out of here than being rescued—or, two, we get into the raft and follow this river out of here."

"Billy's right," said Fred. "I'm pretty sure we're on the Xingu River. From the looks of the terrain, we should be about two-thirds of the way down the river. If I'm right, and I hope I am, then we're about one hundred fifty miles from Xingu National Park, a reservation where fourteen different tribes live."

180

"If they're living on a reservation, does that mean they're friendly Indians?" asked Hector.

Fred hesitated, not sure how much information they needed to know.

"As I've said, there are fourteen tribes living on the reservation. Now, I don't want to alarm you, but I feel that we're getting close enough that I should warn you about what we could face."

Jan's heart started beating madly and she could feel Irene starting to roll. She didn't need any more stress added to what little time she had left to live, which looked less and less by the minute.

"There are actually seventeen tribes that inhabit this part of the jungle on the Xingu River. The tribe that we need to be aware of is the Kayapo tribe. They are a very angry tribe, but with good reason. In the 1940s and '50s, missionaries came to convert them to Christianity."

Fred looked at Sister Mary Alice before continuing.

"With all due respect, Sister, spreading the word of Christ was not the missionaries' sole purpose. They were also accompanied by scientists from a drug company who wanted to try out a new vaccine. They convinced the Kayapo to be vaccinated, and then they infected them with the disease that the vaccine was supposed to prevent. The vaccine didn't work, and it ended up killing between forty and sixty percent of the tribe.

"The Kayapo people who survived went deep into the jungle and became very aggressive, even killing members of neighboring tribes. These native people are the reason that I'm here—well, not right here exactly. I was hired by the Brazilian government to help them understand the tribe better. The government is trying to harness this river and build three hydroelectric plants, but every time they send out a crew to survey it, they disappear."

"They disappear?" asked Hector, starting to get a little nervous.

"How do you know anything about the Kayapo tribe?" asked Billy.

"Good question. I'm a professor of anthropology at Harvard."

"Of what?" Asked Hector.

"Anthropology."

"What is that? I've never even heard that word before."

"I study cultures, and I just happen to be an expert on Kayapo tribal culture. I had hoped to find a peaceful solution to the problem. I'm afraid that if I can't, the Kayapo tribe will be no more."

"What do you mean by no more?" asked Sister Mary Alice.

"Just that. If I can't work out a solution between the native people and the government, the government has plans to wipe out the tribe, every man, woman, and child."

"They can't do that, can they?"

"I'm afraid they can, Sister. The Kayapo tribe is suspected of killing a dozen or more government workers. Who's going to stick up for a tribe like that?"

"The church should. They are all children of God."

"Well the church must have thought that they could spare a few of those children of God when they let the drug companies experiment on them," said Hector disdainfully.

"My point is that I'm not here to discuss the rights and wrongs of the Brazilian government or the church. The reason I brought up the Kayapo tribe in the first place is that we're in their territory and I've seen a few of them already. Now don't be alarmed. I think they're just watching us now, to see if we're any threat to them. As long as we stay on the water and keep moving, my guess is that they'll leave us alone. With that said, I think we should take what's left of the capybara, get in the raft, and get as far as we can while we still have daylight."

Jan had been sitting quietly as Fred talked, though her heart was racing and Irene was rolling. She couldn't believe that Fred knew there were dangerous natives all around them but kept it to himself. "Fred, what do these Indians look like?" she asked.

"You've seen them before."

"I was afraid of that. Those weren't birds that I seen, those were the Indians, right? Why didn't you tell us about them before?"

"Because I didn't want to alarm you."

"Then why alarm us now?"

"Because I've seen two of them about twenty yards away, when Billy and Hector were burying Lou."

182

Dick suddenly jumped up, pulled the raft down from the two pieces of driftwood, and started for the water. Billy grabbed the raft from him and gave him a shove.

"Just where do you think you're going?"

"I think we should leave him here for the Indians," said Hector. "He can't be trusted."

"Hector," said Sister Mary Alice, "I think we are all a little upset right now and none of us is thinking with a clear head. We just buried one of our friends today, it's been raining for what feels like forever, and we're all quite tired. God will see us through this if we put our trust in Him."

"Lou trusted Him," said Jan, "and look where that got him."

"Lou did trust the Lord and I know that he's now with our Savior."

"I'm not ready to join our Lord just yet, so let's get the hell in that raft and get out of here."

They grabbed their few possessions and boarded the raft. The rain was still pouring from the sky, reducing their visibility to about twenty or thirty yards, not enough to warn them of another waterfall but clear enough to see any natives. They paddled down the river for the rest of the afternoon and still the rain had refused to let up.

"It's getting harder to see," said Billy. "I think we should head to shore and find a place to camp for the night."

"Let's just stay on the river until we come to that reservation Fred told us about," said Jan.

"That could be days."

"Better than dying at the hands of those Indians," said Hector. His nerves were shot. He'd seen too many mangled bodies and too many people being eaten by alligators. And he was growing disheartened at burying yet another person. He just wanted it to be over.

Sister Mary Alice took out her rosary beads and prayed. She prayed for Hector because she suspected that he had a demon in his heart that was gripping his soul even before the plane crash. She prayed for Billy because even though he had a strong will to live, he also had his own demons to deal with. She prayed for Fred because he was a good soul and one of the kindest men that she had ever met. She prayed for Jan because

183

she was a survivor and she needed to find love in her life. Lastly, she prayed for Dick because as hard as it was to believe that God loved Dick, she never doubted God and had devoted herself to loving and obeying in His name.

It was quickly getting dark on the river and Billy didn't care what the others thought. He hadn't come this far only to kill them all foolishly. He turned the raft toward the riverbank.

"Billy, where are you going?" Jan shrieked. She was afraid that as soon as they pulled up to the shore, the Indians would capture them and take them to their encampment, where they would torture them and then shrink their heads. She didn't want to wind up being used as a decoration in some Indian's hut.

Billy ignored her and ran the raft onto shore. He got out and held the raft as everyone reluctantly got out. Fred knew that Billy was doing the right thing but the Kayapo back where they had buried Lou had scared him. He would rather have taken his chances with the river.

"You are going to kill us all!" Dick shouted as he stood with one leg on shore and the other in the raft.

Sister Mary Alice, who was still standing in the raft, said, "Please, Dick. It will be all right. The Lord will watch over us."

Billy contemplated grabbing Dick and knocking him to the ground, but he knew that might cause him to lose control of the raft. Fred, sensing Billy's dilemma, moved back toward the raft. Before he could reach out and grab Dick to pull him off the raft, Dick pushed off with the leg that was on shore, breaking Billy's grasp on the rope.

Sister Mary Alice fell to the floor of the raft and Dick grabbed the paddle. He quickly paddled out into the current and down the river. Fred, Hector, and Billy raced into the water and tried to lunge at the raft, but it was too late—they were gone.

"What is he thinking?" said Fred, panting.

"Of himself, what else?" said Billy, blaming himself for letting the rope slip out of his hand. "I should have tied the rope around my hand."

"I should have been quicker to grab him," said Fred.

"What are we going to do now?" asked Hector.

"Well, seeing as we're stuck here without the raft, the first thing we need to do is build a fire," said Billy.

"Won't that attract the Indians?" asked Jan.

"I don't think that they know we're here."

"So you want to announce our presence with a fire?"

"Jan, they aren't the only predators out there."

"What are you saying?"

"I'm saying that most predators are afraid of fire. So let's get a fire going before it's too dark to see what we're doing."

Once they got the fire started, they huddled together.

"It sure is amazing how self-centered some people can be," said Hector.

"Maybe he'll feel guilty and bring the raft back in the morning," said Jan.

"Are you kidding me? That would mean having to paddle upriver. Not to mention that he knows that if he comes back, we'll kill him."

"You wouldn't really kill him. That would be murder."

"Are you going to tell the authorities?"

"I don't want to think about that. Aren't there enough things out here trying to kill us without planning to kill one of our own?"

"You actually consider Dick to be one of our own? He just hijacked our raft and took Sister Mary Alice hostage."

"I'm worried about what he might do to her," said Billy.

"What are you talking about?" said Jan.

"You know what I'm talking about. Haven't you seen the way he's been staring at her? It's like he's undressing her with his eyes."

"She's a nun. You can't touch a nun."

"Says who?"

"God, that's who. Didn't you ever go to Bible school?"

"Are you for real? Do you think our friend Dick went to Bible school? And even if he did, do you think that would stop him from raping a nun out in the middle of the jungle?"

"I'll kill him," said Hector in a voice that none of them had heard before. "I'll not only kill him, I'll kill him a little at a time to prolong his pain."

"Hector, what has come over you? Anyway, you can't catch him now. He's long gone," said Jan.

"At first light, I'll whittle a spear with my pocket knife. I'll run along the riverbank until I catch up to them and then I'll kill him."

"Hector, that raft is traveling at least five miles an hour," said Fred. "How are you going to run five miles an hour along that riverbank? Don't you remember how dense the vegetation is, not to mention the creatures that would love to snack on your skinny ass?"

"We have to do something! We can't just let him get away with this!" Hector shouted.

"I'm afraid all we can do right now is pray for Sister Mary Alice as she prays for us."

"Try to get some sleep," said Billy. "I'll take first watch and keep the fire going."

"Are you kidding? I couldn't sleep if I tried. I'm too wired right now."

"Okay, then you take first watch. I'm exhausted anyway."

"Billy, how can you sleep when you know that Dick is going to pull the raft to shore and rape poor Sister Mary Alice the first opportunity he gets?" said Jan. She began to cry, thinking of Dick touching Sister Mary Alice. If that were her in the raft, she would jump into the black river and take her chances rather than have that pig touch her.

Fred wrapped his arm around Jan and tried to soothe her to sleep. He knew she had to be as exhausted as he was.

Sister Mary Alice clung to her rosary beads, knowing in her heart that God would not forsake her. Dick was busy trying to see where he was going. The raft felt like it was zigzagging all over the river. He couldn't understand why it didn't do that when Billy was paddling.

"Damn it! What's wrong with this raft?" Dick cursed.

Sister Mary Alice remained silent.

"What, are you deaf? I asked you a question!"

Sister Mary Alice refused to speak.

186

Dick was getting angrier by the minute. He'd been waiting a long time to have his way with Little Miss Goody Two Shoes.

"I know you nuns are nothing but a bunch of cock teasers. I went to Catholic school when I was a boy. I know what you nuns like."

Sister Mary Alice ignored him. She was relying on the Lord to protect her.

Dick was getting horny. He could feel his prick getting hard just thinking about her.

"I'll bet you're getting wet just thinking about me, Sister. It won't be long before it'll be just you and me."

Dick was having a hard time controlling himself. He wanted her and he knew she wanted him. *All those bitches who think they're something special want it. They just don't want anybody to know it,* he thought.

"It won't be long now, Sister. How long has it been since you were with a man?" he asked, and then he laughed. "I'll bet you sure had your fill of the women at the convent."

He laughed again.

"I saw that little honey you were traveling with. To be honest with you, Sister, I kinda wished that she were here in your place. I haven't seen a rack like that in a long time. I mean, if you could see that rack buried under that habit you nuns wear, I could only imagine what those babies look like naked. I'll bet you know what they look like."

Sister Mary Alice kept praying silently.

"I'll bet you know what they feel like, don't you? Did they taste good, Sister? I'll bet you're wet now!" said Dick, laughing even louder.

Suddenly, the current grew faster. Dick stopped laughing. He was trying to see where they were going. He frantically tried to find the shore but it was too dark. It felt like they were falling down a black hole with water splashing them in the face. Then the raft hit something and lifted it into the air. Sister Mary Alice screamed.

Chapter Twenty-Eight

Franco hung up the phone and dialed the operator.

"How may I help you?" asked the woman at the other end of the line.

"Hello, my name is Franco Silva and I have an emergency."

"What is the emergency, sir?"

"I was talking to a woman in the United States, telling her about her son who was in a plane crash here, when I heard what sounded like her hitting the floor. After that, she wouldn't respond."

"Sir, I'm not sure how I can help you."

"I need you to connect me to the emergency department in her town."

"And where would that be, sir?"

"One minute, I have it here somewhere."

Franco dug frantically though his desk, looking for the information. All he could find was the Sunday's names and phone number.

"I'm sorry to keep you waiting, miss. All I have is their phone number."

"Go ahead, sir."

Franco fumbled with the piece of paper. *What is wrong with me,* he thought. *I'm never this nervous about anything.* Franco dropped the paper on the floor. As he bent down to pick it up, he could hear the operator.

"Sir? Are you still there, sir?"

Franco retrieved the paper and straightened himself.

"Yes, I'm still here. I dropped the paper is all? I have it now."

"Then please go ahead, sir."

"Yes, the number is 412-774-4324 and the name is Mr. William Sunday. His wife, who I was speaking with, is Mildred."

"Thank you, sir. Please give me a minute while I try to reach the police department in that area."

Franco couldn't believe that was him talking on the phone. He'd handled million-dollar deals without flinching. Why was he rambling so nervously?

"Sir, I have your party on the line. Go ahead."

"Hello, this is Sergeant Jeff Lizzi How can I help you?"

"Hello, Sergeant Lizzi. This is Franco Silva. I'm calling from Rio de Janeiro. I have an emergency."

"Mr. Silva, this is Rochester, Pennsylvania, in the United States. Are you sure you have the right number?"

"Yes, sergeant, I'm sure I have the right number. Please, let's not waste any more time. I was speaking with Mrs. Mildred Sunday a few moments ago and I had some news about her son."

"Billy?"

"Yes, Billy. As I was saying, I was speaking with his mother when I heard what sounded like her fainting. God, let's hope she didn't have a heart attack. Please, sergeant, you need to send help to the Sunday's house right away!"

"I'll get right on it. Please stay on the line, Mr. Silva."

Sergeant Lizzi had dispatch send an ambulance and a police cruiser to the Sunday's house.

"Mr. Silva, are you still there?"

"Yes, sergeant, I'm still here."

"Mr. Silva, thank you for calling. I've sent a rescue team to the Sunday's address. Do you have a number where I can reach you?"

Franco gave the sergeant his number.

"Mr. Silva, I'll call you as soon as I know Mrs. Sunday's condition."

"Thank you, Sergeant Lizzi."

General Russo was at the airport before sunrise to check the weather. He desperately needed to get the search teams out to the crash site so they could search the perimeter to make sure the survivors weren't attacked by the Kayapo tribe. He hoped they were indeed heading east as the message had indicated. That would make the search somewhat easier. He wasn't sure if the weather would cooperate and he was torn about having to put others at risk. In the end, he decided that he didn't have a choice. He would have to send out at least one search plane.

189

Major Reno and Sergeant Rico met General Russo at the hanger with the sole search team at six AM.

"General, what have you decided?" asked Major Reno.

General Russo let out a heavy sigh and then paused. He looked around the room, studying the men. Then he turned back and looked at Major Reno.

"I really hate to send you men out searching for the survivors before we know what happened at the crash site regarding the Kayapo," said General Russo, followed by another long pause. "But I also would hate to think what would happen if I didn't send you and the survivors were somewhere out there in the jungle depending on us to rescue them.

"As you all know, it's been eleven days since the plane crashed, and probably ten days since the survivors supposedly left the crash site. I value your lives and I know that I could be putting you in danger looking for them, especially since they may not even still be alive. To be honest, I don't know of anyone who has survived a plane crash that deep in the jungle and has survived for more than a week. But that doesn't mean that it can't happen. And that's why I've decided to send you out there today."

"Sir," said Major Reno, "may I say something?"

"Go ahead."

"Sir, I know the timeframe we're working with and know that the odds of survival are against them, but at all of the other crashes we've dealt with, the survivors waited at the crash site and died mostly from attacks by predators. These ten survivors have a seasoned solider with them, and I understand that Corporal Sunday was just coming off a thirteen-month tour of duty in Vietnam. That increases their odds dramatically, not to mention that one of the survivors is Fred Dowding, an anthropologist that our own government had hired as a consultant for the Kayapo tribe. So, with all due respect, sir, I think that those ten survivors have a pretty good chance of still being alive."

General Russo let out another heavy sigh.

"Major Reno has a very good point. But with all due respect to Corporal Sunday, he is not with soldiers. He is with civilians. And as for the anthropologist, Mr. Dowding, he has never been in the jungle before. In fact, he has never even left the United States before. Mr. Dowding may know what he studies about the Kayapo tribe at Harvard, but I doubt that he has ever seen one in real life, until this crash. These ten survivors may have a little better chance than most, but I really don't hold out much hope that they are still alive."

"General, we do not have the luxury of gambling with their lives," said Major Reno. "Sir, I think that we should send out two search planes and have them focus on the last four hundred miles of the Xingu River."

"Why the last four hundred miles, major?"

"Well, sir, if you were to draw a straight line east of the crash site, it would put them at about the last four hundred miles of the Xingu River."

General Russo paced and looked at the pilots.

"All right, we'll send out two planes and we'll send two CH-47 helicopters to the crash site. Major Reno, I want you with Search Team One, and Sergeant Rico, I want you with Search Team Two. I want you men to search a one-mile perimeter around that crash site. I want you to look for anything, and I mean anything, that might look like our ten survivors may have had a run-in with our friends the Kayapo. The weather looks like it could be clearing. If we are going to do this, let's do it now. I bid you men good luck and God bless."

The search planes took off first, with the helicopters just behind them. Sergeant Rico hated these kinds of missions, looking for bodies and body parts. The only thing working in their favor on that day's mission was that they knew they weren't looking for any survivors. Before he knew it, the helicopters were getting ready to lower the search rafts, which always made him very nervous. He had visions of falling out of the raft and into the jaws of a great black caiman.

Search Team Two started at the nose of the plane. The stench from the dead bodies that they removed on their previous mission still hung in the air. The cockpit was swarming with ants and centipedes.

"Men, I want you to go through that cockpit with a fine-tooth comb. We are here for two reasons: one, to see if we can find out what caused the crash, and, two, to find out if the survivors made it out of here alive. As you all know, General Russo thinks that the Kayapo have already killed the survivors. We need to find evidence one way or the other."

Private Gomez looked through the bloodstained papers on the navigator's desk. A cockroach skittered across them, and with a natural reflex, he smashed it with the butt of his gun. Standing there in the cockpit, looking at the devastation, he wondered how anyone could have survived. What had caused the crash? How many people were still alive that night when they came to rest on the floor of the jungle? For those who perished, it must have been horrible. He thought of his wife and son. What would it be like to crash in the jungle at night, not knowing if your loved ones were dead or alive, or were being attacked by horrible alligators or eaten by piranhas? He felt a chill run up his spine, imaging his small son flailing helplessly in the water while a giant anaconda swallowed him whole as he cried out.

"Private!" yelled Sergeant Rico. "What are you doing in there?"

"Searching, sir!" shouted Private Gomez as he quickly wiped away a few tears.

"Come on out of there. We need to search the tail, and then we need to search the perimeter. We haven't got all day!" When Private Gomez came out and got into the raft, Sergeant Rico asked, "What took you so long?"

"I was reading the papers on the navigator's desk, sir."

"And did you find anything of significance?"

"No, sir."

They made their way to the tail of the plane. As they did, Private Gomez looked all around the crash site. He looked at the clothing hanging in the trees and the shoes bobbing in the water. Who did they belong to? He wondered if their owners had suffered when the plane hit the water, or were they already dead. He felt another shiver run up his spine.

"Private," said Sergeant Rico, "come on, we need to search the tail."

The men climbed out of the raft and into the tail section. Private Gomez looked around the wreckage. The seats were torn from the floor and there were bloodstains all over the interior. What hell these people must have gone though before dying. He looked over at the list of names written in purple marker on the wall of the cabin. *Purple,* he thought. *What an odd color to write a survivor's list in.* He noticed a nun's habit lying on the floor near the restroom. He looked at the pile of luggage dumped on the floor. He wondered if the barrier made from the seats was meant to keep out the alligators. He couldn't imagine what it must have been like for the survivors that first night in the jungle.

Sergeant Rico's radio crackled. He picked it up and said, "Rico here, come in."

"Sergeant, this is Major Reno. I think we may have found one of the survivors."

"Major, where are you?"

"We're about two hundred yards east of the fuselage."

"We'll be right there," said Sergeant Rico as he motioned to the men to climb back into the raft. The men were solemn. It was eerie to be reminded of death everywhere they looked, knowing that one minute the plane was full of good people ready to celebrate Christmas and the next almost all of them had died a horrible death.

Private Gomez reflected on his own Christmas Eve festivities. He and his wife went to Mass, leaving their small son, Carlos, with his mother-in-law. After church, they picked up their son and took him home, and then set out cookies for Papai Noel before putting Carlos to bed. After they were sure that he was fast asleep, they wrapped presents and put them under the tree. Then Private Gomez thought *we were able to do all the normal holiday preparations while these poor people were fighting for their lives.*

The men looked at the water and saw clothing and debris of all kinds floating near the surface. Sergeant Rico told the men to keep a sharp lookout for any bodies that could still be retrieved.

Retrieved, thought Private Gomez. He wasn't touching them. *God have mercy on their souls, but there is no telling what kind of diseases you could catch from handling dead bodies that have been floating in this swamp.*

They soon came upon Major Reno and his men in their raft, looking up into a tree. Sergeant Rico and the others paddled slowly over to them, and then looked up into the tree as well, trying to spot what they were staring at.

"What is it?" asked Sergeant Rico.

Major Reno looked over at Sergeant Rico. "I think it may be one of the survivors," he answered.

Sergeant Rico looked up into the tree again and then saw a man tangled in its branches.

"How did you find him?"

"One of my men saw buzzards circling, so we paddled over here to check it out."

"What makes you think he's one of the survivors?"

Major Reno looked up at the man in the tree and then looked back at Sergeant Rico. "Look at him. He hasn't been dead for more than a couple of days."

Sergeant Rico thought about that for a moment. If he had only been dead for a few days, then how could he be one of the survivors? "I don't think so," he said.

"What do you mean you don't think so? Who else could it be?"

"I don't know, but the survivors who left their names on the wall left about eleven days ago."

"Maybe they didn't get very far. This guy looks like he's got an arrow sticking out of him."

Sergeant Rico took out his binoculars and looked up at the man. He had what looked like long blond hair. And what was that in his hand? Sergeant Rico tried adjusting his binoculars but he couldn't quite see what was in the man's hand. One thing that he could make out was the arrow sticking out of his torso.

"What's in his hand?"

Major Reno put his binoculars up to his eyes. "I can't tell. We'll have to wait until we can get him down from there to find out."

Private Gomez was secretly praying to God that they wouldn't ask him to go up and get the man down from the tree, not only because he didn't want to handle a dead body but also because he was afraid of heights. God must have heard his prayers. Major Reno had two of his men climb up the tree to lower the man down. Private Gomez prayed for the man. He couldn't imagine the terror that he had lived through before he died.

As the man was being lowered, Sergeant Rico could plainly see what was in his hand. At first, he thought it was a knife, but as the man came within clear view, he could see that he was holding a crucifix. Private Gomez crossed himself when he saw the crucifix. He didn't understand how the man was still able to hold it while being lowered from the tree. The man's body swung back and forth but the crucifix remained gripped in his hand, as if he were holding it out to ward off his oppressors. When the man was finally lowered into Major Reno's raft, Private Gomez thanked the Lord that he wasn't in their raft.

194

"He must have been a man of God," said Major Reno.

"A lot of good that did him," said Sergeant Rico. "You're right. It doesn't look like he's been dead for very long."

"I'd say not more than a day or two. The birds got his eyes and a few insects have been working on him, but he doesn't look bad compared to those fellows in the cockpit."

"We need to figure out whether he's one of the survivors."

"He has to be. Who else could he be?"

"I don't know."

"Take your team and start a grid search. Look in every tree and behind every bush."

"What are you going to do?"

"I'm going to take this poor soul over to the tail section and bag him and leave him there until the helicopter gets back. Then I'm going to check in with General Russo and tell him what we found. You get started, keep your eyes open."

Private Gomez looked up into the trees and saw a red dress billowing in the breeze like a flag. It was an evening dress. He wondered whose dress it was and where she had planned to wear it.

"Private, do you see something?" barked Sergeant Rico.

"No, sir. I mean, there's a red dress caught in the top of that tree over there."

"Is there a body in it?"

"No, sir."

"Then I suggest that you look somewhere else."

By late afternoon, Private Gomez could hear the chopping sounds of the helicopters coming from the west. It was music to his ears. He wondered if there were any survivors within earshot of those sounds. How hopeless they must have felt if they could see the helicopters but the helicopters couldn't see them. Between the thick foliage and the constant noise of the birds and monkeys, the survivors could be within a few miles of the search party without them even knowing it.

As they approached the crash site, Private Gomez thought he saw something in a tree. He put his binoculars up to his eyes and started scanning the trees. He thought he saw a strange bird wearing earrings. *Earrings? Give me a break. I must be losing my mind,* he thought. He rubbed his eyes and looked again but saw nothing out of the ordinary. *It must have been a bird and it flew away.* He looked behind him, away from the sun. When he looked through his binoculars, he saw that there was something shiny and black in the branches of a tree. "Sergeant Rico, over there," he said.

"Where, private?"

"East, at about two o'clock, sir."

"I don't see anything."

"Look about halfway up the tree. See? Something's moving."

Sergeant Rico tilted his binoculars up and down, straining his eyes, as the helicopter stopped above the crash site and hovered. The wind from the rotors stirred the treetops. He looked again, and then he saw what Private Gomez had seen. He put down his binoculars and rubbed his eyes. The wash from the helicopter was drying out his eyes, making everything blurry. He raised his binoculars back to his eyes and looked again.

"Private Gomez, I see it. Take us over there under that tree."

"Sir, what is it?"

"We'll know in a minute."

The raft came to a stop under the tree.

"Gomez, I want you and Private Cruz to climb up that tree and see what's up there."

Private Gomez froze.

"But, sir, I'm afraid of heights."

"Private, you heard me. Get up there!"

Private Gomez stood up in the raft and looked at Private Cruz.

"What are you two looking at? Get up that tree and find out what's up there!"

Private Cruz went first. As he prepared to put on his climbing spikes, Sergeant Rico yelled, "Cruz! Watch what you're doing! Do you want to sink this raft?"

"No, sir," said Private Cruz. He looked over at Private Gomez, who motioned to him to grab his spikes and climb up to the lowest limb. Once they were settled, they strapped on their climbing spikes and reluctantly started to climb the tree. Private Gomez, trying to climb without shaking, he was angry with himself for even mentioning that he saw something in the tree because he knew that Sergeant Rico wouldn't have seen it if he hadn't said anything. Private Cruz followed closely at his heels.

The two men were about twenty feet up the tree when Private Gomez screamed. Private Cruz looked up and to his horror saw what was left of a nun. Her face was completely gone and she was missing one of her arms. Private Gomez lost the contents of his stomach and Private Cruz got an unexpected shower of his regurgitated lunch.

When Sergeant Rico looked up to see what was going on, he got a face full of Private Gomez's lunch, too. He suddenly lost his composure. It had been a long day and he sure didn't need this to add to it.

"Private Gomez! Get up there and prepare to lower that body!"

Private Gomez knew that he was going to see this in his dreams for a long time. He slowly regained his composure, wiped his mouth with his handkerchief, and climbed up to the corpse. He didn't want to touch the dead nun. The smell was terrible and he could swear that her habit was moving the closer he got to it. He decided he wasn't cut out for this kind of work. As soon as he got back, he would ask for a transfer.

Private Gomez grabbed a hold of the rope and began to slide it around the body as he held on to the tree so he wouldn't lose his balance. He grabbed the rope as it came around the other side and looped the end around the rope, making a slipknot. *Almost done,* he thought as he looked down at the men in the raft, giving them the signal to lower the body.

"You need to lift her! She's caught on something!" shouted Sergeant Rico.

Private Gomez didn't want to touch her.

"Gomez, what's taking you so long? The helicopters are here waiting for us. Hurry up!"

Private Gomez took a deep breath, turning his head so as not to look at the dead nun, and lifted her up. Something hit him on the side of his face and went down his shirt. He let out a blood-curdling scream and lost his balance. As he fell, his head slammed into a limb and then he hit the water.

Sergeant Rico grabbed Private Gomez from the water before he went under. As the sergeant turned him over, he saw something moving in his shirt. He ripped it open and out sprang a giant carnivorous centipede with a maroon body and yellow legs. The men in the raft jumped back out of its way as the ugly giant went over the side of the raft and into the water. Private Gomez's head was bleeding badly.

"Call Major Reno! Have his men get that nun down. We need to get Gomez into the helicopter right away!"

The paramedics knocked on the door of the Sunday residence but there was no answer. One of them said, "Sergeant Lizzi was told that she had passed out and that she may be alone. Let's try opening it."

Not surprising for the area, it was unlocked. They went in and found Mildred lying on the floor, the phone receiver dangling from the wall. The paramedics bent down to check for a pulse.

"We've got a pulse and she's breathing," said one of the paramedics. "Let's track down her next of kin."

Bill received the call at work and his heart sank. For the last year, he'd been worried sick that something would happen to Billy in Vietnam, and he watched Mildred age before his eyes. When Billy came home from Vietnam, it was as if a weight had been lifted from his shoulders. Mildred was filled with relief, her tired, vacant stare replaced by a glow of happiness. And now she was lying in a hospital bed recovering from a heart attack.

Doctor Chaves had given Ana a sedative.

"She should sleep for a while. The poor girl is mentally exhausted. I'm going to leave you with something that should help her with the stress. I want her to rest as much as possible for the next few days. Try to shield her from anything that may upset her."

"Doctor, that won't be easy. It's been eleven days since her boyfriend went missing. We've been going crazy with worry," said Franco.

"Do you need something to help you rest?"

Franco thought about it for only a second before replying, "No thank you, Doctor."

"Then if there's nothing else I can help you with, I'll be going. I'll check in tomorrow to see how Ana is doing."

After the doctor left, the phone on Franco's desk rang. He looked at it and a wave of nausea hit him. Was it General Russo with more bad news? Did they find the survivors dead and butchered by the Kayapo? He knew that would put his daughter over the edge. But maybe it was good news and they found them all alive and well. He knew that would be a stretch. This was the real world, not a fairy tale where everything works out in the end.

The phone was on its fifth ring when he said, "I'd better answer it." He reached for it but it had already stopped ringing.

General Russo sat in his office, waiting for the rescue team to get back. He couldn't believe the bad luck that they'd been experiencing. This was one of the worst plane crashes that he'd ever worked on. Of all the times of the year to deal with it, too—over the holidays and during the monsoon season, when the water was high and it could rain for days without end. The survivors could not have had more odds stacked against them. Then the call came in from Major Reno.

"General, I have some good news and I have some bad news. Which would you like to hear first?"

"The good news. I've had enough bad news."

"Sir, we found two more passengers."

"That's the good news? I have a feeling I'm going to hate the bad news."

"Sir, it looks like one of the passengers was a victim of the Kayapo. He had one of their arrows lodged in his chest."

"How long do you think he's been dead?"

"I wouldn't think more than two days, sir."

"Two days!"

"Yes, sir, but we won't know for sure until we get him to the morgue and forensics has a look at him."

"How do you know that it hasn't been longer than two days?"

"He was still in pretty good shape, sir. We found him up in a tree not fifty yards from the crash site."

"And the other one?"

"A nun, sir."

"A nun?"

"Yes, sir."

"And how long do you think she's been dead?"

"By the condition we found her in, I'd say that she was killed the night of the crash, sir."

"Do you think they were part of the survivors' group?"

"No, sir. Well, I don't know about the man. He could be. Like I said, I think he's only been dead for two days at most."

"Were you able to identify him?"

"No, sir, but there were a few things about him that might help us identify him."

"Such as?"

"Well, sir, the man had long blond hair and he was holding a crucifix when we found him, as if he were warding off a vampire or a very evil spirit."

"What about the nun? You know Bishop Cheuiche will be all over me about her."

"She was pretty far gone, sir. She was missing her face, an arm, and part of a leg. The insects had worked her over pretty good. And that's just part of the bad news."

"There's more? Good God, what happened out there?"

"Well, sir, it's Private Gomez."

"What about him?"

"Sir, he said he saw something moving in one of the trees, so we sent him up there with Private Cruz. That's where we found the nun. As he was preparing to lower her from the tree, he suddenly screamed and then lost his balance. He hit a tree limb before landing in the swamp. When Sergeant Rico pulled him into the raft, he saw something moving under his shirt, so he ripped it open and out jumped a giant centipede. It must have been a foot long. I found out later that it was a carnivorous centipede."

"Did it kill Private Gomez?"

"No, sir, but he's in critical condition."

"Where is he now?"

"He's at the army hospital."

"I'll check on him after we hang up. What did the search planes find?"

"Nothing, sir."

"To be honest, I didn't think they would. I don't think we're looking for survivors anymore, at least not ones who are alive. If we can identify the man in the tree as being among the list of survivors, then I'm ending this search before we lose any more men."

Chapter Twenty-Nine

Sister Mary Alice screamed in terror. She felt her body being slammed to the bottom of the raft. It was dark and she knew that Dick would be on her any second. The raft had come to a stop but it was at an odd angle. She knew that they weren't on shore because she could still feel the rapid flow of water beneath the raft. Where was he? She hoped that she had gotten lucky and God had flung him into the water.

Suddenly, Sister Mary Alice felt water rushing into the raft. She frantically climbed up the side of the raft and slowly ran her hand along its exterior, not knowing what she would touch.

Dick felt her hand as it worked its way up the side of the raft. He grabbed it and held it in a vice-like grip. Sister Mary Alice screamed in terror, desperately trying to pull her hand back. Dick held her wrist so tightly that she thought he would break it. He was shouting something at her but the roar of the river was too great for her to hear what he was saying. Then the raft shifted violently and Dick lost his grip on her.

Dick slid to the bottom of the raft. He had tied the raft to a limb and hoped it would hold, but it was too dark to see what was happening. He tried getting back up to find Sister Mary Alice, but when he reached out he felt the raft shift again, as if it were trying to roll over. Dick knew that if that happened, it would dump them both into the river in the pitch-dark night, and their chance of surviving would be slim to none.

Where did that bitch go? He thought.

Dick hadn't heard Sister Mary Alice scream and surely she would have screamed if she had fallen into the river. Then he felt her foot lightly touch his fingers. He grabbed for it but she pulled it back quickly.

She's still here, thought Dick, laughing out loud, hoping to intimidate her. "I know you're there, Sister," laughed Dick. "I'm going to have my way with you and you know it, so why make it so difficult? You wouldn't want to fall into the river and be eaten by one of those black caimans, would you? Come on, slide right on down here to Papa. I won't bite you," he lied. "Well, maybe I'll bite you a little but you'll like it, I promise."

Dick strained his eyes, trying to see where she was. He felt the raft shift and then grow lighter. Without warning, the raft began to turn. It felt like if he moved a muscle, the raft would turn over and dump him into the river.

Sister Mary Alice's heart was beating so fast she thought it would burst. She had leapt when she felt Dick's disgusting hand on her foot. As she jumped, she reached out, hoping to find something to grab onto. She soon discovered that she was hanging from a limb. She had no idea how strong it was or how far out it went but she began to edge her way along it cautiously. She was determined not to drown while Dick raped her. If she were going to drown, she'd drown on her own without that pig violating her.

Hector threw another piece of wood onto the fire. Fred was snoring and Jan was curled into him. They looked like two spoons in a drawer. Billy was curled into a ball, sleeping but not peacefully. He was arguing with someone as he tossed and turned.

Hector turned his gaze back to the fire. He could see Sister Mary Alice's face in the flames. She had such a pleasant and peaceful appearance. It amazed Hector how anyone with so much turmoil around her could be so calm. He tried to think pleasant thoughts so he wouldn't think about what he knew must be going on at that very moment.

I'll kill him, thought Hector, not able to keep himself from thinking that Dick was raping Sister Mary Alice, while he sat helplessly by the fire. It made him want to throw up. What a pig Dick was.

Sister Mary Alice had said that God loved everyone and that they were all His children. But how could God love someone like Dick, who just hurt everyone he came in contact with, stealing whatever he could get his hands on, and all without remorse?

Hector stood up and looked at the heavens.

"God, why are you doing this? What has she done to be punished like this? Maybe you could be merciful and let your daughter Sister Mary Alice drown before that pig rapes her."

Jan opened her eyes. She heard someone talking. It was Hector. Was he praying? He was clearly upset. *I think he's in love with Sister Mary Alice,* she thought as she sighed. *Love. Wouldn't it be great to have a man who loved you so much that he would kill another to protect you?* She didn't actually want someone to kill someone else just to prove that he loved her. Although if she were captured by those Indians, she guessed she'd make an exception. She looked at Fred and thought, *He saved my life*. But she knew he would try to save anyone from harm, even Dick. Then she looked back at Hector. He was down on his knees praying. She felt her heart go out to him and uttered a prayer of her own.

Sister Mary Alice looked to the east. The sky was turning red. Then she looked down at Dick, hanging on for dear life. He was frozen in place, trying to keep the raft from overturning, and he looked tired, dirty, and miserable. Sister Mary Alice wasn't sure, but it looked like he was praying. She felt bad for him. Maybe God had spoken to Dick and this was His way of saving them.

The sun was rising and the air was cool and fresh. The birds were singing, giving Sister Mary Alice a new feeling of hope. She looked to the sky and began to thank God for His mercy.

Dick looked up and saw Sister Mary Alice looking away from him. He moved carefully and slowly, inch by inch, until he was sure he would be able to grab hold of her leg. With one clean and calculated motion, he grabbed her and pulled her down into the raft. Sister Mary Alice was so surprised that she didn't even put up any resistance. Before she knew it, Dick was on top of her, tearing at her blouse like a pit bull.

Fighting for her life, Sister Mary Alice kicked and screamed. Dick ripped off her blouse and tore away her bra. She screamed louder, raking his face with her nails. Dick reached for his face and as he did, Sister Mary Alice was able to escape from his grip and leap into the river. The raft spun around and flipped over.

Dick stuck to the raft like glue. He had fastened his belt through one of the eyelets along the side of the raft, and now he was struggling to keep his face above water as the river tried to separate him from the raft. His head went under and he swallowed a large gulp of the river. As he struggled to get his head above water, he felt a burning sensation in his chest and things were becoming blurry. He was starting to black out. When the raft freed itself from the tree, it rolled in the river and slammed into the shore, where it lodged itself under a low-hanging limb. Dick lay in the bottom of the raft, puking and cursing.

When Sister Mary Alice surfaced, she found herself in the middle of the rapids. The river tore off the rest of her blouse as she fought to keep her head above water. She hit another rapid and felt herself being plunged to the bottom. Her stomach hit a rock, knocking out what little air she still had in her lungs. Then it felt like she was on a merry-go-round. Everything was spinning. She saw her mother, she saw the plane as it was falling out of the sky, she saw the centipede crawling out of Lucy's mouth, and she saw Dick's face as he ripped off her blouse.

Morning came and Hector was still awake.

"Hector, why didn't you wake me?" asked Billy, rubbing his eyes. "I could have relieved you so you could get some sleep."

"Sleep? How could I sleep knowing that animal raped Sister Mary Alice?"

"We don't know that," said Billy.

"Are you kidding me? He probably pulled off at the first bend in the river. I swear I could hear Sister Mary Alice's screams from here."

"Hector, it was just your imagination getting away from you."

"My imagination? Come on, Billy. You've seen the way Dick stares at her. He's just been biding his time for an opportunity like yesterday to come along. I think he figures that he has a pretty good idea of where we're at and he can make it out without us. He's hiding something, he must be."

"Hector, you're giving Dick way too much credit. I don't think he's been planning to take off in the raft without us, and Sister Mary Alice was just in the wrong place at the wrong time."

"You seriously don't think Dick means Sister Mary Alice no harm?"

"No, I don't."

"Then you are a lot dumber than you look, that's for sure."

"I think Dick's worried about Dick and he just wants out of this jungle."

"I can't believe that you are that naïve. Men like Dick are into total self-indulgence. Dick might not have planned to take off in the raft, I'll give you that, but when he got out on the river and realized he was alone with Sister Mary Alice, I guarantee you that the thought of having his way with her hit him like a truck, especially knowing that no one could stop him and he could just leave her behind when he was done with her."

"All right, if you think he beached it at the first bend in the river, then we should be able to catch up to them by noon, providing that they're on this side of the river."

"Now you're beginning to see things my way. Let's go!"

"Hold on," said Fred. "What about us?"

"What about you?"

"Are you just going to go off on a wild goose chase and leave Jan and me here to fend for ourselves?"

"We'll come back for you."

"Fred's got a point," said Billy. "We can't just go off half-cocked. We have a lot more to worry about than just Dick."

"Yeah, we have to worry about saving Sister Mary Alice."

"Hector, we're just as worried about her as you are," said Fred. "But if we go running off into the jungle without a plan, then we'll probably end up dead. And just how will that help Sister Mary Alice?"

"Then what do you propose?"

Fred thought about it for a second and then looked at Billy, and then back at Hector. "I don't know right off the top of my head."

"The only thing we can do is walk our way out of here and keep a sharp eye out for Sister Mary Alice and Dick," said Billy.

"That's it? That's your great plan?"

"Hector, calm down. There's nothing else we can do right now. I wish we could do more but this is it."

"Then we need to leave now. It's daylight and we don't have any time to waste."

"I agree," said Billy. "Let's get going. It's not like we have a lot of gear to pack, so we might as well get a move on."

Dick pulled himself up from the bottom of the raft and grabbed on to the limb, trying to catch his breath and clear his head. He still had the raft. So what if he didn't get to screw the nun. *She probably wasn't worth the effort anyway,* he thought. Now he had bigger problems. He had to get himself out of the jungle alive.

After regaining his composure, he freed the raft from the tree and started down the river. The current wasn't very strong, so he thought he must have already gotten through the rapids. All he had to do was to stay on the river and he would eventually find his way out.

He thought of Fred, Hector, Jan, and Billy sitting on the riverbank without the raft. He wondered what would get them first, an alligator or the Indians. His vote was for the Indians. If the Indians saw that they weren't moving down the river anymore, they would consider them a threat. He wondered if they tortured their victims before they killed them. He'd like to see them pass that bug-bitten bitch around the tribe a time or two before they shrank her head. He laughed at the thought of Jan's face shrunk down and hanging on some Indian's lodge pole.

Dick looked ahead and saw that there was a bend in the river. He hated coming up to a bend because he had no idea what he'd find around it. When they were all in the raft, it wasn't quite so bad. He always figured that the Indians would be more interested in the women than in him, giving him a chance to get away. But now it was just him.

Dick tried to slow the raft a bit so he could get a better look at the terrain as he went around the bend. He almost fell out of the raft when his gaze swept the riverbank. He couldn't believe his luck. There on the shore was Sister Mary Alice. She was lying on her back and she wasn't moving. Dick wondered if she was dead. *But why would she just be lying there on her back with her tits looking up to God if she was still alive? She'd try to cover herself, wouldn't she? One thing's for sure, she has a nice rack, and dead or alive, I'm going in for a better look,* he thought.

Dick paddled slowly to shore, trying not to make any noise. If she was only sleeping, he didn't want her waking up and running into the jungle. What if she were to run into the jungle and hide, and while he was looking for her, she made a dash for the raft? He couldn't risk that. But he wanted her now more than ever. He couldn't believe how beautiful she looked, lying there on the riverbank with water sparkling on her gorgeous tits. He could feel himself getting aroused the closer he got to her. He thought he'd lost his chance with her, but there she was in all her glory, just lying there waiting for him.

As the raft came to a stop, Dick kept his eye on Sister Mary Alice's tits. Were they moving? Was she still breathing? He couldn't tell. *Hell,* he thought, *as gross as it sounds, if she wasn't breathing, she'd still be warm on the inside anyway.* He pulled on the raft, trying to get it over the riverbank, but it seemed to be catching on something. He took a quick look at the raft, and then looked back at Sister Mary Alice. He couldn't afford to lose the raft or he'd be done, and no broad would be worth that. The raft was more than halfway out of the water. He thought it should be far enough away from the current so that it wouldn't be pulled back into the river.

Dick dropped the rope and slowly made his way toward Sister Mary Alice. He slowly unzipped his pants as he drew closer. He was now fully erect. He was going to enjoy this. He stopped and took in her full beauty. Her tits were definitely the real deal. He couldn't remember ever seeing any others that could rival them.

Dick's next thought was to figure out how to get her pants off, at least one leg, without waking her up. He remembered how she had fought him on the raft just before she jumped into the river. He reached up and felt the scratches on his face. *The bitch,* he thought. *I'm not going to give her another chance to do that again.*

Dick had made up his mind. If she was still alive, he would hit her in the jaw, knocking her out, and jump on top of her. Then he could take off her pants without her tearing up his face again. He pulled down his pants as he stood above her. He looked down at his prick. It was at full attention. He laughed to himself, already feeling himself inside her. Suddenly, he felt a pain he had never experienced before. He looked down as he gasped for air and saw Sister Mary Alice's foot fly up to his crotch for a second time. This time Sister Mary Alice kicked Dick as if she were kicking a fifty-yard field goal.

Dick let out a scream. It wasn't a very loud scream since he had hardly any air left in his lungs. He fell to his knees, his pants still around his ankles. Instead of getting up and running to the raft while she could, Sister Mary Alice just stood there staring at Dick as he writhed in pain. Dick looked up at her with a mix of hatred and pain in his eyes. He still couldn't speak but his eyes said it all. Then he wheezed, "You'd better run, bitch,

208

because as soon as I catch my breath, I'm going to make you wish you were dead. I'm going to kill you one little piece at a time."

Sister Mary Alice was in shock. She felt as if her feet were buried in cement.

Dick took in a breath and lunged for her. He caught her by the leg, knocking her down. She tried kicking her leg to get away from him but his grip only tightened. He dug his nails into her flesh.

"I'm going to kill you, bitch! But not before I screw your brains out!"

Dick tried to roll her over and climb on top of her, but his pants were tangled around his ankles, preventing him from doing anything more than grip her leg tightly. He felt his strength coming back, even though his nuts still hurt like hell. She'd make that up to him in a moment. He released his grip for a second, taking a shot at her jaw and catching it right under the chin.

Sister Mary Alice went limp and Dick felt the fight go out of her. He stopped for a moment to catch his breath. Then he pulled himself to his knees and looked down at her. Blood was forming at the corner of her mouth and her head was off to one side. Dick reached down and touched her right breast, squeezing the nipple. He liked the way it felt, amazed at its beauty. As he lifted his weight off her to get her pants off, she kicked him again, not with as much strength as her last kick but enough to give her a second to roll out from under him.

Dick grabbed at Sister Mary Alice but missed. She got to her feet and this time she ran. Dick also got to his feet but his pants were still around his ankles and he could only hobble after her. He tried to kick his pants off as he chased her. Sister Mary Alice realized that she was running toward the jungle and stopped, while Dick, not far behind, lunged for her. She dodged him and ran toward the raft. Dick finally freed himself of his pants and ran after her.

Sister Mary Alice dove into the raft, her momentum casting it into the water. She frantically reached for the paddle and began paddling with all she had. Dick ran into the water and lunged at the raft. He got one hand around its rope and held on. Sister Mary Alice saw him pulling her toward him and screamed. Then she looked up at the sky.

Dick looked up at her and laughed. Just as he was reaching into the raft, Sister Mary Alice struck him in the face with the paddle with all the might of Babe Ruth knocking it out of the park. Somehow, Dick still managed to hold onto the rope, probably because the paddle was made of plastic so it didn't pack the wallop of a wood paddle. Sister Mary Alice raised the paddle again for a second try when Dick suddenly screamed and let go of the rope. He grabbed at his crotch, turning away from Sister Mary Alice, and headed toward the riverbank. She paddled away from him as quickly as she could and headed upriver, looking up to God to give Him praise and thanks.

Billy led the way, with Fred and Jan right behind him and Hector bringing up the rear. The vegetation along the riverbank wasn't very thick, but it still took two hours to walk about a mile.

"We aren't making very good time," said Hector, wanting to run ahead.

"Were doing the best that we can," said Billy as he swatted another mosquito while looking back at Jan, who looked like raw meat swelled up.

"Do you think that they're still looking for us," she asked.

"I doubt it," said Billy. "What's it been, ten, eleven days now?"

"More like eleven or twelve," said Fred.

"Twelve," said Hector, scouring the riverbank across the river for signs of Sister Mary Alice. He grew solemn thinking about her fate.

The vegetation began to get thicker. Billy hacked his way through it with a machete, working his way down a riverbank to a small feeder river. It looked to be no deeper than three or four feet at its center. Billy began to step into the water when Fred shouted, "Stop!"

Billy stopped and looked back at Fred, puzzled.

"What's wrong?"

"That looks like prime breeding ground for the Candiru."

"The what?"

"I told you about the Candiru when Dick was peeing off the raft on our first day out."

"I thought you were just screwing with him," said Billy.

"I wasn't. The Candiru is the most feared creature in this entire jungle."

Billy looked into the water. It was muddy and in the shade. "I don't see anything too scary," he said.

"If you remember, I told you that they're less than an inch long and that they're transparent. I also told you that they are more likely to attack men than women, although they do attack women, too. They swim up your urethra and—"

"Your what?" asked Hector, hoping that it wasn't what he thought it was?

"Your dick, for a lack of a better term."

"I thought that's what it was," said Hector with a shiver running up his spine.

"Well, what do we do?"

"We walk upriver until we come across a safe place to cross."

Moments later, they came upon a tree that had fallen across the river. The water still wasn't very deep but the vegetation was heavy. Thick moss covered the tree and vines grew on its dead, outstretched branches.

"I'll go first," said Billy. "That way I can cut away anything blocking our way."

Jan wasn't going to argue. She liked the fact that two people would be walking in front of her and that one person would be behind her. That way she stood a much greater chance of not being attacked by anything.

Billy started across the tree, hacking a path in front of him. Before long, he was on the other side of the river.

"Okay, Fred, you next."

"Fred," said Jan, "I don't want you to leave me behind."

"All right, you go first."

"No, I meant you should go first while I hang on to you from behind."

"I don't think that's a good idea," said Billy. "That moss is slippery and the tree's not that wide."

"He's right. You go first and just as soon as you get across I'll be right behind you."

Jan didn't like that decision one bit. She never was good at walking on the balance beam in gym class when she was in high school. She was sure she would be even worse at it now. Jan stepped up onto the tree. She looked down at her feet and started swaying.

"Don't look down," said Billy. "Keep your eyes focused on me and you'll be here in no time."

Jan looked Billy right in the eye and put one foot gingerly in front of the other. She was more than halfway across the tree when a snake dropped down in front of her, blocking her way. She screamed but nothing came out and she felt her knees starting to buckle.

"Start backing up slowly," said Billy as he crept back up onto the tree.

Jan tried to back up but her feet wouldn't move. The snake came closer to her and Jan stared at it, mesmerized by its colorful coils. The snake was less than a foot away from her when Billy swung the machete, cutting the snake's head off.

Fred had noticed that Jan's legs were starting to go out from under her and he slowly crept up behind her, catching her as she fainted. He stood swaying in the middle of the tree under Jan's weight. Billy slowly made his way to them and helped Fred walk Jan to safety.

Hector stood frozen with fear. He hated snakes and he knew he wouldn't like the Candiru much, either.

"Come on, Hector, don't even think about it. Just walk across as if you were crossing the street."

Hector stepped out onto the tree, imagining that he was crossing the street and a beer garden was waiting for him on the other side. He imagined how good the cold beer was going to taste until he stopped dead in his tracks and stared. The snake's headless body still squirmed right at eye level.

"Hector, just brush it aside. It can't hurt you," said Billy. "It doesn't have a head."

"Hector!" Jan cried. "Pretend that's Dick hanging in front of you!"

Hector took the snake in his hands, pulling it from the tree, and started whipping it against the tree until there was nothing left but a pulpy mess. Then he stopped and stood still for a minute, staring at the bloody remains.

"Good job, Hector! Now walk across," said Jan.

Once everyone was safely on the other side of the river, Hector said that he wanted to lead. Billy gave him the machete and Hector took off at a fevered pace.

After about ten minutes, Jan said, "I can't keep up with this pace," as she swatted another mosquito.

"Hector, you've got to slow down," said Billy.

Hector ignored him and kept hacking his way back to the river, afraid that they might have already passed the spot where Sister Mary Alice might have been. It was a little past noon when Hector broke through the vegetation and came upon a riverbank. He frantically looked up and down the river, hoping to find signs of Sister Mary Alice's presence. When he saw none, he crouched down and started to cry.

When Billy, Fred, and Jan caught up to him, they saw him on his knees weeping. Jan walked over to him, put her arm around his head, and pulled him in to her. Hector rested his head on her thigh and continued to cry.

Billy looked around for something that they could eat. He walked over to the river and found that it was moving very slowly. The sun was directly overhead, making it hard to see into the water. He strained his eyes; he thought that he saw movement. The sun disappeared briefly behind a cloud and Billy saw a baby alligator swimming along the shore. He picked up his spear and threw it, striking the alligator and pinning it to the riverbed.

Billy reached out, grabbed his spear, and said, "Fred, let's make a fire."

Sister Mary Alice was struggling to get the raft back upriver. Even though the current wasn't flowing very quickly, she had to fight for every inch. When she had first broken away from Dick, she paddled with everything that she had, only to make it around the bend and realize that her arms felt like they were going to fall off. She needed to rest and soon found a low-hanging tree limb on the other side of the river that she could tie the raft to.

She was very thirsty but there was no fresh water in the raft. She stared at the river, longing to plunge her face into it and drink her fill but she knew better. The water was alive with all sorts of bacteria and parasites, and she knew that any momentary relief from her thirst would probably result in a slow and painful death.

Sister Mary Alice spotted some berries growing on some bushes about ten yards away. She sat and contemplated whether she should risk trying to climb out of the raft to pick them. She was starving and thirsty and knew that the berries would help satiate both sensations. She decided to climb out of the raft and walk over to the berries. She studied them for a few minutes because they weren't like any that she had seen before. They were bright red and looked like large raspberries.

She picked one and held it in her hand, then sniffed it and smashed it in her fingers. She slowly raised it to her tongue and tasted it. It tasted very bitter but not so bitter that she couldn't swallow it. After she had eaten her fill, she felt better, even though she was a little worried about the effect that they might have on her later.

She decided to pick more berries to take with her. As she reached in to pluck a berry, a pink-toe tarantula jumped onto her arm. Sister Mary Alice froze. Never in her life had she seen a spider so big or so scary. It sat on her arm, right above her elbow. She could hear her own heart beating so loudly that it drowned out the sounds of the river. Sister Mary Alice closed her eyes and started to pray.

"Dear Lord, please help your lowly servant. I know you haven't brought me this far only to be killed by a giant spider."

With her eyes still closed, Sister Mary Alice felt the tarantula creeping up her arm. She couldn't open her eyes without screaming so she kept them shut. The spider felt like it was almost to her shoulder. Her heart beat even louder. The tarantula started to move again, crawling up on her right shoulder. Resisting the urge to knock it off for fear that it would bite her in the neck, she stood frozen for what seemed like an eternity.

The tarantula started to move again. Sister Mary Alice held her breath as it started to make its way into her hair. She couldn't stand it any longer. Hoping that her hair would act as a buffer, with one quick movement of her hand, she swatted at the tarantula, trying to knock it out of her hair, but the creature wasn't leaving that easily. It buried itself into Sister Mary Alice's hair and she screamed loudly before hitting the ground.

Sister Mary Alice opened her eyes. She was lying on the ground. She had no idea how long she had been there. Then she remembered why she was there—the giant spider. Her heart started to race again and she was having trouble breathing. She stopped and said a prayer, and then she slowly reached up to feel her hair. Nothing moved. She patted her head, and not feeling anything, she slowly got up, looking around cautiously. When she turned her head to her right, she froze. There was the giant spider, with its long, black hairy body and pink toes sitting on a branch about three feet away.

Sister Mary Alice slowly stood up and placed a hand on her heart in relief. It was then that she remembered that Dick had ripped off her blouse and bra. Embarrassed because of her naked breasts, she forgot all about the giant spider with its pink toes. She turned and walked back to the raft, covering her breasts with her arms.

Billy roasted the baby alligator over the fire. It made a sizzling sound as he turned it. The aroma made their mouths water. Hector stood up and walked to the river's edge, where he scanned the water, wishing that he had made Sister Mary Alice ride in the front of the raft.

"Hey, Hector, the alligator is ready!" yelled Billy.

Hector looked back at Billy and waved. "I'll be there in a minute!" When he turned to look back down the river, he thought he saw something yellow. He ran down to the shore to try to get a better look but he saw nothing. He knew he'd seen something, he wasn't going crazy.

Hector scanned the vegetation behind him. There was a tree that was fairly tall not too far from where he stood. He started to climb it but then stopped abruptly. What if there were snakes in the tree? He hated snakes and he'd already had to deal with more snakes than he thought he would ever see in his lifetime. Then he thought of Sister Mary Alice and continued climbing up the tree. He didn't see anything from where he was in the tree because there were too many branches in the way, so he started back down. Just as he was about to jump to the ground, he saw the yellow raft struggling to get up the river. Then it slid back and disappeared.

Hector started yelling as he ran down the bank of the river, not paying any attention to where he was running.

"What's Hector yelling about? What is he saying?" asked Fred.

"I think he said something about the raft," said Jan.

Fred and Billy got to their feet and started to run after him. Jan stood but didn't run. She carefully watched where she was walking, not wanting any more nasty surprises.

Hector could see the raft clearly now and he could see that Sister Mary Alice was alone in the raft. She was fighting to get up the rapids. Without hesitation, Hector dove into the river and began to swim to her aid. He could feel the rapids pulling at him but he was determined to get to the raft.

Fred and Billy stopped when they saw Hector jump into the river. It would be up to Hector now to get to Sister Mary Alice.

Jan could see Fred and Billy standing on the shore but couldn't see Hector. She looked up and down the riverbank. Then she looked across the river. Jan saw two bull alligators come to their feet. They had their eye on something in the river. She kept walking toward Fred and Billy, not taking her eyes off the alligators, and began yelling.

Fred heard Jan yelling and looked up the riverbank. He saw her waving and pointing to the other side of the river.

"Holy shit!"

"What?" said Billy, not taking his eyes off Hector so as not to lose sight of him?

"There are two bull alligators standing on the bank across the river!"

"Damn!" said Billy. He'd left the flare gun back by the fire, and he didn't even think about grabbing his spear. He wondered if he should chance it and run back to get them, but then he thought that it would be too risky to use the weapons. They could hit the raft or Hector or Sister Mary Alice. This was definitely in God's hands now.

Sister Mary Alice was so focused on trying to get the raft up the rapids that she didn't see Hector jump into the river. Nor did she notice Fred, Billy, and Jan standing on the shore not fifty yards up the river from her. She felt she was losing the battle. It took all of her strength just to stay in one place, let alone go any further up the river. She was tiring quickly and she didn't know how much longer she could hold out.

Hector was so focused on the raft that he didn't see the big rock under the water right in his path. Suddenly, Billy shouted, "Hector, look out!" just before Hector hit the rock. Billy dove into the river.

Fred raked his fingers through his hair in agitation, and Jan screamed, "The alligators have gone into the water!"

Fred saw Hector floating helplessly down the river on his back right past the raft.

216

Sister Mary Alice looked down in disbelief as she saw Hector floating in the water. She screamed as a hand reached up into the raft. As she raised the paddle, she saw that it was Billy. She dropped the paddle into the bottom of the raft and grabbed Billy's hand, pulling him up to the side of the raft.

On shore, Fred and Jan yelled as loud as they could to warn Billy of the alligators that were closing in on him. Jan screamed as she saw one of them leap at Billy's leg as he scrambled over the side of the raft. The alligator caught Billy's pant leg, pulling his leg back over the raft. Jan couldn't take it. She buried her face in her hands, not wanting to see the aftermath of what was to come.

Sister Mary Alice looked up and screamed, "No!" as she picked up the paddle and struck the alligator across its nose. The alligator let go of Billy's pant leg for a second before snapping at Billy again but missing this time, giving Billy a chance to pull his leg into the raft.

Billy raised himself to his knees, grabbed the paddle from Sister Mary Alice, and started rowing downriver to get to Hector before the alligators did.

Sister Mary Alice saw the alligators swim toward Hector and yelled, "Hurry, Billy!"

Billy was still about thirty yards ahead of the two alligators but they were closing in quickly. He knew he was only going to get one chance, and if he missed, it would be all over for Hector.

"Get ready!" he yelled, handing the paddle to Sister Mary Alice and hanging over the side of the raft.

Hector was only a few feet away when Sister Mary Alice screamed, "Hurry, Billy! The alligators have caught up to us!"

Billy lunged for Hector, grabbing him by his shirt. Hector was heavier than he looked. Billy pulled with all he had, and then he felt Hector's shirt rip away. Billy reached into his pocket and pulled out his 110 Buck Knife. The alligators were right alongside them. One of the alligators opened its mouth, ready to feast on Hector's limp body, but Billy jumped onto its back.

Sister Mary Alice screamed.

Fred stood in utter amazement, not believing his eyes.

Jan uncovered her eyes just as Billy disappeared under the water.

The alligator didn't know what hit it as it violently tried to flip Billy off its back. Billy plunged his knife into the alligator's back repeatedly, and the water's white froth turned red as man and beast struggled for their lives.

The current had slowed. Sister Mary Alice was out of the rapids now. She hated to leave Billy behind but there was nothing she could do to help him. She started paddling toward Hector as he slowly floated down the river.

Fred ran down the riverbank, desperately trying to reach Hector. Sister Mary Alice brought the raft to Hector's side and tried to pull him into the raft, but she had no strength left, she hung on to him, yelling, "Hector! Hector!"

Fred made his way down to the raft and hesitated for only a moment before jumping into the river to help Sister Mary Alice and Hector. He was only a few yards from reaching Hector when Hector opened his eyes and started thrashing about. Fred grabbed him around the shoulders and started to swim toward the shore. Then he turned his head and yelled for Sister Mary Alice to go back for Billy. She picked up the paddle and wearily started paddling back up the river.

Jan watched what was transpiring from the shore upriver. She saw Billy rolling in the river with the alligator, like in an old Tarzan movie. Then the water, red with blood, became still. Jan held her breath.

Sister Mary Alice stopped paddling.

Fred, with Hector safely on shore, looked back at the river.

Suddenly, the alligator surfaced above the water.

Sister Mary Alice looked up to the sky.

Jan let out a scream.

Fred's head fell forward.

The alligator let out a roar and rolled over on its back.

Ten yards downriver, Billy burst from the water, gasping for air.

Jan screamed, "There he is!"

Fred didn't know what she meant. He hadn't seen Billy and thought that the alligator was heading his way. Then he looked up and saw Billy's head above the water. Without thinking, Fred dove into the water and swam toward Billy.

Sister Mary Alice screamed again, and Jan was yelling and pointing at the water. The second bull alligator was swimming toward Billy, who slipped under the water just as Fred got to him. Fred reached under the water, grabbed Billy under his arms, and started to swim back to shore.

Chapter Thirty

General Russo was waiting to hear whether the man they found was one of the survivors listed on the plane's wall. He couldn't believe that anyone could live for twelve days in the jungle without food, water, or any kind of weapons. They may have had a chance if they had guns. At least they could protect themselves from the Kayapo. His phone rang. It was Major Reno, informing him that Private Gomez had died from a fractured skull.

"Any more good news?" asked General Russo sarcastically.

"Yes, sir. The man we found in the tree was named Alfred Morris. Mr. Morris and his wife, Lara, were heading to Rio and then on to a mission on the Pantanal River."

"He wasn't listed with the other survivors."

"That's right, sir."

"Then there may still be survivors out there somewhere. But could any of them still be alive after twelve days in the jungle?"

"I really don't know, sir. I suppose that one or two of them could still be alive, but I really don't know."

"I have very mixed feelings about continuing this search. We've already lost one good man." General Russo paused and looked out the window before continuing. "Major, have you heard anything more on the nun you found?"

"Yes, sir, her name was Sister Teresa."

"That's what makes my decision so difficult to make. Bishop Cheuiche will insist that I keep looking for Sister Mary Alice."

"Sir, if I'm not mistaken, all of the survivors' families want you to keep searching."

"That's obvious, major. But where do you draw the line?"

"I really don't know sir. I would think that after a reasonable time had passed without locating any survivors, you would have to call off the search."

"Major, I have another call coming in. I'll be in touch."

General Russo pressed the button for his second line.

"This is General Russo."

"General, this is Franco Silva."

General Russo rolled his eyes. He had been trying to avoid Franco.

"Yes, Franco, how can I help you?"

"Sir, I heard that you've decided not to send out any search planes today."

"That's right."

"Sir, with all due respect, may I ask why?"

"Franco, I know that you have a personal interest in this crash, but it's been twelve days now, and we've already lost one of our own men searching for the survivors."

"I didn't know that, sir. I'm very sorry. If you would tell me his name, I will be sure to send his family my appreciation and some monetary assistance."

"That would be very kind of you, Franco," said General Russo as he rolled his eyes again. "I'll make sure that Major Reno gets the information to you."

"General, about the search."

"Yes, Franco?" said General Russo, taking in a deep breath.

"Can I expect it to resume tomorrow?"

"I don't think so," said General Russo, letting out a sigh of frustration. "The Americans have pulled out and I just can't justify risking any more men or resources on this search. I'm very sorry, Franco."

"General, I beg you, just a few more days?"

General Russo remained silent.

"General, I take that to be your final word on the matter then, is that correct?" said Franco tersely.

"I'm afraid it is. Now if there isn't anything else that I can help you with, I bid you good day, Mr. Silva."

General Russo called his secretary and told her to hold all his calls until further notice.

Franco didn't know how he was going to break the news to his daughter, or to the Sundays. The last he heard, Mrs. Sunday was still in the hospital recovering from her heart attack. He raked his fingers through his hair and let out a heavy sigh. This was going to break his daughter's heart.

221

Later that day, he found Ana sitting by the phone, waiting for it to ring. He should have told her earlier but he couldn't bear the thought of causing her any more pain. He decided he couldn't wait any longer; he was going to have to tell her.

"Ana, dear."

"Yes, Daddy?"

"You know I love you."

"Of course, Daddy. I love you, too."

"Ana, I don't know how to tell you this."

Ana's heart stopped and she turned white. She knew what her father was having trouble saying. She started to cry. Franco went over to her and held her head to his chest. Ana sobbed, her shoulders heaving.

Rosesa came over and asked, "What's wrong, child?"

Franco looked up at Rosesa and motioned her away with his eyes. Rosesa looked hurt as she turned away and left the room. Franco held his daughter, telling her that it was going to be all right, that he would have his helicopter keep searching until they found Billy.

Chapter Thirty-One

Fred never looked back. He felt a burning sensation in every muscle in his body as he raced back to shore. Hector got to his knees, spitting out water. He saw the alligator coming toward them, and then he saw its jaws lock on to the dead alligator, pulling it under.

Fred dragged Billy to shore, rolled him over onto his back, and started performing CPR. Billy started to cough up river water, and then he rolled over and puked. Fred looked him over. He was covered with scratches from head to toe. Some of the scratches looked more like gashes.

"He's going to need a few stitches," said Fred.

"How are we going to do that?" asked Hector, still coughing up water.

"We still have the first aid kit from the plane."

Sister Mary Alice paddled the raft onto shore, jumped out, and ran to Billy. After she was sure he would be all right, she turned to Hector and hugged him tightly, squeezing the breath from his lungs. Fred saw that she was topless and hurriedly took off what was left of his own shirt, wrapping it around her. She quickly pulled back from Hector, put Fred's shirt on, and thanked him.

"It was Dick," Sister Mary Alice said weakly. "He ripped it off me." She started to cry. This day was almost more than she could bear.

Hector hugged her tightly and said, "He's not here. He can't hurt you anymore." It was driving him crazy not knowing what Dick had done to her. Did he rape her? He hated thinking about it. All it made him want to do was to kill Dick, if he wasn't already dead.

They decided to stay where they were on the riverbank. Fred gathered some wood so they could make a fire when it got dark. It had been a long, tiring day. All they had the strength to do was to lay on the riverbank and watch the sky in hopes of seeing a spotter plane or a helicopter. They knew the next day would be filled with new challenges.

The sun went down without signs of planes or helicopters. They listened to the same old sounds of the jungle—the howler monkeys, the toucans, and a thousand other birds. The thunder noise was back, along with hissing and splashing sounds coming from the river.

Jan didn't want to think about the noises of the jungle. She wanted to get back to her own jungle. She wanted to hear the honking of horns, the blowing of whistles, the ringing of church bells. She wanted to hear children laughing. She was tired of hearing the shrieks of death. Jan wouldn't even mind listening to her mother tell her how old she was getting and ask why she wasn't married yet. That thought made her feel sadder than ever. Up until now, she'd been so worried about being rescued and getting out of the jungle that she hadn't thought about what her mother must be thinking. Her mother must know about the plane crash. She thought about all the times that she went on business trips without ever telling her mother where she was going. *If I ever get out of this damn jungle, I swear that I will treat my mother better,* she thought.

Fred tossed some more wood onto the fire, causing sparks to float up into the sky.

Jan suddenly sat up, listening intently to a different kind of sound.

"Did you hear that?"

Fred stopped and listened. He didn't hear anything unusual. The wood popped and steamed from being wet. "I don't hear anything," he said.

Jan stood, turning her head from side to side, but she didn't hear the sound again. "I must be going crazy," she said.

"We all are. Try to get some sleep. We can't be more than a day or two, at most, from Xingu National Park."

"A day or two? How would you know that?"

"We've been at this for twelve days now. If the tributary river we've been on is the one that I think it is, we should be within a few hundred miles of the park."

"How do you know which tributary river we're on?"

"It's just an educated guess."

"Oh my God!" cried Jan. "We could be that close to getting out of here? I can't believe it!"

"Don't get too excited," said Hector. "Like he said, he's just guessing."

224

"It's going to be a long day tomorrow. I want to stay on the river all day if we can," said Fred. "We'd better get some sleep. Hector, I'll take the first watch if you don't mind."

Jan tried to sleep but she kept hearing noises, bird noises. *The birds usually stop their ruckus after the sun goes down; that's weird,* she thought.

Billy didn't hear anything. He was out for the count. Jan had given him a few pain pills for the two deep lacerations on his back from the alligator's claws. Sister Mary Alice had cleaned them out the best that she could and then crudely stitched them up. Her handiwork would definitely leave crooked scars when the lacerations healed.

Morning came and Sister Mary Alice was visibly nervous.

"Sister, is everything all right?" asked Fred.

She looked up and started crying. Hector went over to her and wrapped his arms around her. "What's wrong?" he asked gently, as if he were talking to a little girl.

Sister Mary Alice looked at him and started to tremble.

Fred looked at her and said, "It's Dick, isn't it?"

She nodded and started to sob uncontrollably.

"I know," said Fred. "All the excitement when you got back yesterday distracted you. But now that we're getting ready to go back on the river, you're remembering what happened, right?"

She nodded again.

Hector held her at arm's length and looked her straight in the eye.

"Sister, you have nothing to worry about. He is the one that has something to worry about because if I see him I will kill him."

"Hector, you're just upset," said Jan. "You wouldn't really kill Dick. That would be murder."

"I'm going to kill him!" shouted Hector angrily.

"But, Hector, that's murder," Jan repeated.

"Who are you going to tell?" he asked.

Fred was getting nervous. He didn't like Dick any more than the rest of them, but it wasn't up to them to take matters into their own hands. This was something for the police to handle.

"I doubt we will ever see Dick again," said Fred. "He doesn't know how to make a fire, or find food or water. And by the sounds of those caimans that were around last night, I think our troubles with Dick are finished."

Jan despised Dick, but she couldn't think of a worse death than being eaten by one of those giant alligators. She could still picture the caiman that took Coleman away. She shivered at the thought.

They started down the river, the day clear and bright. The jungle was alive with the sounds of life and death, as nature dictated the survival of the fittest. It was such a violent place. There was life all around them but it seemed like something was always killing something else. They could see it everywhere they looked.

Everyone was silent as the raft drifted slowly down the river. Sister Mary Alice had mixed emotions about what had happened with Dick. She fought to keep from looking at the opposite side of the river, where she had left Dick to fend for himself. She knew that it would only be an hour or so until they reached the spot where she had escaped from him. She found it odd that no one had really asked her what had happened to her that night. She knew that they were all curious but also too polite to ask. And she knew that they didn't want to cause her any more pain than she was already dealing with. She caught Hector looking from side to side as they made their way down the river.

Billy tried to keep from wincing as the raft shifted beneath him. He had a slight fever and his back ached where Sister Mary Alice had stitched him up. The pain pills that Jan had given him the night before helped to ease his pain, and he was tempted to ask for another one but he knew that it would make him drowsy. If anything happened while they were on the river, he needed to be alert.

"Stop! Look over there!" yelled Hector as he grabbed the paddle from Fred and started paddling toward the shore.

Sister Mary Alice didn't want to look. She could tell from Hector's voice that he had spotted Dick.

About thirty yards to their left, Dick was laying in a fetal position on the shore. He couldn't have been more than three feet from the water.

Hector had worked himself into a fury. He was like a man possessed.

226

Fred was hoping that they would make it down the river without seeing Dick. That way they wouldn't be stuck with a moral decision to make. "He was lucky that an alligator didn't drag him off during the night," he said.

Hector ran the raft onto shore, grabbing the machete and jumping out before anyone could stop him. He fell face first into the water and the raft started to drift back out into the river.

"Hector, no!" screamed Sister Mary Alice.

Hector quickly found his feet and fished around for the machete he had dropped in the water. Finding it, he walked slowly out of the water, full of rage.

The others couldn't understand why Hector had gone so crazy. When Sister Mary Alice came back for them the day before, she was shook up and topless but she'd made no mention of Dick actually raping her. None of them liked Dick, especially after he took off with the raft, leaving them to fend for themselves, but no one thought he was worth the trouble of killing him. They had all hoped that the jungle would take care of that for them.

Hector started yelling at Dick as he walked up to him. Dick didn't move.

Maybe he's dead, thought Fred.

Hector drew closer as the raft drifted farther away from the shore. Fred picked up the paddle and started paddling back to shore. He could hear bits and pieces of what Hector was saying but none of it was making any sense. He thought he had heard Hector say, "That was my wife." Why was he talking about his wife? Fred thought that Hector had finally cracked and was delirious. How could he think Sister Mary Alice was his wife? Hector never said anything about a wife or anyone else, at least not to him.

"Hector, no!" pleaded Sister Mary Alice.

Fred had the raft back on shore.

"Stop right there!" Hector shouted. "I'll kill him, just as soon as one of you steps out of that raft."

"You're going to kill him anyway," said Fred.

"You're right, but I don't want to hurt anyone else, so don't try to stop me. Just paddle your way out of here."

"We can't just go off and leave you," said Fred.

227

"I said go!" Hector bellowed.

"Hector!" cried Sister Mary Alice. "Don't let Dick take you down to his level."

"Dick hasn't moved," said Billy. "Do you think something's wrong with him?"

"I really don't know," said Fred. "Sister, what happened yesterday? Did he rape you?"

"No, but not for the lack of trying."

"Then why is Hector so riled up?" asked Billy.

"I think Hector's gone mad," said Fred.

"Fred, you have to do something!" cried Jan, not wanting to witness a murder.

Hector raised the machete above his head.

"I'll cut his head clean off and kick it into the water if you come an inch closer!"

Fred sat back down in the raft.

"Hector, please don't," Sister Mary Alice begged. "Please don't put that man's death on yourself. Whatever you think he's done let God take care of it. Vengeance is his, sayeth the Lord. Please, Hector, I'm begging you. Please, don't tarnish your soul."

Sister Mary Alice climbed slowly out of the raft and started to walk toward Hector.

"Stop right there, Sister!" Hector ordered as he held the machete above his head. "Go back. Please go back. Get in the raft and leave. Just get back in the raft and leave, all of you. Just leave!"

"Hector, we can't leave without you," said Sister Mary Alice.

"Please, just leave. This is between Dick and me."

"Hector, don't you think I should have a say in this? After all, I'm the one he kidnapped and tried to rape."

"He needs to pay for that, too."

"Too? What do you mean by that? What else has he done that you should want to kill him?"

"That's between him and me. He knows what he did."

"Hector, the man isn't even moving. Are you sure that God hasn't already done the job for you?"

Hector kicked Dick in the back. Dick suddenly let out a cry of pain.

228

"See? He's just playing possum."

"That didn't sound like the Dick we know. It sounds like he's half dead already."

Hector kicked him again.

"Stop!"

Sister Mary Alice took another step toward Hector.

"I said for you to get back in that raft and get out of here!"

Sister Mary Alice took another step.

"I said stop! And I mean it! Now, I wanted to kill him nice and slow, but I'll kill him right now if you don't stop where you are."

Sister Mary Alice stopped.

"If you take one more step, I'm going to cut off his right foot."

"Hector, please. There's nothing this man could have done to justify torturing him and killing him. Hector, I've gotten to know you. You're not a monster. Only an evil monster could do that kind of thing to another human being. Please, don't do this."

"He's the monster! He killed my daughter!"

Sister Mary Alice was taken aback. Had Hector indeed gone mad? Was he delirious? He had told her that he was flying alone. And even if his daughter were on the plane, how could Dick have killed her?

"Hector, you're not thinking clearly."

"I'm thinking clearer than I ever have. This man killed my daughter. He tortured her to death."

Sister Mary Alice put her hands to her face. The mere thought of torturing a young girl brought back too many painful memories.

"Hector, I'm begging you. Don't do this. If this man tortured your daughter, God will surely punish him."

"What do you mean, *if* he tortured my daughter?"

Hector kicked Dick again. Still in a fetal position, he let out a low moan.

"This man tortured my daughter slowly. It took two years for her to die, two years! I'm going to be merciful. I'm only going to take two days or so to kill him."

"Hector, for God's sake, but most of all for your own sake, don't do this!"

229

"Sister, you should be right here with me. If you hadn't escaped, this man would have raped you, and then raped you again until you couldn't be raped anymore. Then he would have left you to die, 'cause there's no way this man would've let you live. He wouldn't risk having you turn him in to the authorities."

"I know that, but I'm going to let God take care of him. I have already forgiven him."

"You've forgiven him? The man tries to rape you, and if he succeeded he would've left you for dead, and you've forgiven him? I'm not the one who's crazy here, you are. Let me get this straight. You're going to let God take care of it, right?"

"That's right. I've turned it over to God and I have forgiven Dick, just like the Lord wants me to."

"He told you that?"

"Yes, He told me that."

"And just how did He do that? Did He send down an angel who said, 'Sister Mary Alice, I want you to forgive that pig who tried to rape you. God will take care of him'? Is that what He did, Sister? Is it?"

"No, He didn't have to send an angel. He has promised me that He will care for me as He cares for the least of his creatures."

"Cut the crap, Sister. If God were really looking out for you, you wouldn't be in this mess. You would be sitting in some church somewhere praising Him."

"Hector, I resent that! God has put me here for a reason, to do His work, and if that's what He wants me to do, then so be it."

"Well, I think that's what he had in mind for me, too, Sister. I'm here to do His work, to kill this no good son of a bitch!"

"Hector, God doesn't work that way. He wouldn't put blood on your hands to do His work. God wants you to forgive."

"Why can't you just leave me alone? Get back in the raft and leave. You're only a day or two from Xingu National Park, and then you'll be saved. Then you can go and do some more of God's work."

"Hector, God is working right now."

"I know. So why don't you let me get back to finishing the job that He started here?"

"That's not what God wants for you. He wants you to forgive."

"Listen, I'm getting tired of this conversation. Just get back in the raft so I can take care of our little friend Dickey here."

Hector kicked Dick in the back again.

"Hector, look at me."

Hector kept his eyes fixed on Dick.

"Hector, please look at me."

Slowly, and with hesitation, Hector looked up at Sister Mary Alice.

"I've been where you're at. Maybe I didn't lose a wife and daughter, but I lost my virginity along with my dignity. My heart was just as full of hate and revenge as yours is now. I wanted to kill the man who stole my virginity when I was just a child. He not only stole my virginity, but he also stole my innocence. I was just a child. I trusted him. I loved him."

Sister Mary Alice began to cry.

"The one man above all others, whom I trusted, ruined me, scarred me for life, turned me into spoiled goods that no other man could possible want. All I ever wanted was to grow up and find a husband who would love me and have children with me. But that wasn't God's plan for me. When I was raped, time and time again, I wanted to die. I wanted to kill my father. Yes, my father. He was the one who raped me.

"He started raping me when I was eleven years old. I hated him. I used to dream of how I was going to kill him. Yes, just like you, Hector. I'm sure you dreamed of how you were going to do it. How you were going to torture him. How you were going to make him feel all the pain that he made you feel.

"I'm sure that you, like I, have wasted many years, eating yourself up inside, planning how you were going to cause him pain. But when it comes down to it, the pain that you really create is to yourself. You've caused yourself a lot of unnecessary pain. Just like I did. Until I turned it over to God and let Him free me."

231

"Hector, please don't ruin the rest of your life over Dick and what he's done. Trust me, he's not worth it. God will take care of him. Please, Hector. Put down the machete and let God heal your soul."

Hector looked Sister Mary Alice in the eye, tears running down his face. He lifted the machete in the air one more time. As he turned, he looked down at Dick. Pain racked Dick's face.

Sister Mary Alice prayed aloud, "Lord, forgive this man, for he knows not what he is about to do."

Hector shook with rage. The machete in his hand began to shake. As he was about to bring it down on Dick's neck, Dick turned his face, wet with tears, up to Hector. As Sister Mary Alice prayed to God, Hector murmured, "I know what I'm doing. I'm going to kill this dirty scumbag who caused my daughter's death, stealing the money to care for her. I'm going to send a message to other scumbags just like him."

Dick started to beg for his life. His lips were cracked and his face had bites all over it. His eyes had a yellow cast to them. Then Dick let out a cry and a gasp as he rolled back into a fetal position and shouted, "Just kill me! Put me out of my misery!"

Hector took a deep breath, the machete still raised above his head.

Sister Mary Alice, still praying and with tears running down her face, looked at Hector and said, "God loves you and will forgive you, even if you feel the need to go through with this horrible sin."

Hector let out a loud scream and threw the machete away from him. He dropped to his knees and started to cry. Sister Mary Alice went to him and held his head to her bosom.

Fred quickly jumped out of the raft and grabbed the machete. Then he went to Dick's side. When he rolled him over and saw him holding his penis, he had a pretty good idea of what had happened. Dick had fallen victim to the Candiru.

Sister Mary Alice stroked Hector's head and in a soft, gentle voice said, "I'm very proud of you for turning it over to God. But there's one more thing you need to do."

Hector looked up at her with tears in his eyes and shook his head.

"But, Hector, if you really want to be free, you have to."

Hector turned his face back into her bosom.

232

Jan looked at Dick lying in the mud, holding himself and whimpering like a baby. She turned to Fred and asked, "What's wrong with him?"

"Candiru," said Fred.

"Canda what?"

"Candiru, vampire fish, Willy fish. You know, the ones I'd warned all of you about when Dick was peeing in the water."

Jan's face turned white. "You mean it swam up his—"

"Yep, it sure looks that way."

"Is there anything we can do?"

"Out here in the jungle, not a whole lot. But I know what the native people do when this happens."

"What?"

"They cut off the man's penis."

Jan let out a gasp. "You're not going to do that, are you?"

"No, I'm not, but you can if you'd like."

"Are you nuts?"

"I'm afraid that's the only thing that will save him right now."

"I don't believe you. You're pulling my leg."

"I wish I were. That's why I told everyone to be careful. This is one mean little fish. It's been up inside his penis for over twenty-four hours now. It's wedged in there and the only way to remove it is surgically."

"You mean by cutting off Dick's dick?"

"That's right."

"And if he doesn't get his dick cut off?"

"He'll die a slow and very painful death."

"How can a transparent fish less than an inch long kill a full-grown man?"

"The Candiru fish has tiny barbs and it can only move forward in the urethra tube. As it moves forward, it eats its way through the urethra tube, blocking the pathway for the excretion of urine. Eventually, the bladder will rupture and secrete poison throughout the body, which will kill the host."

233

Jan visibly shuddered. "What do they do for women who have these fish in them?"

"They have to go in surgically and try to flush it out. Unfortunately, they have a pretty poor success rate with women."

Jan held herself. She'd make sure that she never got in any water above her knees. This would be something that would haunt her for the rest of her life. *From now on, I'm only taking showers,* she thought.

Billy and Fred lifted Dick and then lowered him into the raft. He screamed in agony at the slightest movement.

"How long do you think he has?" asked Jan.

"A day or two," said Fred. "Not much longer without medical treatment."

A shiver ran up Jan's spine at the thought of Dick having his penis removed.

Sister Mary Alice couldn't help but overhear Jan and Fred talking about Dick, and she began to pray for him.

With everyone back in the raft, Dick moaning on the floor, they began their journey back downriver, hoping to find Xingu National Park around the next bend. Jan tore off a piece of her shirt, tore it in half, rolled up the pieces, and stuffed them in her ears. She couldn't take another minute of Dick's moaning it was driving her mad.

The river grew wider the farther they went, and as it did, it also ran slower so someone always had to paddle. Jan and Sister Mary Alice volunteered to paddle but the men wouldn't hear of it, taking turns when one of them grew tired.

The day was drawing to an end. Billy thought that they should start to look for a place to make camp. They were going to need to build a fire to keep the predators away and cook whatever they could capture.

As they were guiding the raft to shore, Billy whispered hoarsely, "Quiet. I see four or five capybaras swimming in that cove."

Billy picked up his spear.

"Fred, bring us in nice and slow and I'll see if I can get us dinner."

Billy let his spear fly and managed to hit a small capybara in the hindquarter. It began to squeal as it swam toward shore.

"Hurry, Fred, before he gets too deep into the jungle for me to catch him!"

Fred ran the raft up onto the shore. Dick screamed in pain. Billy jumped out of the raft and ran after the capybara, hoping to cut him off.

"Jan, you stay with the raft, and Sister Mary Alice and Hector, why don't you start looking for firewood," said Fred. "I'm going to help Billy."

"What about Dick?" Jan asked.

"I don't think he's going to give you any trouble."

The jungle was dense along the shoreline. Hector said, "Sister, maybe it would be better if you stayed here with Jan."

"Are you sure?" she asked. She actually didn't want to go look for wood with all the creepy things in the jungle, but she also didn't want them to think that she wasn't doing her fair share.

After Hector disappeared into the jungle, Jan told Sister Mary Alice that she was glad that she had stayed back with her. She didn't like being alone with Dick, especially with him in the raft.

"What if he's faking it and he overpowered me and stole the raft?"

"I don't think he's faking it. But I'm glad that we're here together. We stand a better chance if something were to happen."

The light was starting to fade. Jan heard something like a whipping noise.

"Sister, do you hear that?"

Sister Mary Alice held her breath and concentrated. She did hear something off in the distance. It sounded as if it were coming down the river. Both women looked into the sky but they couldn't see anything. As they looked toward the setting sun, the two women didn't notice the Kayapo sneaking up on them. Just as the big red helicopter came overhead, Sister Mary Alice screamed. Jan thought she was screaming for joy until she felt the hand around her waist.

Chapter Thirty-Two

As the red Cytron Oil Company helicopter came around the bend in the river, they saw the raft.

"There!" shouted the spotter. "There's a yellow rescue raft! It looks like the one they showed us at the briefing. Bring her in a little lower so I can get a better look."

The pilot brought the helicopter around for another look and they saw a group of Kayapo dragging off what looked like two women. The women were fighting back but they were no match for the six natives.

The pilot said, "I'm going to try to buzz them and scare them off."

He put the helicopter into a dive, heading straight for the Kayapo. They stopped and shot their arrows up at the helicopter, which bounced harmlessly off the helicopter's shell. One woman broke away and started running back toward the raft. The pilot hovered over the Kayapo as the wash from the helicopter threw debris everywhere.

One of the Kayapo's feathered headdress flew from his head. He ran for cover into the jungle with three others while two of the Kayapo stood their ground, firing to the last arrow. What a great story they would tell at their campfire that night, about how they had fought off the great red bird that sat in the sky trying to catch them. They would tell how they stood their ground firing at it, using up all of their arrows before retreating into the jungle, while the great red bird stood still, hanging in the air and angrily flapping its great wings.

The pilot radioed for help. He told the control tower that they had found the survivors about seventy-five miles up the river from Xingu National Park. He confirmed one survivor lying in the bottom of the raft and one woman. The man in the raft looked to be badly injured. The control tower told him to head back. They would call General Russo and relay the news.

General Russo was just getting ready to call it a day. He had had enough of being harassed by Bishop Cheuiche, the Americans and their airline company, and the press. It was all he could take for one day.

"General Russo, you have a call," said his secretary.

"Tell whoever it is that I just left and I'll call back in the morning."

"Sir, I think you should take this call. It's the airport. It seems that Franco Silva's helicopter has found the survivors and the crew needs help."

General Russo walked back into his office, making the sign of the cross as he entered the room. He looked up at the ceiling and asked the Lord for help. Then he picked up the phone.

"This is General Russo speaking."

"General, sir, we have just received a message from the Cytron Oil Company's helicopter. They have informed us that they've located the rescue raft from Flight 153."

But how could they still be alive? He thought. *Please, Lord, let the nun be one of the survivors or Bishop Cheuiche will have my head and my job.*

"General, are you still there?"

"Yes, I'm here. How many survivors?"

"Sir, the pilot said he wasn't sure. There wasn't enough room for him to land but from the air he counted three. One man was lying in the bottom of the raft and he looked to be badly injured."

"And what about the other two?" barked General Russo.

"Well, sir, this is where it gets a bit complicated."

"What do you mean?"

"They were under attack when the helicopter found them."

"Mother of God," General Russo murmured under his breath.

"What was that, sir? I didn't catch it."

"Tell me, man, who was attacking them?"

"Indians, sir. The pilot said he thought they were from the Kayapo tribe. He said they were dragging off two of the survivors when they spotted them."

"Why didn't they scare them off with the helicopter?"

"They tried to, sir, but the Kayapo stood their ground and fought."

"They what? How could natives fight a helicopter?"

"I don't know, sir. I was a little surprised myself when they told me. I mean, really, arrows at a helicopter. Anyway, sir, the Kayapo managed to capture one of the women while the other one escaped and ran back to the raft. So I guess we might be looking at only two survivors at this point. We won't know more until we get back and search the area."

"Ay, caramba," said General Russo. The press was going to crucify him.

"Sir, I didn't get that. Sir, I need to know what to tell the Cytron pilot."

General Russo raked his fingers through his hair and took a deep breath. It would be dark in another fifteen minutes. He hated to send men out into the jungle at night, but it looked like he didn't have a choice. "I will notify the army," he replied. "Get the coordinates from the pilot. Tell him that we should have at least one helicopter there in the next ninety minutes."

General Russo hung up the phone and then picked it back up.

"Major Reno has left for the day," said his secretary.

"Get a hold of him now!" barked General Russo, losing his patience. "Have him call me right away."

He hung up the phone and then picked it back up. On the third ring, Sergeant Rico answered.

"Sergeant Rico, this is General Russo. Thank God you're still there. I need you to get a rescue team together as soon as possible, and I mean yesterday."

"Yesterday?" asked Sergeant Rico.

"No, sergeant, not literally yesterday. It's a figure of speech. I mean I need you to get a team together now."

"Now? I'm sorry, general, but I'm a little confused. First you wanted it done yesterday but now you want it done now?"

"Sergeant, I'm going to tell you one more time and one more time only, and unless you want to be a private cleaning latrines for the rest of your life, I suggest that you listen. I want you to get a rescue team together right now, and I want a helicopter at the coordinates that the tower will provide for you in no more than ninety minutes. Do you understand?"

"I do, sir. Has there been another plane crash, if you don't mind me asking?"

"No, sergeant, this is still about the old plane crash."

"But, sir, I thought you said that they were all dead and that's why you called off the search."

238

"Sergeant, now you have exactly eight-seven minutes to get there!" General Russo thundered.

"Yes, sir," said Sergeant Rico.

General Russo's mind was racing. He had to call a number of people, none of whom he was looking forward to talking to. He debated over whom he should call first. The bishop? Franco Silva? Or should it be the press? He hated the press, so he decided to call them last, and since Franco probably already knew of his helicopter crew's discovery, that left Bishop Cheuiche. He picked up the phone and reluctantly dialed the bishop's number. The line was busy, so he hung up and was about to call Franco when the phone rang.

"This is General Russo speaking."

"Major Reno, sir. I've been trying to call you but your line was busy."

"I was talking to that idiot Sergeant Rico."

"Sir, what is going on?"

"Franco Silva's helicopter crew found the survivors."

"That's good news, sir."

"Yes, well, it is and it isn't."

"What do you mean, sir?"

"It was almost dark by the time they found them. And when they found them they were under attack."

"Under attack, sir?"

"I'm afraid so. I need you to put together a task force and I want them armed to the teeth. They'll need lights on their rifles."

"Sir, what are we after?"

The Kayapo. They were attacking the survivors when the helicopter first spotted them."

"How many survivors, sir?"

"When the helicopter arrived, they spotted three, one man lying in the bottom of the raft who looked injured and two women who were being dragged off by the Kayapo."

"Was one of them could be the bishop's nun?"

239

"It's impossible to know at this point. You had better get going, major and, major, be careful. Please don't shoot any of the survivors. The press would make fools of us and the bishop would have our heads on a platter."

The pilot of the Cytron helicopter, ignoring tower's request to return, hovered for as long as he could. As he was pulling away, the spotter yelled, "Bring her back around!"

"I only have enough fuel to get us to Xingu National Park," said the pilot.

"There are three people coming out of the jungle!"

"Are they the Kayapo? If so, I would say that those two survivors down there are goners."

As the pilot headed for Xingu National Park, he radioed the tower.

"This is Cytron One," said the pilot.

"Go ahead," said the tower.

"We are leaving the site of the survivors now. Have you requested assistance yet?"

"We have notified General Russo. He has his men on their way now."

"One more thing. Tell them that there were three unidentified people coming out of the jungle and heading toward the survivors when we left. Over and out."

The tower called General Russo to relay the latest news. He felt like throwing up. They'd probably find the survivors just in time to watch them be slaughtered by the Kayapo. *What else could go wrong?* He thought.

The phone rang again and he reluctantly picked it up, hoping that it wasn't Bishop Cheuiche.

"This is General Russo speaking."

"General, we've just got word that the survivors of Flight 153 have been found after thirteen days. What can you tell us?"

General Russo held his hand over the receiver. He wanted to scream and tell them to go screw themselves. Instead, he took a deep breath, removed his hand from the receiver, and said, "Yes, we have located some of the survivors of Flight 153."

"Have you recovered all ten?" asked the reporter.

"We do not know at this time how many of the survivors are alive."

240

"You don't know or you won't say? We were told that you've found the survivors and are in the process of bringing them back."

"I don't know where you got your information but it's incorrect."

"General, then tell us how many you're bringing back."

"I cannot give you that information at this time. Look, as you can imagine, I'm very busy at the moment with this rescue operation. Please, just let me do my job. When we get the details sorted out, you'll be notified. Until then, good night."

"But, general, we heard that Indians were attacking the survivors as your men were trying to rescue them, and there was a big gun fight, and—"

General Russo hung up the phone and looked up at the ceiling. *Lord, please let my men find all the survivors alive and well,* he prayed.

"Daddy, is it true that your men have found Billy?" asked Ana, bursting with excitement.

"No," said Franco. "They have found some survivors."

"But, Billy was one of them, right?"

"It was late when they spotted them, and they were low on fuel, and there wasn't anywhere to land, so they don't know how many survivors there are."

Franco felt like a fool rambling on like that, but he didn't want to upset his daughter.

"Ana, General Russo is sending out a full rescue squad as we speak. We should know more by morning."

"By morning? I don't think I can wait that long."

"It's night, my darling. They are in the middle of the jungle and there is a man injured."

Franco regretted the words as soon as they left his mouth.

"Daddy, it's not Billy, is it?" cried Ana.

Chapter Thirty-Three

Billy found the capybara in a thicket about fifty yards into the jungle. Fred felt sorry for the animal. Under normal circumstances, there would be no way that he could harm a defenseless animal. But these weren't normal circumstances; they were starving in the middle of the jungle. Fred now understood the term "the survival of the fittest." He also understood what the top of the food chain meant. He realized that out there he wasn't at the top of the food chain but somewhere in the middle.

The capybara squealed louder the closer Billy came to it and then there was silence.

"Fred, grab it by the back legs and help me drag it out from this damn brush."

Billy heard a very familiar sound. It was the sound of rotors whipping in the air. A helicopter was right above them. Billy dropped the capybara and started running back toward the raft.

"Hey! Where are you going?" yelled Fred.

Billy ran as fast as he could. Fred stopped and listened, and then realizing it was a helicopter, he ran after Billy. When Billy and Fred broke through to the clearing, the helicopter was flying away. Once again, Billy didn't have the flare gun with him when he needed it.

He looked at Jan standing in a trance, as if she hadn't even seen the helicopter. As he looked closer, he could see that she had bits of grass and twigs in her hair from the wash of the helicopter's rotors. Fred shouted out as he watched the helicopter disappear over the treetops.

"Jan!" yelled Fred. "Didn't you see the helicopter?"

Before Jan could reply, Fred yelled at her again.

"Why didn't you shoot off a flare?"

Hector came running out of the jungle. He had heard the helicopter as it sped away. He was yelling hysterically. Then he ran up to Billy, out of breath, and grabbed him by the arm, dragging him back toward the jungle.

"Sister," mumbled Hector, trying to take in enough air to speak.

"What is it?" yelled Billy, pulling his arm from Hector's grasp.

242

Hector bent over, hands on his knees, trying to catch his breath. After a few seconds, he yelled, "Sister! Sister Mary Alice! They've got her!"

"Who has Sister Mary Alice?"

"The Indians. I heard the helicopter and started running toward the raft. As I came up to the edge of the jungle, I saw five or six Indians running into the jungle. I stopped and hid behind a tree so they wouldn't see me, and then I saw them dragging a woman with them. It was Sister Mary Alice. I'm such a coward! I know I should have gone after them."

"If you did, you would be dead right now," said Fred. "They would have killed you. You did the right thing coming back for help."

"What are we going to do?" cried Hector.

"We'll have to track them down before it gets too dark," said Billy. "If we wait until morning, we'll never see Sister Mary Alice again."

"No!" cried Hector as he started to run back toward the jungle.

Billy ran after him and tackled him.

"Get off me!" cried Hector. "We have to find her! I couldn't live with myself if something happened to her."

Billy shook Hector. "Stop! Calm down. You're no good to anyone running through the jungle half-cocked."

"But it's my fault."

"It's nobody's fault."

"But it is. She wanted to come with me to look for firewood but I made her stay with Jan. I thought she would be safer there."

"She should have been," said Billy. "I would have asked her to do the same thing."

Billy went back to the raft and retrieved the flare gun.

"What are you planning to do?" asked Fred.

"I'm going after them before it gets too dark to find their trail."

"I'm going with you," said Fred.

"I'm going, too," said Hector.

"You both can't go. Someone needs to stay here with Jan. She's in shock."

243

Jan stood in place, speechless and staring out into space.

"Why couldn't they have taken Dick?" said Fred. "Never mind, stupid question."

"Fred, I want you to stay here with Jan. I'll take Hector with me since he saw which direction they went. Maybe we'll get lucky and the helicopter will come back."

"Even if they did see Jan and Dick, I doubt that they'll be back before morning," said Fred.

"Well, just sit tight. Come on, Hector."

Billy grabbed Hector by the arm and started running toward the jungle. Then he stopped abruptly and turned to Fred.

"Put Jan in the raft with Dick. If the natives come back, I want you to get into the raft and head downriver."

"What about you two?"

"I doubt we'll be coming back."

"What are you talking about? Of course you'll come back. And with Sister Mary Alice, too."

"Fred, let's be real. Our chances of finding Sister Mary Alice are slim at best. Our chances of rescuing her and getting back here alive are even slimmer. Fred, when they finally rescue you, please tell Ana and my parents that I love them."

Billy turned back to Hector and they trotted off into the jungle. Normally, native people moving through the jungle would be very hard to detect. But now with Sister Mary Alice in tow, their trail was relatively easy to follow. Billy stopped and looked at a broken branch. There was blood on it. He showed it to Hector.

"Those bastards!"

Billy quickly covered Hector's mouth.

"Be quiet," Billy whispered. "Nothing like calling them with a bullhorn and letting them know we're coming."

"I'm sorry, I wasn't thinking."

It was getting dark fast and it wouldn't be long before they would have to stop for the night. Suddenly, they heard a loud scream.

"It's Sister Mary Alice!" cried Hector as he turned toward the direction of the scream.

Billy grabbed Hector by the arm.

"Chill out! You're no good to anybody all worked up. You need to take your emotions out of it, unless you want to get us all killed."

"How do you do that, knowing that someone's in harm's way?"

"You think about it. Do you want to live or die? People who go through life letting their emotions guide them usually don't get very far. So do us both a favor and take your emotions out of it. We need to think clearly."

"You're right, I'll try."

"Well you won't get any older if you don't."

They heard the scream again.

"What are they doing to her?" yelled Hector, clenching and unclenching his fists.

Billy had to do something about Hector. He was going to get everybody killed. Before Hector knew what hit him, Billy brought the handle of the machete up and hit him over the head, knocking him out cold. Billy tore off a strip of Hector's shirt and tied Hector's wrists together. Then he shoved a piece of the shirt into Hector's mouth so he couldn't shout out.

Billy heard Sister Mary Alice scream again. He had a pretty good idea what was causing her to scream. Billy moved slowly and quietly toward the sound. It was getting dark and the canopy of the jungle made it even darker. Billy could see the small glow of a campfire ahead, maybe thirty or forty yards away. Now he could hear Sister Mary Alice sobbing. They must have taken a break from whatever they were doing to her.

Billy heard the Kayapo fighting amongst each other. The fighting grew more intense the closer he crept. He was within ten yards of their camp when he heard one of them let out a scream. It wasn't a scream of pain it was more like a battle cry. Then he heard a wet, crashing sound, as if a watermelon had been hit with a baseball bat. Sister Mary Alice started screaming again, only much louder this time.

Billy could almost see what was going on. He noticed that when one of the Kayapo let out a command, everyone but Sister Mary Alice went quiet. Sister Mary Alice sobbed until one of them covered her mouth.

Billy's heart started to beat much louder. He laid flat on the ground. When he was in Vietnam, he had many encounters with the Vietcong where he laid still on the jungle floor while the Vietcong searched for him. The only difference between now and then was then he had a machine gun in his hands and a belt full of ammunition, and now he had a flare gun in his hand that fired one shot at a time and he had only three flares left.

After several minutes that seemed more like hours, the Kayapo surrounded Sister Mary Alice. Billy could hear her yelling for them to stop. Then she called on God to take her home. She begged God to take her away from the savagery she was enduring. Then Billy saw four of them holding Sister Mary Alice spread-eagle while a fifth one prepared to mount her. He knew that they were so engrossed in what they were doing that they wouldn't hear him as he sprang forward.

Chapter Thirty-Four

It had been more than two hours since General Russo had hung up with Sergeant Rico. *They should be there by now,* he thought. *What could be taking them so long?*

Sergeant Rico and his crew sat in the Chinook. The pilot was having a hard time finding the location that the Cytron helicopter pilot had called in. He had entered in the coordinates that the tower had given him but he couldn't even find the river. The co-pilot shined a huge spotlight down below, but all they could see was the canopy of the jungle.

Fred could hear the chopping noise of the rotors off in the distance. He searched the sky but from where he stood, he couldn't see anything. He knew they had to be close because the wash from the rotors was getting louder by the minute. Fred kept looking, hoping he wasn't imagining the sound that he so desperately wanted to hear.

The pilot called the tower and told them that they couldn't find the river, let alone the survivors. The tower had them read off the coordinates again. They checked them against the coordinates that they had received from the Cytron pilot and said, "Your coordinates are off by a mile." Then they gave them the correct coordinates and wished them luck.

Within minutes, the light was shining down on a raft with a man waving furiously.

"I think we've found them," said the pilot. "Let's get the men down there ASAP."

They dropped the static line down and six soldiers and a medic slid down the rope. As soon as they hit the ground, the medic and Sergeant Rico made their way over to the raft.

"I'm Sergeant Rico and I'm in charge of this operation. Who are you, if I may ask?"

"Fred Dowding."

"Are there any more survivors?"

"Yes," said Fred as he looked at the medic checking out Jan and Dick.

"How many?"

"Three others."

"And where are they?"

"It's a long story."

"Then hurry up and tell it. It's dark and my general is very anxious to get you people out of here."

"I don't think he could be anywhere near as anxious as we are to get out of here."

"I don't know about that."

"Sergeant, the Kayapo attacked us about two hours ago. They've taken Sister Mary Alice."

"Holy mother of God. Not the nun."

"Yes, Sister Mary Alice is a nun."

"The bishop will have my head on a platter."

"Why?"

"Never mind that now. Tell me, where are the other two and who are they?"

"Billy Sunday and Hector Garcia. They're out in the jungle trying to rescue Sister Mary Alice."

"Do they have any weapons?"

"A flare gun and a machete."

"A flare gun and a machete? And that's what they're going to fight off the Kayapo with?"

"That's all we had."

"How many were there?"

"I'm not sure. Jan was here when they took Sister Mary Alice. In fact, they tried to take Jan as well but the helicopter must have scared them off."

"We're going to put you and the other two on the helicopter and take you to the hospital."

"I'm not going anywhere until we find Billy, Hector, and Sister Mary Alice."

"Fred, I need you to go with the others. We will have enough to deal with finding Billy, Hector, and the holy nun. We don't need to be worrying about you as well. Now you get on that helicopter. That's an order!"

"I'm not in your army. I won't take orders from you or anyone else. Besides, I'm an American."

"Fred, with all due respect to you being an American, I will give you two choices and I will not give you much time to make up your mind. Choice number one, you get on the helicopter on your own accord. Choice number two, I will have one of my men, or two if necessary, handcuff you and physically put you on that helicopter."

Fred reluctantly got on the helicopter, followed by Jan. Then they carefully loaded Dick into the helicopter and headed for the hospital. Five minutes after they took off, the second helicopter with Major Reno aboard arrived.

The helicopter hovered as Major Reno and his men slid down the static line. Once the men were on the ground, the helicopter went up and away from where the men were and hovered, waiting for its next order.

"Sergeant, did you see that flare go off?" asked Major Reno.

"No, sir," said Sergeant Rico. "I thought it was your searchlight."

Billy stepped out of the foliage into the light of the Kayapo campfire and yelled, "Stop!"

The Kayapo stopped and stared in disbelief. Three of them reached for their bows and spears. Billy pulled the trigger of the flare gun, hitting the one who was about to mount Sister Mary Alice directly in the stomach. His stomach erupted, sending sulfuric burning flesh onto two others standing beside him, allowing Billy time to reload the flare gun and duck back into the thick foliage.

The Kayapo spread out, looking for Billy. The one holding Sister Mary Alice dragged her to her feet. The only clothing that she still wore was her shoes. Billy's anger grew upon seeing her so vulnerable. He wanted to take a shot at him but it was too risky. The light from the campfire was poor, and the Kayapo seemed nervous, pulling Sister Mary Alice around with him and using her as a human shield.

Billy suddenly remembered that he had left Hector tied and gagged about fifty yards behind him. He was afraid that the Kayapo would find Hector and kill him. Then he heard the wash from the helicopter's rotors and saw the spotlight. It was as if God himself had come to rescue them.

The Kayapo holding on to Sister Mary Alice looked up at the bright light in amazement. Billy laughed, wondering what they must think was causing the noise and bright light that was coming from the sky. The spotlight seemed to be searching for them. He imagined that the Kayapo thought the light was an evil spirit.

The biggest Kayapo, wearing a brightly colored headdress that stood a full eighteen inches on top of his head, brought up his bow and started firing at the light, screaming in a very bizarre language. The only thing that Billy could make of what he was saying was what he perceived from his tone of voice, and that was he wasn't very happy about what was in the sky.

The helicopter left after a minute, making the Kayapo think that he had chased it away. He started dancing in a circle, beating on his chest like a great gorilla. Then the Kayapo started to argue with one another. The one who shot at the searchlight wanted Sister Mary Alice, but the other one who had her by the arm wouldn't let her go. The two Kayapo looked as if they were going to have a face off to see who would win her. Suddenly, there was a great ruckus of yelling and screaming.

Major Reno and Sergeant Rico were trying to agree upon how they would go about finding and rescuing the three survivors without killing or wounding their own men or the survivors.

"I say we have two groups of men go in from two different sides and work toward the center," said Major Reno.

"That would be suicidal, sir," said Sergeant Rico. "What if they started shooting? They'd be shooting at each other and not even know it. It's impossible to conduct a search and rescue in the middle of the jungle at night, especially with wild killer Indians holding a hostage."

"Those Indians would be considered tame compared to General Russo's rage if we wait until morning. Besides, if we wait that long, we'll never see the hostages or the Indians again. We'd be lucky to come out alive ourselves."

"We have guns and they have bows and arrows and a few spears. There is no way on God's green Earth that they could survive. I say we wait until morning."

"I'm calling General Russo. I'm sure he'll agree with my plan."

Major Reno called up to the helicopter.

"Patch me through to General Russo."

250

"This is General Russo."

"General, this is Major Reno."

"I know who you are, you idiot. Tell me that you've found and rescued the survivors."

"Sir, three of the survivors are on their way to the hospital."

"Is one of those survivors the nun?"

Major Reno took a very deep breath before answering. "General Russo, I'm afraid not, sir. I'm sorry."

"What do you mean you're sorry?"

"Sir, the Kayapo have taken the holy sister."

"Major, what I want to know is why you are standing there talking to me instead of out there rescuing her!"

Major Reno took that to mean that his plan was the one the general wanted them to go with, even though he hadn't explicitly laid it out for him.

"Major, are you still there?"

"Yes, sir."

"Why? I thought I made it perfectly clear what I wanted you to do!"

"Yes, sir."

As Major Reno hung up, Sergeant Rico looked at him.

"Well?"

Suddenly, the sky lit up.

"Someone's shot off a flare!" cried Sergeant Rico. "Fred said that Billy had gone after the Kayapo with a machete and a flare gun."

"How far away would you say that was?"

"About half a mile."

The pilot from the helicopter called down to Major Reno.

"Major, did you see the flare?"

"Yes. One of the survivors has a flare gun. Did you see where the flare was shot from?"

"It was pretty close by."

"Then I want you to find them. Take your helicopter down as close as you can. And if you spot them, I want you to stay on them. Lower a rope to them if you can."

"Roger that," said the pilot as the helicopter took off in pursuit.

Hector emerged from the jungle running and screaming like a wild man. He ran straight toward the Kayapo holding Sister Mary Alice. He was just feet away from reaching her when one of them picked up a spear and launched it at him. Billy immediately fired the flare gun, knocking the Kayapo onto his back. His chest was on fire and the other Kayapo ran, screaming and dragging Sister Mary Alice in tow.

Billy ran to Hector. The spear had hit him in the shoulder and had gone clean through, pinning Hector to a tree. Hector screamed in pain as Billy struggled to free him from the tree.

The helicopter's bright searchlight flashed all around them. Then a loud voice came over the PA system.

"This is the Brazilian Army. Please stay where you are. We are here to rescue you."

Billy had only one flare left. He wrestled between using it to show the helicopter where they were and using it on the remaining Kayapo who still had Sister Mary Alice with them. Hector was bleeding badly. He would die if he didn't get help quickly.

Billy assumed that the soldiers would have guns, so he shot the flare into the air, illuminating their location. Within minutes, the helicopter hovered overhead and lowered a static line. Two soldiers carrying machine guns slid down the rope.

"Help him! He's wounded!" shouted Billy.

As the soldiers approached Hector, Billy grabbed one of the machine guns and took off into the jungle.

"Hey! Stop! Are you crazy?" yelled the soldier.

Billy ran through the jungle, hoping to pick up the Kayapos' trail. He started to have flashbacks of being in the jungle at night in Vietnam, trying to locate his squad, not knowing whether a booby trap would go off, blowing him to pieces, or falling into a grass-covered pit raked with bamboo spikes that would impale him as he fell. At least in this jungle he only had to worry about a few Kayapo armed with bows and arrows and spears, while he had a machine gun. Billy stopped when he realized he was a safe distance from the helicopter. He was ready for whatever came next.

Major Reno was frantic. "Lieutenant Marez, come in!" he ordered.

"This is Lieutenant Marez. Go ahead, major."

"Lieutenant Marez, what is going on?"

"We found two of the survivors, sir."

"Lieutenant, is one of the survivors a nun?"

"No, sir. We *had* two survivors but one got away."

"Got away? Don't they realize we're here to rescue them? I don't understand, lieutenant."

Major Reno was sure that General Russo wouldn't understand, either. How could they let a survivor escape?

Billy stopped to get his bearings and check out the gun he had taken from the soldier. In the dark, he was forced to identify it by touch. He ran his hand up and down the gun, feeling it as a blind man would. As he felt near the end of the barrel, he discovered that the gun was equipped with a tactical night-light. God was with him. Now all he needed was a little cry from Sister Mary Alice to let him know where she was and he'd riddle those Kayapo like Swiss cheese.

Billy heard the helicopter leaving, and the jungle returned to its sounds of nature. The nightlife in the jungle was unusually loud that night. More than likely, its inhabitants were startled from all the noise and lights of the helicopters. He thought it was odd that the birds were still awake and making so much noise.

Billy crouched down on his knees. There was a rustling sound behind him about five yards away. He stood and slowly turned toward the sound, flicking on the light at the end of the gun barrel. The light fell on one of the Kayapo. Without a second's hesitation, Billy pulled the trigger. The Kayapo flew back as if a cannon had shot him. Billy immediately shut off the light and moved away from where he had been standing, just in time to hear two arrows whiz past his head. He took a deep breath and then let it out very slowly. He silently circled back around to where he thought the arrows had come from.

Major Reno was beginning to crack. He called Lieutenant Marez and asked, "What's going on out there? I heard shots."

"It must be Sunday."

"Sunday?"

"Yes, sir. Billy Sunday."

"How did he get a gun?"

"He took it from one of your men when they were dealing with the other survivor who was badly injured."

Major Reno took off his hat and threw it on the ground, cursing. *If General Russo finds out that a survivor has taken a gun from one of my soldiers and is running half-cocked through the jungle, shooting at whatever moves, he'll strip me of my rank,* he thought.

"Lieutenant, what is the condition of the survivor you picked up?"

"Not good, sir. We need to get him to the hospital as soon as possible."

"All right, lieutenant. Call General Russo and explain what's going on. Have him send another helicopter and more men. And, lieutenant, do not, I repeat, do not mention that Mr. Sunday has one of my men's gun."

"More men, sir?"

"Yes, lieutenant. Those savages are more than likely regrouping as we speak. We could be facing who knows how many Indians by daybreak. I'm not interested in re-enacting America's Little Bighorn."

Billy circled back and hid behind a tree. He listened very closely to every sound that the jungle made. A long time had passed and he was starting to worry because he hadn't heard any kind of noise from Sister Mary Alice. Then he heard the familiar whipping sound of a helicopter. The noise from the helicopter grew louder and soon the backwash drowned out any sounds that could lead him to Sister Mary Alice.

Major Reno was trying to organize his search for the remaining survivors.

254

"Sergeant Rico, I want you and your men to fan out. Try to stay in a straight line about ten yards apart. Make sure that your men stay in line. We don't need them shooting one another. I want you to keep in contact with me via radio," said Major Reno.

"Sir, I really think that we should wait here until daybreak before we continue our search."

"If I wanted your opinion, I would've asked for it, sergeant!"

"Yes, sir. Where will you and your men be?"

"About a hundred yards downriver, then we'll move west into the jungle."

"What about the helicopter and the men on board?"

"I've directed the helicopter crew to go about half a mile west and drop off their men there, and then have them form a line and head east. After the men are on the ground, the helicopter will fly overhead with its searchlight on. Then, we'll circle in, forming a trap which we'll close like a noose."

"Sir, I really don't think this is a very good plan."

"Sergeant, I do not remember asking you what you thought of my plan!"

"But, sir, with all due respect, won't we end up shooting at each other if we're heading toward each other?"

"Sergeant, no one is to fire his weapon, except in self-defense. Those are your orders, now get a move on!"

Billy heard the helicopter pass overhead and saw its spotlight as it passed by. *What are they doing?* He thought.

The helicopter sounded like it was going away, and then it stopped and hovered in the air about a quarter of a mile west of Billy. Five minutes later, he could see the helicopter flying in a zigzag pattern, searching the ground with its spotlight. He could barely hear what they were shouting over the PA system. It sounded like they were saying that they were the Brazilian Army and they were urging the survivors to show themselves.

They all must be mad, thought Billy. *How can we show ourselves in the dead of night in a pitch-black jungle? Don't they know that Sister Mary Alice is being held by the Kayapo?*

255

It sounded like the rescue operation was deteriorating. They were going to kill one another and he needed to get out from the middle of them before it was too late. Billy started to head south, or at least he hoped he was heading south. He hadn't gone fifty yards before he heard a man scream. Then he saw lights and heard shooting, ten or fifteen shots. He instinctively hit the ground when he heard bullets tear through the foliage.

The helicopter tried to hover over where the shooting was taking place, fanning its searchlight to see what was going on. Sergeant Rico's voice came on the radio.

"Man down! Man down!"

The helicopter hovered even lower, trying to spot the wounded soldier. Then a flare lit up the sky, allowing the helicopter to zero in on the wounded man.

Billy heard rustling to his left and a sound that could only be that of a woman weeping. He took a chance and flicked on the gun's light as he swung it toward the sound. For one quick second, he saw a Kayapo dragging Sister Mary Alice through the brush. He targeted the Kayapo and pulled the trigger. Suddenly, guns erupted from everywhere. Billy hit the ground. Then he heard the helicopter's PA system ordering the men to hold their fire. The jungle grew quiet, except for the wash from the helicopter's rotors.

Billy heard a moaning sound coming from his left. It sounded like it was coming from where the Kayapo and Sister Mary Alice had been. Billy was having a hard time hearing what was making the sound over the wash from the rotors. He didn't want to risk turning his light back on, not knowing whether he hit the Kayapo dragging Sister Mary Alice or if it was another one that he hadn't seen. He also didn't want to run the risk of being shot by one of the soldiers trying to rescue him.

General Russo sat in his office, waiting to hear what was going on with the rescue teams. Bishop Cheuiche had called three times, and Franco Silva had called twice. The press was camped outside his door. He was having second thoughts about letting Major Reno and that idiot, Sergeant Rico handle the rescue operation, especially at night. If they didn't recover that nun, they all would be through. The bishop would see to that, especially after he had called off the search earlier.

The phone rang. General Russo hesitated to answer it. It was either bad news or Bishop Cheuiche calling back to demand that he produce the nun, as if he were a magician.

"This is General Russo speaking."

"General, this is Lieutenant Marez. Good news, sir. We've recovered another survivor."

General Russo could feel a weight being lifted from his shoulders. *Please, God, let it be the nun,* he thought.

"Unfortunately, the survivor is in the operating room in critical condition."

General Russo felt the weight come back on his shoulders, along with another ten pounds or more. *Please, Lord, don't let the nun die,* he thought. "Lieutenant, is it the nun?"

"No, sir. It's a Hispanic man. Hector Garcia I believe is his name."

"Where is the nun?" barked General Russo.

"We think the Kayapo have her, sir. Mr. Garcia kept mumbling about the Indians raping the holy sister and that he was going to kill them. I think that's what happened anyway."

"What do you mean you *think* that's what happened?"

"I'm just repeating what Mr. Garcia said on the way to the hospital, sir."

"I want you to get back in your helicopter and get back out in that jungle and bring back that nun! And that's an order!" shouted General Russo as he slammed down the phone.

Billy stayed low, crawling on all fours very slowly, so as not to attract any attention. As he moved, he strained to hear who was making the moaning sounds. He was only feet away now and he was sure that the moans were those of a woman. He couldn't risk turning on the light. What if the Kayapo was sitting there with his hand over Sister Mary Alice's mouth? What if there were two Kayapo? What if it were the trigger-happy soldiers?

257

Billy heard a small cry for help. *It has to be Sister Mary Alice,* he thought. He said a quick prayer to God to guide him, and then he turned on the light. Two bursts of gunfire rang out and he could hear the bullets ripping through the trees.

"Stop!" yelled Billy. He looked down. There laid Sister Mary Alice's bloody, naked body.

Chapter Thirty-Five

Five hours later, Fred sat in the waiting room of the hospital, waiting to hear word of Hector's progress. He was exhausted. He vowed he would never fly again. He planned to take a ship back to the States. Jan was being treated for shock and her many insect bites. Dick was in intensive care, recovering from his surgery. And Hector was still in the operating room.

Fred got up to stretch his legs. He walked down the hall to get a cup of coffee. Never again would he take the simple pleasure of a cup of coffee for granted. As he approached the coffee machine, he spotted Lieutenant Marez coming in through the emergency doors, following a gurney being pushed by soldiers. He rushed over to see whether it was Billy or Sister Mary Alice, hoping that it was neither of them.

"Lieutenant!"

Lieutenant Marez stopped and turned to Fred.

Very reluctantly, Fred asked, "Who are you bringing in?"

"A soldier. Shot by one of our own. Never in all my days have I witnessed such a botched rescue mission."

"Lieutenant, has there been any word about my two friends, Billy and Sister Mary Alice?"

Lieutenant Marez looked at Fred, took a deep breath, and shook his head.

"I'm not really sure what happened. I heard they found them and they're bringing them in as we speak."

"Are they all right?"

"There was a lot of confusion out there. I was in the helicopter trying to locate the missing survivors. Major Reno had some cockamamie plan to crush the natives in a vice grip maneuver. But all he managed to do was get a couple of his own men shot. After the first solider was shot, it was pure chaos down there. People were shooting in every direction. Major Reno was lucky that his soldiers were such bad shots or he could have had his whole squad wiped out. The press is going to have a field day tomorrow."

"But what about Billy and Sister Mary Alice?"

"I don't know, but I sure don't want to be the one spreading the wrong information. Their helicopter should be here in about twenty minutes."

Fred was going out of his mind with worry. He had lost more friends in the last two weeks than he had in his entire life. Captain Davis, Lou, Lucy, Julie. But the thought of losing Billy or Sister Mary Alice was too much to bear and to think that Dick who cared nothing for anyone but himself, had survived. In fact, he was the first one to be rescued.

"Where is there justice in this world?" cried Fred, not bothering to get his cup of coffee.

General Russo got word from the helicopter pilot of the unfortunate accident that had happened to his troops under Major Reno's command. Who would order his men to walk toward each other at night in the jungle with guns? *Only an idiot,* thought General Russo. *When I get done with Major Reno, he'll wish he'd never been born.*

There was a loud knock on General Russo's door. He was paying his secretary overtime to screen anyone from trying to reach him and suddenly the door burst open. It was Bishop Cheuiche, trailed by General Russo's secretary, apologizing for letting the bishop get past her.

"General, where is Sister Mary Alice?" he shouted, slamming his staff into the floor.

"She is en route as we speak," said General Russo, hoping that was the case.

Bishop Cheuiche leaned into General Russo's face, shouting, "Is Sister Mary Alice all right?"

General Russo could feel the bishop's spittle land on his face.

"I'm sure she is doing fine. She should be arriving at the hospital any moment now," he replied weakly.

"Then why wasn't I informed of her arrival?"

"I didn't want to bother you until I knew she was there safe and sound."

"A lame excuse! I will promise you this, general. If there is one hair harmed on Sister Mary Alice's head, I will have your job and your pension!"

Bishop Cheuiche stormed out of the office.

General Russo called to his secretary, "Get that damn Major Reno on the phone now!"

Fred paced the floor. Hector was out of surgery and in intensive care, with a fifty-fifty chance of making it. But there was still no sign of Billy or Sister Mary Alice. Fred had a dreadful feeling that they were dead and the lieutenant just didn't want to tell him.

Chapter Thirty-Six

Franco had sent Victor Chavez, one of his men from the company, to the hospital to get news of the situation that was quickly unfolding. Chavez told him that more survivors were being brought to the hospital, but he wasn't given any names.

Franco didn't want to tell Ana anything until he knew that Billy was one of the survivors. She was on the verge of a nervous breakdown, and he didn't think that she could take too much more without going mad. Then there were the Sundays, who were waiting for his call. Mrs. Sunday had been released from the hospital two days earlier, and the last thing he wanted to do was to call her with news that might send her back.

The phone rang, startling Franco. He knew it was probably Chavez, since General Russo had refused to take his calls. He was torn between wanting it all to be over, no matter the outcome, and taking a call that he knew would break his daughter's heart. On the fourth ring, he reached for the phone.

"Hello, this is Franco Silva speaking."

"Franco, its Bill Sunday."

Franco felt his heart skip a beat. What was he going to tell Bill?

"Franco? Are you still there?"

"Yes, Bill, how are you?"

"A bit exhausted, but otherwise fine."

"And Mrs. Sunday? How is she doing?"

"She's doing much better, thank you for asking."

Franco could feel the tension in his neck building.

"Franco, I just saw on the news that they found survivors from the plane crash. They haven't said how many or who they are. To be frank, they haven't even said if they're dead or alive. I'm just glad that Mildred is in bed already and hasn't heard. I'm afraid it would send her right back to the hospital."

Franco took a deep breath.

"Bill, you know as much as we do. They've been keeping a very tight lid on this whole thing. I've got a man down at the hospital and he's to call me if there is any news.

262

So far, he hasn't been able to find out any more than what's been reported on the news, but I'll call you just as soon as I find out anything. Until then, all we can do is pray."

"I'm afraid you're right, Franco. We'll be in touch."

Chapter Thirty-Seven

Fred could hear the unmistakable sound of the helicopter as it landed at the hospital. The reporters were jostling on the tarmac, trying to get the best footage before their competition did. Four soldiers got off the helicopter, pushing back the press to clear a path for the hospital personnel to load the bodies onto gurneys.

Fred tried to see what was going on but there were too many people standing in the way. The two gurneys were wheeled across the tarmac, followed by a procession of news media in tow. Fred worked his way down to the emergency room, trying to see what was going on. There were more press members waiting at the entrance. Then one of the reporters turned to Fred.

"Aren't you one of the survivors they brought in last night?"

Fred didn't know what to say. Then the emergency room doors opened and the soldiers wheeled the two gurneys through them, surrounded by hospital staff, obscuring Fred's view of who occupied the gurneys. The news reporter turned back to Fred as the rest of the reporters circled around him. They all seemed to be asking questions at the same time.

"How does it feel to be back in civilization?"

"Did you have to fight off any of the Kayapo?"

"How many of the ten survivors died before they found you?"

"Did the captain die first?"

Fred couldn't take it. He pushed his way through the sea of reporters and headed back to his room. When he opened the door, Jan was sitting on a chair looking out the window.

"Jan, should you be up?"

"I couldn't find you. I woke up and you weren't there. I realized then that without you, I couldn't have made it out of that horrible jungle. Fred, I don't know how you feel about the whole ordeal, but I know if it weren't for you, I wouldn't have made it. I owe my life to you."

Jan, teary eyed, turned her head to look out the window. She didn't want Fred to see her crying.

Fred felt his heart swell to the size of a football. He never took the time to get involved in a relationship before. The time that he had spent with Jan was as close as he'd ever gotten to a woman, not counting his mother. He hoped he hadn't been reading more into what Jan was saying. He realized that he had fallen in love with her and he hoped that she felt the same way.

"Jan, you don't owe me anything. Hell, if it weren't for you, I don't know that I would have gotten out myself."

Jan felt a little downhearted. Maybe she'd watched too many chick flicks, but she was hoping that Fred would grab her in his arms and ask her to marry him. She got up to go back to her room and as she walked by Fred, he grabbed her arm lightly and turned her toward him. Fred looked down at her face riddled with mosquito bites.

"Jan, you're the best thing that has ever happened to me. This whole thing was worth it. It made me realize how important it is to have someone you care about in your life."

Jan wrapped her arms around Fred's big body. She had never felt happier.

"Mr. Silva, they've just brought in the last two survivors," said Chavez.

"Were you able to find out who they are?"

"I'm not one hundred percent sure, but I overheard a couple of nurses talking. I think it's the nun and Billy."

"Billy? Is he alive?"

"I couldn't tell when they brought them through, but they usually don't bring dead people into the emergency room."

"Keep checking. Call me as soon as you hear anything on Billy."

Franco was faced with a real dilemma. Ana's sedative would be wearing off very soon and he was going to have to tell her something. He was worried about her hearing anything second-hand.

Bishop Cheuiche and his entourage pushed their way into the emergency room.

"Who is in charge here?" he barked.

A nurse came running over, making the sign of the cross.

"I'm the head nurse, bishop. How can I help you? Are you sick?"

"No, of course not," said Bishop Cheuiche, full of his own authority. "I'm fine."

"Then what is it, bishop?"

"It is my understanding that they have brought in a nun from the plane crash."

"I'm sorry, Bishop Cheuiche, but I am not at liberty to give out any information regarding the survivors of the plane crash. General Russo is scheduled to give a press conference in about twenty minutes."

The bishop was outraged. "But I am the bishop! I demand an answer!" he bellowed, red-faced.

"With all due respect, Bishop Cheuiche, stop acting like a spoiled little boy and have a seat. We have sick people here that we need to take care of," the head nurse replied crisply as she walked back to her desk.

Bishop Cheuiche stood in amazement. No one had ever spoken to him that way before. One of the priests in his entourage had to turn his head so the bishop couldn't see him laughing.

Before the press conference, Major Reno briefed General Russo about the rescue operation, and General Russo replied that he would deal with him after he dealt with the press.

General Russo stood in full uniform at the podium set up in the hospital lobby. He addressed the crowd of news reporters with a very solemn face. It almost looked as if he had tears in his eyes.

"I'd like to begin by thanking everyone for taking the time to be here for this very important news conference. Thank you also to all the people who have given their time and have risked their lives to participate in this search and rescue mission. At this time, I'd like to ask for a moment of silence to honor the loss of one of our own, Private Gomez. Because of his unselfish act of courage during this mission, he paid the ultimate price with his life."

The room grew silent. Then General Russo continued.

"I'd like to ask for another moment of silence, for the two soldiers who were wounded tonight, rescuing the three survivors who were captured by the fearful Kayapo."

266

One of the reporters in the back of the room shouted, "Cut the crap, general, and get to the point! How many survivors are there, who are they, and what condition are they in?"

General Russo cleared his throat and stared sternly at the reporter.

"As I was saying, we all have made a valiant effort to bring these six lucky survivors home safely."

"What are their names?"

"What's their condition?"

One of General Russo's men handed him a piece of paper. Reading it, he ordered two of his men to go into the hallway, where two policemen were waiting by the door.

General Russo said, "Where was I?" and then paused. "Yes, the names. The first survivor to be rescued was Mr. Dick Frost. Mr. Frost was in very critical condition when we found him. If we hadn't gotten to him when we did, I am certain he would have died. Mr. Frost is now resting in his hospital room in satisfactory condition. He should be strong enough to be sent back home to the United States in just a few days.

"Along with Mr. Frost, Miss Jan Lombardi was also rescued. By the brave efforts of the Cytron Oil Company aircrew, she was rescued from the savage Kayapo. Miss Lombardi is resting quietly in her hospital room in fair condition and will also be able to return home to the United States in just a few days."

General Russo took a drink of water, cleared his throat, and continued.

"Mr. Fred Dowding was also rescued and is resting in his hospital room. Mr. Dowding is being treated for stress and malnutrition, like all of the survivors. He will be released tomorrow to return to the United States.

"The other survivors brought in tonight, rescued by my brave men from the savage Kayapo, weren't so lucky. Mr. Hector Garcia was seriously wounded by a spear thrust through his shoulder. After many hours of surgery, our good doctors here have given Mr. Garcia a fifty-fifty chance of surviving his injuries."

Bishop Cheuiche was squirming in his chair. *General Russo is so full of shit his eyes are brown. Get to the nun,* he thought.

"Just less than an hour ago," General Russo continued, "after a valiant effort by my men and a long, bloody battle with the Kayapo, we were able to rescue the last two survivors."

Franco was watching the press conference with Ana. She sat watching with her father's arms wrapped around her, crying and wanting to leave for the hospital the moment that General Russo gave word of Billy's condition.

On television, General Russo looked up at the ceiling, took a deep breath, and lowered his head. He sniffed, pushed his lips together, and shook his head.

"I'm afraid that the fate of Mr. Billy Sunday is still in the hands of God." General Russo paused. "Our good doctors here are fighting for Mr. Sunday's life as we speak."

Ana let out a loud scream and fainted.

Franco yelled, "Rosesa! Call the doctor!"

General Russo continued.

"God was good to us today. Our last survivor, Sister Mary Alice, is quietly resting in her hospital room. My brave men saved her from great harm at the hands of a Kayapo and she is suffering from only minor injuries. Sister Mary Alice should be able to return to the convent by the end of the week. That is all the information I have for now. Thank you."

As General Russo left the podium, the reporters flooded him with questions. He ignored them as he made his way to his car waiting just outside the lobby.

The doctor gave Ana a mild sedative and said that it would help her sleep.

Franco asked the doctor, "What should I do when she wakes up? You know that she's going to want to go straight to the hospital."

"Yes, you're right. And she should go. She loves that boy. I think you would be doing her a grave injustice if you didn't let her go to the hospital. I'll give you some Valium for her to take when she wakes up. It should help her deal with the stress."

Franco thanked the doctor and saw him to the door. As Franco closed the door, he heard the phone ring. *That has to be Chavez,* he thought. "Hello, this is Franco Silva."

268

Franco heard crying in the background, and then a man's quivering voice came over the receiver.

"This is Bill Sunday. Franco, did you hear the news?"

"I'm not sure. What is it?"

"It was just on the news. They think my boy's dead. Mildred is taking it real bad."

Franco was silent for a full minute, and then he took a deep breath.

"Bill, I didn't hear that. The news here said that Billy was still in the operating room. And that was only twenty minutes ago. Bill, there is a small chance that what you heard could be wrong," said Franco, looking up and silently praying.

"I don't think so. They interrupted the TV program we were watching for a special news update."

Franco couldn't believe the callousness of the media. They shouldn't have reported anything without first notifying the next of kin.

"I'm so sorry, Bill. Is there anything that I can do for you and Mildred? Anything, you just name it." Franco felt his eyes filling up with tears and he started to get choked up. "I'm sorry, Bill. I have to go. Ana needs me."

Franco hung up and walked over to his liquor cabinet. He poured himself a tall glass of bourbon, even though it was still very early in the morning. He took a long pull and thought, *After all this. Thirteen days of pure terror and to get this close. Now he's dead.*

He shook his head in disbelief.

The phone rang.

"This is Franco Silva speaking."

"Mr. Silva, this is Chavez. Sir, I don't know how to tell you this."

"I already know, Chavez. Billy's father just called me with the sad news."

"I'm very sorry, sir. Is there anything I can do for you?"

"Yes, there is in fact. Find out how he died."

"Yes, sir. I can do that, sir."

269

Epilogue

Fred and Jan were released from the hospital a few days later. They both had seen enough of Brazil. After they checked each ship's travel record for accidents, and then checked the weather, they boarded the first ship that passed their scrutiny for their return trip to the United States. While on board, they had the captain marry them. Both Fred and Jan decided that life was too short to put off such an important event. They also decided to live each day as if it were their last. Neither had ever felt as lucky as when they came out of the jungle alive. But they couldn't help feeling sorry for the close friends that they lost along the way.

"It's a funny thing," said Fred, "all the people in the world who you think are your friends. But how many would offer up their lives for yours, like Billy, Lou, and Hector? Unfortunately, I'm afraid that there are a whole lot more people like Dick Frost out there."

"Fred, I don't agree with you," said Jan. "There are more Billys out there by far, thank God."

Dick Frost made a full recovery, less his manhood, which he lost to the jungle's most feared creature, the mighty one-inch-long Candiru. Dick not only lost his manhood but also his freedom after being convicted for the attempted rape of Sister Mary Alice. Dick was also convicted of embezzlement. It was discovered that he had embezzled five million dollars from his former law firm. He is now serving twenty years in a maximum-security prison in Brazil. Dick will serve another twenty years in Pittsburgh, upon his release.

Hector Garcia recovered from his spear wound after three months in the hospital. Most important of all, Hector recovered from his hatred of Dick Frost. Hector eventually forgave Dick for the greedy selfish acts leading to the death of his daughter. In the end, Sister Mary Alice's strong faith is what really saved Hector.

Sister Mary Alice recovered from the trauma of rape and forgave Dick and the Kayapo who had befouled her. She went on to start a foundation for battered women and named it in memory of the man who had saved her life, Billy Sunday.

It took Ana Silva a long time to get over the death of Billy Sunday. Ana continued her education and went on to become an aviation engineer to help design better navigational systems for aircraft. Ana also worked with the company that invented the beacons used to help find lost aircraft.

Billy Sunday died on the operating table after suffering fatal gunshot wounds from Major Reno's confused and scared soldiers. Billy had saved Sister Mary Alice from the Kayapo, and then Billy saved her again by covering her body with his when the gunfire broke out.

There was an investigation of the rescue mission after Billy's death. Major Reno was found guilty of poor judgment in conducting the mission. He was court-martialed and served time in a Brazilian army prison. Upon his release, he was dishonorably discharged from service and denied all benefits. The government of Brazil awarded Billy Sunday's parents an undisclosed amount in damages, which they donated to the foundation bearing their son's name.

The End

About the Author

Alex Lizzi lives with his wife, Janice, in Pine, Colorado, atop Pine Valley, which looks down onto Pikes Peak and its surrounding range of mountains. He has been a hairdresser for the last 35 years and attributes much of his writing creativity to his vast client base that he has been privileged to serve over the years.

Alex started his career as a hairdresser in a small town just north of Pittsburgh, Pennsylvania, where most of his clientele were involved in the steel industry. This gave him a very rich and colorful view of life through the eyes of the blue-collar working man. After the decline of the steel industry, Alex moved to Evergreen, Colorado, in 1983, which led him to the opposite end of the spectrum, where his clients were mainly high-level executives.

Listening to the views, interests, and opinions of such a variety of people, along with his genuine love of books, has awakened his desire to write, opening yet another chapter in Alex's life that he hopes to enjoy for years to come.

Why? Is Alex's third published book. His other two titles are *Bonding: A Rizzo Family Vacation* and *Schoolhouse*.

Made in the USA
Charleston, SC
08 March 2012